FOUR GROUNDBREAKING HUGO AND NEBULA WINNING STORIES

UNRIVALED

JOE HALDEMAN
LOIS McMASTER BUJOLD
MIKE RESNICK
NANCY KRESS

ARC MANOR
ROCKVILLE, MARYLAND

SHAHID MAHMUD
PUBLISHER

www.caeziksf.com

This is a work of fiction.

Cover art by Christina P. Myrvold; artstation.com/christinapm

ISBN: 978-1-64710-065-0

First Edition. First Printing April 2023
1 2 3 4 5 6 7 8 9 10

An imprint of Arc Manor LLC

www.CaezikSF.com

CONTENTS

THE HEMINGWAY HOAX

Joe Haldeman 1

THE MOUNTAINS OF MOURNING

Lois McMaster Bujold 121

SEVEN VIEWS OF OLDUVAI GORGE

Mike Resnick 199

BEGGARS IN SPAIN

Nancy Kress 257

THE HEMINGWAY HOAX

Joe Haldeman

Introduction

The idea to write a science fiction story about the lost Hemingway manuscripts came all of a sudden, during a casual conversation with one of my students at MIT.

He had offered to drive me to the airport. We had to kill several hours waiting for a plane there, and on the way back from hiking to the mens' room, I got the idea to tell him about Hemingway's Lost Manuscripts as a way to pass the time.

The story has become familiar from repeated exposure on television, especially from a recent three-part Ken Burns special on Hemingway's life. But this was more than thirty years ago, and few people who weren't students of the Lost Generation had heard about the lost Hemingway manuscript drama.

It's a great story for writers, though—the most famous lucky-break legend in American letters—and this guy was one of my most promising graduate students. So I related it to him in some detail.

I'm not sure when that conversation boiled down to a book idea. It might have been in the back of my mind while I was talking to him. But it was a couple of days later when it crystalized: True, it would be unbelievably lucky to come across the lost Hemingway manuscripts in some forgotten file folder—but hey! You could forge them! Or you could write a *story* about forging or finding them without looking through any dusty Paris attics.

I had a perfect title: "The Hemingway Hoax."

I also had a perfect place to do research for such a story. The University of Massachusetts had just opened a research center for Hemingway studies at the Kennedy Library, just an hour down the Red Line from my MIT office. So once or twice a week, for a couple of semesters, I took the train down there and wrote notes for the novel.

I wrote another book in the meantime, and when it came time to write the Hemingway book, I got a cheap motel room in Key West and wrote most of it there. It was almost too much fun.

The great editor and good friend Gardner Dozois wanted to look at it for magazine rights. He said he liked it, but had to cut it by at least a third. I thought that was impossible! The book was already seamlessly tight. He said "Why don't you let me try?"

I wound up sitting on the phone with him, a thousand miles apart, for many hours while we condensed the book, rewriting it line by line! It taught me a little humility about my deathless prose. We got it down to his required length, and I wound up using many of Gardner's changes in the final version of the novel itself.

—JOE HALDEMAN

1

The Torrents of Spring

Our story begins in a rundown bar in Key West, not so many years from now. The bar is not the one Hemingway drank at, nor yet the one that claims to be the one he drank at, because they are both too expensive and full of tourists. This bar, in a more interesting part of town, is a Cuban place. It is neither clean nor well-lighted, but has cold beer and good strong Cuban coffee. Its cheap prices and rascally charm are what bring together the scholar and the rogue.

Their first meeting would be of little significance to either at the time, though the scholar, John Baird, would never forget it. John Baird was not capable of forgetting anything.

Key West is lousy with writers, mostly poor writers, in one sense of that word or the other. Poor people did not interest our rogue, Sylvester Castlemaine, so at first he didn't take any special note of the man sitting in the corner scribbling on a yellow pad. Just another would-be writer, come down to see whether some of Papa's magic would rub off. Not worth the energy of a con.

But Castle's professional powers of observation caught at a detail or two and focused his attention. The man was wearing jeans and a faded flannel shirt, but his shoes were expensive Italian loafers. His beard had been trimmed by a barber. He was drinking Heineken. The pen he was scribbling with was a fat Mont Blanc Diplomat, two hundred bucks on the hoof, discounted. Castle got his cup of coffee and sat at a table two away from the writer.

He waited until the man paused, set the pen down, took a drink. "Writing a story?" Castle said.

The man blinked at him. "No ... just an article." He put the cap on the pen with a crisp snap. "An article about stories. I'm a college professor."

"Publish or perish," Castle said.

The man relaxed a bit. "Too true." He riffled through the yellow pad. "This won't help much. It's not going anywhere."

"Tell you what ... bet you a beer it's Hemingway or Tennessee Williams."

"Too easy." He signaled the bartender. "Dos cervezas. Hemingway, the early stories. You know his work?"

"Just a little. We had to read him in school—*The Old Man and the Fish?* And then I read a couple after I got down here." He moved over to the man's table. "Name's Castle."

"John Baird." Open, honest expression; not too promising. You can't con somebody unless he thinks he's conning you. "Teach up at Boston."

"I'm mostly fishing. Shrimp nowadays." Of course Castle didn't normally fish, not for things in the sea, but the shrimp part was true. He'd been reduced to heading shrimp on the Catalina for five dollars a bucket. "So what about these early stories?"

The bartender set down the two beers and gave Castle a weary look.

"Well ... they don't exist." John Baird carefully poured the beer down the side of his glass. "They were stolen. Never published."

"So what can you write about them?"

"Indeed. That's what I've been asking myself." He took a sip of the beer and settled back. "Seventy-four years ago they were stolen. December 1922. That's really what got me working on them; thought I would do a paper, a monograph, for the seventy-fifth anniversary of the occasion."

It sounded less and less promising, but this was the first imported beer Castle had had in months. He slowly savored the bite of it.

"He and his first wife, Hadley, were living in Paris. You know about Hemingway's early life?"

"Huh uh. Paris?"

"He grew up in Oak Park, Illinois. That was kind of a prissy, self-satisfied suburb of Chicago."

"Yeah, I been there."

"He didn't like it. In his teens he sort of ran away from home, went down to Kansas City to work on a newspaper.

"World War I started, and like a lot of kids, Hemingway couldn't get into the army because of bad eyesight, so he joined the Red Cross and went off to drive ambulances in Italy. Take cigarettes and chocolate to the troops.

"That almost killed him. He was just doing his cigarettes-and-chocolate routine and an artillery round came in, killed the guy next to him, tore up another, riddled Hemingway with shrapnel. He claims then that he picked up the wounded guy and carried him back to the trench, in spite of being hit in the knee by a machine gun bullet."

"What do you mean, 'claims'?"

"You're too young to have been in Vietnam."

"Yeah."

"Good for you. I was hit in the knee by a machine gun bullet myself, and went down on my ass and didn't get up for five weeks. He didn't carry anybody one step."

"That's interesting."

"Well, he was always rewriting his life. We all do it. But it seemed to be a compulsion with him. That's one thing that makes Hemingway scholarship challenging."

Baird poured the rest of the beer into his glass. "Anyhow, he actually was the first American wounded in Italy, and they made a big deal over him. He went back to Oak Park a war hero. He had a certain amount of success with women."

"Or so he says?"

"Right, God knows. Anyhow, he met Hadley Richardson, an older woman but quite a number, and they had a steamy courtship and got married and said the hell with it, moved to Paris to live a sort of Bohemian life while Hemingway worked on perfecting his art. That part isn't bullshit. He worked diligently and he did become one of the best writers of his era. Which brings us to the lost manuscripts."

"Do tell."

"Hemingway was picking up a little extra money doing journalism. He'd gone to Switzerland to cover a peace conference for a news service. When it was over, he wired Hadley to come join him for some skiing.

"This is where it gets odd. On her own initiative, Hadley packed up all of Ernest's work. All of it. Not just the typescripts, but the handwritten first drafts and the carbons."

"That's like a Xerox?"

"Right. She packed them in an overnight bag, then packed her own suitcase. A porter at the train station, the Gare de Lyon, put them aboard for her. She left the train for a minute to find something to read—and when she came back, they were gone."

"Suitcase and all?"

"No, just the manuscripts. She and the porter searched up and down the train. But that was it. Somebody had seen the overnight bag sitting there and snatched it. Lost forever."

That did hold a glimmer of professional interest. "That's funny. You'd think they'd get a note then, like 'If you ever want to see your stories again, bring a million bucks to the Eiffel Tower' sort of thing."

"A few years later, that might have happened. It didn't take long for Hemingway to become famous. But at the time, only a few of the literary intelligentsia knew about him."

Castle shook his head in commiseration with the long-dead thief. "Guy who stole 'em probably didn't even read English. Dumped 'em in the river."

John Baird shivered visibly. "Undoubtedly. But people have never stopped looking for them. Maybe they'll show up in some attic someday."

"Could happen." Wheels turning.

"It's happened before in literature. Some of Boswell's diaries were recovered because a scholar recognized his handwriting on an old piece of paper a merchant used to wrap a fish. Hemingway's own last book, he put together from notes that had been lost for thirty years. They were in a couple of trunks in the basement of the Ritz, in Paris." He leaned forward, excited. "Then after he died, they found another batch of papers down here, in a back room in Sloppy Joe's. It could still happen."

Castle took a deep breath. "It could be made to happen, too."

"Made to happen?"

"Just speakin', you know, in theory. Like some guy who really knows Hemingway, suppose he makes up some stories that're like those old ones, finds some seventy-five-year-old paper and an old, what do you call them, not a word processor—"

"Typewriter."

"Whatever. Think he could pass 'em off for the real thing?"

"I don't know if he could fool me," Baird said, and tapped the side of his head. "I have a freak memory: eidetic, photographic. I have just about every word Hemingway ever wrote committed to memory." He looked slightly embarrassed. "Of course that doesn't make me an expert in the sense of being able to spot a phony. I just wouldn't have to refer to any texts."

"So take yourself, you know, or somebody else who spent all his life studyin' Hemingway. He puts all he's got into writin' these stories—he knows the people who are gonna be readin' 'em; knows what they're gonna look for. And he hires like an expert forger to make the pages look like they came out of Hemingway's machine. So could it work?"

Baird pursed his lips and for a moment looked professorial. Then he sort of laughed, one syllable through his nose. "Maybe it could. A man did a similar thing when I was a boy, counterfeiting the memoirs of Howard Hughes. He made millions."

"Millions?"

"Back when that was real money. Went to jail when they found out, of course."

"And the money was still there when he got out."

"Never read anything about it. I guess so."

"So the next question is, how much stuff are we talkin' about? How much was in that old overnight bag?"

"That depends on who you believe. There was half a novel and some poetry. The short stories, there might have been as few as eleven or as many as thirty."

"That'd take a long time to write."

"It would take forever. You couldn't just 'do' Hemingway; you'd have to figure out what the stories were about, then reconstruct his early style—do you know how many Hemingway scholars there are in the world?"

"Huh uh. Quite a few."

"Thousands. Maybe ten thousand academics who know enough to spot a careless fake."

Castle nodded, cogitating. "You'd have to be real careful. But then you wouldn't have to do all the short stories and poems, would you? You could say all you found was the part of the novel. Hell, you could sell that as a book."

The odd laugh again. "Sure you could. Be a fortune in it."

"How much? A million bucks?"

"A million … maybe. Well, sure. The last new Hemingway made at least that much, allowing for inflation. And he's more popular now."

Castle took a big gulp of beer and set his glass down decisively. "So what the hell are we waiting for?"

Baird's bland smile faded. "You're serious?"

2

In Our Time

Got a ripple in the Hemingway channel.

Twenties again?

No, funny, this one's in the 1990s. See if you can track it down?

Sure. Go down to the armory first and—

Look—no bloodbaths this time. You solve one problem and start ten more.

Couldn't be helped. It's no tea party, twentieth-century America.

Just use good judgment. That Ransom guy …

Manson. Right. That was a mistake.

3

A Way You'll Never Be

You can't cheat an honest man, as Sylvester Castlemaine well knew, but then again, it never hurts to find out just how honest a man is. John Baird refused his scheme, with good humor at first, but when Castle persisted, his refusal took on a sarcastic edge, maybe a tinge of outrage. He backed off and changed the subject, talking for a half hour about commercial fishing around Key West and then said he had to run. He slipped his business card into John's shirt pocket on the way out (Sylvester Castlemaine, Consultant, it claimed.)

John left the place soon, walking slowly through the afternoon heat. He was glad he hadn't brought the bicycle; it was pleasant to walk in the shade of the big aromatic trees, a slight breeze on his face from the Gulf side.

One could do it. One could. The problem divided itself into three parts: writing the novel fragment, forging the manuscript, and devising a suitable story about how one had uncovered the manuscript.

The writing part would be the hardest. Hemingway is easy enough to parody—one-fourth of the take-home final he gave in English 733 was to write a page of Hemingway pastiche, and some of his graduate students did a credible job—but parody was exactly what one would not want to do.

It had been a crucial period in Hemingway's development those three years of apprenticeship the lost manuscripts represented. Two stories survived, and they were maddeningly dissimilar. "My Old Man," which had slipped down behind a drawer, was itself a pastiche, reading like pretty good Sherwood Anderson, but with an O. Henry twist at the end—very unlike the bleak understated quality that would distinguish the stories that were to make Hemingway's reputation. The other, "Up in Michigan," had been out in the mail at the time of the loss. It was a lot closer to Hemingway's ultimate style, a spare and, by the standards of the time, pornographic description of a woman's first sexual experience.

John riffled through the notes on the yellow pad, a talismanic gesture, since he could have remembered any page with little effort. But the sight of the words and the feel of the paper sometimes helped him think.

One would not do it, of course. Except perhaps as a mental exercise. Not to show to anybody. Certainly not to profit from.

You wouldn't want to use "My Old Man" as the model, certainly; no one would care to publish a pastiche of a pastiche of Anderson, now undeservedly obscure. So "Up in Michigan." And the first story he wrote after the loss, "Out of Season," would also be handy. That had a lot of the Hemingway strength.

You wouldn't want to tackle the novel fragment, of course, not just as an exercise, over a hundred pages …

Without thinking about it, John dropped into a familiar fugue state as he walked through the rundown neighborhood, his freak memory taking over while his body ambled along on autopilot. This is the way he usually remembered pages. He transported himself back to the Hemingway collection at the JFK Library in Boston, last November, snow swirling outside the big picture windows overlooking the harbor, the room so cold he was wearing coat and gloves and could see his breath. They didn't normally let you wear a coat up there, afraid you might squirrel away a page out of the manuscript collection, but they had to make an exception because the heat pump was down.

He was flipping through the much-thumbed Xerox of Carlos Baker's interview with Hadley, page 52: "Stolen suitcase," Baker asked; "lost novel?"

The typescript of her reply appeared in front of him, more clear than the cracked sidewalk his feet negotiated: "This novel was a knockout, about Nick, up north in Michigan—hunting, fishing, all sorts of experiences—stuff on the order of 'Big Two-Hearted River,' with more action. Girl experiences well done, too." With an enigmatic addition, evidently in Hadley's handwriting, "Girl experiences too well done."

That was interesting. John hadn't thought about that, since he'd been concentrating on the short stories. Too well done? There had been a lot of talk in the eighties about Hemingway's sexual ambiguity—*gender* ambiguity, actually—could Hadley have been upset, sixty years after the fact, remembering some confidence that Hemingway had revealed to the world in that novel; something girls knew that boys were not supposed to know? Playful pillow talk that was filed away for eventual literary exploitation?

He used his life that way. A good writer remembered everything and then forgot it when he sat down to write, and reinvented it so the writing would be more real than the memory. Experience was important but imagination was more important.

Maybe I would be a better writer, John thought, if I could learn how to forget. For about the tenth time today, like any day, he regretted not having tried to succeed as a writer, while he still had the independent income. Teaching and research had fascinated him when he was younger, a rich boy's all-consuming hobbies, but the end of this fiscal year would be the end of the monthly checks from the trust fund. So the salary from Boston University wouldn't be mad money any more, but rent and groceries in a city suddenly expensive.

Yes, the writing would be the hard part. Then forging the manuscript, that wouldn't be easy. Any scholar would have access to copies of thousands of pages that Hemingway typed before and after the loss. Could one find the typewriter Hemingway had used? Then duplicate his idiosyncratic typing style—a moment's reflection put a sample in front of him, spaces before and after periods and commas....

He snapped out of the reverie as his right foot hit the first step on the back staircase up to their rented flat. He automatically stepped over the fifth step, the rotted one, and was thinking about a nice tall glass of iced tea as he opened the screen door.

"Scorpions!" his wife screamed, two feet from his face.

"What?"

"We have scorpions!" Lena grabbed his arm and hauled him to the kitchen.

"Look!" She pointed at the opaque plastic skylight. Three scorpions, each about six inches long, cast sharp silhouettes on the milky plastic. One was moving.

"My word."

"Your *word!*" She struck a familiar pose, hands on hips, and glared up at the creatures. "What are we going to do about it?"

"We could name them."

"John."

"I don't know." He opened the refrigerator. "Call the bug man."

"The bug man was just here yesterday. He probably flushed them out."

He poured a glass of cold tea and dumped two envelopes of artificial sweetener into it. "I'll talk to Julio about it. But you know they've been there all along. They're not bothering anybody."

"They're bothering the hell out of me!"

He smiled. "Okay. I'll talk to Julio." He looked into the oven. "Thought about dinner?"

"Anything you want to cook, sweetheart. I'll be damned if I'm going to stand there with three … poisonous … arthropods staring down at me."

"Poised to jump," John said, and looked up again. There were only two visible now, which made his skin crawl.

"Julio wasn't home when I first saw them. About an hour ago."

"I'll go check." John went downstairs and Julio, the landlord, was indeed home, but was not impressed by the problem. He agreed that it was probably the bug man, and they would probably go back to where they came from in a while, and gave John a flyswatter.

John left the flyswatter with Lena, admonishing her to take no prisoners, and walked a couple of blocks to a Chinese restaurant. He brought back a few boxes of takeout, and they sat in the living room and wielded chopsticks in silence, listening for the pitter-patter of tiny feet.

"Met a real live con man today." He put the business card on the coffee table between them.

"Consultant?" she read.

"He had a loony scheme about counterfeiting the missing stories." Lena knew more about the missing stories than ninety-eight percent of the people who Hemingway'ed for a living. John liked to think out loud.

"Ah, the stories," she said, preparing herself.

"Not a bad idea, actually, if one had a larcenous nature." He concentrated for a moment on the slippery Moo Goo Gai Pan. "Be millions of bucks in it."

He was bent over the box. She stared hard at his bald spot. "What exactly did he have in mind?"

"We didn't bother to think it through in any detail, actually. You go and find ..." He got the slightly walleyed look that she knew meant he was reading a page of a book a thousand miles away. "Yes. A 1921 Corona portable, like the one Hadley gave him before they were married. Find some old paper. Type up the stories. Take them to Sotheby's. Spend money for the rest of your life. That's all there is to it."

"You left out jail."

"A mere detail. Also the writing of the stories. That could take weeks. Maybe you could get arrested first, write the stories in jail, and then sell them when you got out."

"You're weird, John."

"Well. I didn't give him any encouragement."

"Maybe you should've. A few million would come in handy next year."

"We'll get by."

"'We'll get by.' You keep saying that. How do you know? You've never had to 'get by.'"

"Okay, then. We won't get by." He scraped up the last of the fried rice. "We won't be able to make the rent and they'll throw us out on the street. We'll live in a cardboard box over a heating grate. You'll have to sell your body to keep me in cheap wine. But we'll be happy, dear." He looked up at her, mooning. "Poor but happy."

"Slap-happy." She looked at the card again. "How do you know he's a con man?"

"I don't know. Salesman type. Says he's in commercial fishing now, but he doesn't seem to like it much."

"He didn't say anything about any, you know, criminal stuff he'd done in the past?"

"Huh uh. I just got the impression that he didn't waste a lot of time mulling over ethics and morals." John held up the Mont Blanc pen. "He was staring at this, before he came over and introduced himself. I think he smelled money."

Lena stuck both chopsticks into the half-finished carton of boiled rice and set it down decisively. "Let's ask him over."

"He's a sleaze, Lena. You wouldn't like him."

"I've never met a real con man. It would be fun."

He looked into the darkened kitchen. "Will you cook something?"

She followed his gaze, expecting monsters. "If you stand guard."

4

Romance Is Dead

SUBTITLE

The Hell It Is

"Be a job an' a half," Castle said, mopping up residual spaghetti sauce with a piece of garlic bread. "It's not like your Howard Hughes guy, or Hitler's notebooks."

"You've been doing some research." John's voice was a little slurred. He'd bought a half gallon of Portuguese wine, the bottle wrapped in straw like cheap Chianti, the wine not quite that good. If you could get past the first couple of glasses, it was okay. It had been okay to John for some time now.

"Yeah, down to the library. The guys who did the Hitler notebooks, hell, nobody'd ever seen a real Hitler notebook; they just studied his handwriting in letters and such, then read up on what he did day after day. Same with the Howard Hughes, but that was even easier, because most of the time nobody knew what the hell Howard Hughes was doing anyhow. Just stayed locked up in that room."

"The Hughes forgery nearly worked, as I recall," John said. "If Hughes himself hadn't broken silence …"

"Ya gotta know that took balls. 'Scuse me, Lena." She waved a hand and laughed. "Try to get away with that while Hughes was still alive."

"How did the Hitler people screw up?" she asked.

"Funny thing about that one was how many people they fooled. Afterwards everybody said it was a really lousy fake. But you can bet that before the newspapers bid millions of dollars on it, they showed it to the best Hitlerologists they could find, and they all said it was real."

"Because they wanted it to be real," Lena said.

"Yeah. But one of the pages had some chemical in it that wouldn't be in paper before 1945. That was kinda dumb."

"People would want the Hemingway stories to be real," Lena said quietly, to John.

John's gaze stayed fixed on the center of the table, where a few strands of spaghetti lay cold and drying in a plastic bowl. "Wouldn't be honest."

"That's for sure," Castle said cheerily. "But it ain't exactly armed robbery, either."

"A gross misuse of intellectual … intellectual …"

"It's past your bedtime, John," Lena said. "We'll clean up." John nodded and pushed himself away from the table and walked heavily into the bedroom.

Lena didn't say anything until she heard the bedsprings creak. "He isn't always like this," she said quietly.

"Yeah. He don't act like no alky."

"It's been a hard year for him." She refilled her glass. "Me, too. Money."

"That's bad."

"Well, we knew it was coming. He tell you about the inheritance?" Castle leaned forward. "Huh uh."

"He was born pretty well off. Family had textile mills up in New Hampshire. John's grandparents died in an auto accident in the forties and the family sold off the mills—good timing, too. They wouldn't be worth much today.

"Then John's father and mother died in the sixties, while he was in college. The executors set up a trust fund that looked like it would keep him in pretty good shape forever. But he wasn't interested in money. He even joined the army, to see what it was like."

"Jesus."

"Afterwards, he carried a picket sign and marched against the war—you know, Vietnam.

"Then he finished his Ph.D. and started teaching. The trust fund must have been fifty times as much as his salary, when he started out. It was still ten times as much, a couple of years ago."

"Boy ... howdy." Castle was doing mental arithmetic and algebra with variables like Porsches and fast boats.

"But he let his sisters take care of it. He let them reinvest the capital."

"They weren't too swift?"

"They were idiots! They took good solid blue-chip stocks and tax-free municipals, too 'boring' for them, and threw it all away gambling on commodities." She grimaced. "*Pork* bellies? I finally had John go to Chicago and come back with what was left of his money. There wasn't much."

"You ain't broke, though."

"Damned near. There's enough income to pay for insurance and eventually we'll be able to draw on an IRA. But the cash payments stop in two months. We'll have to live on John's salary. I suppose I'll get a job, too."

"What you ought to get is a typewriter."

Lena laughed and slouched back in her chair. "That would be something."

"You think he could do it? I mean if he would, do you think he could?"

"He's a good writer." She looked thoughtful. "He's had some stories published, you know, in the literary magazines. The ones that pay four or five free copies."

"Big deal."

She shrugged. "Pays off in the long run. Tenure. But I don't know whether being able to write a good literary story means that John could write a good Hemingway imitation."

"He knows enough, right?"

"Maybe he knows too much. He might be paralyzed by his own standards." She shook her head. "In some ways he's an absolute nut about Hemingway. Obsessed, I mean. It's not good for him."

"Maybe writing this stuff would get it out of his system."

She smiled at him. "You've got more angles than a protractor."

"Sorry; I didn't mean to—"

"No." She raised both hands. "Don't be sorry; I like it. I like you, Castle. John's a good man, but sometimes he's too good."

He poured them both more wine. "Nobody ever accused me of that."

"I suspect not." She paused. "Have you ever been in trouble with the police? Just curious."

"Why?"

"Just curious."

He laughed. "Nickel-and-dime stuff, when I was a kid. You know, jus' to see what you can get away with." He turned serious. "Then I pulled two months' hard time for somethin' I didn't do. Wasn't even in town when it happened."

"What was it?"

"Armed robbery. Then the guy came back an' hit the same god-damned store! I mean, he was one sharp cookie. He confessed to the first one and they let me go."

"Why did they accuse you in the first place?"

"Used to think it was somebody had it in for me. Like the clerk who fingered me." He took a sip of wine. "But hell. It was just dumb luck. And dumb cops. The guy was about my height, same color hair, we both lived in the neighborhood. Cops didn't want to waste a lot of time on it. Jus' chuck me in jail."

"So you do have a police record?"

"Huh uh. Girl from the ACLU made sure they wiped it clean. She wanted me to go after 'em for what? False arrest an' wrongful imprisonment. I just wanted to get out of town."

"It wasn't here?"

"Nah. Dayton, Ohio. Been here eight, nine years."

"That's good."

"Why the third degree?"

She leaned forward and patted the back of his hand. "Call it a job interview, Castle. I have a feeling we may be working together."

"Okay." He gave her a slow smile. "Anything else you want to know?"

5

The Doctor and the Doctor's Wife

John trudged into the kitchen the next morning, ignored the coffeepot and pulled a green bottle of beer out of the fridge. He looked up at the skylight. Four scorpions, none of them moving. Have to call the bug man today.

Red wine hangover, the worst kind. He was too old for this. Cheap red wine hangover. He eased himself into a soft chair and carefully poured the beer down the side of the glass. Not too much noise, please.

When you drink too much, you ought to take a couple of aspirin, and some vitamins, and all the water you can hold, before retiring. If you drink too much, of course, you don't remember to do that.

The shower turned off with a bass clunk of plumbing. John winced and took a long drink, which helped a little. When he heard the bathroom door open he called for Lena to bring the aspirin when she came out.

After a few minutes she brought it out and handed it to him. "And how is Dr. Baird today?"

"Dr. Baird needs a doctor. Or an undertaker." He shook out two aspirin and washed them down with the last of the beer. "Like your outfit."

She was wearing only a towel around her head. She simpered and struck a dancer's pose and spun daintily around. "Think it'll catch on?"

"Oh my yes." At thirty-five, she still had the trim model's figure that had caught his eye in the classroom, fifteen years before. A safe, light tan was uniform all over her body, thanks to liberal sunblock and the private sunbathing area on top of the house—private except for the helicopter that came low overhead every weekday at 1:15. She always tried to be there in time to wave at it. The pilot had such white teeth. She wondered how many sunbathers were on his route.

She undid the towel and rubbed her long blond hair vigorously. "Thought I'd cool off for a few minutes before I got dressed. Too much wine, eh?"

"Couldn't you tell from my sparkling repartee last night?" He leaned back, eyes closed, and rolled the cool glass back and forth on his forehead.

"Want another beer?"

"Yeah. Coffee'd be smarter, though."

"It's been sitting all night."

"Pay for my sins." He watched her swivel tightly into the kitchen and, more than ever before, felt the difference in their ages. Seventeen years; he was half again as old as she. A young man would say the hell with the hangover, go grab that luscious thing and carry her back to bed. The organ that responded to this meditation was his stomach, though, and it responded very audibly.

"Some toast, too. Or do you want something fancier?"

"Toast would be fine." Why was she being so nice? Usually if he drank too much, he reaped the whirlwind in the morning.

"Ugh." She saw the scorpions. "Five of them now."

"I wonder how many it will hold before it comes crashing down. Scorpions everywhere, stunned. Then angry."

"I'm sure the bug man knows how to get rid of them."

"In Africa they claimed that if you light a ring of fire around them with gasoline or lighter fluid, they go crazy, run amok, stinging themselves to death in their frenzies. Maybe the bug man could do that."

"Castle and I came up with a plan last night. It's kinda screwy, but it might just work."

"Read that in a book called *Jungle Ways*. I was eight years old and believed every word of it."

"We figured out a way that it would be legal. Are you listening?"

"Uh huh. Let me have real sugar and some milk."

She poured some milk in a cup and put it in the microwave to warm. “Maybe we should talk about it later.”

“Oh no. Hemingway forgery. You figured out a way to make it legal. Go ahead. I’m all ears.”

“See, you tell the publisher first off what it is, that you wrote it and then had it typed up to look authentic.”

“Sure, be a big market for that.”

“In fact, there could be. You’d have to generate it, but it could happen.” The toast sprang up and she brought it and two cups of coffee into the living room on a tray. “See, the bogus manuscript is only one part of a book.”

“I don’t get it.” He tore the toast into strips, to dunk in the strong Cuban coffee.

“The rest of the book is in the nature of an exegesis of your own text.”

“If that con man knows what exegesis is, then I can crack a safe.”

“That part’s my idea. You’re really writing a book *about* Hemingway. You use your own text to illustrate various points—‘I wrote it this way instead of that way because …’”

“It would be different,” he conceded. “Perhaps the second most egotistical piece of Hemingway scholarship in history. A dubious distinction.”

“You could write it tongue-in-cheek, though. It could be really amusing, as well as scholarly.”

“God, we’d have to get an unlisted number, publishers calling us night and day. Movie producers. Might sell ten copies, if I bought nine.”

“You really aren’t getting it, John. You don’t have a particle of larceny in your heart.”

He put a hand on his heart and looked down. “Ventricles, auricles. My undying love for you, a little heartburn. No particles.”

“See, you tell the publisher the truth … but the publisher doesn’t have to tell the truth. Not until publication day.”

“Okay. I still don’t get it.”

She took a delicate nibble of toast. “It goes like this. They print the bogus Hemingway up into a few copies of bogus bound galleys. Top secret.”

“My exegesis carefully left off.”

"That's the ticket. They send it out to a few selected scholars, along with Xeroxes of a few sample manuscript pages. All they say, in effect, is 'Does this seem authentic to you? Please keep it under your hat, for obvious reasons.' Then they sit back and collect blurbs."

"I can see the kind of blurbs they'd get from Scott or Mike or Jack, for instance. Some variation of 'What kind of idiot do you think I am?'"

"Those aren't the kind of people you send it to, dope! You send it to people who think they're experts, but aren't. Castle says this is how the Hitler thing almost worked—they knew better than to show it to historians in general. They showed it to a few people and didn't quote the ones who thought it was a fake. Surely you can come up with a list of people who would be easy to fool."

"Any scholar could. Be a different list for each one; I'd be on some of them."

"So they bring it out on April Fool's Day. You get the front page of the *New York Times Book Review*. *Publishers Weekly* does a story. Everybody wants to be in on the joke. Best-seller list, here we come."

"Yeah, sure, but you haven't thought it through." He leaned back, balancing the coffee cup on his slight potbelly. "What about the guys who give us the blurbs, those second-rate scholars? They're going to look pretty bad."

"We did think of that. No way they could sue, not if the letter accompanying the galleys is carefully written. It doesn't have to say—"

"I don't mean getting sued. I mean I don't want to be responsible for hurting other people's careers maybe wrecking a career, if the person was too extravagant in his endorsement, and had people looking for things to use against him. You know departmental politics. People go down the chute for less serious crimes than making an ass of yourself and your institution in print."

She put her cup down with a clatter. "You're always thinking about other people. Why don't you think about yourself for a change?" She was on the verge of tears. "Think about *us*."

"All right, let's do that. What do you think would happen to my career at BU if I pissed off the wrong people with this exercise? How long do you think it would take me to make full professor? Do you think BU would make a full professor out of a man who uses his specialty to pull vicious practical jokes?"

"Just do me the favor of thinking about it. Cool down and weigh the pluses and minuses. If you did it with the right touch, your department would love it—and God, Harry wants to get rid of the chairmanship so bad he'd give it to an axe murderer. You know you'll make full professor about thirty seconds before Harry hands you the keys to the office and runs."

"True enough." He finished the coffee and stood up in a slow creak. "I'll give it some thought. Horizontally." He turned toward the bedroom.

"Want some company?"

He looked at her for a moment. "Indeed I do."

6

In Our Time

Back already?

Need to find a meta-causal. One guy seems to be generating the danger flag in various timelines. John Baird, who's a scholar in some of them, a soldier in some, and a rich playboy in a few. He's always a Hemingway nut, though. He does something that starts off the ripples in '95, '96, '97; depending on which timeline you're in—but I can't seem to get close to it. There's something odd about him, and it doesn't have to do with Hemingway specifically.

But he's definitely causing the eddy?

Has to be him.

All right. Find a meta-causal that all the doom lines have in common, and forget about the others. Then go talk to him.

There'll be resonance—

But who cares? Moot after A.D. 2006.

That's true. I'll hit all the doom lines at once, then: neutralize the meta-causal, then jump ahead and do some spot checks.

Good. And no killing this time.

I understand. But—

You're too close to 2006. Kill the wrong person, and the whole thing could unravel.

Well, there are differences of opinion. We would certainly feel it if the world failed to come to an end in those lines.

As you say, differences of opinion. My opinion is that you better not kill anybody or I'll send you back to patrol the fourteenth century again.

Understood. But I can't guarantee that I can neutralize the meta-causal without eliminating John Baird.

Fourteenth century. Some people love it. Others think it was nasty, brutish, and long.

7

A Clean, Well-Lighted Place

Most of the sleuthing that makes up literary scholarship takes place in settings either neutral or unpleasant. Libraries' old stacks, attics metaphorical and actual; dust and silverfish, yellowed paper and fading ink. Books and letters that appear in card files but not on shelves.

Hemingway researchers have a haven outside of Boston, the Hemingway Collection at the University of Massachusetts' John F. Kennedy Library. It's a triangular room with one wall dominated by a picture window that looks over Boston Harbor to the sea. Comfortable easy chairs surround a coffee table, but John had never seen them in use; worktables under the picture window provided realistic room for computer and clutter. Skins from animals the Hemingways had dispatched in Africa snarled up from the floor, and one wall was dominated by Hemingway memorabilia and photographs. What made the room Nirvana, though, was row upon row of boxes containing tens of thousands of Xerox pages of Hemingway correspondence, manuscripts, clippings—everything from a boyhood shopping list to all extant versions of every short story and poem and novel.

John liked to get there early so he could claim one of the three computers. He snapped it on, inserted a CD, and typed in his code number. Then he keyed in the database index and started searching.

The more commonly requested items would appear onscreen if you asked for them—whenever someone requested a physical copy of an item, an electronic copy automatically was sent into the database—but most of the things John needed were obscure, and he had to haul down the letter boxes and physically flip through them, just like some poor scholar inhabiting the first nine-tenths of the twentieth century.

Time disappeared for him as he abandoned his notes and followed lines of instinct leaping from letter to manuscript to note to interview, doing what was in essence the opposite of the scholar's job: a scholar would normally be trying to find out what these stories had been about. John instead was trying to track down every reference that might restrict what he himself could write about, simulating the stories.

The most confining restriction was the one he'd first remembered, walking away from the bar where he'd met Castle. The one-paragraph answer that Hadley had given to Carlos Baker about the unfinished novel; that it was a Nick Adams story about hunting and fishing up in Michigan. John didn't know anything about hunting, and most of his fishing experience was limited to watching a bobber and hoping it wouldn't go down and break his train of thought.

There was the one story that Hemingway had left unpublished, "Boys and Girls Together," mostly clumsy self-parody. It covered the right period and the right activities, but using it as a source would be sensitive business, tiptoeing through a minefield. Anyone looking for a fake would go straight there. Of course John could go up to the Michigan woods and camp out, see things for himself and try to re-create them in the Hemingway style. Later, though. First order of business was to make sure there was nothing in this huge collection that would torpedo the whole project—some postcard where Hemingway said "You're going to like this novel because it has a big scene about cleaning fish."

The short stories would be less restricted in subject matter. According to Hemingway, they'd been about growing up in Oak Park and Michigan and the battlefields of Italy.

That made him stop and think. The one dramatic experience he shared with Hemingway was combat—fifty years later, to be sure, in

Vietnam, but the basic situations couldn't have changed that much. Terror, heroism, cowardice. The guns and grenades were a little more streamlined, but they did the same things to people. Maybe do a World War I story as a finger exercise, see whether it would be realistic to try a longer growing-up-in-Michigan pastiche.

He made a note to himself about that on the computer, oblique enough not to be damning, and continued the eye-straining job of searching through Hadley's correspondence, trying to find some further reference to the lost novel—damn!

Writing to Ernest's mother, Hadley noted that "the taxi driver broke his typewriter" on the way to the Constantinople conference—did he get it fixed, or just chuck it? A quick check showed that the typeface of his manuscripts did indeed change after July 1924. So they'd never be able to find it. There were typewriters in Hemingway shrines in Key West, Billings, Schruns; the initial plan had been to find which was the old Corona, then locate an identical one and have Castle arrange a swap.

So they would fall back on Plan B. Castle had claimed to be good with mechanical things, and thought if they could find a 1921 Corona, he could tweak the keys around so they would produce a convincing manuscript—lowercase "s" a hair low, "e" a hair high, and so forth.

How he could be so sure of success without ever having seen the inside of a manual typewriter, John did not know. Nor did he have much confidence.

But it wouldn't have to be a perfect simulation, since they weren't out to fool the whole world, but just a few reviewers who would only see two or three Xeroxed pages. He could probably do a close enough job. John put it out of his mind and moved on to the next letter.

But it was an odd coincidence for him to think about Castle at that instant, since Castle was thinking about him. Or at least asking.

The Coming Man

"How was he when he was younger?"

"He never was younger." She laughed and rolled around inside the compass of his arms to face him. "Than you, I mean. He was in his mid-thirties when we met. You can't be much over twenty-five."

He kissed the end of her nose. "Thirty this year. But I still get carded sometimes."

"I'm a year older than you are. So you have to do anything I say."

"So far so good." He'd checked her wallet when she'd gone into the bathroom to insert the diaphragm, and knew she was thirty-five. "Break out the whips and chains now?"

"Not till next week. Work up to it slowly." She pulled away from him and mopped her front with the sheet. "You're good at being slow."

"I like being asked to come back."

"How 'bout tonight and tomorrow morning?"

"If you feed me lots of vitamins. How long you think he'll be up in Boston?"

"He's got a train ticket for Wednesday. But he said he might stay longer if he got onto something."

Castle laughed. "Or into something. Think he might have a girl up there? Some student like you used to be?"

"That would be funny. I guess it's not impossible." She covered her eyes with the back of her hand. "The wife is always the last to know."

They both laughed. "But I don't think so. He's a sweet guy but he's just not real sexy. I think his students see him as kind of a favorite uncle."

"You fell for him once."

"Uh huh. He had all of his current virtues plus a full head of hair, no potbelly—and, hm, what am I forgetting?"

"He was hung like an elephant?"

"No, I guess it was the millions of dollars. That can be pretty sexy."

9

Wanderings

It was a good thing John liked to nose around obscure neighborhoods shopping; you couldn't walk into any old Kmart and pick up a 1921 Corona portable. In fact, you couldn't walk into any typewriter shop in Boston and find one, not any. Nowadays they all sold self-contained word processors, with a few dusty electrics in the back room. A few had fancy manual typewriters from Italy or Switzerland; it had been almost thirty years since the American manufacturers had made a machine that wrote without electronic help.

He had a little better luck with pawnshops. Lots of Smith-Coronas, a few L.C. Smiths, and two actual Coronas that might have been old enough. One had too large a typeface and the other, although the typeface was the same as Hemingway's, was missing a couple of letters: Th quick b own fox jump d ov th lazy dog. The challenge of writing a convincing Hemingway novel without using the letters "e" and "r" seemed daunting. He bought the machine anyhow, thinking they might ultimately have two or several broken ones that could be concatenated into one reliable machine.

The old pawnbroker rang up his purchase and made change and slammed the cash drawer shut. "Now you don't look to me like the kind of man who would hold it against a man who …" He shrugged. "Well, who sold you something and then suddenly remembered that there was a place with lots of those somethings?"

"Of course not. Business is business."

"I don't know the name of the guy or his shop; I think he calls it a museum. Up in Brunswick, Maine. He's got a thousand old typewriters. He buys, sells, trades. That's the only place I know of you might find one with the missing whatever-you-call-ems."

"Fonts." He put the antique typewriter under his arm—the handle was missing—and shook the old man's hand. "Thanks a lot. This might save me weeks."

With some difficulty John got together packing materials and shipped the machine to Key West, along with Xeroxes of a few dozen pages of Hemingway's typed copy and a note suggesting Castle see what he could do. Then he went to the library and found a Brunswick telephone directory. Under "Office Machines & Supplies" was listed Crazy Tom's Typewriter Museum and Sales Emporium. John rented a car and headed north.

The small town had rolled up its sidewalks by the time he got there. He drove past Crazy Tom's and pulled into the first motel. It had a neon VACANCY sign but the innkeeper had to be roused from a deep sleep. He took John's credit card number and directed him to Room 14 and pointedly turned on the NO sign. There were only two other cars in the motel lot.

John slept late and treated himself to a full "trucker's" breakfast at the local diner: two pork chops and eggs and hash browns. Then he worked off ten calories by walking to the shop.

Crazy Tom was younger than John had expected, thirtyish with an unruly shock of black hair. A manual typewriter lay upside down on an immaculate worktable, but most of the place was definitely maculate. Thousands of peanut shells littered the floor. Crazy Tom was eating them compulsively from a large wooden bowl. When he saw John standing in the doorway, he offered some. "Unsalted," he said. "Good for you."

John crunched his way over the peanut-shell carpet. The only light in the place was the bare bulb suspended over the worktable, though two unlit high-intensity lamps were clamped on either side of it. The walls were floor-to-ceiling gloomy shelves holding hundreds of typewriters, mostly black.

"Let me guess," the man said as John scooped up a handful of peanuts. "You're here about a typewriter."

"A specific one. A 1921 Corona portable."

"Ah." He closed his eyes in thought. "Hemingway. His first. Or I guess the first after he started writing. A '27 Corona, now, that'd be Faulkner."

"You get a lot of calls for them?"

"Couple times a year. People hear about this place and see if they can find one like the master used, whoever the master is to them. Sympathetic magic and all that. But you aren't a writer."

"I've had some stories published."

"Yeah, but you look too comfortable. You do something else. Teach school." He looked around in the gloom. "Corona Corona." Then he sang the six syllables to the tune of "Corina, Corina." He walked a few steps into the darkness and returned with a small machine and set it on the table. "Newer than 1920 because of the way it says 'Corona' here. Older than 1927 because of the tab setup." He found a piece of paper and a chair. "Go on, try it."

John typed out a few quick foxes and aids to one's party. The typeface was identical to the one on the machine Hadley had given Hemingway before they'd been married. The up-and-down displacements of the letters were different, of course, but Castle should be able to fix that once he'd practiced with the backup machine.

John cracked a peanut. "How much?"

"What you need it for?"

"Why is that important?"

"It's the only one I got. Rather rent it than sell it." He didn't look like he was lying, trying to push the price up. "A thousand to buy, a hundred a month to rent."

"Tell you what, then. I buy it and if it doesn't bring me luck, you agree to buy it back at a pro ratum. My one thousand dollars minus ten percent per month."

Crazy Tom stuck out his hand. "Let's have a beer on it."

"Isn't it a little early for that?"

"Not if you eat peanuts all morning." He took two long-necked Budweisers from a cooler and set them on paper towels on the table. "So what kind of stuff you write?"

"Short stories and some poetry." The beer was good after the heavy greasy breakfast. "Nothing you would've seen unless you read magazines like *Iowa Review* and *Triquarterly*."

"Oh yeah. Foldouts of Gertrude Stein and H.D. I might've read your stuff."

"John Baird."

He shook his head. "Maybe. I'm no good with names."

"If you recognized my name from *The Iowa Review* you'd be the first person who ever had."

"I was right about the Hemingway connection?"

"Of course."

"But you don't write like Hemingway for no *Iowa Review*. Short declarative sentences, truly this truly that."

"No, you were right about the teaching, too. I teach Hemingway up at Boston University."

"So that's why the typewriter? Play show-and-tell with your students?"

"That, too. Mainly I want to write some on it and see how it feels."

From the back of the shop, a third person listened to the conversation with great interest. He, it, wasn't really a "person," though he could look like one: he had never been born and he would never die. But then he didn't really exist, not in the down-home pinch-yourself-ouch! way that you and I do.

In another way, he did *more* than exist, since he could slip back and forth between places you and I don't even have words for.

He was carrying a wand that could be calibrated for heart attack, stroke, or metastasized cancer on one end; the other end induced a kind of aphasia. He couldn't use it unless he materialized. He walked toward the two men, making no crunching sounds on the peanut shells because he weighed less than a thought. He studied John Baird's face from about a foot away.

"I guess it's a mystical thing, though I'm uncomfortable with that word. See whether I can get into his frame of mind."

"Funny thing," Crazy Tom said; "I never thought of him typing out his stories. He was always sitting in some cafe writing in notebooks, piling up saucers."

"You've read a lot about him?" That would be another reason not to try the forgery. This guy comes out of the woodwork and says "I sold John Baird a 1921 Corona portable."

"Hell, all I do is read. If I get two customers a day, one of 'em's a mistake and the other just wants directions. I've read all of Hemingway's fiction and most of the journalism and I think all of the poetry. Not just the *Querschnitt* period; the more interesting stuff."

The invisible man was puzzled. Quite obviously John Baird planned some sort of Hemingway forgery. But then he should be growing worried over this man's dangerous expertise. Instead, he was radiating relief.

What course of action, inaction? He could go back a few hours in time and steal this typewriter, though he would have to materialize for that, and it would cause suspicions. And Baird could find another. He could kill one or both of them, now or last week or next, but that would mean duty in the fourteenth century for more than forever—when you exist out of time, a century of unpleasantness is long enough for planets to form and die.

He wouldn't have been drawn to this meeting if it were not a strong causal nexus. There must be earlier ones, since John Baird did not just stroll down a back street in this little town and decide to change history by buying a typewriter. But the earlier ones must be too weak, or something was masking them.

Maybe it was a good timeplace to get John Baird alone and explain things to him. Then use the wand on him. But no, not until he knew exactly what he was preventing. With considerable effort of will and expenditure of something like energy, he froze time at this instant and traveled to a couple of hundred adjacent realities that were all in this same bundle of doomed timelines.

In most of them, Baird was here in Crazy Tom's Typewriter Museum and Sales Emporium. In some, he was in a similar place in New York. In two, he was back in the Hemingway collection. In one, John Baird didn't exist: the whole planet was a lifeless blasted cinder. He'd known about that timeline; it had been sort of a dry run.

"He did both," John then said in most of the timelines. "Sometimes typing, sometimes fountain pen or pencil. I've seen the rough draft of his first novel. Written out in a stack of seven French schoolkids' copybooks." He looked around, memory working. A red herring wouldn't hurt. He'd never come across a reference to any other specific Hemingway typewriter, but maybe this guy had. "You know what kind of machine he used in Key West or Havana?"

Crazy Tom pulled on his chin. "Nope. Bring me a sample of the typing and I might be able to pin it down, though. And I'll keep an eye out—got a card?"

John took out a business card and his checkbook. "Take a check on a Boston bank?"

"Sure. I'd take one on a Tierra del Fuego bank. Who'd stiff you on a seventy-year-old typewriter?" Sylvester Castlemaine might, John thought. "I've had this business almost twenty years," Tom continued. "Not a single bounced check or bent plastic."

"Yeah," John said. "Why would a crook want an old typewriter?" The invisible man laughed and went away.

10

Banal Story

Dear Lena & Castle,

Typing this on the new/old machine to give you an idea about what has to be modified to mimic EH's:

abcdefghijklmnopqrstuvwxyz

ABCDEFGHIJKLMNOPQRSTUVWXYZ234567890,./ "#$%_&'( )*?

Other mechanical things to think about—

1. Paper—One thing that made people suspicious about the Hitler forgery is that experts know that old paper smells old. And of course there was that fatal chemical-composition error that clinched it.

As we discussed, my first thought was that one of us would have to go to Paris and nose around in old attics and so forth, trying to find either a stack of 75-year-old paper or an old blank book we could cut pages out of. But in the JFK Library collection I found out that EH actually did bring some American-made paper along with him. A lot of the rough draft of in our time—written in Paris a year or two after our "discovery"—was typed on the back of 6 X 7" stationery from his parents' vacation place in Windemere, Xerox enclosed. It should be pretty easy to duplicate on a hand press, and of course it will be a lot easier to find 75-year-old American paper. One complication, unfortunately, is that I haven't really seen the paper;

only a Xerox of the pages. Have to come up with some pretext to either visit the vault or have a page brought up, so I can check the color of the ink, memorize the weight and deckle of the paper, check to see how the edges are cut ...

I'm starting to sound like a real forger. In for a penny, though, in for a pound. One of the critics who's sent the fragment might want to see the actual document, and compare it with the existing Windemere pages.

2. Inks. This should not be a problem. Here's a recipe for typewriter ribbon ink from a 1918 book of commercial formulas:

8 oz. lampblack

4 oz. gum arabic

1 quart methylated spirits

That last one is wood alcohol. The others ought to be available in Miami if you can't find them on the Rock.

Aging the ink on the paper gets a little tricky. I haven't been able to find anything about it in the libraries around here; no FORGERY FOR FUN & PROFIT. May check in New York before coming back.

(If we don't find anything, I'd suggest baking it for a few days at a temperature low enough not to greatly affect the paper, and then interleaving it with blank sheets of the old paper and pressing them together for a few days, to restore the old smell, and further absorb the residual ink solvents.)

Toyed with the idea of actually allowing the manuscript to mildew somewhat, but that might get out of hand and actually destroy some of it—or for all I know we'd be employing a species of mildew that doesn't speak French. Again, thinking like a true forger, which may be a waste of time and effort, but I have to admit is kind of fun. Playing cops and robbers at my age.

Well, I'll call tonight. Miss you, Lena.

Your partner in crime,

John

11

A Divine Gesture

When John returned to his place in Boston, there was a message on his answering machine: "John, this is Nelson Van Nuys. Harry told me you were in town. I left something in your box at the office and I strongly suggest you take it before somebody else does. I'll be out of town for a week, but give me a call if you're here next Friday. You can take me and Doris out to dinner at Panache."

Panache was the most expensive restaurant in Cambridge. Interesting. John checked his watch. He hadn't planned to go to the office, but there was plenty of time to swing by on his way to returning the rental car. The train didn't leave for another four hours.

Van Nuys was a fellow Hemingway scholar and sometimes drinking buddy who taught at Brown. What had he brought ninety miles to deliver in person, rather than mail? He was probably just in town and dropped by. But it was worth checking.

No one but the secretary was in the office, noontime, for which John was obscurely relieved. In his box were three interdepartmental memos, a textbook catalog, and a brown cardboard box that sloshed when he picked it up. He took it all back to his office and closed the door.

The office made him feel a little weary, as usual. He wondered whether they would be shuffling people around again this year. The department liked to keep its professors in shape by having them haul tons of books and files up and down the corridor every couple of years.

He glanced at the memos and pitched them, irrelevant since he wasn't teaching in the summer, and put the catalog in his briefcase. Then he carefully opened the cardboard box.

It was a half-pint Jack Daniel's bottle, but it didn't have bourbon in it. A cloudy greenish liquid. John unscrewed the top and with the sharp Pernod tang the memory came back. He and Van Nuys had wasted half an afternoon in Paris years ago, trying to track down a source of true absinthe. So he had finally found some.

Absinthe. Nectar of the gods, ruination of several generations of French artists, students, workingmen—outlawed in 1915 for its addictive and hallucinogenic qualities. Where had Van Nuys found it?

He screwed the top back on tightly and put it back in the box and put the box in his briefcase. If its effect really was all that powerful, you probably wouldn't want to drive under its influence. In Boston traffic, of course, a little lane weaving and a few mild collisions would go unnoticed.

Once he was safely on the train, he'd try a shot or two of it. It couldn't be all that potent. Child of the sixties, John had taken LSD, psilocybin, ecstasy, and peyote, and remembered with complete accuracy the quality of each drug's hallucinations. The effects of absinthe wouldn't be nearly as extreme as its modern successors. But it was probably just as well to try it first in a place where unconsciousness or Steve Allen imitations or speaking in tongues would go unremarked.

He turned in the rental car and took a cab to South Station rather than juggle suitcase, briefcase, and typewriter through the subway system. Once there, he nursed a beer through an hour of the Yankees murdering the Red Sox, and then rented a cart to roll his burden down to track 3, where a smiling porter installed him aboard the *Silver Meteor*, its range newly extended from Boston to Miami.

He had loved the train since his boyhood in Washington. His mother hated flying and so they often clickety-clacked from place to place in the snug comfort of first-class compartments. Eidetic memory blunted his enjoyment of the modern Amtrak version. This compartment was as large as the ones he had read and done puzzles in, forty years before—amazing and delighting his mother with his proficiency in word games—but the smell of good old leather was gone, replaced by plastic, and the fittings that had been polished brass were chromed steel now. On the middle of the red plastic seat was a Hospitality Pak, a plastic box encased in plastic wrap that contained a wedge of indestructible "cheese food," as if cheese had to eat, a small plastic bottle of cheap California wine, a plastic glass to contain it, and an apple, possibly not plastic.

John hung up his coat and tie in the small closet provided beside where the bed would fold down, and for a few minutes he watched with interest as his fellow passengers and their accompaniment hurried or ambled to their cars. Mostly old people, of course. Enough young ones, John hoped, to keep the trains alive a few decades more.

"Mr. Baird?" John turned to face a black porter, who bowed slightly and favored him with a blinding smile of white and gold. "My name is George, and I will be at your service as far as Atlanta. Is everything satisfactory?"

"Doing fine. But if you could find me a glass made of glass and a couple of ice cubes, I might mention you in my will."

"One minute, sir." In fact it took less than a minute. That was one aspect, John had to admit, that had improved in recent years: The service on Amtrak in the sixties and seventies had been right up there with Alcatraz and the Hanoi Hilton.

He closed and locked the compartment door and carefully poured about two ounces of the absinthe into the glass. Like Pernod, it turned milky on contact with the ice.

He swirled it around and breathed deeply. It did smell much like Pernod, but with an acrid tang that was probably oil of wormwood. An experimental sip: the wormwood didn't dominate the licorice flavor, but it was there.

"Thanks, Nelson," he whispered, and drank the whole thing in one cold fiery gulp. He set down the glass and the train began to move. For a weird moment that seemed hallucinatory, but it always did, the train starting off so smoothly and silently.

For about ten minutes he felt nothing unusual, as the train did its slow tour of Boston's least attractive backyards. The conductor who checked his ticket seemed like a normal human being, which could have been a hallucination.

John knew that some drugs, like amyl nitrite, hit with a swift slap, while others creep into your mind like careful infiltrators. This was the way of absinthe; all he felt was a slight alcohol buzz, and he was about to take another shot, when it subtly began.

There were *things* just at the periphery of his vision, odd things with substance, but somehow without shape, that of course moved away when he turned his head to look at them. At the same time a whispering began in his ears, just audible over the train noise, but not intelligible, as if in a language he had heard before but not understood. For some reason the effects were pleasant, though of course they could be frightening if a person were not expecting weirdness. He enjoyed the illusions for a few minutes, while the scenery outside mellowed into woodsy suburbs, and the visions and voices stopped rather suddenly.

He poured another ounce and this time diluted it with water. He remembered the sad woman in "Hills like White Elephants" lamenting that everything new tasted like licorice, and allowed himself to wonder what Hemingway had been drinking when he wrote that curious story.

Chuckling at his own—what? Effrontery?—John took out the 1921 Corona and slipped a sheet of paper into it and balanced it on his knees. He had earlier thought of the first two lines of the WWI pastiche; he typed them down and kept going:

The dirt on the sides of the trenches was never completely dry in the morning. If Rick could find an old newspaper he would put it between his chest and the dirt when he went out to lean on the side of the trench and wait for the light. First light was the best time. You might have luck and see a muzzle flash. But patience was better than luck. Wait to see a helmet or a head without a helmet.

Nick looked at the enemy line through a rectangular box of wood that went through the trench at about ground level. The other end of the box was covered by a square of gauze the color of dirt. A person looking directly at it might see the muzzle flash when Nick fired through the box. But with luck, the flash would be the last thing he saw.

Nick had fired through the gauze six times, perhaps killing three enemy, and the gauze now had a ragged hole in the center.

Okay, John thought, he'd be able to see slightly better through the hole in the center but staring that way would reduce the effective field of view, so he would deliberately try to look to one side or the other. How to type that down in a simple way? Someone cleared his throat.

John looked up from the typewriter. Sitting across from him was Ernest Hemingway, the weathered, wise Hemingway of the famous Karsh photograph.

"I'm afraid you must not do that," Hemingway said.

John looked at the half-full glass of absinthe and looked back. Hemingway was still there. "Jesus Christ," he said.

"It isn't the absinthe." Hemingway's image rippled and he became the handsome teenager who had gone to war, the war John was writing about. "I am quite real. In a way, I am more real than you are." As it spoke it aged: the mustachioed leading-man-handsome Hemingway of the twenties; the slightly corpulent still magnetic media hero of the thirties and forties; the beard turning white, the features hard and sad and then twisting with impotence and madness, and then a sudden loud report and the cranial vault exploding, the mahogany veneer of the wall splashed with blood and brains and imbedded chips of skull. There was a strong smell of cordite and blood. The almost-headless corpse shrugged, spreading its hands. "I can look like anyone I want." The mess disappeared and it became the young Hemingway again.

John slumped and stared.

"This thing you just started must never be finished. This Hemingway pastiche. It will ruin something very important."

"What could it ruin? I'm not even planning to—"

"Your plans are immaterial. If you continue with this project, it will profoundly affect the future."

"You're from the future?"

"I'm from the future and the past and other temporalities that you can't comprehend. But all you need to know is that you must not write this Hemingway story. If you do, I or someone like me will have to kill you."

It gestured and a wand the size of a walking stick, half-black and half-white, appeared in its hand. It tapped John's knee with the white end. There was a slight tingle.

"Now you won't be able to tell anybody about me, or write anything about me down. If you try to talk about me, the memory will disappear—and reappear moments later, along with the knowledge that I will kill you if you don't cooperate." It turned into the bloody corpse again. "Understood?"

"Of course."

"If you behave, you will never have to see me again." It started to fade.

"Wait. What do you really look like?"

"This...." For a few seconds John stared at an ebony presence deeper than black, at once points and edges and surfaces and volume and hints of further dimensions. "You can't really see or know," a voice whispered inside his head. He reached into the blackness and jerked his hand back, rimed with frost and numb. The thing disappeared.

He stuck his hand under his armpit and feeling returned. That last apparition was the unsettling one. He had Hemingway's appearance at every age memorized, and had seen the corpse in his mind's eye often enough. A drug could conceivably have brought them all together and made up this fantastic demand—which might actually be nothing more than a reasonable side of his nature trying to make him stop wasting time on this silly project.

But that thing. His hand was back to normal. Maybe a drug could do that, too; make your hand feel freezing. LSD did more profound things than that. But not while arguing about a manuscript.

He considered the remaining absinthe. Maybe take another big blast of it and see whether ol' Ernie comes back again. Or no—there was a simpler way to check.

The bar was four rocking and rolling cars away, and bouncing his way from wall to window helped sober John up. When he got there, he had another twinge for the memories of the past. Stained

Formica tables. No service; you had to go to a bar at the other end. Acrid with cigarette fumes. He remembered linen tablecloths and endless bottles of Coke with the names of cities from everywhere stamped on the bottom and, when his father came along with them, the rich sultry smoke of his Havanas. The fat Churchills from Punch that emphysema stopped just before Castro could. "A Coke, please." He wondered which depressed him more, the red can or the plastic cup with miniature ice cubes.

The test. It was not in his nature to talk to strangers on public conveyances. But this was necessary. There was a man sitting alone who looked about John's age, a Social Security–bound hippy with wire-rimmed John Lennon glasses, white hair down to his shoulders, bushy grey beard. He nodded when John sat down across from him, but didn't say anything. He sipped beer and looked blankly out at the gathering darkness.

"Excuse me," John said, "but I have a strange thing to ask you."

The man looked at him. "I don't mind strange things. But please don't try to sell me anything illegal."

"I wouldn't. It may have something to do with a drug, but it would be one I took."

"You do look odd. You tripping?"

"Doesn't feel like it. But I may have been … slipped something." He leaned back and rubbed his eyes. "I just talked to Ernest Hemingway."

"The writer?"

"In my roomette, yeah."

"Wow. He must be pretty old."

"He's dead! More than thirty years."

"Oh wow. Now that is something weird. What he say?"

"You know what a pastiche is?"

"French pastry?"

"No, it's when you copy … when you create an imitation of another person's writing. Hemingway's, in this case."

"Is that legal? I mean, with him dead and all."

"Sure it is, as long as you don't try to foist it off as Hemingway's real stuff."

"So what happened? He wanted to help you with it?"

"Actually, no … he said I'd better stop."

"Then you better stop. You don't fuck around with ghosts." He pointed at the old brass bracelet on John's wrist. "You in the 'Nam."

"Sixty-eight," John said. "Hue."

"Then you oughta know about ghosts. You don't fuck with ghosts."

"Yeah." What he'd thought was aloofness in the man's eyes, the set of his mouth, was aloneness, something slightly different. "You okay?"

"Oh yeah. Wasn't for a while, then I got my shit together." He looked out the window again, and said something weirdly like Hemingway: "I learned to take it a day at a time. The day you're in's the only day that's real. The past is shit and the future, hell, some day your future's gonna be that you got no future. So fuck it, you know? One day at a time."

John nodded. "What outfit were you in?"

"Like I say, man, the past is shit. No offense?"

"No, that's okay." He poured the rest of his Coke over the ice and stood up to go.

"You better talk to somebody about those ghosts. Some kinda shrink, you know? It's not that they're not real. But just you got to deal with 'em."

"Thanks. I will." John got a little more ice from the barman and negotiated his way down the lurching corridor back to his compartment, trying not to spill his drink while also juggling fantasy, reality, past, present, memory. …

He opened the door and Hemingway was there, drinking his absinthe. He looked up with weary malice. "Am I going to have to kill you?"

What John did next would have surprised Castlemaine, who thought he was a nebbish. He closed the compartment door and sat down across from the apparition. "Maybe you can kill me and maybe you can't."

"Don't worry. I can."

"You said I wouldn't be able to talk to anyone about you. But I just walked down to the bar car and did."

"I know. That's why I came back."

"So if one of your powers doesn't work, maybe another doesn't. At any rate, if you kill me, you'll never find out what went wrong."

"That's very cute, but it doesn't work." It finished off the absinthe and then ran a finger around the rim of the glass, which refilled out of nowhere.

"You're making assumptions about causality that are necessarily naïve, because you can't perceive even half of the dimensions that you inhabit."

"Nevertheless, you haven't killed me yet."

"And assumptions about my 'psychology' that are absurd. I am no more a human being than you are a paramecium."

"I'll accept that. But I would make a deal with a paramecium if I thought I could gain an advantage from it."

"What could you possibly have to deal with, though?"

"I know something about myself that you evidently don't, that enables me to overcome your don't-talk restriction. Knowing that might be worth a great deal to you."

"Maybe something."

"What I would like in exchange is, of course, my life, and an explanation of why I must not do the Hemingway pastiche. Then I wouldn't do it."

"You wouldn't do it if I killed you, either."

John sipped his Coke and waited.

"All right. It goes something like this. There is not just one universe, but actually uncountable zillions of them. They're all roughly the same size and complexity as this one, and they're all going off in a zillion different directions, and it is one hell of a job to keep things straight."

"You do this by yourself? You're God?"

"There's not just one of me. In fact, it would be meaningless to assign a number to us, but I guess you could say that altogether, we are God ... and the Devil, and the Cosmic Puppet Master, and the Grand Unification Theory, the Great Pumpkin and everything else. When we consider ourselves as a group, let me see, I guess a human translation of our name would be the Spatio-Temporal Adjustment Board."

"STAB?"

"I guess that is unfortunate. Anyhow, what STAB does is more the work of a scalpel than a knife." The Hemingway scratched its nose, leaving the absinthe suspended in midair. "Events are supposed to happen in certain ways, in certain sequences. You look at things happening and say cause and effect, or coincidence, or golly, that couldn't have happened in a million years—but you don't even have a clue. Don't even try to think about it. It's like an ant trying to figure out General Relativity."

"It wouldn't have a clue. Wouldn't know where to start."

The apparition gave him a sharp look and continued. "These universes come in bundles. Hundreds of them, thousands, that are pretty much the same. And they affect each other. Resonate with each other. When something goes wrong in one, it resonates and screws up all of them."

"You mean to say that if I write a Hemingway pastiche, hundreds of universes are going to go straight to hell?"

The apparition spread its hands and looked to the ceiling. "Nothing is simple. The only thing that's simple is that nothing is simple.

"I'm a sort of literature specialist. American literature of the nineteenth and twentieth centuries. Usually. Most of my timespace is taken up with guys like Hemingway, Teddy Roosevelt, Heinlein, Bierce. Crane, Spillane, Twain."

"Not William Dean Howells?"

"Not him or James or Carver or Coover or Cheever or any of those guys. If everybody gave me as little trouble as William Dean Howells, I could spend most of my timespace on a planet where the fishing was good."

"Masculine writers?" John said. "But not all hairy-chested macho types."

"I'll give you an A– on that one. They're writers who have an accumulating effect on the masculine side of the American national character. There's no one word for it, though it is a specific thing: individualistic, competence-worshiping, short-term optimism and long-term existentialism. 'There may be nothing after I die but I sure as hell will do the job right while I'm here, even though I'm surrounded by idiots.' You see the pattern?"

"Okay. And I see how Hemingway fits in. But how could writing a pastiche interfere with it?"

"That's a limitation I have. I don't know specifically. I do know that the accelerating revival of interest in Hemingway from the seventies through the nineties is vitally important. In the Soviet Union as well as the United States. For some reason, I can feel your pastiche interfering with it." He stretched out the absinthe glass into a yard-long amber crystal, and it changed into the black-and-white cane. The glass reappeared in the drink holder by the window. "Your turn."

"You won't kill me after you hear what I have to say?"

"No. Go ahead."

"Well ... I have an absolutely eidetic memory. Everything I've ever seen—or smelled or tasted or heard or touched, or even dreamed—I can instantly recall.

"Every other memory freak I've read about was limited—numbers, dates, calendar tricks, historical details—and most of them were *idiots savants.* I have at least normal intelligence. But from the age of about three, I have never forgotten anything."

The Hemingway smiled congenially. "Thank you. That's exactly it." It fingered the black end of the cane, clicking something. "If you had the choice, would you rather die of a heart attack, stroke, or cancer?"

"That's it?" The Hemingway nodded. "Well, you're human enough to cheat. To lie."

"It's not something you could understand. Stroke?"

"It might not work."

"We're going to find out right now." He lowered the cane.

"Wait! What's death? Is there ... anything I should do, anything you know?"

The rod stopped, poised an inch over John's knee. "I guess you just end. Is that so bad?"

"Compared to not ending, it's bad."

"That shows how little you know. I and the ones like me can never die. If you want something to occupy your last moment, your last thought, you might pity me."

John stared straight into his eyes. "Fuck you."

The cane dropped. A fireball exploded in his head.

12

Marriage Is a Dangerous Game

"We'll blackmail him." Castle and Lena were together in the big antique bathtub, in a sea of pink foam, her back against his chest.

"Sure," she said. "'If you don't let us pass this manuscript off as the real thing, we'll tell everybody you faked it.' Something wrong with that, but I can't quite put my finger on it."

"Here, I'll put mine on it."

She giggled. "Later. What do you mean, blackmail?"

"Got it all figured out. I've got this friend Pansy, she used to be a call girl. Been out of the game seven, eight years; still looks like a million bucks."

"Sure. We fix John up with this hooker—"

"Call girl isn't a hooker. We're talkin' class."

"In the first place, John wouldn't pay for sex. He did that in Vietnam and it still bothers him."

"Not talkin' about pay. Talkin' about fallin' in love. While she meanwhile fucks his eyeballs out."

"You have such a turn of phrase, Sylvester. Then while his eyeballs are out, you come in with a camera."

"Yeah, but you're about six steps ahead."

"Okay, step two; how do we get them together? Church social?"

"She moves in next door." There was another upstairs apartment, unoccupied. "You and me and Julio are conveniently somewhere else when she shows up with all these boxes and that big flight of stairs."

"Sure, John would help her. But that's his nature; he'd help her if she were an ugly old crone with leprosy. Carry a few boxes, sit down for a cup of coffee, maybe. But not jump into the sack."

"Okay, you know John." His voice dropped to a husky whisper and he cupped her breasts. "But I know men, and I know Pansy … and Pansy could give a hard-on to a corpse."

"Sure, and then fuck his eyeballs out. They'd come out easier."

"What?"

"Never mind. Go ahead."

"Well … look. Do you know what a call girl does?"

"I suppose you call her up and say you've got this eyeball problem."

"Enough with the eyeballs. What she does, she works for like an escort service. That part of it's legal. Guy comes into town, business or maybe on vacation, he calls up the service and they ask what kind of companion he'd like. If he says, like, give me some broad with a tight ass, can suck the chrome off a bumper hitch—the guy says like 'I'm sorry, sir, but this is not that kind of a service.' But mostly the customers are pretty hip to it, they say, oh, a pretty young blonde who likes to go dancing."

"Meanwhile they're thinking about bumper hitches and eyeballs."

"You got it. So it starts out just like a date, just the guy pays the escort service like twenty bucks for getting them together. Still no law broken.

"Now about one out of three, four times, that's it. The guy knows what's going on but he don't get up the nerve to ask, or he really doesn't know the score, and it's like a real dull date. I don't think that happened much with Pansy."

"In the normal course of things, though, the subject of bumper hitches comes up."

"Uh huh, but not from Pansy. The guy has to pop the question. That way if he's a cop it's, what, entrapment."

"Do you know whether Pansy ever got busted?"

"Naw. Mainly the cops just shake down the hookers, just want a blowjob anyhow. This town, half of 'em want a blowjob from guys.

"So they pop the question and Pansy blushes and says for you, I guess I could. Then, on the way to the motel or wherever she says, you know, I wouldn't ask this if we weren't really good friends, but I got to make a car payment by tomorrow, and I need like two hundred bucks before noon tomorrow?"

"And she takes MasterCard and VISA."

"No, but she sure as hell knows where every bank machine in town is. She even writes up an IOU" Castle laughed. "Told me a guy from Toledo's holdin' five grand of IOUs from her."

"All right, but that's not John. She could suck the chrome off his eyeballs and he still wouldn't be interested in her if she didn't know Hemingway from hummingbirds."

Castle licked behind her ear, a weird gesture that made her shiver. "That's the trump card. Pansy reads like a son of a bitch. She's got like a thousand books. So this morning I called her up and asked about Hemingway."

"And?"

"She's read them all."

She nodded slowly. "Not bad, Sylvester. So we promote this love affair and sooner or later you catch them in the act. Threaten to tell me unless John accedes to a life of crime."

"Think it could work? He wouldn't say hell, go ahead and tell her?"

"Not if I do my part ... starting tomorrow. I'm the best, sweetest, lovingest wife in this sexy town. Then in a couple of weeks Pansy comes into his life, and there he is, luckiest man alive. Best of both worlds. Until you accidentally catch them *in flagrante delicioso*."

"So to keep both of you, he goes along with me."

"It might just do it. It might just." She slowly levered herself out of the water and smoothed the suds off her various assets.

"Nice."

"Bring me that bumper hitch, Sylvester. Hold on to your eyeballs."

13

In Another Country

John woke up with a hangover of considerable dimension. The diluted glass of absinthe was still in the drink holder by the window. It was just past dawn, and a verdant forest rushed by outside. The rails made a steady hum; the car had a slight rocking that would have been pleasant to a person who felt well.

A porter knocked twice and inquired after Mr. Baird. "Come in," John said. A short white man, smiling, brought in coffee and Danish.

"What happened to George?"

"Pardon me, sir? George who?"

John rubbed his eyes. "Oh, of course. We must be past Atlanta."

"No, sir." The man's smile froze as his brain went into nutty-passenger mode. "We're at least two hours from Atlanta."

"George … is a tall black guy with gold teeth who—"

"Oh, you mean George Mason, sir. He does do this car, but he picks up the train in Atlanta, and works it to Miami and back. He hasn't had the northern leg since last year."

John nodded slowly and didn't ask what year it was. "I understand." He smiled up and read the man's name tag. "I'm sorry, Leonard. Not at my best in the morning." The man withdrew with polite haste.

Suppose that weird dream had not been a dream. The Hemingway creature had killed him—the memory of the stroke was awesomely strong and immediate—but all that death amounted to was slipping into another universe where George Mason was on a different shift. Or perhaps John had gone completely insane.

The second explanation seemed much more reasonable.

On the tray underneath the coffee, juice, and Danish was a copy of *USA Today*, a paper John normally avoided because, although it had its comic aspects, it didn't have any funnies. He checked the date, and it was correct. The news stories were plausible—wars and rumors of war—so at least he hadn't slipped into a dimension where Martians ruled an enslaved Earth or Barry Manilow was president. He turned to the weather map and stopped dead.

Yesterday the country was in the middle of a heat wave that had lasted weeks. It apparently had ended overnight. The entry for Boston, yesterday, was "72/58/sh." But it hadn't rained and the temperature had been in the nineties.

He went back to the front page and began checking news stories. He didn't normally pay much attention to the news, though, and hadn't seen a paper in several days. They'd canceled their Globe delivery for the six weeks in Key West and he hadn't been interested enough to go seek out a newsstand.

There was no mention of the garbage collectors' strike in New York; he'd overheard a conversation about that yesterday. A long obituary for a rock star he was sure had died the year before.

An ad for DeSoto automobiles. That company had gone out of business when he was a teenager.

Bundles of universes, different from each other in small ways. Instead of dying, or maybe because of dying, he had slipped into another one. What would be waiting for him in Key West?

Maybe John Baird.

He set the tray down and hugged himself, trembling. Who or what was he in this universe? All of his memories, all of his personality, were from the one he had been born in. What happened to the John Baird that was born in this one? Was he an associate professor in American Literature at Boston University? Was he down in Key West wrestling with a paper to give at Nairobi—or working on a forgery? Or was he a Fitzgerald specialist snooping around the literary attics of St. Paul, Minnesota?

The truth came suddenly. Both John Bairds were in this compartment, in this body. And the body was slightly different.

He opened the door to the small washroom and looked in the mirror. His hair was a little shorter, less grey, beard better trimmed.

He was less paunchy and … something felt odd. There was feeling in his thigh. He lowered his pants and there was no scar where the sniper bullet had opened his leg and torn up the nerves there.

That was the touchstone. As he raised his shirt, the parallel memory flooded in. Puckered round scar on the abdomen; in this universe the sniper had hit a foot higher—and instead of the convalescent center in Cam Ranh Bay, the months of physical therapy and then back into the war, it had been peritonitis raging; surgery in Saigon and Tokyo and Walter Reed, and no more army.

But slowly they converged again. Amherst and U. Mass.—perversely using the G.I. Bill in spite of his access to millions—the doctorate on *The Sun Also Rises* and the instructorship at B.U., meeting Lena and virtuously waiting until after the semester to ask her out. Sex on the second date, and the third … but there they verged again. This John Baird hadn't gone back into combat to have his midsection sprayed with shrapnel from an American grenade that bounced off a tree; never had dozens of bits of metal cut out of his dick—and in the ensuing twenty-five years had made more use of it. Girlfriends and even one disastrous homosexual encounter with a stranger. As far as he knew, Lena was in the dark about this side of him; thought that he had remained faithful other than one incident seven years after they married. He knew of one affair she had had with a colleague, and suspected more.

The two Johns' personalities and histories merged, separate but one, like two vines from a common root climbing a single support.

Schizophrenic but not insane.

John looked into the mirror and tried to address his new or his old self—John A, John B. There were no such people. There was suddenly a man who had existed in two separate universes and, in a way, it was no more profound than having lived in two separate houses.

The difference being that nobody else knows there is more than one house.

He moved over to the window and set his coffee in the holder, picked up the absinthe glass and sniffed it, considered pouring it down the drain, but then put it in the other holder, for possible future reference.

Posit this: is it more likely that there are bundles of parallel universes prevailed over by a Hemingway look-alike with a magic cane, or that John Baird was exposed to a drug that he had never experienced before and it had had an unusually disorienting effect?

He looked at the paper. He had not hallucinated two weeks of drought. The rock star had been dead for some time. He had not seen a DeSoto in twenty years, and that was a hard car to miss. Tail fins that had to be registered as lethal weapons.

But maybe if you take a person who remembers every trivial thing, and zap his brain with oil of wormwood, that is exactly the effect: perfectly recalled things that never actually happened.

The coffee tasted repulsive. John put on a fresh shirt and decided not to shave and headed for the bar car. He bought the last imported beer in the cooler and sat down across from the long-haired white-bearded man who had an earring that had escaped his notice before, or hadn't existed in the other universe.

The man was staring out at the forest greening by. "Morning," John said.

"How do." The man looked at him with no sign of recognition.

"Did we talk last night?"

He leaned forward. "What?"

"I mean did we sit in this car last night and talk about Hemingway and Vietnam and ghosts?"

He laughed. "You're on somethin', man. I been on this train since two in the mornin' and ain't said boo to nobody but the bartender."

"You were in Vietnam?"

"Yeah, but that's over; that's shit." He pointed at John's bracelet. "What, you got ghosts from over there?"

"I think maybe I have."

He was suddenly intense. "Take my advice, man; I been there. You got to go talk to somebody. Some shrink. Those ghosts ain't gonna go 'way by themself."

"It's not that bad."

"It ain't the ones you killed." He wasn't listening. "Fuckin' dinks, they come back but they don't, you know, they just stand around." He looked at John and tears came so hard they actually spurted from his eyes. "It's your fuckin' friends, man, they all died and they come back now ..." He took a deep breath and wiped his face. "They used to come back every night. That like you?" John shook his head, helpless, trapped by the man's grief. "Every fuckin' night, my old lady, finally she said you go to a shrink or go to hell." He fumbled with the button on his shirt pocket and took out a brown plastic prescription bottle and stared at the label. He shook out a capsule. "Take a swig?" John pushed the beer over to him. He washed the pill down without touching the bottle to his lips.

He sagged back against the window. "I musta not took the pill last night, sometimes I do that. Sorry." He smiled weakly. "One day at a time, you know? You get through the one day. Fuck the rest. Sorry." He leaned forward again suddenly and put his hand on John's wrist. "You come outa nowhere and I lay my fuckin' trip on you. You don' need it."

John covered the hand with his own. "Maybe I do need it. And maybe I didn't come out of nowhere." He stood up. "I will see somebody about the ghosts. Promise."

"You'll feel better. It's no fuckin' cure-all, but you'll feel better."

"Want the beer?"

He shook his head. "Not supposed to."

"Okay." John took the beer and they waved at each other and he started back.

He stopped in the vestibule between cars and stood in the rattling roar of it, looking out the window at the flashing green blur. He put his forehead against the cool glass and hid the blur behind the dark red of his eyelids.

Were there actually a zillion of those guys each going through a slightly different private hell? Something he rarely asked himself was "What would Ernest Hemingway have done in this situation?"

He'd probably have the sense to leave it to Milton.

14

The Dangerous Summer

Castle and Lena met him at the station in Miami and they drove back to Key West in Castle's old pickup. The drone of the air conditioner held conversation to a minimum, but it kept them cool, at least from the knees down.

John didn't say anything about his encounter with the infinite, or transfinite, not wishing to bring back that fellow with the cane just yet. He did note that the two aspects of his personality hadn't quite become equal partners yet, and small details of this world kept surprising him. There was a monorail being built down to Pigeon Key, where Disney was digging an underwater park. Gasoline stations still sold Regular. Castle's car radio picked up TV as well as AM/FM, but sound only.

Lena sat between the two men and rubbed up against John affectionately. That would have been remarkable for John-one and somewhat unusual for John-two. It was a different Lena here, of course; one who had had more of a sex life with John, but there was something more than that too. She was probably sleeping with Castle, he thought, and the extra attention was a conscious or unconscious compensation, or defense.

Castle seemed a little harder and more serious in this world than the last, not only from his terse moodiness in the pickup, but from recollections of parallel conversations. John wondered how shady he actually was, whether he'd been honest about his police record.

(He hadn't been. In this universe, when Lena had asked him whether he had ever been in trouble with the police, he'd answered a terse "no." In fact, he'd done eight hard years in Ohio for an armed robbery he hadn't committed—the real robber hadn't been so stupid, here—and he'd come out of prison bitter, angry, an actual criminal. Figuring the world owed him one, a week after getting out he stopped for a hitchhiker on a lonely country road, pulled a gun, walked him a few yards off the road into a field of high corn, and shot him point-blank at the base of the skull. It didn't look anything like the movies.)

(He drove off without touching the body, which a farmer's child found two days later. The victim turned out to be a college student who was on probation for dealing—all he'd really done was buy a kilo of green and make his money back by selling bags to his friends, and one enemy—so the papers said **DRUG DEALER FOUND SLAIN IN GANGLAND-STYLE KILLING** and the police pursued the matter with no enthusiasm. Castle was in Key West well before the farmer's child smelled the body, anyhow.)

As they rode along, whatever Lena had or hadn't done with Castle was less interesting to John than what *he* was planning to do with her. Half of his self had never experienced sex, as an adult, without the sensory handicaps engendered by scar tissue and severed nerves in the genitals, and he was looking forward to the experience with a relish that was obvious, at least to Lena. She encouraged him in not-so-subtle ways, and by the time they crossed the last bridge into Key West, he was ready to tell Castle to pull over at the first bush.

He left the typewriter in Castle's care and declined help with the luggage. By this time Lena was smiling at his obvious impatience; she was giggling by the time they were momentarily stalled by a truculent door key; laughed her delight as he carried her charging across the room to the couch, then clawing off a minimum of clothing and taking her with fierce haste, wordless, and keeping her on a breathless edge he drifted the rest of the clothes off her and carried her into the bedroom, where they made so much noise Julio banged on the ceiling with a broomstick.

They did quiet down eventually, and lay together in a puddle of mingled sweat, panting, watching the fan push the humid air around. "Guess we both get to sleep in the wet spot," John said.

"No complaints." She raised up on one elbow and traced a figure eight on his chest. "You're full of surprises tonight, Dr. Baird."

"Life is full of surprises."

"You should go away more often—or at least come back more often."

"It's all that Hemingway research. Makes a man out of you."

"You didn't learn this in a book," she said, gently taking his penis and pantomiming a certain motion.

"I did, though, an anthropology book." In another universe. "It's what they do in the Solomon Islands."

"Wisdom of Solomon," she said, lying back. After a pause: "They have anthropology books at JFK?"

"Uh, no." He remembered he didn't own that book in this universe. "Browsing at Wordsworth's."

"Hope you bought the book."

"Didn't have to." He gave her a long slow caress. "Memorized the good parts."

On the other side of town, six days later, she was in about the same position on Castle's bed, and even more exhausted.

"Aren't you overdoing the loving little wifey bit? It's been a week."

She exhaled audibly. "What a week."

"Missed you." He nuzzled her and made an unsubtle preparatory gesture.

"No, you don't." She rolled out of bed. "Once is plenty." She went to the mirror and ran a brush through her damp hair. "Besides, it's not me you missed. You missed *it*." She sat at the open window, improving the neighborhood's scenery. "*It*'s gonna need a Teflon lining installed."

"Old boy's feelin' his oats?"

"Not feeling *his* anything. God, I don't know what's gotten into him. Four, five times a day; six."

"Screwed, blewed, and tattooed. You asked for it."

"As a matter of fact, I didn't. I haven't had a chance to start my little act. He got off that train with an erection, and he still has it. No woman would be safe around him. Nothing wet and concave would be safe."

"So does that mean it's a good time to bring in Pansy? Or is he so stuck on you he wouldn't even notice her?"

She scowled at the brush, picking hair out of it. "Actually, Castle, I was just about to ask you the same thing. Relying on your well-known expertise in animal behavior."

"Okay." He sat up. "I say we oughta go for it. If he's a walkin' talkin' hard-on like you say … Pansy'd pull him like a magnet. You'd have to be a fuckin' monk not to want Pansy."

"Like Rasputin."

"Like who?"

"Never mind." She went back to the brush. "I guess, I guess one problem is that I really am enjoying the attention. I guess I'm not too anxious to hand him over to this champion sexpot."

"Aw, Lena—"

"Really. I do love him in my way, Castle. I don't want to lose him over this scheme."

"You're not gonna lose him. Trust me. You catch him dickin' Pansy, get mad, forgive him. Hell, you'll have him wrapped around your finger."

"I guess. You make the competition sound pretty formidable."

"Don't worry. She's outa there the next day."

"Unless she winds up in love with him. That would be cute."

"He's almost twice her age. Besides, she's a whore. Whores don't fall in love."

"They're women, Castle. Women fall in love."

"Yeah, sure. Just like on TV."

She turned away from him; looked out the window. "You really know how to make a woman feel great, you know?"

"Come on." He crossed over and smoothed her hair. She turned around but didn't look up. "Don't run yourself down, Lena. You're still one hell of a piece of ass."

"Thanks." She smiled into his leer and grabbed him. "If you weren't such a poet, I'd trade you in for a vibrator."

15

In Praise of His Mistress

Pansy was indeed beautiful, even under normal conditions; delicate features, wasp waist combined with generous secondary sexual characteristics. The conditions under which John first saw her were calculated to maximize sexiness and vulnerability. Red nylon running shorts, tight and very short, and a white sleeveless T-shirt from a local bar that was stamped LAST HETEROSEXUAL IN KEY WEST—all clinging to her golden skin with a healthy sweat, the cloth made translucent enough to reveal no possibility of underwear.

John looked out the screen door and saw her at the other door, struggling with a heavy box while trying to make the key work. "Let me help you," he said through the screen, and stepped across the short landing to hold the box while she got the door open.

"You're too kind." John tried not to stare as he handed the box back. Pansy, of course, was relieved at his riveted attention. It had taken days to set up this operation, and would take more days to bring it to its climax, so to speak, and more days to get back to normal. But she did owe Castle a big favor and this guy seemed nice enough. Maybe she'd learn something about Hemingway in the process.

"More to come up?" John asked.

"Oh, I couldn't ask you to help. I can manage."

"It's okay. I was just goofing off for the rest of the day."

It turned out to be quite a job, even though there was only one load from a small rented truck. Most of the load was uniform and heavy boxes of books, carefully labeled LIT A-B, GEN REF, ENCY 1-12, and so forth. Most of her furniture, accordingly, was cinder blocks and boards, the standard student bookshelf arrangement.

John found out that despite a couple of dozen boxes marked LIT, Pansy hadn't majored in literature, but rather Special Education; during the school year, she taught third grade at a school for the retarded in Key Largo. She didn't tell him about the several years she'd spent as a call girl, but if she had, John might have seen a connection that Castle would never have made—that the driving force behind both of the jobs was the same, charity. The more or less easy forty dollars an hour for going on a date and then having sex was a factor, too, but she really did like making lonely men feel special, and had herself felt more like a social worker than a woman of easy virtue. And the hundreds of men who had fallen for her, for love or money, weren't responding only to her cheerleader's body. She had a sunny disposition and a natural, artless way of concentrating on a man that made him for a while the only man in the world.

John would not normally be an easy conquest. Twenty years of facing classrooms full of coeds had given him a certain wariness around attractive young women. He also had an impulse toward faithfulness, Lena having suddenly left town, her father ill. But he was still in the grip of the weird overweening horniness that had animated him since inheriting this new body and double-image personality. If Pansy had said "Let's do it," they would be doing it so soon that she would be wise to unwrap the condom before speaking. But she was being as indirect as her nature and mode of dress would allow.

"Do you and your wife always come down here for the summer?"

"We usually go somewhere. Boston's no fun in the heat."

"It must be wonderful in the fall."

And so forth. It felt odd for Pansy, probably the last time she would ever seduce a man for reasons other than personal interest. She wanted it to be perfect. She wanted John to have enough pleasure in her to compensate for the embarrassment of their "accidental" exposure, and whatever hassle his wife would put him through afterwards.

She was dying to know why Castle wanted him set up. How Castle ever met a quiet, kindly gentleman like John was a mystery, too—she had met some of Castle's friends, and they had oilier virtues.

Quiet and kindly, but horny. Whenever she contrived, in the course of their working together, to expose a nipple or a little beaver, he would turn around to adjust himself, and blush. More like a teenager, discovering his sexuality, than a middle-aged married man.

He was a pushover, but she didn't want to make it too easy. After they had finished putting the books up on shelves, she said thanks a million; I gotta go now, spending the night house-sitting up in Islamorada. You and your wife come over for dinner tomorrow? Oh, then come on over yourself. No, that's all right, I'm a big girl. Roast beef okay? See ya.

Driving away in the rented truck, Pansy didn't feel especially proud of herself. She was amused at John's sexiness and looking forward to trying it out. But she could read people pretty well, and sensed a core of deep sadness in John. Maybe it was from Vietnam; he hadn't mentioned it but she knew what the bracelet meant.

Whatever the problem, maybe she'd have time to help him with it—before she had to turn around and add to it.

Maybe it would work out for the best. Maybe the problem was with his wife, and she'd leave, and he could start over....

Stop kidding yourself. Just lay the trap, catch him, deliver him. Castle was not the kind of man you want to disappoint.

16

Fiesta

She had baked the roast slowly with wine and fruit juice, along with dried apricots and apples plumped in port wine, seasoned with cinnamon and nutmeg and cardamom. Onions and large cubes of acorn squash simmered in the broth. She served new potatoes steamed with parsley and dressed Italian style, with garlicky olive oil and a splash of vinegar. Small Caesar salad and air-light *pan de agua*, the Cuban bread that made you forget every other kind of bread.

The way to a man's heart, her mother had contended, was through his stomach, and although she was accustomed to aiming rather lower, she thought it was probably a good approach for a longtime married man suddenly forced to fend for himself. That was exactly right for John. He was not much of a cook, but he was an accomplished eater.

He pushed the plate away after three helpings. "God, I'm such a pig. But that was irresistible."

"Thank you." She cleared the table slowly, accepting John's offer to help. "My mother's 'company' recipe. So you think Hadley might have just thrown the stories away, and made up the business about the train?"

"People have raised the possibility. There she was, eight years older than this handsome hubby—with half the women on the Left Bank after him, at least in her mind—and he's starting to get published, starting to build a reputation …"

"She was afraid he was going to 'grow away' from her? Or did they have that expression back then?"

"I think she was afraid he would start making money from his writing. She had an inheritance, a trust fund from her grandfather, that paid over two thousand a year. That was plenty to keep the two of them comfortable in Paris. Hemingway talked poor in those days, starving artist, but he lived pretty well."

"He probably resented it, too. Not making the money himself."

"That would be like him. Anyhow, if she chucked the stories to ensure his dependency, it backfired. He was still furious thirty years later—three wives later. He said the stuff had been 'fresh from the mint,' even if the writing wasn't so great, and he was never able to reclaim it."

She opened a cabinet and slid a bottle out of its burlap bag, and selected two small glasses. "Sherry?" He said why not? and they moved into the living room.

The living room was mysteriously devoid of chairs, so they had to sit together on the small couch. "You don't actually think she did it."

"No." John watched her pour the sherry. "From what I've read about her, she doesn't seem at all calculating. Just a sweet gal from St. Louis who fell in love with a cad."

"Cad. Funny old-fashioned word."

John shrugged. "Actually, he wasn't really a cad. I think he sincerely loved every one of his wives … at least until he married them."

They both laughed. "Of course it could have been something in between," Pansy said, "I mean, she didn't actually throw away the manuscripts, but she did leave them sitting out, begging to be stolen. Why did she leave the compartment?"

"That's one screwy aspect of it. Hadley herself never said, not on paper. Every biographer seems to come up with a different reason: she went to get a newspaper, she saw some people she recognized and stepped out to talk with them, wanted some exercise before the long trip … even Hemingway had two different versions—she went out to get a bottle of Evian water or to buy something to read. That one pissed him off, because she did have an overnight bag full of the best American writing since Mark Twain."

"How would you have felt?"

"Felt?"

"I mean, you say you've written stories, too. What if somebody, your wife, made a mistake and you lost everything?"

He looked thoughtful. "It's not the same. In the first place, it's just a hobby with me. And I don't have that much that hasn't been published—when Hemingway lost it, he lost it for good. I could just go to a university library and make new copies of everything."

"So you haven't written much lately?"

"Not stories. Academic stuff."

"I'd love to read some of your stories."

"And I'd love to have you read them. But I don't have any here. I'll mail you some from Boston."

She nodded, staring at him with a curious intensity. "Oh hell," she said, and turned her back to him. "Would you help me with this?"

"What?"

"The zipper." She was wearing a dingy white summer dress. "Undo the zipper a little bit."

He slowly unzipped it a few inches. She did it the rest of the way, stood up and hooked her thumbs under the shoulder straps and shrugged. The dress slithered to the floor. She wasn't wearing anything else.

"You're blushing." Actually, he was doing a good imitation of a beached fish. She straddled him, sitting back lightly on his knees, legs wide, and started unbuttoning his shirt.

"Uh," he said.

"I just get impatient. You don't mind?"

"Uh … no?"

17

On Being Shot Again

John woke up happy but didn't open his eyes for nearly a minute, holding on to the erotic dream of the century. Then he opened one eye and saw it hadn't been a dream: the tousled bed in the strange room, unguents and sex toys on the nightstand, the smell of her hair on the other pillow. A noise from the kitchen; coffee and bacon smells.

He put on pants and went into the living room to pick up the shirt where it had dropped. "Good morning, Pansy."

"Morning, stranger." She was wearing a floppy terry cloth bathrobe with the sleeves rolled up to her elbows. She turned the bacon carefully with a fork. "Scrambled eggs okay?"

"Marvelous." He sat down at the small table and poured himself a cup of coffee. "I don't know what to say."

She smiled at him. "Don't say anything. It was nice."

"More than nice." He watched her precise motions behind the counter. She broke the eggs one-handed, two at a time, added a splash of water to the bowl, plucked some chives from a window box and chopped them with a small Chinese cleaver, rocking it in a staccato chatter; scraped them into the bowl, and followed them with a couple of grinds of pepper. She set the bacon out on a paper towel, with another towel to cover. Then she stirred the eggs briskly with the fork and set them aside. She picked up the big cast-iron frying pan and poured off a judicious amount of grease. Then she poured the egg mixture into the pan and studied it with alertness.

"Know what I think?" John said.

"Something profound?"

"Huh uh. I think I'm in a rubber room someplace, hallucinating the whole thing. And I hope they never cure me."

"I think you're a butterfly who's dreaming he's a man. I'm glad I'm in your dream." She slowly stirred and scraped the eggs with a spatula.

"You like older men?"

"One of them." She looked up, serious. "I like men who are considerate … and playful." She returned to the scraping. "Last couple of boyfriends I had were all dick and no heart. Kept to myself the last few months."

"Glad to be of service."

"You could rent yourself out as a service." She laughed. "You must have been impossible when you were younger."

"Different." Literally.

She ran hot water into a serving bowl, then returned to her egg stewardship. "I've been thinking."

"Yes?"

"The lost manuscript stuff we were talking about last night, all the different explanations." She divided the egg into four masses and turned each one. "Did you ever read any science fiction?"

"No. Vonnegut."

"The toast." She hurriedly put four pieces of bread in the toaster. "They write about alternate universes. Pretty much like our own, but different in one way or another. Important or trivial."

"What, uh, what silliness."

She laughed and poured the hot water out of the serving bowl, and dried it with a towel. "I guess maybe. But what if … what if all of those versions were equally true? In different universes. And for some reason they all came together here." She started to put the eggs into the bowl when there was a knock on the door.

It opened and Ernest Hemingway walked in. Dapper, just twenty, wearing the Italian army cape he'd brought back from the war. He pointed the black-and-white cane at Pansy. "Bingo."

She looked at John and then back at the Hemingway. She dropped the serving bowl; it clattered on the floor without breaking. Her knees buckled and she fainted dead away, executing a half turn as she fell so that the back of her head struck the wooden floor with a loud thump and the bathrobe drifted open from the waist down.

The Hemingway stared down at her frontal aspect. "Sometimes I wish I were human," it said. "Your pleasures are intense. Simple, but intense." It moved toward her with the cane.

John stood up. "If you kill her—"

"Oh?" It cocked an eyebrow at him. "What will you do?"

John took one step toward it and it waved the cane. A waist-high brick wall surmounted by needle-sharp spikes appeared between them. It gestured again and an impossible moat appeared, deep enough to reach down well into Julio's living room. It filled with water and a large crocodile surfaced and rested its chin on the parquet floor, staring at John. It yawned teeth.

The Hemingway held up its cane. "The white end. It doesn't kill, remember?" The wall and moat disappeared and the cane touched Pansy lightly below the navel. She twitched minutely but continued to sleep. "She'll have a headache," it said. "And she'll be somewhat confused by the uncommunicatable memory of having seen me. But that will all fade, compared to the sudden tragedy of having her new lover die here, just sitting waiting for his breakfast."

"Do you enjoy this?"

"I love my work. It's all I have." It walked toward him, footfalls splashing as it crossed where the moat had been. "You have not personally helped, though. Not at all."

It sat down across from him and poured coffee into a mug that said ON THE SIXTH DAY GOD CREATED MAN—SHE MUST HAVE HAD PMS.

"When you kill me this time, do you think it will 'take'?"

"I don't know. It's never failed before." The toaster made a noise. "Toast?"

"Sure." Two pieces appeared on his plate; two on the Hemingway's. "Usually when you kill people they stay dead?"

"I don't kill that many people." It spread margarine on its toast, gestured, and marmalade appeared. "But when I do, yeah. They die all up and down the Omniverse, every timespace. All except you." He pointed toast at John's toast. "Go ahead. It's not poison."

"Not my idea of a last meal."

The Hemingway shrugged. "What would you like?"

"Forget it." He buttered the toast and piled marmalade on it, determined out of some odd impulse to act as if nothing unusual were happening. Breakfast with Hemingway, big deal.

He studied the apparition and noticed that it was somewhat translucent, almost like a traditional TV ghost. He could barely see a line that was the back of the chair, bisecting its chest below shoulder-blade level. Was this something new? There hadn't been too much light in the train; maybe he had just failed to notice it before.

"A penny for your thoughts."

He didn't say anything about seeing through it. "Has it occurred to you that maybe you're not *supposed* to kill me? That's why I came back?"

The Hemingway chuckled and admired its nails. "That's a nearly content-free assertion."

"Oh really." He bit into the toast. The marmalade was strong, pleasantly bitter.

"It presupposes a higher authority, unknown to me, that's watching over my behavior, and correcting me when I do wrong. Doesn't exist, sorry."

"That's the oldest one in the theologian's book." He set down the toast and kneaded his stomach; shouldn't eat something so strong first thing in the morning. "You can only *assert* the nonexistence of something; you can't prove it."

"What you mean is *you* can't." He held up the cane and looked at it. The simplest explanation is that there's something wrong with the cane. There's no way I can test it; if I kill the wrong person, there's hell to pay up and down the Omniverse. But what I can do is kill you without the cane. See whether you come back again, some timespace."

Sharp, stabbing pains in his stomach now. "Bastard." Heart pounding slow and hard: shirt rustled in time to its spasms.

"Cyanide in the marmalade. Gives it a certain *frisson*, don't you think?"

He couldn't breathe. His heart pounded once, and stopped. Vicious pain in his left arm, then paralysis. From an inch away, he could just see the weave of the white tablecloth. It turned red and then black.

18

The Sun Also Rises

From blackness to brilliance: the morning sun pouring through the window at a flat angle. He screwed up his face and blinked.

Suddenly smothered in terry cloth, between soft breasts. "John, John."

He put his elbow down to support himself, uncomfortable on the parquet floor, and looked up at Pansy. Her face was wet with tears. He cleared his throat. "What happened?"

"You, you started putting on your foot and … you just fell over. I thought …"

John looked down over his body, hard ropy muscle and deep tan under white body hair, the puckered bullet wound a little higher on the abdomen. Left leg ended in a stump just above the ankle.

Trying not to faint. His third past flooding back. Walking down a dirt road near Kontum, the sudden loud bang of the mine and he pitched forward, unbelievable pain, rolled over and saw his bloody boot yards away; grey, jagged shinbone sticking through the bloody smoking rag of his pant leg, bright crimson splashing on the dry dust, loud in the shocked silence; another bloodstain spreading between his legs, the deep mortal pain there—and he started to buck and scream and two men held him while the medic took off his belt and made a tourniquet and popped morphine through the cloth and unbuttoned his fly and slowly worked his pants down: penis torn by shrapnel, scrotum ripped open in a bright red flap of skin, bloody grey-blue egg of a testicle separating, rolling out. He fainted, then and now.

And woke up with her lips against his, her breath sweet in his lungs, his nostrils pinched painfully tight. He made a strangled noise and clutched her breast.

She cradled his head, panting, smiling through tears, and kissed him lightly on the forehead. "Will you stop fainting now?"

"Yeah. Don't worry." Her lips were trembling. He put a finger on them. "Just a longer night than I'm accustomed to. An overdose of happiness."

The happiest night of his life, maybe of three lives. Like coming back from the dead.

"Should I call a doctor?"

"No. I faint every now and then." Usually at the gym, from pushing too hard. He slipped his hand inside the terry cloth and covered her breast. "It's been … do you know how long it's been since I … did it? I mean … three times in one night?"

"About six hours." She smiled. "And you can say 'fuck.' I'm no schoolgirl."

"I'll say." The night had been an escalating progression of intimacies, gymnastics, accessories. "Had to wonder where a sweet girl like you learned all that."

She looked away, lips pursed, thoughtful. With a light fingertip she stroked the length of his penis and smiled when it started to uncurl. "At work."

"What?"

"I was a prostitute. That's where I learned the tricks. Practice makes perfect."

"Prostitute. Wow."

"Are you shocked? Outraged?"

"Just surprised." That was true. He respected the sorority and was grateful to it for having made Vietnam almost tolerable, an hour or so at a time. "But now you've got to do something really mean. I could never love a prostitute with a heart of gold."

"I'll give it some thought." She shifted. "Think you can stand up?"

"Sure." She stood and gave him her hand. He touched it but didn't pull; rose in a smooth practiced motion, then took one hop and sat down at the small table. He started strapping on his foot.

"I've read about those new ones," she said, "the permanent kind."

"Yeah; I've read about them, too. Computer interface, graft your nerves onto sensors." He shuddered. "No, thanks. No more surgery."

"Not worth it for the convenience?"

"Being able to wiggle my toes, have my foot itch? No. Besides, the VA won't pay for it." That startled John as he said it: here, he hadn't grown up rich. His father had spent all the mill money on a photocopy firm six months before Xerox came on the market. "You say you 'were' a prostitute. Not anymore?"

"No, that was the truth about teaching. Let's start this egg thing over." She picked up the bowl she had dropped in the other universe. "I gave up whoring about seven years ago." She picked up an egg, looked at it, set it down. She half turned and stared out the kitchen window. "I can't do this to you."

"You … can't do what?"

"Oh, lie. Keep lying." She went to the refrigerator. "Want a beer?"

"Lying? No, no thanks. What lying?"

She opened a beer, still not looking at him. "I like you, John. I really like you. But I didn't just … spontaneously fall into your arms." She took a healthy swig and started pouring some of the bottle into a glass.

"I don't understand."

She walked back, concentrating on pouring the beer, then sat down gracelessly. She took a deep breath and let it out, staring at his chest. "Castle put me up to it."

"*Castle*?"

She nodded. "Sylvester Castlemaine, boy wonder."

John sat back stunned. "But you said you don't do that anymore," he said without too much logic. "Do it for money."

"Not for money," she said in a flat, hurt voice.

"I should've known. A woman like you wouldn't want …" He made a gesture that dismissed his body from the waist dow n.

"You do all right. Don't feel sorry for yourself." Her face showed a pinch of regret for that, but she plowed on. "If it were just the obligation, once would have been enough. I wouldn't have had to fuck and suck all night long to win you over."

"No," he said, "that's true. Just the first moment, when you undressed. That was enough."

"I owe Castle a big favor. A friend of mine was going to be prosecuted for involving a minor in prostitution. It was a setup, pure and simple."

"She worked for the same outfit you did?"

"Yeah, but this was freelance. I think it was the escort service that set her up, sort of delivered her and the man in return for this or that."

She sipped at the beer. "Guy wanted a three-way. My friend had met this girl a couple of days before at the bar where she worked part-time … she looked old enough, said she was in the biz."

"She was neither?"

"God knows. Maybe she got caught as a juvie and made a deal. Anyhow, he'd just slipped it to her and suddenly cops comin' in the windows. Threw the book at him. 'Two inches, twenty years,' my friend said. He was a county commissioner somewhere, with enemies. Almost dragged my friend down with him. I'm *sorry*." Her voice was angry.

"Don't be," John said, almost a whisper. "It's understandable. Whatever happens, I've got last night."

She nodded. "So two of the cops who were going to testify got busted for possession, cocaine. The word came down and everybody remembered the woman was somebody else."

"So what did Castle want you to do? With me?"

"Oh, whatever comes natural—or *un*-natural, if that's what you wanted. And later be doing it at a certain time and place, where we'd be caught in the act."

"By Castle?"

"And his trusty little VCR. Then I guess he'd threaten to show it to your wife, or the university."

"I wonder. Lena … she knows I've had other women."

"But not lately."

"No. Not for years."

"It might be different now. She might be starting to feel, well, insecure."

"Any woman who looked at you would feel insecure."

She shrugged. "That could be part of it. Could it cost you your job, too?"

"I don't see how. It would be awkward, but it's not as if you were one of my students—and even that happens, without costing the guy his job." He laughed. "Poor old Larry. He had a student kiss and tell, and had to run the Speakers' Committee for four or five years. Got allergic to wine and cheese. But he made tenure."

"So what is it?" She leaned forward. "Are you an addict or something?"

"Addict?"

"I mean how come you even *know* Castle? He didn't pick your name out of a phone book and have me come seduce you, just to see what would happen."

"No, of course not."

"So? I confess, you confess."

John passed a hand over his face and pressed the other hand against his knee, bearing down to keep the foot from tapping. "You don't want to be involved."

"What do you call last night, Spin the Bottle? I'm in*volved*!"

"Not the way I mean. It's illegal."

"Oh golly. Not really."

"Let me think." John picked up their dishes and limped back to the sink. He set them down there and fiddled with the straps and pad that connected the foot to his stump, then poured himself a cup of coffee and came back, not limping.

He sat down slowly and blew across the coffee. "What it is, is that *Castle* thinks there's a scam going on. He's wrong. I've taken steps to ensure that it couldn't work." His foot tapped twice.

"You think. You hope."

"No. I'm sure. Anyhow, I'm stringing Castle along because I need his expertise in a certain matter."

"'A certain matter,' yeah. Sounds wholesome."

"Actually, that part's not illegal."

"So tell me about it."

"Nope. Still might backfire."

She snorted. "You know what might *back*fire. Fucking with Castle."

"I can take care of him."

"You don't know. He may be more dangerous than you think he is."

"He talks a lot."

"You men." She took a drink and poured the rest of the bottle into the glass. "Look, I was at a party with him, couple of years ago. He was drunk, got into a little coke, started babbling."

"In vino veritas?"

"Yeah, and Coke is It. But he said he'd killed three people, strangers, just to see what it felt like. He liked it. I more than halfway believe him."

John looked at her silently for a moment, sorting out his new memories of Castle. "Well … he's got a mean streak. I don't know about murder. Certainly not over this thing."

"Which is?"

"You'll have to trust me. It's not because of Castle that I can't tell you." He remembered her one universe ago, lying helpless while the Hemingway lowered its cane onto her nakedness. "Trust me?"

She studied the top of the glass, running her finger around it. "Suppose I do. Then what?"

"Business as usual. You didn't tell me anything. Deliver me to Castle and his video camera; I'll try to put on a good show."

"And when he confronts you with it?"

"Depends on what he wants. He knows I don't have much money." John shrugged. "If it's unreasonable, he can go ahead and show the tape to Lena. She can live with it."

"And your department head?"

"He'd give me a medal."

19

In Our Time

So it wasn't the cane. He ate enough cyanide to kill a horse, but evidently only in one universe.

You checked the next day in all the others?

All 119. He's still dead in the one where I killed him on the train—

That's encouraging.

—but there's no causal resonance in the others.

Oh, but there is some resonance. He remembered you in the universe where you poisoned him. Maybe in all of them.

That's impossible.

Once is impossible. Twice is a trend. A hundred and twenty means something is going on that we don't understand.

What I suggest—

No. You can't go back and kill them all one by one.

If the wand had worked the first time, they'd all be dead anyhow. There's no reason to think we'd cause more of an eddy by doing them one at a time.

It's not something to experiment with. As you well know.

I don't know how we're going to solve it otherwise.

Simple. Don't kill him. Talk to him again. He may be getting frightened, if he remembers both times he died.

Here's an idea. What if someone else killed him?

I don't know. If you just hired someone—made him a direct agent of your will—it wouldn't be any different from the cyanide. Maybe as a last resort. Talk to him again first.

All right. I'll try.

Of Wounds and Other Causes

Although John found it difficult to concentrate, trying not to think about Pansy, this was the best time he would have for the foreseeable future to summon the Hemingway demon and try to do something about exorcising it. He didn't want either of the women around if the damned thing went on a killing spree again. They might just do as he did, and slip over into another reality—as unpleasant as that was, it was at least living—but the Hemingway had said otherwise. There was no reason to suspect it was not the truth.

Probably the best way to get the thing's attention was to resume work on the Hemingway pastiche. He decided to rewrite the first page to warm up, typing it out in Hemingway's style:

ALONG WITH YOUTH

1. Mitraigliatrice

The dirt on the side of the trench was never dry in the morning. If Fever could find a dry newspaper he could put it between his chest and the dirt when he went out to lean on the side of the trench and wait for the light .First light was the best time . You might have luck and see a muzzle flash to aim at . But patience was better than luck. Wait to see a helmet or a head without a helmet.

Fever looked at the enemy trench line through a rectangular box of wood that pushed through the trench wall at about ground level. The other end of the box was covered with a square of gauze the color of dirt. A man looking directly at it might see the muzzle flash when Fever fired through the box. But with luck, the flash would be the last thing he saw.

Fever had fired through the gauze six times. He'd potted at least three Austrians. Now the gauze had a ragged hole in the center. One bullet had come in the other way, an accident, and chiseled a deep gouge in the floor of the wooden box. Fever knew that he would be able to see the splinters sticking up before he could see any detail at the enemy trench line.

That would be maybe twenty minutes. Fever wanted a cigarette. There was plenty of time to go down in the bunker and light one. But it would fox his night vision. Better to wait.

Fever heard movement before he heard the voice. He picked up one of the grenades on the plank shelf to his left and his thumb felt the ring on the cotter pin. Someone was crawling in front of his position. Slow crawling but not too quiet. He slid his left forefinger through the ring and waited.

—Help me, came a strained whisper.

Fever felt his shoulders tense. Of course many Austrians could speak Italian.

—I am wounded. Help me. I can go no farther.

—What is your name and unit, Fever whispered through the box.

—Jean-Franco Dante. Four forty-seventh.

That was the unit that had taken such a beating at the evening show.—At first light they will kill me.

—All right. But I'm coming over with a grenade in my hand. If you kill me, you die as well.

—I will commend this logic to your superior officer. Please hurry.

Fever slid his rifle into the wooden box and eased himself to the top of the trench. He took the grenade out of his pocket and carefully worked the pin out, the arming lever held secure. He kept the pin around his finger so he could replace it.

He inched his way down the slope, guided by the man's whispers. After a few minutes his probing hand found the man's shoulder.—Thank God. Make haste, now.

The soldier's feet were both shattered by a mine. He would have to be carried.

—Don't cry out, Fever said. This will hurt.

—No sound, the soldier said. And when Fever raised him up onto his back there was only a breath. But his canteen was loose. It fell on a rock and made a loud hollow sound.

Firecracker pop above them and the night was all glare and bobbing shadow. A big machine gun opened up rong, cararong, rong, rong. Fever headed for the parapet above as fast as he could but knew it was hopeless. He saw dirt spray twice to his right and then felt the thud of the bullet into the Italian, who said "Jesus" as if only annoyed, and they almost made it then but on the lip of the trench a hard snowball hit Fever behind the kneecap and they both went down in a tumble. They fell two yards to safety but the Italian was already dead.

Fever had sprained his wrist and hurt his nose falling and they hurt worse than the bullet. But he couldn't move his toes and he knew that must be bad. Then it started to hurt.

A rifleman closed the Italian's eyes and with the help of another clumsy one dragged Fever down the trench to the medical bunker. It hurt awfully and his shoe filled up with blood and he puked. They stopped to watch him puke and then dragged him the rest of the way.

The surgeon placed him between two kerosene lanterns. He removed the puttee and shoe and cut the bloody pants leg with a straight razor. He rolled Fever onto his stomach and had four men hold him down while he probed for the bullet. The pain was great but Fever was insulted enough by the four men not to cry out. He heard the bullet clink into a metal dish. It sounded like the canteen.

"That's a little too pat, don't you think?" John turned around and there was the Hemingway, reading over his shoulder. "'It sounded like the canteen,' indeed." Khaki army uniform covered with mud and splattered with bright blood. Blood dripped and pooled at its feet.

"So shoot me. Or whatever it's going to be this time. Maybe I'll rewrite the line in the next universe."

"You're going to run out soon. You only exist in eight more universes."

"Sure. And you've never lied to me." John turned back around and stared at the typewriter, tensed.

The Hemingway sighed. "Suppose we talk, instead."

"I'm listening."

The Hemingway walked past him toward the kitchen. "Want a beer?"

"Not while I'm working."

"Suit yourself." It limped into the kitchen, out of sight, and John heard it open the refrigerator and pry the top off of a beer. It came back out as the five-year-old Hemingway, dressed up in girl's clothing, both hands clutching an incongruous beer bottle. It set the bottle on the end table and crawled up onto the couch with childish clumsiness.

"Where's the cane?"

"I knew it wouldn't be necessary this time," it piped. "It occurs to me that there are better ways to deal with a man like you."

"Do tell," John smiled. "What is 'a man like me'? One on whom your cane for some reason doesn't work?"

"Actually, what I was thinking of was curiosity. That is supposedly what motivates scholars. You *are* a real scholar, not just a rich man seeking legitimacy?"

John looked away from the ancient eyes in the boy's face. "I've sometimes wondered myself. Why don't you cut to the chase, as we used to say. A few universes ago."

"I've done spot checks on your life through various universes," the child said. "You're always a Hemingway buff, though you don't always do it for a living."

"What else do I do?"

"It's probably not healthy for you to know. But all of you are drawn to the missing manuscripts at about this time, the seventy-fifth anniversary."

"I wonder why that would be."

The Hemingway waved the beer bottle in a disarmingly mature gesture. "The Omniverse is full of threads of coincidence like that. They have causal meaning in a dimension you can't deal with."

"Try me."

"In a way, that's what I want to propose. You will drop this dangerous project at once, and never resume it. In return, I will take you back in time, back to the Gare de Lyon on December 14, 1921."

"Where I will see what happens to the manuscripts."

Another shrug. "I will put you on Hadley's train, well before she said the manuscripts were stolen. You will be able to observe for an hour or so, without being seen. As you know, some people have theorized that there never was a thief; never was an overnight bag; that Hadley simply threw the writings away. If that's the case, you won't see anything dramatic. But the absence of the overnight bag would be powerful indirect proof.

John looked skeptical. "You've never gone to check it out for yourself?"

"If I had, I wouldn't be able to take you back. I can't exist twice in the same timespace, of course."

"How foolish of me. Of course."

"Is it a deal?"

John studied the apparition. The couch's plaid upholstery showed through its arms and legs. It did appear to become less substantial each time. "I don't know. Let me think about it a couple of days."

The child pulled on the beer bottle and it stretched into a long amber stick. It turned into the black-and-white cane. "We haven't tried cancer yet. That might be the one that works." It slipped off the couch and sidled toward John. "It does take longer and it hurts. It hurts 'awfully.'"

John got out of the chair. "You come near me with that and I'll drop kick you into next Tuesday."

The child shimmered and became Hemingway in his mid-forties, a big-gutted barroom brawler. "Sure you will, Champ." It held out the cane so that the tip was inches from John's chest. "See you around." It disappeared with a barely audible pop, and a slight breeze as air moved to fill its space.

John thought about that as he went to make a fresh cup of coffee. He wished he knew more about science. The thing obviously takes up space, since its disappearance caused a vacuum, but there was no denying that it was fading away.

Well, not fading. Just becoming more transparent. That might not affect its abilities. A glass door is as much of a door as an opaque one, if you try to walk through it.

He sat down on the couch, away from the manuscript so he could think without distraction. On the face of it, this offer by the Hemingway was an admission of defeat. An admission, at least, that it couldn't solve its problem by killing him over and over. That was comforting. He would just as soon not die again, except for the one time.

But maybe he should. That was a chilling thought. If he made the Hemingway kill him another dozen times, another hundred … what land of strange creature would he become? A hundred overlapping autobiographies, all perfectly remembered? Surely the brain has a finite capacity for storing information; he'd "fill up," as Pansy said. Or maybe it wasn't finite, at least in his case—but that was logically absurd. There are only so many cells in a brain. Of course he might be "wired" in some way to the John Bairds in all the other universes he had inhabited.

And what would happen if he died in some natural way, not dispatched by an interdimensional assassin? Would he still slide into another identity? That was a lovely prospect: sooner or later he would be 130 years old, on his deathbed, dying every fraction of a second for the rest of eternity.

Or maybe the Hemingway wasn't lying, this time, and he had only eight lives left. In context, the possibility was reassuring.

The phone rang; for a change, John was grateful for the interruption. It was Lena, saying her father had come home from the hospital, much better, and she thought she could come on home day after tomorrow. Fine, John said, feeling a little wicked; I'll borrow a car and pick you up at the airport. Don't bother, Lena said; besides, she didn't have a flight number yet.

John, didn't press it. If, as he assumed, Lena was in on the plot with Castle, she was probably here in Key West, or somewhere nearby. If she had to buy a ticket to and from Omaha to keep up her end of the ruse, the money would come out of John's pocket.

He hung up and, on impulse, dialed her parents' number. Her father answered. Putting on his professorial tone, he said he was Maxwell Perkins, Blue Cross claims adjuster, and he needed to know the exact date when Mr. Monaghan entered the hospital for this recent confinement. He said you must have the wrong guy; I haven't been inside a hospital in twenty years, knock on wood. Am I not speaking to John Franklin Monaghan? No, this is John *Frederick* Monaghan. Terribly sorry, natural mistake. That's okay; hope the other guy's okay, good-bye, good night, sir.

So tomorrow was going to be the big day with Pansy. To his knowledge, John hadn't been watched during sex for more than twenty years, and never by a disinterested, or at least dispassionate, observer. He hoped that knowing they were being spied upon wouldn't affect his performance. Or knowing that it would be the last time.

A profound helpless sadness settled over him. He knew that the last thing you should do, in a mood like this, was go out and get drunk. It was barely noon, anyhow. He took enough money out of his wallet for five martinis, hid the wallet under a couch cushion, and headed for Duval Street.

21

Dying, Well or Badly

John had just about decided it was too early in the day to get drunk. He had polished off two martinis in Sloppy Joe's and then wandered uptown because the tourists were getting to him and a band was setting up, depressingly young and cheerful. He found a grubby bar he'd never noticed before, dark and smoky and hot. In the other universes it was a yuppie boutique. Three Social Security drunks were arguing politics almost loudly enough to drown out the game show on the television. It seemed to go well with the headache and sour stomach he'd reaped from the martinis and the walk in the sun. He got a beer and some peanuts and a couple of aspirin from the bartender, and sat in the farthest booth with a copy of the local classified ad newspaper. Somebody had obscurely carved FUCK ANARCHY into the tabletop.

Nobody else in this world knows what anarchy *is*, John thought, and the helpless anomie came back, intensified somewhat by drunken sentimentality. What he would give to go back to the first universe and undo this all by just not …

Would that be possible? The Hemingway was willing to take him back to 1921; why not back a few weeks? Where the hell was that son of a bitch when you needed him, it, whatever.

The Hemingway appeared in the booth opposite him, an Oak Park teenager smoking a cigarette. "I felt a kind of vibration from you. Ready to make your decision?"

"Can the people at the bar see you?"

"No. And don't worry about appearing to be talking to yourself. A lot of that goes on around here."

"Look. Why can't you just take me back to a couple of weeks before we met on the train, back in the first universe? I'll just ..." The Hemingway was shaking its head slowly. "You can't."

"No. As I explained, you already exist there—"

"You said that *you* couldn't be in the same place twice. How do you know I can't?"

"How do you know you can't swallow that piano? You just can't."

"You thought I couldn't talk about you, either, you thought your stick would kill me. I'm not like normal people."

"Except in that alcohol does nothing for your judgment."

John ate a peanut thoughtfully. "Try this on for size. At 11:46 on June 3, a man named Sylvester Castlemaine sat down in Dos Hermosas and started talking with me about the lost manuscripts. The forgery would never have occurred to me if I hadn't talked to him. Why don't you go back and keep him from going into that cafe? Or just go back to 11:30 and kill him."

The Hemingway smiled maliciously. "You don't like him much."

"It's more fear than like or dislike." He rubbed his face hard, remembering. "Funny how things shift around. He was kind of likable the first time I met him. Then you killed me on the train and in the subsequent universe, he became colder, more serious. Then you killed me in Pansy's apartment and in this universe, he has turned mean. Dangerously mean, like a couple of men I knew in Vietnam. The ones who really love the killing. Like you, evidently."

It blew a chain of smoke rings before answering. "I don't 'love' killing, or anything else. I have a complex function and I fulfill it, because that is what I do. That sounds circular because of the limitations of human language.

"I can't go killing people right and left just to see what happens. When a person dies at the wrong time it takes forever to clean things up. Not that it wouldn't be worth it in your case. But I can tell you with certainty that killing Castlemaine would not affect the final outcome."

"How can you say that? He's responsible for the whole thing." John finished off most of his beer and the Hemingway touched the mug and it refilled. "Not poison."

"Wouldn't work," it said morosely. "I'd gladly kill Castlemaine any way you want—cancer of the penis is a possibility—if there was even a fighting chance that it would clear things up. The reason I know it wouldn't is that I am not in the least attracted to that meeting. There's no probability nexus associated with it, the way there was with your buying the Corona or starting the story on the train, or writing it down here. You may think that you would never have come up with the idea for the forgery on your own, but you're wrong."

"That's preposterous."

"Nope. There are universes in this bundle where Castle isn't involved. You may find that hard to believe, but your beliefs aren't important."

John nodded noncommittally and got his faraway remembering look. "You know … reviewing in my mind all the conversations we've had, all five of them, the only substantive reason you've given me not to write this pastiche, and I quote, is that 'I or someone like me will have to kill you.' Since that doesn't seem to be possible, why don't we try some other line of attack?"

It put out the cigarette by squeezing it between thumb and forefinger. There was a smell of burning flesh. "All right, try this: give it up or I'll kill Pansy. Then Lena."

"I've thought of that, and I'm gambling that you won't, or can't. You had a perfect opportunity a few days ago—maximum dramatic effect—and you didn't do it. Now you say it's an awfully complicated matter."

"You're willing to gamble with the lives of the people you love?"

"I'm gambling with a lot. Including them." He leaned forward. "Take me into the future instead of the past. Show me what will happen if I succeed with the Hemingway hoax. If I agree that it's terrible, I'll give it all up and become a plumber."

The old, wise Hemingway shook a shaggy head at him. "You're asking me to please fix it so you can swallow a piano. I can't. Even I can't go straight to the future and look around; I'm pretty much tied to your present and past until this matter is cleared up."

"One of the first things you said to me was that you were from the future. And the past. And 'other temporalities,' whatever the hell that means. You were lying then?"

"Not really." It sighed. "Let me force the analogy. Look at the piano."

John twisted half around. "Okay."

"You can't eat it—but after a fashion, I can." The piano suddenly transformed itself into a piano-shaped mountain of cold capsules, which immediately collapsed and rolled all over the floor. "Each capsule contains a pinch of sawdust or powdered ivory or metal, the whole piano in about a hundred thousand capsules. If I take one with each meal, I will indeed eat the piano, over the course of the next three hundred-some years. That's not a long time for me."

"That doesn't prove anything."

"It's not a *proof*, it's a demonstration." It reached down and picked up a capsule that was rolling by, and popped it into its mouth. "One down, 99,999 to go. So how many ways could I eat this piano?"

"Ways?"

"I mean I could have swallowed any of the hundred thousand first. Next I can choose any of the remaining 99,999. How many ways can—"

"That's easy. One hundred thousand factorial. A huge number."

"Go to the head of the class. It's ten to the godzillionth power. That represents the number of possible paths—the number of futures—leading to this one guaranteed, preordained event: my eating the piano. They are all different, but in terms of whether the piano gets eaten, their differences are trivial.

"On a larger scale, every possible trivial action that you or anybody else in this universe takes puts us into a slightly different future than would have otherwise existed. An overwhelming majority of actions, even seemingly significant ones, make no difference in the long run. All of the futures bend back to one central, unifying event—except for the ones that you're screwing up!"

"So what is this big event?"

"It's impossible for you to know. It's not important, anyhow." Actually, it would take a rather cosmic viewpoint to consider the event unimportant: the end of the world.

Or at least the end of life on Earth. Right now there were two earnest young politicians, in the United States and Russia, who on 11 August 2006 would be President and Premier of their countries. On that day, one would insult the other beyond forgiveness, and a button would be pushed, and then another button, and by the time the sun set on Moscow, or rose on Washington, there would be nothing left alive on the planet at all—from the bottom of the ocean to the top of the atmosphere—not a cockroach, not a paramecium, not a virus, and all because there are some things a man just doesn't have to take, not if he's a real man.

Hemingway wasn't the only writer who felt that way, but he was the one with the most influence on this generation. The apparition who wanted John dead or at least not typing didn't know exactly what effect his pastiche was going to have on Hemingway's influence, but it was going to be decisive and ultimately negative. It would prevent or at least delay the end of the world in a whole bundle of universes, which would put a zillion adjacent realities out of kilter, and there would be hell to pay all up and down the Omniverse. Many more people than six billion would die—and it's even possible that all of Reality would unravel, and collapse back to the Primordial Hiccup from whence it came.

"If it's not important, then why are you so hell-bent on keeping me from preventing it? I don't believe you."

"*Don't* believe me, then!" At an imperious gesture, all the capsules rolled back into the corner and reassembled into a piano, with a huge crashing chord. None of the barflies heard it. "I should think you'd cooperate with me just to prevent the unpleasantness of dying over and over."

John had the expression of a poker player whose opponent has inadvertently exposed his hole card. "You get used to it," he said. "And it occurs to me that sooner or later I'll wind up in a universe that I really like. This one doesn't have a hell of a lot to recommend it." His foot tapped twice and then twice again.

"No," the Hemingway said. "It will get worse each time."

"You can't know that. This has never happened before."

"True so far, isn't it?"

John considered it for a moment. "Some ways. Some ways not."

The Hemingway shrugged and stood up. "Well. Think about my offer." The cane appeared. "Happy cancer." It tapped him on the chest and disappeared.

The first sensation was utter tiredness, immobility. When he strained to move, pain slithered through his muscles and viscera, and stayed. He could hardly breathe, partly because his lungs weren't working and partly because there was something in the way. In the mirror beside the booth he looked down his throat and saw a large white mass, veined, pulsing. He sank back into the cushion and waited. He remembered the young wounded Hemingway writing his parents from the hospital with ghastly cheerfulness: "If I should have died it would have been very easy for me. Quite the easiest thing I ever did." I don't know, Ernie; maybe it gets harder with practice. He felt something tear open inside and hot stinging fluid trickled through his abdominal cavity. He wiped his face and a patch of necrotic skin came off with a terrible smell. His clothes tightened as his body swelled.

"Hey buddy, you okay?" The bartender came around in front of him and jumped." Christ, Harry, punch nine-one-one!"

John gave a slight ineffectual wave. "No rush," he croaked.

The bartender cast his eyes to the ceiling. "Always on my shift?"

22

Death in the Afternoon

John woke up behind a Dumpster in an alley. It was high noon and the smell of fermenting garbage was revolting. He didn't feel too well in any case; as if he'd drunk far too much and passed out behind a Dumpster, which was exactly what had happened in this universe.

In this universe. He stood slowly to a quiet chorus of creaks and pops, brushed himself off, and staggered away from the malefic odor. Staggered, but not limping—he had both feet again, in this present. There was a hand-sized numb spot at the top of his left leg where a .51 caliber machine gun bullet had missed his balls by an inch and ended his career as a soldier.

And started it as a writer. He got to the sidewalk and stopped dead. This was the first universe where he wasn't a college professor. He taught occasionally—sometimes creative writing; sometimes Hemingway—but it was only a hobby now, and a nod toward respectability.

He rubbed his fringe of salt-and-pepper beard. It covered the bullet scar there on his chin. He ran his tongue along the metal teeth the army had installed thirty years ago. Jesus. Maybe it does get worse every time. Which was worse, losing a foot or getting your dick sprayed with shrapnel, numb from severed nerves, plus bullets in the leg and face and arm? If you knew there was a Pansy in your future, you would probably trade a foot for a whole dick. Though she had done wonders with what was left.

Remembering furiously, not watching where he was going, he let his feet guide him back to the oldster's bar where the Hemingway had showed him how to swallow a piano. He pushed through the door and the shock of air-conditioning brought him back to the present.

Ferns. Perfume. Lacy underthings. An epicene sales clerk sashayed toward him, managing to look worried and determined at the same time. His nose was pierced, decorated with a single diamond button. "Si-i-r," he said in a surprisingly deep voice, "may I *help* you?"

Crotchless panties. Marital aids. The bar had become a store called The French Connection. "Guess I took a wrong turn. Sorry." He started to back out.

The clerk smiled. "Don't be shy, Everybody needs *some*thing here."

The heat was almost pleasant in its heavy familiarity. John stopped at a convenience store for a six-pack of greenies and walked back home.

An interesting universe; much more of a divergence than the other had been. Reagan had survived the Hinckley assassination and actually went on to a second term. Bush was elected rather than succeeding to the presidency, and the country had not gone to war in Nicaragua. The Iran/Contra scandal nipped it in the bud.

The United States was actually cooperating with the Soviet Union in a flight to Mars. There were no DeSotos. Could there be a connection?

And in this universe he had actually met Ernest Hemingway.

Havana, 1952. John was eight years old. His father, a doctor in this universe, had taken a break from the New England winter to treat his family to a week in the tropics. John got a nice sunburn the first day, playing on the beach while his parents tried the casinos. The next day they made him stay indoors, which meant tagging along with his parents, looking at things that didn't fascinate eight-year-olds.

For lunch they went to La Florida, on the off chance that they might meet the famous Ernest Hemingway, who supposedly held court there when he was in Havana.

To John it was a huge dark cavern of a place, full of adult smells. Cigar smoke, rum, beer, stale urine. But Hemingway was indeed there, at the end of the long dark wood bar, laughing heartily with a table full of Cubans.

John was vaguely aware that his mother resembled some movie actress, but he couldn't have guessed that that would change his life. Hemingway glimpsed her and then stood up and was suddenly silent, mouth open. Then he laughed and waved a huge arm. "Come on over here, daughter."

The three of them rather timidly approached the table, John acutely aware of the careful inspection his mother was receiving from the silent Cubans. "Take a look, Mary," he said to the small blond woman knitting at the table. "The Kraut."

The woman nodded, smiling, and agreed that John's mother looked just like Marlene Dietrich ten years before. Hemingway invited them to sit down and have a drink, and they accepted with an air of genuine astonishment. He gravely shook John's hand, and spoke to him as he would to an adult. Then he shouted to the bartender in fast Spanish, and in a couple of minutes his parents had huge daiquiris and he had a Coke with a wedge of lime in it, tropical and grown-up. The waiter also brought a tray of boiled shrimp. Hemingway even ate the heads and tails, crunching loudly, which impressed John more than any Nobel Prize. Hemingway might have agreed, since he hadn't yet received one, and Faulkner had.

For more than an hour, two Cokes, John watched as his parents sat hypnotized in the aura of Hemingway's famous charm. He put them at ease with jokes and stories and questions—for the rest of his life John's father would relate how impressed he was with the sophistication of Hemingway's queries about cardiac medicine—but it was obvious even to a child that they were in awe, electrified by the man's presence.

Later that night John's father asked him what he thought of Mr. Hemingway. Forty-four years later, John of course remembered his exact reply: "He has fun all the time. I never saw a grown-up who plays like that."

Interesting. That meeting was where his eidetic memory started. He could remember a couple of days before it pretty well, because they had still been close to the surface. In other universes, he could remember back well before grade school. It gave him a strange feeling. All of the universes were different but this was the first one where the differentness was so tightly connected to Hemingway.

He was flabby in this Universe, fat over old, tired muscle, like Hemingway at his age, perhaps, and he felt a curious anxiety that he realized was a real *need* to have a drink. Not just desire, not thirst. If he didn't have a drink, something very very bad would happen. He knew that was irrational. Knowing didn't help.

John carefully mounted the stairs up to their apartment, stepping over the fifth one, also rotted in this universe. He put the beer in the refrigerator and took from the freezer a bottle of icy vodka—that was different—and poured himself a double shot and knocked it back, medicine drinking.

That spiked the hangover pretty well. He pried the top off a beer and carried it into the living room, thoughtful as the alcoholic glow radiated through his body. He sat down at the typewriter and picked up the air pistol, a fancy Belgian target model. He cocked it and, with a practiced two-handed grip, aimed at a paper target across the room. The pellet struck less than half an inch low.

All around the room the walls were pocked from where he'd fired at roaches, and once a scorpion. Very Hemingwayish, he thought; in fact, most of the ways he was different from the earlier incarnations of himself were in Hemingway's direction.

He spun a piece of paper into the typewriter and made a list:

EH & me—

- both had doctor fathers
- both forced into music lessons
- in high school wrote derivative stuff that didn't show promise
- Our war wounds were evidently similar in severity and location. Maybe my groin one was worse; army doctor there said that in Korea (and presumably WWI), without helicopter dust-

off, I would have been dead on the battlefield. (Having been wounded in the kneecap and foot myself, I know that H's story about carrying the wounded guy on his back is unlikely. It was a month before I could put any stress on the knee.) He mentioned genital wounds, possibly similar to mine, in a letter to Bernard Baruch, but there's nothing in the Red Cross report about them.

- But in both cases, being wounded and surviving was the central experience of our youth. Touching death.
- We each wrote the first draft of our first novel in six weeks (but his was better and more ambitious).
- Both had unusual critical success from the beginning.
- Both shy as youngsters and gregarious as adults.
- Always loved fishing and hiking and guns; I loved the bullfight from my first corrida, but may have been influenced by H's books.
- Spain in general
- have better women than we deserve

  drink too much

- hypochondria
- accident proneness
- a tendency toward morbidity
- One difference. I will never stick a shotgun in my mouth and pull the trigger. Leaves too much of a mess.

He looked up at the sound of the cane tapping. The Hemingway was in the Karsh wise-old-man mode, but was nearly transparent in the bright light that streamed from the open door. "What do I have to do to get your attention?" it said. "Give you cancer again?"

"That was pretty unpleasant."

"Maybe it will be the last." It half sat on the arm of the couch and spun the cane around twice. "Today is a big day. Are we going to Paris?"

"What do you mean?"

"Something big happens today. In every universe where you're alive, this day glows with importance. I assume that means you've decided to go along with me. Stop writing this thing in exchange for the truth about the manuscripts."

As a matter of fact, he had been thinking just that. Life was confusing enough already, torn between his erotic love for Pansy and the more domestic, but still deep, feeling for Lena … writing the pastiche was kind of fun, but he did have his own fish to fry. Besides, he'd come to truly dislike Castle, even before Pansy had told him about the setup. It would be fun to disappoint him.

"You're right. Let's go."

"First destroy the novel." In this universe, he'd completed seventy pages of the Up-in-Michigan novel.

"Sure." John picked up the stack of paper and threw it into the tiny fireplace. He lit it several places with a long barbecue match, and watched a month's work go up in smoke. It was only a symbolic gesture, anyhow; he could retype the thing from memory if he wanted to.

"So what do I do? Click my heels together three times and say 'There's no place like the Gare de Lyon'?"

"Just come closer."

John took three steps toward the Hemingway and suddenly fell up down sideways—

It was worse than dying. He was torn apart and scattered throughout space and time, being nowhere and everywhere, everywhen, being a screaming vacuum forever—

Grit crunched underfoot and coal smoke was choking thick in the air. It was cold. Grey Paris skies glowered through the long skylights, through the complicated geometry of the black steel trusses that held up the high roof. Bustling crowds chattering French. A woman walked through John from behind. He pressed himself with his hands and felt real.

"They can't see us," the Hemingway said. "Not unless I will it."

"That was awful."

"I hoped you would hate it. That's how I spend most of my time-space. Come on." They walked past vendors selling paper packets of roasted chestnuts, bottles of wine, stacks of baguettes and cheeses. There were strange resonances as John remembered the various times he'd been here more than a half century in the future. It hadn't changed much.

"There she is." The Hemingway pointed. Hadley looked worn, tired, dowdy. She stumbled, trying to keep up with the porter who strode along with her two bags. John recalled that she was just recovering from a bad case of the grippe. She'd probably still be home in bed if Hemingway hadn't sent the telegram urging her to come to Lausanne because the skiing was so good, at Chamby.

"Are there universes where Hadley doesn't lose the manuscripts?"

"Plenty of them," the Hemingway said. "In some of them he doesn't sell 'My Old Man' next year, or anything else, and he throws all the stories away himself. He gives up fiction and becomes a staff writer for the Toronto *Star*. Until the Spanish Civil War; he joins the Abraham Lincoln Battalion and is killed driving an ambulance. His only effect on American literature is one paragraph in *The Autobiography of Alice B. Toklas*."

"But in some, the stories actually do see print?"

"Sure, including the novel, which is usually called *Along With Youth*. There." Hadley was mounting the steps up into a passenger car. There was a microsecond of agonizing emptiness, and they materialized in the passageway in front of Hadley's compartment. She and the porter walked through them.

"*Merci*," she said, and handed the man a few sou. He made a face behind her back.

"*Along With Youth*?" John said.

"It's a pretty good book, sort of prefiguring *A Farewell to Arms*, but he does a lot better in universes where it's not published. *The Sun Also Rises* gets more attention."

Hadley stowed both the suitcase and the overnight bag under the seat. Then she frowned slightly, checked her wristwatch, and left the compartment, closing the door behind her.

"Interesting," the Hemingway said. "So she didn't leave it out in plain sight, begging to be stolen."

"Makes you wonder," John said. "This novel. Was it about World War I?"

"The trenches in Italy," the Hemingway said.

A young man stepped out of the shadows of the vestibule, looking in the direction Hadley took. Then he turned around and faced the two travelers from the future.

It was Ernest Hemingway. He smiled. "Close your mouth, John. You'll catch flies." He opened the door to the compartment, picked up the overnight bag, and carried it into the next car.

John recovered enough to chase after him. He had disappeared.

The Hemingway followed. "What *is* this?" John said. "I thought you couldn't be in two timespaces at once."

"That wasn't me."

"It sure as hell wasn't the real Hemingway. He's in Lausanne with Lincoln Steffens."

"Maybe he is and maybe he isn't."

"He knew my *name*!"

"That he did." The Hemingway was getting fainter as John watched.

"Was he another one of you? Another STAB agent?"

"No. Not possible." It peered at John. "What's happening to you?"

Hadley burst into the car and ran right through them, shouting in French for the conductor. She was carrying a bottle of Evian water.

"Well," John said, "that's what—"

The Hemingway was gone. John just had time to think *Marooned in 1922?* when the railroad car and the Gare de Lyon dissolved in an inbursting cascade of black sparks and it was no easier to handle the second time, spread impossibly thin across all those light years and millennia, wondering whether it was going to last forever this time, realizing that it did anyhow, and coalescing with an impossibly painful *snap*:

Looking at the list in the typewriter. He reached for the Heineken; it was still cold. He set it back down. “God,” he whispered. “I hope that’s that.”

The situation called for higher octane. He went to the freezer and took out the vodka. He sipped the gelid syrup straight from the bottle, and almost dropped it when out of the corner of his eye he saw the overnight bag.

He set the open bottle on the counter and sleepwalked over to the dining room table. It was the same bag, slightly beat-up, monogrammed EHR, Elizabeth Hadley Richardson. He opened it and inside was a thick stack of manila envelopes.

He took out the top one and took it and the vodka bottle back to his chair. His hands were shaking. He opened the folder and stared at the familiar typing.

ERNEST M. HEMINGWAY

One-Eye for Mine

Fever stood up. In the moon light he could xx see blood starting on his hands. His pants were torn at the knee and he knew it would be bleeding ~~there~~ too. He watched the lights of the caboose disppear in the trees where the track curved.

That lousy crut of a brakeman. He would get him x~~day~~xx some day.

Fever scuffed xxxxxxx off the end of a tie and sat down to pick the cinders out of his hands and knee. He could use some water. The brakeman had his canteen.

He could smell a campfire. He wondered if it would be smart to go find it. He knew about the wolves, the human kind that lived along the rails and the disgusting things they liked. He wasn’t afraid of them but you didn’t look for trouble.

You don’t have to look for trouble, his father would say. Trouble will find you. His father didn’t tell him about wolves, though, ~~or about women~~.

There was a noise in the brush. Fever stood up and slipped his hand around the horn grip of the fat Buck clasp knife in his pocket.

The screen door creaked open and he looked up to see Pansy walk in with a strange expression on her face. Lena followed, looking even stranger. Her left eye was swollen shut and most of that side of her face was bruised blue and brown.

He stood up, shaking with the sudden collision of emotions. "What the hell—"

"Castle," Pansy said. "He got outta hand."

"Real talent for understatement." Lena's voice was tightly controlled but distorted.

"He went nuts. Slappin' Lena around. Then he started to rummage around in a closet, rave about a shotgun, and we split."

"I'll call the police."

"We've already been there," Lena said. "It's all over."

"Of course. We can't work with—"

"No, I mean he's a *criminal.* He's wanted in Mississippi for second-degree murder. They went to arrest him, hold him for extradition. So no more Hemingway hoax."

"What Hemingway?" Pansy said.

"We'll tell you all about it," Lena said, and pointed at the bottle. "A little early, don't you think? You could at least get us a couple of glasses."

John went into the kitchen, almost floating with vodka buzz and anxious confusion. "What do you want with it?" Pansy said oh-jay and Lena said ice. Then Lena screamed.

He turned around and there was Castle standing in the door, grinning. He had a pistol in his right hand and a sawed-off shotgun in his left.

"You cunts," he said. "You fuckin' cunts. Go to the fuckin' cops."

There was a butcher knife in the drawer next to the refrigerator, but he didn't think Castle would stand idly by and let him rummage for it. Nothing else that might serve as a weapon, except the air pistol. Castle knew that it wouldn't do much damage.

He looked at John. "You three're gonna be my hostages. We're gettin' outta here, lose 'em up in the Everglades. They'll have a make on my pickup, though."

"We don't have a car," John said.

"I *know* that, asshole! There's a Hertz right down on One. You go rent one and don't try nothin' cute. I so much as *smell* a cop, I blow these two cunts away."

He turned back to the women and grinned crookedly, talking hard-guy through his teeth. "Like I did those two they sent, the spic and the nigger. They said somethin' about comin' back with a warrant to look for the shotgun and I was just bein' as nice as could be, I said hell, come on in, don't need no warrant. I got nothin' to hide, and when they come in I take the pistol from the nigger and kill the spic with it and shoot the nigger in the balls. You shoulda heard him. Some nigger. Took four more rounds to shut him up."

Wonder if that means the pistol is empty, John thought. He had Pansy's orange juice in his hand. It was an old-fashioned Smith & Wesson .357 Magnum six-shot, but from this angle he couldn't tell whether it had been reloaded. He could try to blind Castle with the orange juice.

He stepped toward him. "What kind of car do you want?"

"Just a car, damn it. Big enough." A siren whooped about a block away. Castle looked wary. "Bitch. You told 'em where you'd be."

"No," Lena pleaded. "We didn't tell them anything."

"Don't do anything stupid," John said.

Two more sirens, closer. "I'll show you *stupid!*" He raised the pistols toward Lena. John dashed the orange juice in his face.

It wasn't really like slow motion. It was just that John didn't miss any of it. Castle growled and swung around and in the cylinder's chambers John saw five copper-jacketed slugs. He reached for the gun and the first shot shattered his hand, blowing off two fingers, and struck the right side of his chest. The explosion was deafening and the shock of the bullet was like being hit simultaneously in the hand and chest with baseball bats. He rocked, still on his feet, and coughed blood spatter on Castle's face. He fired again, and the second slug hit him on the other side of the chest, this time spinning him half around. Was somebody screaming? Hemingway said it felt like an icy snowball, and that was pretty close, except for the inside part, your body saying Well, time to close up shop. There was a terrible familiar radiating pain in the center of his chest, and John realized that he was having a totally superfluous heart attack. He pushed off from the dinette and staggered toward Castle again. He made a grab for the shotgun and Castle emptied both barrels into his abdomen. He dropped to his knees and then fell over on his side. He couldn't feel anything. Things started to go dim and red. Was this going to be the last time?

Castle cracked the shotgun and the two spent shells flew up in an arc over his shoulder. He took two more out of his shirt pocket and dropped one. When he bent over to pick it up, Pansy leaped past him. In a swift motion that was almost graceful—it came to John that he had probably practiced it over and over, acting out fantasies—he slipped both shells into their chambers and closed the gun with a flip of the wrist. The screen door was stuck. Pansy was straining at the knob with both hands. Castle put the muzzles up to the base of her skull and pulled one trigger. Most of her head covered the screen or went through the hole the blast made. The crown of her skull, a bloody bowl, bounced off two walls and went spinning into the kitchen. Her body did a spastic little dance and folded, streaming.

Lena was suddenly on his back, clawing at his face. He spun and slammed her against the wall. She wilted like a rag doll and he hit her hard with the pistol on the way down. She unrolled at his feet, out cold, and with his mouth wide open laughing silently he lowered the shotgun and blasted her point-blank in the crotch. Her body jackknifed and John tried with all his will not to die but blackness crowded in and the last thing he saw was that evil grin as Castle reloaded again, peering out the window, presumably at the police.

It wasn't the terrible sense of being spread infinitesimally thin over an infinity of pain and darkness; things had just gone black, like closing your eyes. If this is death, John thought, there's not much to it.

But it changed. There was a little bit of pale light, some vague figures, and then colors bled into the scene, and after a moment of disorientation he realized he was still in the apartment, but apparently floating up by the ceiling. Lena was conscious again, barely, twitching, staring at the river of blood that pumped from between her legs. Pansy looked unreal, headless but untouched from the neck down, lying in a relaxed, improbable posture like a knocked-over department store dummy, blood still spurting from a neck artery out through the screen door.

His own body was a mess, the abdomen completely excavated by buckshot. Inside the huge wound, behind the torn coils of intestine, the shreds of fat and gristle, the blood, the shit, he could see sharp splintered knuckles of backbone. Maybe it hadn't hurt so much because the spinal cord had been severed in the blast.

He had time to be a little shocked at himself for not feeling more. Of course most of the people he'd known who had died did die this way, in loud spatters of blood and brains. Even after thirty years of the occasional polite heart attack or stroke carrying off a friend or acquaintance, most of the dead people he knew had died in the jungle.

He had been a hero there, in this universe. That would have surprised his sergeants in the original one. Congressional Medal of Honor, so-called, which hadn't hurt the sales of his first book. Knocked out the NVA machine gun emplacement with their own satchel charge, then hauled the machine gun around and wiped out their mortar and command squads. He managed it all with bullet wounds in the face and triceps. Of course without the bullet wounds he wouldn't have lost his cool and charged the machine gun emplacement, but that wasn't noted in the citation.

A pity there was no way to trade the medals in—melt them down into one big fat bullet and use it to waste that crazy motherfucker who was ignoring the three people he'd just killed, laughing like a hyena while he shouted obscenities at the police gathering down below.

Castle fires a shot through the lower window and then ducks and a spray of automatic weapon fire shatters the upper window, filling the air with a spray of glass; bullets and glass fly painlessly through John where he's floating and he hears them spatter into the ceiling and suddenly everything is white with plaster dust—it starts to clear and he is much closer to his body, drawing down closer and closer; he merges with it and there's an instant of blackness and he's looking out through human eyes again.

A dull noise and he looked up to see hundreds of shards of glass leap up from the floor and fly to the window; plaster dust in billows sucked up into bullet holes in the ceiling, which then disappeared.

The top windowpane reformed as Castle uncrouched, pointed the shotgun, then jerked forward as a blossom of yellow flame and white smoke rolled back into the barrel.

His hand was whole, the fingers restored. He looked down and saw rivulets of blood running back into the hole in his abdomen, then individual drops; then it closed and the clothing restored itself; then one of the holes in his chest closed up and then the other.

The clothing was unfamiliar. A tweed jacket in this weather? His hands had turned old, liver spots forming as he watched. Slow like a plant growing, slow like the moon turning, thinking slowly too, he reached up and felt the beard, and could see out of the corner of his eye that it was white and long. He was too fat, and a belt buckle bit painfully into his belly. He sucked in and pried out and looked at the buckle, yes, it was old brass and said GOTT MIT UNS, the buckle he'd taken from a dead German so long ago. The buckle Hemingway had taken.

John got to one knee. He watched fascinated as the stream of blood gushed back into Lena's womb, disappearing as Castle grinning jammed the barrels in between her legs, flinched, and did a complicated dance in reverse (while Pansy's decapitated body writhed around and jerked upright); Lena, sliding up off the floor, leaped up between the man's back and the wall, then fell off and ran backwards as he flipped the shotgun up to the back of Pansy's neck and seeming gallons of blood and tissue came flying from every direction to assemble themselves into the lovely head and face, distorted in terror as she jerked awkwardly at the door and then ran backwards, past Castle as he did a graceful pirouette, unloading the gun and placing one shell on the floor, which flipped up to his pocket as he stood and put the other one there.

John stood up and walked through some thick resistance toward Castle. Was it *time* resisting him? Everything else was still moving in reverse: Two empty shotgun shells sailed across the room to snick into the weapon's chambers; Castle snapped it shut and wheeled to face John—

But John wasn't where he was supposed to be. As the shotgun swung around, John grabbed the barrels—hot!—and pulled the pistol out of Castle's waistband. He lost his grip on the shotgun barrels just as he jammed the pistol against Castle's heart and fired. A spray of blood from all over the other side of the room converged on Castle's back and John felt the recoil sting of the Magnum just as the shotgun muzzle cracked hard against his teeth, mouthful of searing heat then blackness forever, back in the featureless infinite timespace hell that the Hemingway had taken him to, forever, but in the next instant, a new kind of twitch, a twist …

23

The Time Exchanged

What does that mean, you "lost" him?

We were in the railroad car in the Gare de Lyon, in the normal observation mode. This entity that looked like Hemingway walked up, greeted us, took the manuscripts, and disappeared.

Just like that.

No. He went into the next car. John Baird ran after him. Maybe that was my mistake. I translated instead of running.

That's when you lost him.

Both of them. Baird disappeared, too. Then Hadley came running in—

Don't confuse me with Hadleys. You checked the adjacent universes.

All of them, yes. I think they're all right.

Think?

Well … I can't quite get to that moment. When I disappeared. It's as if I were still there for several more seconds, so I'm excluded.

And John Baird is still there?

Not by the time I can insert myself. Just Hadley running around—

No Hadleys. No Hadleys. So naturally you went back to 1996.

Of course. But there is a period of several minutes there from which I'm excluded as well. When I can finally insert myself, John Baird is dead.

Ah.

In every doom line, he and Castlemaine have killed each other. John is lying there with his head blown off, Castle next to him with his heart torn out from a point-blank pistol shot, with two very distraught women screaming while police pile in through the door. And this.

The overnight bag with the stories.

I don't think anybody noticed it. With Baird dead, I could spot-check the women's futures; neither of them mentions the bag. So perhaps the mission is accomplished.

Well, Reality is still here. So far. But the connection between Baird and this Hemingway entity is disturbing. That Baird is able to return to 1996 without your help is *very* disturbing. He has obviously taken on some of your characteristics, your abilities, which is why you're excluded from the last several minutes of his life.

I've never heard of that happening before.

It never has. I think that John Baird is no more human than you and I.

Is?

I suspect he's still around somewhen.

24

Islands in the Stream

and the unending lightless desert of pain becomes suddenly one small bright spark and then everything is dark red and a taste, a bitter taste, Hoppe's No. 9 gun oil and the twin barrels of the fine Boss pigeon gun cold and oily on his tongue and biting hard against the roof of his mouth, the dark red is light on the other side of his eyelids, sting of pain before he bumps a tooth and opens his eyes and mouth and lowers the gun and with shaking hands unloads—no, *dis*-loads—both barrels and walks backwards, shuffling in the slippers, slumping, stopping to stare out into the Idaho morning dark, helpless tears coursing up from the snarled white beard, walking backwards down the stairs with the shotgun heavily cradled in his elbow, backing into the storeroom and replacing it in the rack, then back up the stairs and slowly put the keys there in plain sight on the kitchen windowsill, a bit of mercy from Miss Mary, then sit and stare at the cold bad coffee as it warms back to one acid sip—

A tiny part of the mind saying *wait! I am John Baird it is 1996*

and back to a spiritless shower, numb to the needle spray, and cramped constipation and a sleep of no ease; an evening with Mary and George Brown tiptoeing around the blackest of black-ass worse and worse each day, only one thing to look forward to

got to throw out an anchor

faster now, walking through the Ketchum woods like a jerky cartoon in reverse, fucking FBI and IRS behind every tree, because you sent Ezra that money, felt sorry for him because he was crazy, what a fucking joke, should have finished the *Cantos* and shot himself.

effect preceding cause but I can read or hear scraps of thought somehow speeding to a blur now, driving in reverse hundreds of miles per hour back from Ketchum to Minnesota, the Mayo Clinic, holding the madness in while you talk to the shrink, promise not to hurt myself have to go home and write if I'm going to beat this, figuring what he wants to hear, then the rubber mouthpiece and smell of your own hair and flesh slightly burnt by the electrodes then deep total blackness

sharp stabs of thought sometimes stretching

hospital days blur by in reverse, cold chrome and starch white, a couple of mouthfuls of claret a day to wash down the pills that seem to make it worse and worse

what will happen to me when he's born?

When they came back from Spain was when he agreed to the Mayo Clinic, still all beat-up from the plane crashes six years before in Africa, liver and spleen shot to hell, brain, too, nerves, can't write or can't stop: all day on one damned sentence for the Kennedy book but a hundred thousand fast words, pure shit, for the bullfight article. Paris book okay but stuck. Great to find the trunks in the Ritz but none of the stuff Hadley lost.

Here it stops. A frozen tableau:

Afternoon light slanting in through the tall cloudy windows of the Cambon bar, where he had liberated, would liberate, the hotel in August 1944. A good large American-style martini gulped too fast in the excitement. The two small trunks unpacked and laid out item by item. Hundreds of pages of notes that would become the Paris book. But nothing before '23, of course, *the manuscripts.* The novel and the stories and the poems still gone. One moment nailed down with the juniper sting of the martini and then time crawling rolling flying backwards again—

no control?

Months blurring by, Madrid Riviera Venice feeling sick and busted up, the plane wrecks like a quick one-two punch brain and body, blurry sick even before them at the Finca Vigia, can't get a fucking thing done after the Nobel Prize, journalists day and night, the prize bad luck and bullshit anyhow but need the $35,000 damn, had to shoot Willie, cat since the boat-time before the war, but winged a burglar too, same gun, just after the Pulitzer, now that was all right

slowing down again—Havana—the Floridita—

Even Mary having a good time, and the Basque jai alai players, too, though they don't know much English, most of them, interesting couple of civilians, the doctor and the Kraut look-alike, but there's something about the boy that makes it hard to take my eyes off him, looks like someone I guess, another round of Papa Dobles, that boy, what is it about him? and then the first round, with lunch, and things speeding up to a blur again.

out on the Gulf a lot, enjoying the triumph of *The Old Man and the Sea*, the easy good-paying work of providing fishing footage for the movie, and then back into 1951, the worst year of his life that far, weeks of grudging conciliation, uncontrollable anger, and black-ass depression from the poisonous critical slime that followed *Across the River*, bastards gunning for him, Harold Ross dead, mother Grace dead, son Gregory a dope addict hip-deep into the dianetics horseshit, Charlie Scribner dead but first declaring undying love for that asshole Jones

most of the forties an anxious blur, Cuba Italy Cuba France Cuba China found Mary kicked Martha out, thousand pages on the fucking *Eden* book wouldn't come together Bronze Star better than Pulitzer

Martha a chrome-plated bitch in Europe but war is swell otherwise, liberating the Ritz, grenades rifles pistols and bomb runs with the RAF, China boring compared to it and the Q-ship runs off Cuba, hell, maybe the bitch was right for once, just kid stuff and booze

marrying the bitch was the end of my belle epoch, easy to see from here, the thirties all sunshine Key West Spain Key West Africa Key West, good hard writing with Pauline holding down the store, good woman but sorry I had to

sorry I had to divorce

stopping

Walking Paris streets after midnight:

I was never going to throw back at her losing the manuscripts. Told Steffens that would be like blaming a human for the weather, or death. These things happen. Nor say anything about what I did the night after I found out she really had lost them. But this one time we got to shouting and I think I hurt her. Why the hell did she have to bring the carbons what the hell did she think carbons were for stupid stupid stupid and she crying and she giving me hell about Pauline Jesus any woman who could fuck up Paris for you could fuck up a royal flush

it slows down around the manuscripts or me—

golden years the mid-twenties everything clicks Paris Vorarlburg Paris Schruns Paris Pamplona Paris Madrid Paris Lausanne

couldn't believe she actually

most of a novel dozens of poems stories sketches—*contes*, Kitty called them by God woman you show me your *conte* and I'll show you mine

so drunk that night I know better than to drink that much absinthe so drunk I was half crawling going up the stairs to the apartment I saw weird I saw God I saw *I saw myself standing there on the fourth landing with Hadley's goddamn bag*

I waited almost an hour, that seemed like no time or all time, and when he, when I, when he came crashing up the stairs he blinked twice, then I walked through me groping, shook my head without looking back and managed to get the door unlocked

flying back through the dead winter French countryside, standing in the bar car fighting hopelessness to Hadley crying so hard she can't get out what was wrong with Steffens standing gaping like a fish in a bowl

twisting again, painlessly inside out, I suppose through various dimensions, seeing the man's life as one complex chord of beauty and purpose and ugliness and chaos, my life on one side of the Mobius strip consistent through its fading forty-year span, starting, *starting*, here:

the handsome young man sits on the floor of the apartment holding himself, rocking racked with sobs, one short manuscript crumpled in front of him, the room a mess with drawers pulled out, their contents scattered on the floor, it's like losing an arm a leg (a foot a testicle), it's like losing your youth and along with youth

with a roar he stands up, eyes closed fists clenched, wipes his face dry and stomps over to the window

breathes deeply until he's breathing normally
strides across the room, kicking a brassiere out of his way
stands with his hand on the knob and thinks this:
life can break you but you can grow back strong at the broken places
and goes out slamming the door behind him, somewhat conscious of having been present at his own birth.

With no effort I find myself standing earlier that day in the vestibule of a train. Hadley is walking away, tired, looking for a vendor. I turn and confront two aspects of myself.

"Close your mouth, John. You'll catch flies." They both stand paralyzed while I slide open the door and pull the overnight bag from under the seat. I walk away and the universe begins to tingle and sparkle.

I spend forever in the black void between timespaces. I am growing to enjoy it.

I appear in John Baird's apartment and set down the bag. I look at the empty chair in front of the old typewriter, the green beer bottle sweating cold next to it, and John Baird appears, looking dazed, and I have business elsewhere, elsewhen. A train to catch. I'll come back for the bag in twelve minutes or a few millennia, after the bloodbath that gives birth to us all.

25

A Moveable Feast

He wrote the last line and set down the pencil and read over the last page sitting on his hands for warmth. He could see his breath. Celebrate the end with a little heat.

He unwrapped the bundle of twigs and banked them around the pile of coals in the brazier. Crazy way to heat a room, but it's France. He cupped both hands behind the stack and blew gently. The coals glowed red and then orange and with the third breath the twigs smoldered and a small yellow flame popped up. He held his hands over the fire, rubbing the stiffness out of his fingers, enjoying the smell of the birch as it cracked and spit.

He put a fresh sheet and carbon into the typewriter and looked at his penciled notes. Final draft? Worth a try:

```
Ernest M. Hemingway,
74 rue da Cardinal Lemoine,
Paris, France
```

))UP IN MICHIGAN))

```
Jim Gilmore came to Horton's Bay from Canada . He
bought the blacksmith shop from old man Hortom
```

Shit, a typo. He flinched suddenly, as if struck, and shook his head to clear it. What a strange sensation to come out of nowhere. A sudden cold stab of grief. But larger somehow than grief for a person.

Grief for everybody, maybe. For being human.

From a typo?

He went to the window and opened it in spite of the cold. He filled his lungs with the cold damp air and looked around the familiar orange-and-grey mosaic of chimney pots and tiled roofs under the dirty winter Paris sky.

He shuddered and eased the window back down and returned to the heat of the brazier. He had felt it before, exactly that huge and terrible feeling. But where?

For the life of him he couldn't remember.

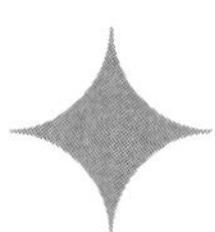

THE MOUNTAINS OF MOURNING

Lois McMaster Bujold

Introduction

"The Mountains of Mourning" had some oddly commercial roots, for such a tale. The science fiction convention PhilCon, in 1989, had invited me to be their writer guest, and at the time I was fretting about what I should write next, having finished out my current contracts for Baen Books with *Falling Free* and a return to the adventures of Miles Vorkosigan with *Brothers in Arms*. At our very first meeting at the Worldcon in Atlanta in 1986, my new publisher Jim Baen had alarmed me very much by mentioning that he thought the ideal rate of production for an author was a book every eight months, which was notably faster than I wrote.

In the meanwhile, then-senior-editor at Baen, Betsy Mitchell, had invited me to write my first novella ever, for a novella anthology series she was editing. "The Borders of Infinity," another Miles adventure, was published in September 1987 in Free Lancers, along with military SF stories by David Drake and Orson Scott Card, which put my work before a wider audience, very useful for my newbie career. At the time, before ebooks, novellas were a quirky and hard-to-place length in the pulp magazine or paper book markets, but I discovered I really enjoyed the structure, brisk and compact, like a novel on speed, but still giving room for significant character development. (And a very belated "Thank you, Betsy!" for that.)

Because it would allow me to produce a book in two-thirds of my usual time, I suggested to Jim at that dinner meeting at Philcon as part of my next three-book contract to recycle the "Borders" tale and add two more novellas to it, making an all-Miles volume. So I wrote "The Mountains of Mourning" next, followed by "Labyrinth," giving me yet more taste for a form that I found other chances to return to later in my career. Their pre-collection publication in *Analog* magazine further showcased my work.

I can still name where many of the elements of "Mountains" came from. Fat Ninny was based on a real horse, and I share Miles's love of the semi-wild country. Ma Mattulich was an extreme version of a certain female type I knew from real life, both victim and enforcer of her culture's life-denying mores. The river of roses might seem to have wandered in from some fairytale, sign and signifier of transformations to come, but I have met those wild roses in person, in banked-up masses, while riding my pony in the rural fields and woods of my childhood. A sense of the setting came from, first, living in central Ohio, a state bordering Appalachia, and unconsciously taking in how regional-cultural tensions worked along that divide, and second, less expectedly, from a very mainstream novel titled *Christie* by Catherine Marshall, based on her mother's experiences as a young teacher in the mountain region in the very early twentieth century, and read by me long before I became a writer.

I borrowed the title from a friend's working title of a fantasy, "The Mountains of Morning," that she didn't use for her story's final version. My "Mountains" was a contrary story, based on the "What's the worst possible thing we can do to this guy?" plot-generator, taking my new-minted Ensign Miles, his face to the stars, and forcing his head around to take a look at what his feet were planted in.

(That dictum has been quoted out of context since, leading to some misunderstanding. It wasn't meant as a call for authorial sadism. I realize it would be much better expressed as, "What's the most character-revealing plot turn we can inflict on this person?")

At the time I was having an amiable debate with Jim Baen about whether the series should be called "Miles Naismith Adventures" or "Miles Vorkosigan Adventures" on the books' cover banners. "Mountains" was in some sense the proof of my argument. It won me my first Hugo award, and my second Nebula, for best novella of 1989.

I wasn't able to be at the Worldcon that year in Den Haag, so Baen editor Toni Weisskopf kindly accepted for me and schlepped the rocket home, with some hassle. (I should have just told her to just ship it, but I was still in the most stringent penny-pinching stage of my life, and didn't process that as a tax-deductible business expense from a publisher's point of view.) I did make it to the Nebula Weekend in San Francisco the next year, thanks to my older brother's gift of frequent flyer points, a memorable experience.

—LOIS MCMASTER BUJOLD

The Mountains of Mourning

Miles heard the woman weeping as he was climbing the hill from the long lake. He hadn't dried himself after his swim, as the morning already promised shimmering heat. Lake water trickled cool from his hair onto his naked chest and back, more annoyingly down his legs from his ragged shorts. His leg braces chafed on his damp skin as he pistoned up the faint trail through the scrub, military double-time. His feet squished in his old wet shoes. He slowed curiously as he became conscious of the voices.

The woman's voice grated with grief and exhaustion. "Please, lord, please. All I want is m'justice ..."

The front gate guard's voice was irritated and embarrassed. "I'm no lord. C'mon, get *up*, woman. Go back to the village and report it at the district magistrate's office."

"I tell you, I just came from there!" The woman did not move from her knees as Miles emerged from the bushes and paused to take in the tableau across the paved road. "The magistrate's not to return for weeks, weeks. I walked four days to get here. I only have a little money ..." A desperate hope rose in her voice, and her spine bent and straightened as she scrabbled in her skirt pocket and held out her cupped hands to the guard. "A mark and twenty pence, it's all I have, but—"

The exasperated guard's eye fell on Miles, and he straightened abruptly, as if afraid Miles might suspect him of being tempted by so pitiful a bribe. "Be off, woman!" he snapped.

Miles quirked an eyebrow, and limped across the road to the main gate. "What's all this about, Corporal?" he inquired easily.

The guard corporal was on loan from Imperial Security, and wore the high-necked dress greens of the Barrayaran Service. He was sweating and uncomfortable in the bright morning light of this southern district, but Miles fancied he'd be boiled before he'd undo his collar on this post. His accent was not local; he was a city man from the capital, where a more-or-less efficient bureaucracy absorbed such problems as the one on her knees before him.

The woman, now, was local and more than local—she had back-country written all over her. She was younger than her strained voice had at first suggested. Tall, fever-red from her weeping, with stringy blond hair hanging down across a ferret-thin face and protuberant gray eyes. If she were cleaned up, fed, rested, happy and confident, she might achieve a near-prettiness, but she was far from that now, despite her remarkable figure. Lean but full-breasted—no, Miles revised himself as he crossed the road and came up to the gate. Her bodice was all blotched with dried milk leaks, though there was no baby in sight. Only temporarily full-breasted. Her worn dress was factory-woven cloth, but handsewn, crude and simple. Her feet were bare, thickly callused, cracked and sore.

"No problem," the guard assured Miles. "Go away," he hissed to the woman.

She lurched off her knees and sat stonily.

"I'll call my sergeant"—the guard eyed her, wary—"and have her removed."

"Wait a moment," said Miles.

She stared up at Miles from her cross-legged position, clearly not knowing whether to identify him as hope or not. His clothing, what there was of it, offered her no clue as to what he might be. The rest of him was all too plainly displayed. He jerked up his chin and smiled thinly. Too-large head, too-short neck, back thickened with its crooked spine, crooked legs with their brittle bones too-often broken, drawing the eye in their gleaming chromium braces. Were the hill woman standing, the top of his head would barely be even with the top of her shoulder. He waited in boredom for her hand to make the backcountry hex sign against evil mutations, but it only jerked and clenched into a fist.

"I must see my lord Count," she said to an uncertain point halfway between Miles and the guard. "It's my right. My daddy, he died in the Service. It's my right."

"Prime Minister Count Vorkosigan," said the guard stiffly, "is on his country estate to rest. If he were working, he'd be back in Vorbarr Sultana." The guard looked as if he wished *he* were back in Vorbarr Sultana.

The woman seized the pause. "You're only a city man. He's *my* count. My right."

"What do you want to see Count Vorkosigan for?" asked Miles patiently.

"Murder," growled the girl/woman. The security guard spasmed slightly. "I want to report a murder."

"Shouldn't you report to your village speaker first?" inquired Miles, with a hand-down gesture to calm the twitching guard.

"I did. He'll do *nothing*." Rage and frustration cracked her voice. "He says it's over and done. He won't write down my accusation, says it's nonsense. It would only make trouble for everybody, he says. I don't care! I want my justice!"

Miles frowned in thought, looking the woman over. The details checked, corroborated her claimed identity, added up to a solid if subliminal sense of authenticity which perhaps escaped the professionally paranoid security man. "It's true, Corporal," Miles said. "She has a right to appeal, first to the district magistrate, then to the Count's Court. And the district magistrate won't be back for two weeks."

This sector of Count Vorkosigan's native district had only one overworked district magistrate, who rode a circuit that included the lakeside village of Vorkosigan Surleau but one day a month. Since the region of the Prime Minister's country estate was crawling with Imperial Security when the great lord was in residence, and loosely monitored even when he was not, prudent troublemakers took their troubles elsewhere.

"Scan her, and let her in," said Miles. "On my authority."

The guard was one of Imperial Security's best, trained to look for assassins in his own shadow. He now looked scandalized, and lowered his voice to Miles. "Sir, if I let every country lunatic wander the estate at will—"

"I'll take her up. I'm going that way."

The guard shrugged helplessly, but stopped short of saluting; Miles was decidedly not in uniform. The gate guard pulled a scanner from his belt and made a great show of going over the woman. Miles wondered if he'd have been inspired to harass her with a strip-search without Miles's inhibiting presence. When the guard finished demonstrating how alert, conscientious, and loyal he was, he palmed open the gate's lock, entered the transaction, including the woman's retina scan, into the computer monitor, and stood aside in a pose of rather pointed parade rest. Miles grinned at the silent editorial, and steered the bedraggled woman by the elbow through the gates and up the winding drive.

She twitched away from his touch at the earliest opportunity, yet still refrained from superstitious gestures, eyeing him with a strange and hungry curiosity. Time was, such openly repelled fascination with the peculiarities of his body had driven Miles to grind his teeth; now he could take it with a serene amusement only slightly tinged with acid. They would learn, all of them. They would learn.

"Do you serve Count Vorkosigan, little man?" she asked cautiously.

Miles thought about that one a moment. "Yes," he answered finally. The answer was, after all, true on every level of meaning but the one she'd asked it. He quelled the temptation to tell her he was the court jester. From the look of her, this one's troubles were much worse than his own.

She had apparently not quite believed in her own rightful destiny, despite her mulish determination at the gate, for as they climbed unimpeded toward her goal a nascent panic made her face even more drawn and pale, almost ill. "How—how do I talk to him?" she choked. "Should I curtsey …?" She glanced down at herself as if conscious for the first time of her own dirt and sweat and squalor.

Miles suppressed a facetious set-up starting with, *Kneel and knock your forehead three times on the floor before speaking; that's what the General Staff does*, and said instead, "Just stand up straight and speak the truth. Try to be clear. He'll take it from there. He does not, after all"—Miles's lip twitched—"lack experience."

She swallowed.

A hundred years ago, the Vorkosigans' summer retreat had been a guard barracks, part of the outlying fortifications of the great castle on the bluff above the village of Vorkosigan Surleau. The castle was now a burnt-out ruin, and the barracks transformed into a comfortable low stone residence, modernized and re-modernized, artistically landscaped and bright with flowers. The arrow slits had been widened into big glass windows overlooking the lake, and comlink antennae bristled from the roof. There was a new guard barracks concealed in the trees downslope, but it had no arrow slits.

A man in the brown-and-silver livery of the Count's personal retainers exited the residence's front door as Miles approached with the strange woman in tow. It was the new man, what was his name? Pym, that was it.

"Where's m'lord Count?" Miles asked him.

"In the upper pavilion, taking breakfast with m'lady." Pym glanced at the woman, waited on Miles in a posture of polite inquiry.

"Ah. Well, this woman has walked four days to lay an appeal before the district magistrate's court. The court's not here, but the Count is, so she now proposes to skip the middlemen and go straight to the top. I like her style. Take her up, will you?"

"During *breakfast*?" said Pym.

Miles cocked his head at the woman. "Have you had breakfast?"

She shook her head mutely.

"I thought not." Miles turned his hands palm-out, dumping her, symbolically, on the retainer. "Now, yes."

"My daddy, he died in the Service," the woman repeated faintly. "It's my right." The phrase seemed as much to convince herself as anyone else, now.

Pym was, if not a hill man, district-born. "So it is." He sighed, gesturing her to follow him without further ado. Her eyes widened, as she trailed him around the house, and she glanced back nervously over her shoulder at Miles. "Little man ...?"

"Just stand straight," he called to her. He watched her round the corner, grinned, and took the steps two at a time into the residence's main entrance.

After a shave and cold shower, Miles dressed in his own room overlooking the long lake. He dressed with great care, as great as he'd expended on the Service Academy ceremonies and Imperial Review two days ago. Clean underwear, long-sleeved cream shirt, dark green trousers with the side piping. High-collared green tunic tailor-cut to his own difficult fit. New pale-blue plastic ensign's rectangles aligned precisely on the collar and poking most uncomfortably into his jaw. He dispensed with the leg braces and pulled on mirror-polished boots to the knee, and swiped a bit of dust from them with his pajama pants, ready-to-hand on the floor where he'd dropped them before going swimming.

He straightened and checked himself in the mirror. His dark hair hadn't even begun to recover from that last cut before the graduation ceremonies. A pale, sharp-featured face, not-too-much dissipated bags under the gray eyes, nor too bloodshot—alas, the limits of his body compelled him to stop celebrating well before he could hurt himself.

Echoes of the late celebration still boiled up silently in his head, crooking his mouth into a grin. He was on his way now, had his hand clamped firmly around the lowest rung of the highest ladder on Barrayar, Imperial Service itself. There were no giveaways in the Service even for sons of the Old Vor. You got what you earned. His brother-officers could be relied on to know that, even if outsiders wondered. He was in position at last to prove himself to all doubters. Up and away and never look down, never look back.

One last look back. As carefully as he'd dressed, Miles gathered up the necessary objects for his task. The white cloth rectangles of his former Academy cadet's rank. The hand-calligraphied second copy, purchased for this purpose, of his new officer's commission in the Barrayaran Imperial Service. A copy of his Academy three-year scholastic transcript on paper, with all its commendations (and demerits). No point in anything but honesty in this next transaction. In a cupboard downstairs he found the brass brazier and tripod, wrapped in its polishing cloth, and a plastic bag of very dry juniper bark. Chemical fire sticks.

Out the back door and up the hill. The landscaped path split, right going up to the pavilion overlooking it all, left forking sideways to a garden-like area surrounded by a low fieldstone wall. Miles let himself in by the gate. "Good morning, crazy ancestors," he called, then quelled his humor. It might be true, but lacked the respect due the occasion.

He strolled over and around the graves until he came to the one he sought, knelt, and set up the brazier and tripod, humming. The stone was simple, *General Count Piotr Pierre Vorkosigan*, and the dates. If they'd tried to list all the accumulated honors and accomplishments, they'd have had to go to microprint.

He piled in the bark, the very expensive papers, the cloth bits, a clipped mat of dark hair from that last cut. He set it alight and rocked back on his heels to watch it burn. He'd played a hundred versions of this moment over in his head, over the years, ranging from solemn public orations with musicians in the background, to dancing naked on the old man's grave. He'd settled on this private and traditional ceremony, played straight. Just between the two of them.

"So, Grandfather," he purred at last. "And here we are after all. Satisfied now?"

All the chaos of the graduation ceremonies behind, all the mad efforts of the last three years, all the pain, came to this point; but the grave did not speak, did not say, *Well done; you can stop now*. The ashes spelled out no messages, there were no visions to be had in the rising smoke. The brazier burned down all too quickly. Not enough stuff in it, perhaps.

He stood, and dusted his knees, in the silence and the sunlight. So what had he expected? Applause? Why was he here, in the final analysis? Dancing out a dead man's dreams—who did his service really serve? Grandfather? Himself? Pale Emperor Gregor? Who cared?

"Well, old man," he whispered, then shouted: "ARE YOU SATISFIED YET?" The echoes rang from the stones.

A throat cleared behind him, and Miles whirled like a scalded cat, heart pounding.

"Uh … my lord?" said Pym carefully. "Pardon me, I did not mean to interrupt … anything. But the Count your father requires you to attend on him in the upper pavilion."

Pym's expression was perfectly bland. Miles swallowed, and waited for the scarlet heat he could feel in his face to recede. "Quite." He shrugged. "The fire's almost out. I'll clean it up later. Don't … let anybody else touch it."

He marched past Pym and didn't look back.

The pavilion was a simple structure of weathered silver wood, open on all four sides to catch the breeze, this morning a few faint puffs from the west. Good sailing on the lake this afternoon, maybe. Only ten days of precious home leave left, and much Miles wanted to do, including the trip to Vorbarr Sultana with his cousin Ivan to pick out his new lightflyer. And then his first assignment would be coming through—ship duty, Miles prayed. He'd had to overcome a major temptation, not to ask his father to make sure it was ship duty. He would take whatever assignment fate dealt him, that was the first rule of the game. And win with the hand he was dealt.

The interior of the pavilion was shady and cool after the glare outside. It was furnished with comfortable old chairs and tables, one of which bore the remains of a noble breakfast—Miles mentally marked two lonely-looking oil cakes on a crumb-scattered tray as his own. Miles's mother, lingering over her cup, smiled across the table at him.

Miles's father, casually dressed in an open-throated shirt and shorts, sat in a worn armchair. Aral Vorkosigan was a thick-set, gray-haired man, heavy-jawed, heavy-browed, scarred. A face that lent itself to savage caricature—Miles had seen some, in Opposition press, in the histories of Barrayar's enemies. They had only to draw one lie, to render dull those sharp penetrating eyes, to create everyone's parody of a military dictator.

And how much is he haunted by Grandfather? Miles wondered. *He doesn't show it much. But then, he doesn't have to.* Admiral Aral

Vorkosigan, space master strategist, conqueror of Komarr, hero of Escobar, for sixteen years Imperial Regent and supreme power on Barrayar in all but name. And then he'd capped it, confounded history and all self-sure witnesses and heaped up honor and glory beyond all that had gone before by voluntarily stepping *down* and transferring command smoothly to Emperor Gregor upon his majority. Not that the prime ministership hadn't made a dandy retirement from the regency, and he was showing no signs yet of stepping down from *that*.

And so Admiral Aral's life took General Piotr's like an overpowering hand of cards, and where did that leave Ensign Miles? Holding two deuces and the joker. He must surely either concede or start bluffing like crazy …

The hill woman sat on a hassock, a half-eaten oil cake clutched in her hands, staring open-mouthed at Miles in all his power and polish. As he caught and returned her gaze, her lips pressed closed and her eyes lit. Her expression was strange—anger? Exhilaration? Embarrassment? Glee? Some bizarre mixture of all? *And what did you think I was, woman?*

Being in uniform (showing off his uniform?), Miles came to attention before his father. "Sir?"

Count Vorkosigan spoke to the woman. "That is my son. If I send him as my Voice, would that satisfy you?"

"Oh," she breathed, her wide mouth drawing back in a weird, fierce grin, the most expression Miles had yet seen on her face, "*yes*, my lord."

"Very well. It will be done."

What will be done? Miles wondered warily. The Count was leaning back in his chair, looking satisfied with himself, but with a dangerous tension around his eyes hinting that something had aroused his true anger. Not anger at the woman, clearly they were in some sort of agreement, and—Miles searched his conscience quickly—not at Miles himself. He cleared his throat gently, cocking his head and baring his teeth in an inquiring smile.

The Count steepled his hands and spoke to Miles at last. "A most interesting case. I can see why you sent her up."

"Ah …" said Miles. What had he got hold of? He'd only greased the woman's way through security on a quixotic impulse, for God's sake, and to tweak his father at breakfast. "… ah?" he continued noncommittally.

Count Vorkosigan's brows rose. "Did you not know?"

"She spoke of a murder, and a marked lack of cooperation from her local authorities about it. Figured you'd give her a lift on to the district magistrate."

The Count settled back still further, rubbing his hand thoughtfully across his scarred chin. "It's an infanticide case."

Miles's belly went cold. *I don't want anything to do with this.* Well, that explained why there was no baby to go with the breasts. "Unusual … for it to be reported."

"We've fought the old customs for twenty years and more," said the Count. "Promulgated, propagandized …. In the cities, we've made good progress."

"In the cities," murmured the Countess, "people have access to alternatives."

"But in the backcountry—well—little has changed. We all know what's going on, but without a report, a complaint—and with the family invariably drawing together to protect its own—it's hard to get leverage."

"What"—Miles cleared his throat, nodded at the woman—"what was your baby's mutation?"

"The cat's mouth." The woman dabbed at her upper lip to demonstrate. "She had the hole inside her mouth, too, and was a weak sucker, she choked and cried, but she was getting enough, she *was* …"

"Harelip," the Count's off-worlder wife murmured half to herself, translating the Barrayaran term to the galactic standard, "and a cleft palate, sounds like. Harra, that's not even a mutation. They had that back on Old Earth. A … a normal birth defect, if that's not a contradiction in terms. Not a punishment for your Barrayaran ancestors' pilgrimage through the Fire. A simple operation could have corrected—" Countess Vorkosigan cut herself off. The hill woman was looking anguished.

"I'd heard," the woman said. "My lord had made a hospital to be built at Hassadar. I meant to take her there, when I was a little stronger, though I had no money. Her arms and legs were sound, her head was well shaped, anybody could see—surely they would have"—her hands clenched and twisted, her voice went ragged—"but Lem killed her first."

A seven-day walk, Miles calculated, from the deep Dendarii Mountains to the lowland town of Hassadar. Reasonable, that a woman newly risen from childbed might delay that hike a few days. An hour's ride in an aircar …

"So one is reported as a murder at last," said Count Vorkosigan, "and we will treat it as exactly that. This is a chance to send a message to the farthest corners of my own district. You, Miles, will be my Voice, to reach where it has not reached before. You will dispense count's justice upon this man—and not quietly, either. It's time for the practices that brand us as barbarians in galactic eyes to end."

Miles gulped. "Wouldn't the district magistrate be better qualified …?"

The Count smiled slightly. "For this case, I can think of no one better qualified than yourself."

The messenger and the message all in one: *Times have changed.* Indeed. Miles wished himself elsewhere, anywhere—back sweating blood over his final examinations, for instance. He stifled an unworthy wail, *My home leave …!*

Miles rubbed the back of his neck. "Who, ah … who is it killed your little girl?" *Meaning, who is it I'm expected to drag out, put up against a wall, and shoot?*

"My husband," she said tonelessly, looking at—through—the polished silvery floorboards.

I knew this was going to be messy …

"She cried and cried," the woman went on, "and wouldn't go to sleep, not nursing well—he shouted at me to shut her up—"

"Then?" Miles prompted, sick to his stomach.

"He swore at me, and went to go sleep at his mother's. He said at least a working man could sleep there. I hadn't slept either …"

This guy sounds like a real winner. Miles had an instant picture of him, a bull of a man with a bullying manner—nevertheless, there was something missing in the climax of the woman's story.

The Count had picked up on it too. He was listening with total attention, his strategy-session look, a slit-eyed intensity of thought you could mistake for sleepiness. That would be a grave mistake.

"Were you an eyewitness?" he asked in a deceptively mild tone that put Miles on full alert. "Did you actually see him kill her?"

"I found her dead in the midmorning, lord."

"You went into the bedroom—" Count Vorkosigan led her on.

"We've only got one room." She shot him a look as if doubtful for the first time of his total omniscience. "She had slept, slept at last. I went out to get some brillberries, up the ravine a way. And when I came back … I should have taken her with me, but I was so glad she slept at last, didn't want to risk waking her—" Tears leaked from the woman's tightly closed eyes. "I let her sleep when I came back, I was glad to eat and rest, but I began to get full"—her hand touched a breast—"and I went to wake her …"

"What, were there no marks on her? Not a cut throat?" asked the Count. That was the usual method for these backcountry infanticides, quick and clean compared to, say, exposure.

The woman shook her head. "Smothered, I think, lord. It was cruel, something cruel. The village Speaker said I must have overlain her, and wouldn't take my plea against Lem. I did not, I did not! She had her own cradle, Lem made it with his own hands when she was still in my belly …" She was close to breaking down.

The Count exchanged a glance with his wife, and a small tilt of his head. Countess Vorkosigan rose smoothly.

"Come, Harra, down to the house. You must wash and rest before Miles takes you home."

The hill woman looked taken aback. "Oh, not in your house, lady!"

"Sorry, it's the only one I've got handy. Besides the guard barracks. The guards are good boys, but you'd make 'em uncomfortable …" The Countess eased her out.

"It is clear," said Count Vorkosigan as soon as the women were out of earshot, "that you will have to check out the medical facts before, er, popping off. And I trust you will also have noticed the little problem with a positive identification of the accused. This could be the ideal public-demonstration case we want, but not if there's any ambiguity about it. No bloody mysteries."

"I'm not a coroner," Miles pointed out immediately. If he could wriggle off this hook …

"Quite. You will take Dr. Dea with you."

Lieutenant Dea was the Prime Minister's physician's assistant. Miles had seen him around—an ambitious young military doctor, in a constant state of frustration because his superior would never let him touch his most important patient—oh, he was going to be thrilled with this assignment, Miles predicted morosely.

"He can take his osteo kit with him, too," the Count went on, brightening slightly, "in case of accidents."

"How economical," said Miles, rolling his eyes. "Look, uh—suppose her story checks out and we nail this guy. Do I have to, personally …?"

"One of the liveried men will be your bodyguard. And—if the story checks—the executioner."

That was only slightly better. "Couldn't we wait for the district magistrate?"

"Every judgment the district magistrate makes, he makes in my place. Every sentence his office carries out, is carried out in my name. Someday, it will be done in your name. It's time you gained a clear understanding of the process. Historically, the Vor may be a military caste, but a Vor lord's duties were never only military ones."

No escape. Damn, damn, damn. Miles sighed. "Right. Well … we could take the aircar, I suppose, and be up there in a couple of hours. Allow some time to find the right hole. Drop out of the sky on 'em, make the message loud and clear … be back before bedtime." Get it over with quickly.

The Count had that slit-eyed look again. "No …" he said slowly, "not the aircar, I don't think."

"No roads for a groundcar, up that far. Just trails." He added uneasily—surely his father could not be thinking of—"I don't think I'd cut a very impressive figure of central Imperial authority on foot, sir."

His father glanced up at his crisp dress uniform and smiled slightly. "Oh, you don't do so badly."

"But picture this after three or four days of beating through the bushes," Miles protested. "You didn't see us in Basic. Or smell us."

"I've been there," said the Admiral dryly. "But no, you're quite right. Not on foot. I have a better idea."

My own cavalry troop, thought Miles ironically, turning in his saddle, *just like Grandfather.* Actually, he was pretty sure the old man would have had some acerbic comments about the riders now strung out behind Miles on the wooded trail, once he'd got done rolling on the ground laughing at the equitation being displayed. The Vorkosigan stables had shrunk sadly since the old man was no longer around to take an interest, the polo string sold off, the few remaining ancient and ill-tempered ex-cavalry beasts put permanently out to pasture. The handful of riding horses left were retained for their sure-footedness and good manners, not their exotic bloodlines, and kept exercised and gentle for the occasional guest by a gaggle of girls from the village.

Miles gathered his reins, tensed one calf, and shifted his weight slightly, and Fat Ninny responded with a neat half turn and two precise back steps. The thick-set roan gelding could not have been mistaken by the most ignorant urbanite for a fiery steed, but Miles adored him, for his dark and liquid eye, his wide velvet nose, his phlegmatic disposition equally unappalled by rushing streams or screaming aircars, but most of all for his exquisite dressage-trained responsiveness. Brains before beauty. Just being around him made Miles calmer; the beast was an emotional blotter, like a purring cat. Miles patted Fat Ninny on the neck. "If anybody asks," he murmured, "I'll tell them your name is Chieftain." Fat Ninny waggled one fuzzy ear, heaving a whooshing, barrel-chested sigh.

Grandfather had a great deal to do with the unlikely parade Miles now led. The great guerilla general had poured out his youth in these mountains, fighting the Cetagandan invaders to a standstill and then reversing their tide. Anti-flyer heatless seeker-strikers smuggled in at bloody cost from off-planet had a lot more to do with the final victory than cavalry horses, which, according to Grandfather, had saved his forces through the worst winter of that campaign mainly by being edible. But through retroactive romance, the horse had become the symbol of that struggle.

Miles thought his father was being overly optimistic, if he thought Miles was going to cash in thusly on the old man's residual glory. The guerilla caches and camps were shapeless lumps of rust and *trees*, dammit, not just weeds and scrub anymore—they had passed some, earlier in today's ride—the men who had fought that war had long since gone to ground for the last time, just like Grandfather. What was he doing here? It was jump-ship duty he wanted, taking him high, high above all this. The future, not the past, held his destiny.

Miles's meditations were interrupted by Dr. Dea's horse, which, taking exception to a branch lying across the logging trail, planted all four feet in an abrupt stop and snorted loudly. Dr. Dea toppled off with a faint cry.

"Hang onto the *reins*," Miles called, and pressed Fat Ninny back down the trail.

Dr. Dea was getting rather better at falling off; he'd landed more or less on his feet this time. He made a lunge at the dangling reins, but his sorrel mare shied away from his grab. Dea jumped back as she swung on her haunches and then, realizing her freedom, bounced back down the trail, tail bannering, horse body-language for *Nyah, nyah, ya can't catch me!* Dr. Dea, red and furious, ran swearing in pursuit. She broke into a canter.

"No, no, don't run after her!" called Miles.

"How the hell am I supposed to catch her if I don't run after her?" snarled Dea. The space surgeon was not a happy man. "My medkit's on that bloody beast!"

"How do you think you can catch her if you do?" asked Miles. "She can run faster than you can."

At the end of the little column, Pym turned his horse sideways, blocking the trail. "Just wait, Harra," Miles advised the anxious hill woman in passing. "Hold your horse still. Nothing starts a horse running faster than another running horse."

The other two riders were doing rather better. The woman Harra Csurik sat her horse wearily, allowing it to plod along without interference, but at least riding on balance instead of trying to use the reins as a handle like the unfortunate Dea. Pym, bringing up the rear, was competent if not comfortable.

Miles slowed Fat Ninny to a walk, reins loose, and wandered after the mare, radiating an air of calm relaxation. *Who, me? I don't want to catch you. We're just enjoying the scenery, right. That's it, stop for a bite.* The sorrel mare paused to nibble at a weed, but kept a wary eye on Miles's approach.

At a distance just short of starting the mare bolting off again, Miles stopped Fat Ninny and slid off. He made no move toward the mare, but instead stood still and made a great show of fishing in his pockets. Fat Ninny butted his head against Miles eagerly, and Miles cooed and fed him a bit of sugar. The mare cocked her ears with interest. Fat Ninny smacked his lips and nudged for more. The mare snuffled up for her share. She lipped a cube from Miles's palm as he slid his other arm quietly through the loop of her reins.

"Here you go, Dr. Dea. One horse. No running."

"No fair," wheezed Dea, trudging up. "You had sugar in your pockets."

"Of course I had sugar in my pockets. It's called foresight and planning. The trick of handling horses isn't to be faster than the horse, or stronger than the horse. That pits your weakness against his strengths. The trick is to be smarter than the horse. That pits your strength against his weakness, eh?"

Dea took his reins. "It's snickering at me," he said suspiciously.

"That's nickering, not snickering." Miles grinned. He tapped Fat Ninny behind his left foreleg, and the horse obediently grunted down onto one knee. Miles clambered up readily to his conveniently lowered stirrup.

"Does mine do that?" asked Dr. Dea, watching with fascination.

"Sorry, no."

Dea glowered at his horse. "This animal is an idiot. I shall lead it for a while."

As Fat Ninny lurched back to his four feet Miles suppressed a riding-instructorly comment gleaned from his grandfather's store such as, *Be smarter than the horse, Dea.* Though Dr. Dea was officially sworn to Lord Vorkosigan for the duration of this investigation, Space Surgeon Lieutenant Dea certainly outranked Ensign Vorkosigan. To command older men who outranked one called for a certain measure of tact.

The logging road widened out here, and Miles dropped back beside Harra Csurik. Her fierceness and determination of yesterday morning at the gate seemed to be fading even as the trail rose toward her home. Or perhaps it was simply exhaustion catching up with her. She'd said little all morning, been sunk in silence all afternoon. If she was going to drag Miles all the way up to the back of beyond and then wimp out on him …

"What, ah, branch of the Service was your father in, Harra?" Miles began conversationally.

She raked her fingers through her hair in a combing gesture more nervousness than vanity. Her eyes looked out at him through the straw-colored wisps like skittish creatures in the protection of a hedge.

"District Militia, m'lord. I don't really remember him, he died when I was real little."

"In combat?"

She nodded. "In the fighting around Vorbarr Sultana, during Vordarian's Pretendership."

Miles refrained from asking which side he had been swept up on—most foot soldiers had had little choice, and the amnesty had included the dead as well as the living.

"Ah … do you have any sibs?"

"No, lord. Just me and my mother left."

A little anticipatory tension eased in Miles's neck. If this judgment indeed drove all the way through to an execution, one misstep could trigger a blood feud among the in-laws. *Not* the legacy of justice the Count intended him to leave behind. So the fewer in-laws involved, the better. "What about your husband's family?"

"He's got seven. Four brothers and three sisters."

"Hm." Miles had a mental flash of an entire team of huge, menacing hill hulks. He glanced back at Pym, feeling a trifle understaffed for his task. He had pointed out this factor to the Count, when they'd been planning this expedition last night.

"The village Speaker and his deputies will be your backup," the Count had said, "just as for the district magistrate on court circuit."

"What if they don't want to cooperate?" Miles had asked nervously.

"An officer who expects to command Imperial troops," the Count had glinted, "should be able to figure out how to extract cooperation from a backcountry headman."

In other words, his father had decided this was a test, and wasn't going to give him any more clues. Thanks, Da.

"You have no sibs, lord?" said Harra, snapping him back to the present.

"No. But surely that's known, even in the back-beyond."

"They *say* a lot of things about you." Harra shrugged.

Miles bit down on the morbid question in his mouth like a wedge of raw lemon. He would not ask it, he would not … he couldn't help himself. "Like what?" forced out past his stiff lips.

"Everyone knows the Count's son is a mutant." Her eyes flicked defiant-wide. "Some said it came from the off-worlder woman he married. Some said it was from radiation from the wars, or a disease from, um, corrupt practices in his youth among his brother-officers—"

That last was a new one to Miles. His brow lifted.

"—but most say he was poisoned by his enemies."

"I'm glad most have it right. It was an assassination attempt using soltoxin gas, when my mother was pregnant with me. But it's not—" a *mutation*, his thought hiccoughed through the well-worn grooves—how many times had he explained this?—*it's teratogenic, not genetic*, I'm not a mutant, not … What the hell did a fine point of biochemistry matter to this ignorant, bereaved woman? For all practical purposes—for her purposes—he might as well be a mutant. "—important," he finished.

She eyed him sideways, swaying gently in the clop-a-clop rhythm of her mount. "Some said you were born with no legs, and lived all the time in a float chair in Vorkosigan House. Some said you were born with no bones—"

"—and kept in a jar in the basement, no doubt," Miles muttered.

"But Karal said he'd seen you with your grandfather at Hassadar Fair, and you were only sickly and undersized. Some said your father had got you into the Service, but others said no, you'd gone off-planet to your mother's home and had your brain turned into a computer and your body fed with tubes, floating in a liquid—"

"I knew there'd be a jar turn up in this story somewhere." Miles grimaced. *You knew you'd be sorry you asked, too, but you went and did it anyway.* She was baiting him, Miles realized suddenly. How *dare* she … but there was no humor in her, only a sharp-edged watchfulness.

She had gone out, way out on a limb to lay this murder charge, in defiance of family and local authorities alike, in defiance of established custom. And what had her Count given her for a shield and support, going back to face the wrath of all her nearest and dearest? Miles. Could he handle this? She must be wondering indeed. Or would he botch it, cave and cut and run, leaving her to face the whirlwind of rage and revenge alone?

He wished he'd left her weeping at the gate.

The woodland, fruit of many generations of terraforming forestry, opened out suddenly on a vale of brown native scrub. Down the middle of it, through some accident of soil chemistry, ran a half-kilometer-wide swathe of green and pink—feral roses, Miles realized with astonishment as they rode nearer. Earth roses. The track dove into the fragrant mass of them and vanished.

He took turns with Pym, hacking their way through with their Service bush knives. The roses were vigorous and studded with thick thorns, and hacked back with a vicious elastic recoil. Fat Ninny did his part by swinging his big head back and forth and nipping off blooms and chomping them down happily. Miles wasn't sure just how many he ought to let the big roan eat—just because the species wasn't native to Barrayar didn't mean it wasn't poisonous to horses. Miles sucked at his wounds and reflected upon Barrayar's shattered ecological history.

The fifty thousand Firsters from Earth had only meant to be the spearhead of Barrayar's colonization. Then, by a gravitational anomaly, the wormhole jump through which the colonists had come had shifted closed—violently, irrevocably, and without warning. The terraforming which had begun, so careful and controlled in the beginning, collapsed along with everything else. Imported Earth plant and animal species had escaped everywhere to run wild, as the humans turned their attention to the most urgent problems of survival. Biologists still mourned the mass extinctions of native species that had followed, the erosions and droughts and floods, but really, Miles thought, over the centuries of the Time of Isolation the fittest of both worlds had fought it out to a perfectly good new balance. If it was alive and covered the ground who cared where it came from?

We are all here by accident. Like the roses.

They camped that night high in the hills, and pushed on in the morning to the flanks of the true mountains. They were now out of the region Miles was personally familiar with from his childhood, and he checked Harra's directions frequently on his orbital survey map. They stopped only a few hours short of their goal at sunset of the second day. Harra insisted she could lead them on in the dusk from here, but Miles did not care to arrive after nightfall, unannounced, in a strange place of uncertain welcome.

He bathed the next morning in a stream, and unpacked and dressed carefully in his new officer's Imperial dress greens. Pym wore the Vorkosigan brown-and-silver livery, and pulled the Count's standard on a telescoping aluminum pole from the recesses of his saddlebag and mounted it on his left stirrup. *Dressed to kill,* thought Miles joylessly. Dr. Dea wore ordinary black fatigues and looked uncomfortable. If they constituted a message, Miles was damned if he knew what it was.

They pulled the horses up at midmorning before a two-room cabin set on the edge of a vast grove of sugar maples, planted who-knew-how-many centuries ago but now raggedly marching up the vale by self-seeding. The mountain air was cool and pure and bright. A few chickens stalked and bobbed in the weeds. An algae-choked wooden pipe from the woods dribbled water into a trough, which overflowed into a squishy green streamlet and away.

Harra slid down and smoothed her skirt and climbed the porch. "Karal?" she called. Miles waited high on horseback for the initial contact. Never give up a psychological advantage.

"Harra? Is that you?" came a man's voice from within. He banged open the door and rushed out. "Where have you been, girl? We've been beating the bushes for you! Thought you'd broke your neck in the scrub somewhere—" He stopped short before the three silent men on horseback.

"You wouldn't write down my charges, Karal," said Harra rather breathlessly. Her hands kneaded her skirt. "So I walked to the district magistrate at Vorkosigan Surleau to Speak them myself."

"Oh, girl," Karal breathed in regret, "that was a *stupid* thing to do ..." His head lowered and swayed, as he stared uneasily at the riders. He was a balding man of maybe sixty, leathery and worn, and his left arm ended in a stump. Another veteran.

"Speaker Serg Karal?" began Miles sternly. "I am the Voice of Count Vorkosigan. I am charged to investigate the crime Spoken by Harra Csurik before the Count's Court, namely the murder of her infant daughter Raina. As Speaker of Silvy Vale, you are requested and required to assist me in all matters pertaining to the Count's justice."

At this point Miles ran out of prescribed formalities, and was on his own. That hadn't taken long. He waited. Fat Ninny snuffled. The silver-on-brown cloth of the standard made a few soft snapping sounds, lifted by a vagrant breeze.

"The district magistrate wasn't there," put in Harra, "but the Count was."

Karal was gray-faced, staring. He pulled himself together with an effort, came to a species of attention, and essayed a creaking half-bow. "Who—who are you, sir?"

"Lord Miles Vorkosigan."

Karal's lips moved silently. Miles was no lip reader, but he was pretty sure it came to a dismayed variant of *Oh, shit.* "This is my liveried man, Armsman Pym, and my medical examiner, Lieutenant Dea of the Imperial Service."

"You are my lord Count's son?" Karal croaked.

"The one and only." Miles was suddenly sick of the posing. Surely that was a sufficient first impression. He swung down off Ninny, landing lightly on the balls of his feet. Karal's gaze followed him down, and down. *Yeah, so I'm short. But wait'll you see me dance.* "All right if we water our horses in your trough here?" Miles looped Ninny's reins through his arm and stepped toward it.

"Uh, that's for the people, m'lord," said Karal. "Just a minute and I'll fetch a bucket." He hitched up his baggy trousers and trotted off around the side of the cabin. A minute's uncomfortable silence, then Karal's voice floating faintly, "Where'd you put the goat bucket, Zed?"

Another voice, light and young. "Behind the woodstack, Da." The voices fell to a muffled undertone. Karal came trotting back with a battered aluminum bucket, which he placed beside the trough. He knocked out a wooden plug in the side, letting a bright stream arc out to splash and fill. Fat Ninny flickered his ears and snuffled and rubbed his big head against Miles, smearing his tunic with red and white horsehairs and nearly knocking him off his feet. Karal glanced up and smiled at the horse, though his smile fell away as his gaze passed on to the horse's owner. As Fat Ninny gulped his drink Miles caught a glimpse of the source of the second voice, a boy of around twelve who flitted off into the woods behind the cabin.

Karal fell to, assisting Miles and Harra and Pym in securing the horses. Miles left Pym to unsaddle and feed, and followed Karal into his house. Harra stuck to Miles like glue. Dr. Dea unpacked his medical kit and trailed along. Miles's boots rang loud and unevenly on the wooden floorboards.

"My wife, she'll be back in the nooning," said Karal, moving uncertainly around the room as Miles and Dea settled themselves on a bench and Harra curled up with her arms around her knees on the floor beside the fieldstone hearth. "I'll … I'll make some tea, m'lord." He skittered back out the door to fill a kettle at the trough before Miles could say, *No, thank you.* No, let him ease his nerves in ordinary movements. Then maybe Miles could begin to tease out how much of this static was social nervousness and how much was—perhaps—guilty conscience. By the time Karal had the kettle on the coals he was noticeably better controlled, so Miles began.

"I'd prefer to commence this investigation immediately, Speaker. It need not take long."

"It need not … take place at all, m'lord. The baby's death was natural—there were no marks on her. She was weakly, she had the cat's mouth, who knows what else was wrong with her? She died in her sleep, or by some accident."

"It is remarkable," said Miles dryly, "how often such accidents happen in this district. My father the Count himself has … remarked on it."

"There was no call to drag you up here." Karal looked in exasperation at Harra. She sat silent, unmoved by his persuasion.

"It was no problem," said Miles blandly.

"Truly, m'lord"—Karal lowered his voice—"I believe the child might have been overlain. 'S no wonder, in her grief, that her mind rejected it. Lem Csurik, he's a good boy, a good provider. She really doesn't want to do this, her reason is just temporarily overset by her troubles."

Harra's eyes, looking out from her hair-thatch, were poisonously cold.

"I begin to see." Miles's voice was mild, encouraging.

Karal brightened slightly. "It all could still be all right. If she will just be patient. Get over her sorrow. Talk to poor Lem. I'm sure he didn't kill the babe. Not rush to something she'll regret."

"I begin to see"—Miles let his tone go ice cool—"why Harra Csurik found it necessary to walk four days to get an unbiased hearing. 'You think.' 'You believe.' 'Who knows what?' Not you, it appears. I hear speculation—accusation—innuendo—assertion. I came for *facts*, Speaker Karal. The Count's justice doesn't turn on guesses. It doesn't have to. This isn't the Time of Isolation. Not even in the back-beyond.

"My investigation of the facts will begin now. No judgment will be—rushed into, before the facts are complete. Confirmation of Lem Csurik's guilt or innocence will come from his own mouth, under fast-penta, administered by Dr. Dea before two witnesses—yourself and a deputy of your choice. Simple, clean, and quick." *And maybe I can be on my way out of this benighted hole before sundown.* "I require you, Speaker, to go now and bring Lem Csurik for questioning. Armsman Pym will assist you."

Karal killed another moment pouring the boiling water into a big brown pot before speaking. "I'm a travelled man, lord. A twenty-year Service man. But most folks here have never been out of Silvy Vale. Interrogation chemistry might as well be magic to them. They might say it was a false confession, got that way."

"Then you and your deputy can say otherwise. This isn't exactly like the good old days, when confessions were extracted under torture, Karal. Besides, if he's as innocent as you *guess*—he'll clear himself, no?"

Reluctantly, Karal went into the adjoining room. He came back shrugging on a faded Imperial Service uniform jacket with a corporal's rank marked on the collar, the buttons of which did not quite meet across his middle anymore. Preserved, evidently, for such official functions. Even as in Barrayaran custom one saluted the uniform, and not the man in it, so might the wrath engendered by an unpopular duty fall on the office and not the individual who carried it out. Miles appreciated the nuance.

Karal paused at the door. Harra still sat wrapped in silence by the hearth, rocking slightly.

"M'lord," said Karal. "I've been Speaker of Silvy Vale for sixteen years now. In all that time nobody has had to go to the district magistrate for a Speaking, not for water rights or stolen animals or swiving or even the time Neva accused Bors of tree piracy over the maple sap. We've not had a blood feud in all that time."

"I have no intention of starting a blood feud, Karal. I just want the facts."

"That's the thing, m'lord. I'm not so in love with facts as I used to be. Sometimes, they bite." Karal's eyes were urgent.

Really, the man was doing everything but stand on his head and juggle cats—one-handed—to divert Miles. How overt was his obstruction likely to get?

"Silvy Vale cannot be permitted to have its own little Time of Isolation," said Miles in warning. "The Count's justice is for everyone, now. Even if they're small. And weakly. And have something wrong with them. And cannot even speak for themselves—*Speaker*."

Karal flinched, white about the lips—point taken, evidently. He trudged away up the trail, Pym following watchfully, one hand loosening the stunner in his holster.

They drank the tea while they waited, and Miles pottered about the cabin, looking but not touching. The hearth was the sole source of heat for cooking and washwater. There was a beaten metal sink for washing up, filled by hand from a covered bucket but emptied through a drainpipe under the porch to join the streamlet running down out of the trough. The second room was a bedroom, with a double bed and chests for storage. A loft held three more pallets; the boy around back had brothers, apparently. The place was cramped, but swept, things put away and hung up.

On a side table sat a government-issue audio receiver, and a second and older military model, opened up, apparently in the process of getting minor repairs and a new power pack. Exploration revealed a drawer full of old parts, nothing more complex than for simple audio sets, unfortunately. Speaker Karal must double as Silvy Vale's comlink specialist. How appropriate. They must pick up broadcasts from the station in Hassadar, maybe the high-power government channels from the capital as well.

No other electricity, of course. Powersat receptors were expensive pieces of precision technology. They would come even here, in time; some communities almost as small, but with strong economic co-ops, already had them. Silvy Vale was obviously still stuck in subsistence-level, and must-needs wait till there was enough surplus in the district to gift them, if the surplus was not grabbed off first by some competing want. If only the city of Vorkosigan Vashnoi had not been obliterated by Cetagandan atomics, the whole district could be years ahead, economically …

Miles walked out on the porch and leaned on the rail. Karal's son had returned. Down at the end of the cleared yard Fat Ninny was standing tethered, hip-shot, ears aflop, grunting with pleasure as the grinning boy scratched him vigorously under his halter. The boy looked up to catch Miles watching him, and scooted off fearfully to vanish again in the scrub downslope. "Huh," muttered Miles.

Dr. Dea joined him. "They've been gone a long time. About time to break out the fast-penta?"

"No, your autopsy kit, I should say. I fancy that's what we'll be doing next."

Dea glanced at him sharply. "I thought you sent Pym along to enforce the arrest."

"You can't arrest a man who's not there. Are you a wagering man, Doctor? I'll bet you a mark they don't come back with Csurik. No, hold it—maybe I'm wrong. I hope I'm wrong. Here are three coming back …"

Karal, Pym, and another were marching down the trail. The third was a hulking young man, big-handed, heavy-browed, thick-necked, surly. "Harra," Miles called, "is this your husband?" He looked the part, by God, just what Miles had pictured. And four brothers just like him—only bigger, no doubt …

Harra appeared by Miles's shoulder, and let out her breath. "No, m'lord. That's Alex, the Speaker's deputy."

"Oh." Miles's lips compressed in silent frustration. *Well, I had to give it a chance to be simple.*

Karal stopped beneath him and began a wandering explanation of his empty-handed state. Miles cut him off with a lift of his eyebrows. "Pym?"

"Bolted, m'lord," said Pym laconically. "Almost certainly warned."

"I agree." He frowned down at Karal, who prudently stood silent. Facts first. Decisions, such as how much deadly force to pursue the fugitive with, second. "Harra. How far is it to your burying place?"

"Down by the stream, lord, at the bottom of the valley. About two kilometers."

"Get your kit, Doctor, we're taking a walk. Karal, fetch a shovel."

"M'lord, surely it isn't needful to disturb the peace of the dead," began Karal.

"It is entirely needful. There's a place for the autopsy report right in the Procedural I got from the district magistrate's office. Where I will file my completed report upon this case when we return to Vorkosigan Surleau. I have permission from the next-of-kin—do I not, Harra?"

She nodded numbly.

"I have the two requisite witnesses, yourself and your …" —*gorilla*—"… deputy, we have the doctor and the daylight—if you don't stand there arguing till sundown. All we need is the shovel. Unless you're volunteering to dig with your hand, Karal." Miles's voice was flat and grating and getting dangerous.

Karal's balding head bobbed in his distress. "The—the father is the legal next-of-kin, while he lives, and you don't have his—"

"Karal," said Miles.

"M'lord?"

"Take care the grave you dig is not your own. You've got one foot in it already."

Karal's hand opened in despair. "I'll … get the shovel, m'lord."

The midafternoon was warm, the air golden and summer-sleepy. The shovel bit with a steady *scrunch-scrunch* through the soil at the hands of Karal's deputy. Downslope, a bright stream burbled away over clean rounded stones. Harra hunkered watching, silent and grim.

When big Alex levered out the little crate—so little!—Armsman Pym went off for a patrol of the wooded perimeter. Miles didn't blame him. He hoped the soil at that depth had been cool, these last eight days. Alex pried open the box, and Dr. Dea waved him away and took over. The deputy too went off to find something to examine at the far end of the graveyard.

Dea looked the cloth-wrapped bundle over carefully, lifted it out, and set it on his tarp laid out on the ground in the bright sun. The instruments of his investigation were arrayed upon the plastic in precise order. He unwrapped the brightly patterned cloths in their special folds, and Harra crept up to retrieve them, straighten and fold them ready for reuse, then crept back.

Miles fingered the handkerchief in his pocket, ready to hold over his mouth and nose, and went to watch over Dea's shoulder. Bad, but not too bad. He'd seen and smelled worse. Dea, filter-masked, spoke procedurals into his recorder, hovering in the air by his shoulder, and made his examination first by eye and gloved touch, then by scanner.

"Here, my lord," said Dea, and motioned Miles closer. "Almost certainly the cause of death, though I'll run the toxin tests in a moment. Her neck was broken. See here on the scanner where the spinal cord was severed, then the bones twisted back into alignment."

"Karal, Alex." Miles motioned them up to witness; they came reluctantly.

"Could this have been accidental?" said Miles.

"Very remotely possible. The realignment had to be deliberate, though."

"Would it have taken long?"

"Seconds only. Death was immediate."

"How much physical strength was required? A big man's or …"

"Oh, not much at all. Any adult could have done it, easily."

"Any sufficiently motivated adult." Miles's stomach churned at the mental picture Dea's words conjured up. The little fuzzy head would easily fit under a man's hand. The twist, the muffled cartilaginous crack—if there was one thing Miles knew by heart, it was the exact tactile sensation of breaking bone, oh yes.

"Motivation," said Dea, "is not my department." He paused. "I might note, a careful external examination could have found this. Mine did. An experienced layman"—his gaze fell cool on Karal—"paying attention to what he was doing, should not have missed it."

Miles too stared at Karal, waiting.

"Overlain," hissed Harra. Her voice was ragged with scorn.

"M'lord," said Karal carefully, "it's true I suspected the possibility—"

Suspected, hell. You knew.

"But I felt—and still feel, strongly"—his eye flashed a wary defiance—"that only more grief would come from a fuss. There was nothing I could do to help the baby at that point. My duties are to the living."

"So are mine, Speaker Karal. As, for example, my duty to the next small Imperial subject in mortal danger from those who should be his or her protectors, for the grave fault of being"— Miles flashed an edged smile—"physically different. In Count Vorkosigan's view this is not just a case. This is a test case, fulcrum of a thousand cases. Fuss …" He hissed the sibilant; Harra rocked to the rhythm of his voice, "you haven't begun to see *fuss* yet."

Karal subsided as if folded.

There followed an hour of messiness yielding mainly negative data; no other bones were broken, the infant's lungs were clear, her gut and bloodstream free of toxins except those of natural decomposition. Her brain held no secret tumors. The defect for which she had died did not extend to spina bifida, Dea reported. Fairly simple plastic surgery would indeed have corrected the cat's mouth, could she somehow have won access to it. Miles wondered what comfort this confirmation was to Harra; cold, at best.

Dea put his puzzle back together, and Harra rewrapped the tiny body in intricate, meaningful folds. Dea cleaned his tools and placed them in their cases and washed his hands and arms and face thoroughly in the stream, for rather a longer time than needed for just hygiene, Miles thought, while the gorilla reburied the box.

Harra made a little bowl in the dirt atop the grave and piled in some twigs and bark scraps and a sawed-off strand of her lank hair.

Miles, caught short, felt in his pockets. "I have no offering on me that will burn," he said apologetically.

Harra glanced up, surprised at even the implied offer. “No matter, m’lord.” Her little pile of scraps flared briefly and went out, like her infant Raina’s life.

But it does matter, thought Miles.

Peace to you, small lady, after our rude invasions. I will give you a better sacrifice, I swear by my word as Vorkosigan. And the smoke of that burning will rise and be seen from one end of these mountains to the other.

Miles charged Karal and Alex straightly with producing Lem Csurik, and gave Harra Csurik a ride home up behind him on Fat Ninny. Pym accompanied them.

They passed a few scattered cabins on the way. At one a couple of grubby children playing in the yard loped alongside the horses, giggling and making hex signs at Miles, egging each other on to bolder displays, until their mother spotted them and ran out and hustled them indoors with a fearful look over her shoulder. In a weird way it was almost relaxing to Miles, the welcome he’d expected, not like Karal’s and Alex’s strained, self-conscious, careful not-noticing. Raina’s life would not have been an easy one.

Harra’s cabin was at the head of a long draw, just before it narrowed into a ravine. It seemed very quiet and isolated, in the dappled shade.

“Are you sure you wouldn’t rather go stay with your mother?” asked Miles dubiously.

Harra shook her head. She slid down off Ninny, and Miles and Pym dismounted to follow her in.

The cabin was of a standard design, a single room with a fieldstone fireplace and a wide roofed front porch. Water apparently came from the rivulet in the ravine. Pym held up a hand and entered first behind Harra, his hand on his stunner. If Lem Csurik had run, might he have run home first? Pym had been making scanner checks of perfectly innocent clumps of bushes all the way here.

The cabin was deserted. Although not long deserted; it did not have the lingering, dusty silence one would expect of eight days’ mournful disoccupation. The remains of a few hasty meals sat on the sinkboard. The bed was slept in, rumpled and unmade. A few man's garments were scattered about. Automatically Harra began to move about the room, straightening it up, reasserting her presence, her worth. If she could not control the events of her life, at least she might control one small room.

The one untouched item was a cradle that sat beside the bed, little blankets neatly folded. Harra had fled for Vorkosigan Surleau just a few hours after the burial.

Miles wandered about the room, checking the view from the windows. "Will you show me where you went to get your brillberries, Harra?"

She led them up the ravine; Miles timed the hike. Pym divided his attention unhappily between the brush and Miles, alert to catch any bone-breaking stumble. After flinching away from about three aborted protective grabs Miles was ready to tell him to go climb a tree. Still, there was a certain understandable self-interest at work here; if Miles broke a leg, it would be Pym who'd be stuck with carrying him out.

The brillberry patch was nearly a kilometer up the ravine. Miles plucked a few seedy red berries and ate them absently, looking around, while Harra and Pym waited respectfully. Afternoon sun slanted through green and brown leaves, but the bottom of the ravine was already gray and cool with premature twilight. The brillberry vines clung to the rocks and hung down invitingly, luring one to risk one's neck reaching. Miles resisted their weedy temptations, not being all that fond of brillberries. "If someone called out from your cabin, you couldn't hear them up here, could you?" remarked Miles.

"No, m'lord."

"About how long did you spend picking?"

"About"—Harra shrugged—"a basketful."

The woman didn't own a chrono. "An hour, say. And a twenty-minute climb each way. About a two-hour time window, that morning. Your cabin was not locked?"

"Just a latch, m'lord."

"Hm."

Method, motive, and opportunity, the district magistrate's Procedural had emphasized. Damn. The method was established, and almost anybody could have used it. The opportunity angle, it appeared, was just as bad. Anyone at all could have walked up to that cabin, done the deed, and departed, unseen and unheard. It was much too late for an aura detector to be of use, tracing the shining ghosts of movements in and out of that room, even if Miles had brought one.

Facts, hah. They were back to motive, the murky workings of men's minds. Anybody's guess.

Miles had, as per the instructions in the Procedural, been striving to keep an open mind about the accused, but it was getting harder and harder to resist Harra's assertions. She'd been proved right about everything so far.

They left Harra reinstalled in her little home, going through the motions of order and the normal routine of life as if they could somehow re-create it, like an act of sympathetic magic.

"Are you sure you'll be all right?" Miles asked, gathering Fat Ninny's reins and settling himself in the saddle. "I can't help but think that if your husband's in the area, he could show up here. You say nothing's been taken, so it's unlikely he's been here and gone before we arrived. Do you want someone to stay with you?"

"No, m'lord." She hugged her broom, on the porch. "I'd … I'd like to be alone for a while."

"Well … all right. I'll, ah, send you a message if anything important happens."

"Thank you, m'lord." Her tone was unpressing; she really did want to be left alone. Miles took the hint.

At a wide place in the trail back to Speaker Karal's, Pym and Miles rode stirrup to stirrup. Pym was still painfully on the alert for boogies in the bushes.

"My lord, may I suggest that your next logical step be to draft all the able-bodied men in the community for a hunt for this Csurik? Beyond doubt, you've established that the infanticide was a murder."

Interesting turn of phrase, Miles thought dryly. *Even Pym doesn't find it redundant. Oh, my poor Barrayar.* "It seems reasonable at first glance, Armsman Pym, but has it occurred to you that half the able-bodied men in this community are probably relatives of Lem Csurik's?"

"It might have a psychological effect. Create enough disruption, and perhaps someone would turn him in just to get it over with."

"Hm, possibly. Assuming he hasn't already left the area. He could have been halfway to the coast before we were done at the autopsy."

"Only if he had access to transport." Pym glanced at the empty sky.

"For all we know one of his subcousins had a rickety lightflyer in a shed somewhere. But … he's never been out of Silvy Vale. I'm not sure he'd know how to run, where to go. Well, if he has left the district it's a problem for Imperial Civil Security, and I'm off the hook." Happy thought. "But—one of the things that bothers me, a lot, are the inconsistencies in the picture I'm getting of our chief suspect. Have you noticed them?"

"Can't say I have, m'lord."

"Hm. Where did Karal take you, by the way, to arrest this guy?"

"To a wild area, rough scrub and gullies. Half a dozen men were out searching for Harra. They'd just called off their search and were on their way back when we met up with them. By which I concluded our arrival was no surprise."

"Had Csurik actually been there, and fled, or was Karal just ring-leading you in a circle?"

"I think he'd actually been there, m'lord. The men claimed not, but as you point out they were relatives, and besides, they did not, ah, lie well. They were tense. Karal may begrudge you his cooperation, but I don't think he'll quite dare disobey your direct orders. He is a twenty-year man, after all."

Like Pym himself, Miles thought. Count Vorkosigan's personal guard was legally limited to a ceremonial twenty men, but given his political position their function included very practical security. Pym was typical of their number, a decorated veteran of the Imperial Service who had retired to this elite private force. It was not Pym's fault that when he had joined he had stepped into a dead man's shoes, replacing the late Sergeant Bothari. Did anyone in the universe besides himself miss the deadly and difficult Bothari? Miles wondered sadly.

"I'd like to question *Karal* under fast-penta," said Miles morosely. "He displays every sign of being a man who knows where the body's buried."

"Why don't you, then?" asked Pym logically.

"I may come to that. There is, however, a certain unavoidable degradation in a fast-penta interrogation. If the man's loyal it may not be in our best long-range interest to shame him publicly."

"It wouldn't be in public."

"No, but he would remember being turned into a drooling idiot. I need ... more information."

Pym glanced back over his shoulder. "I thought you had all the information, by now."

"I have facts. Physical facts. A great big pile of—meaningless, useless facts." Miles brooded. "If I have to fast-penta every back-beyonder in Silvy Vale to get to the bottom of this, I will. But it's not an elegant solution."

"It's not an elegant problem, m'lord," said Pym dryly.

They returned to find Speaker Karal's wife back and in full possession of her home. She was running in frantic circles, chopping, beating, kneading, stoking, and flying upstairs to change the bedding on the three pallets, driving her three sons before her to fetch and run and carry. Dr. Dea, bemused, was following her about trying to slow her down, explaining that they had brought their own tent and food, thank you, and that her hospitality was not required. This produced a most indignant response from Ma Karal.

"My lord's own son come to my house, and I to turn him out in the fields like his horse! I'd be ashamed!" And she returned to her work.

"She seems rather distraught," said Dea, looking over his shoulder.

Miles took him by the elbow and propelled him out onto the porch. "Just get out of her way, Doctor. We're doomed to be Entertained. It's an obligation on both sides. The polite thing to do is sort of pretend we're not here till she's ready for us."

Dea lowered his voice. "It might be better, in light of the circumstances, if we were to eat only our packaged food."

The chatter of a chopping knife, and a scent of herbs and onions, wafted enticingly through the open window. "Oh, I would imagine anything out of the common pot would be all right, wouldn't you?" said Miles. "If anything really worries you, you can whisk it off and check it, I suppose, but—discreetly, eh? We don't want to insult anyone."

They settled themselves in the homemade wooden chairs, and were promptly served tea again by a boy draftee of ten, Karal's youngest. He had apparently already received private instructions in manners from one or the other of his parents, for his response to Miles's deformities was the same flickering covert not-noticing as the adults, not quite as smoothly carried off.

"Will you be sleeping in my bed, m'lord?" he asked. "Ma says we got to sleep on the porch."

"Well, whatever your ma says, goes," said Miles. "Ah … do you like sleeping on the porch?"

"Naw. Last time, Zed kicked me and I rolled off in the dark."

"Oh. Well, perhaps, if we're to displace you, you would care to sleep in our tent by way of trade."

The boy's eyes widened. "Really?"

"Certainly. Why not?"

"Wait'll I tell Zed!" He danced down the steps and shot away around the side of the house. "Zed, hey, Zed …!"

"I suppose," said Dea, "we can fumigate it, later …"

Miles's lips twitched. "They're no grubbier than you were at the same age, surely. Or than I was. When I was permitted." The late afternoon was warm. Miles took off his green tunic and hung it on the back of his chair, and unbuttoned the round collar of his cream shirt.

Dea's brows rose. "Are we keeping shopman's hours, then, m'lord, on this investigation? Calling it quits for the day?"

"Not exactly." Miles sipped tea thoughtfully, gazing out across the yard. The trees and treetops fell away down to the bottom of this feeder valley. Mixed scrub climbed the other side of the slope. A crested fold, then the long flanks of a backbone mountain, beyond, rose high and harsh to a summit still flecked with dwindling dirty patches of snow.

"There's still a murderer loose out there somewhere," Dea pointed out helpfully.

"You sound like Pym." Pym, Miles noted, had finished with their horses and was taking his scanner for another walk. "I'm waiting."

"What for?"

"Not sure. The piece of information that will make sense of all this. Look, there's only two possibilities. Csurik's either innocent or he's guilty. If he's guilty, he's not going to turn himself in. He'll certainly involve his relations, hiding and helping him. I can call in reinforcements by comlink from Imperial Civil Security in Hassadar, if I want to. Any time. A squad of men, plus equipment, here by aircar in a couple of hours. Create a circus. Brutal, ugly, disruptive, exciting—could be quite popular. A manhunt, with blood at the end.

"Of course, there's also the possibility that Csurik's innocent, but scared. In which case …"

"Yes?"

"In which case, there's still a murderer out there." Miles drank more tea. "I merely note, if you want to catch something, running after it isn't always the best way."

Dea cleared his throat, and drank his tea too.

"In the meantime, I have another duty to carry out. I'm here to be seen. If your scientific spirit is yearning for something to do to while away the hours, try keeping count of the number of Vor-watchers that turn up tonight."

Miles's predicted parade began almost immediately. It was mainly women, at first, bearing gifts as to a funeral. In the absence of a comlink system Miles wasn't sure by what telepathy they managed to communicate with each other, but they brought covered dishes of food, flowers, extra bedding, and offers of assistance. They were all introduced to Miles with nervous curtseys, but seldom lingered to chat; apparently a look was all their curiosity desired. Ma Karal was polite, but made it clear that she had the situation well in hand, and set their culinary offerings well back of her own.

Some of the women had children in tow. Most of these were sent to play in the woods in back, but a small party of whispering boys sneaked back around the cabin to peek up over the rim of the porch at Miles. Miles had obligingly remained on the porch with Dea, remarking that it was a better view, without saying for whom. For a few moments, Miles pretended not to notice his audience, restraining Pym with a hand signal from running them off. *Yes, look well, look your fill*, thought Miles. *What you see is what you're going to get, for the rest of your lives or at any rate mine. Get used to it* .... Then he caught Zed Karal's whisper, as self-appointed tour guide to his cohort—"That big one's the one that's come to kill Lem Csurik!"

"Zed," said Miles.

There was an abrupt frozen silence from under the edge of the porch. Even the animal rustlings stopped.

"Come here," said Miles.

To a muted background of dismayed whispers and nervous giggles, Karal's middle boy slouched warily up onto the porch.

"You three"—Miles's pointing finger caught them in midflight—"wait there." Pym added his frown for emphasis, and Zed's friends stood paralyzed, eyes wide, heads lined up at the level of the porch floor as if stuck up on some ancient battlement as a warning to kindred malefactors.

"What did you just say to your friends, Zed?" asked Miles quietly. "Repeat it."

Zed licked his lips. "I jus' said you'd come to kill Lem Csurik, lord." Zed was clearly now wondering if Miles's murderous intent included obnoxious and disrespectful boys as well.

"That is not true, Zed. That is a dangerous lie."

Zed looked bewildered. "But Da—said it."

"What is true, is that I've come to catch the person who killed Lem Csurik's baby daughter. That may be Lem. But it may not. Do you understand the difference?"

"But Harra said Lem did it, and she ought to know; he's her husband and all."

"The baby's neck was broken by someone. Harra thinks Lem, but she didn't see it happen. What you and your friends here have to understand is that I won't make a mistake. I *can't* condemn the wrong person. My own truth drugs won't let me. Lem Csurik has only to come here and tell me the truth to clear himself, if he didn't do it.

"But suppose he did. What should I do with a man who would kill a baby, Zed?"

Zed shuffled. "Well, she was only a mutie …" then shut his mouth and reddened, not looking at Miles.

It was, perhaps, a bit much to ask a twelve-year-old boy to take an interest in any baby, let alone a mutie one … *no*, dammit. It wasn't too much. But how to get a hook into that prickly defensive surface? And if Miles couldn't even convince one surly twelve-year-old, how was he to magically transmute a whole district of adults? A rush of despair made him suddenly want to rage. These people were so bloody *impossible*. He checked his temper firmly.

"Your Da was a twenty-year man, Zed. Are you proud that he served the Emperor?"

"Yes, lord." Zed's eyes sought escape, trapped by these terrible adults.

Miles forged on. "Well, these practices—mutie-killing—shame the Emperor, when he stands for Barrayar before the galaxy. I've been out there. I know. They call us all savages, for the crimes of a few. It shames the Count my father before his peers, and Silvy Vale before the District. A soldier gets honor by killing an armed enemy, not a baby. This matter touches my honor as a Vorkosigan, Zed. Besides"—Miles's lips drew back on a mirthless grin, and he leaned forward intently in his chair—Zed recoiled as much as he dared—"you will all be astonished at what *only a mutie* can do. *That* I have sworn on my grandfather's grave."

Zed looked more suppressed than enlightened, his slouch now almost a crouch. Miles slumped back in his chair and released him with a weary wave of his hand. "Go play, boy."

Zed needed no urging. He and his companions shot away around the house as though released from springs.

Miles drummed his fingers on the chair arm, frowning into the silence that neither Pym nor Dea dared break.

"These hill-folk are ignorant, lord," offered Pym after a moment.

"These hill-folk are *mine*, Pym. Their ignorance is … a shame upon my house." Miles brooded. How had this whole mess become his anyway? He hadn't created it. Historically, he'd only just got here himself. "Their continued ignorance, anyway," he amended in fairness.

It still made a burden like a mountain. "Is the message so complex? So difficult? 'You don't have to kill your children anymore.' It's not like we're asking them all to learn 5-Space navigational math." That had been the plague of Miles's last Academy semester.

"It's not easy for them," shrugged Dea. "It's easy for the central authorities to make the rules, but these people have to live every minute of the consequences. They have so little, and the new rules force them to give their margin to marginal people who can't pay back. The old ways were wise, in the old days. Even now you have to wonder how many premature reforms we can afford, trying to ape the galactics."

And what's your definition of a marginal person, Dea? "But the margin is growing," Miles said aloud. "Places like this aren't up against famine every winter anymore. They're not isolated in their disasters, relief can get from one district to another under the Imperial seal … we're all getting more connected, just as fast as we can. Besides," Miles paused, and added rather weakly, "perhaps you underestimate them."

Dea's brows rose ironically. Pym strolled the length of the porch, running his scanner in yet another pass over the surrounding scrubland. Miles, turning in his chair to pursue his cooling teacup, caught a slight movement, a flash of eyes, behind the casement-hung front window swung open to the summer air—Ma Karal, standing frozen, listening. For how long? Since he'd called her boy Zed, Miles guessed, arresting her attention. She raised her chin as his eyes met hers, sniffed, and shook out the cloth she'd been holding with a snap. They exchanged a nod. She turned back to her work before Dea, watching Pym, noticed her.

Karal and Alex returned, understandably, around suppertime.

"I have six men out searching," Karal reported cautiously to Miles on the porch, now well on its way to becoming Miles's official HQ. Clearly, Karal had covered ground since midafternoon. His face was sweaty, lined with physical as well as the underlying emotional strain. "But I think Lem's gone into the scrub. It could take days to smoke him out. There's hundreds of places to lie low out there."

Karal ought to know. "You don't think he's gone to some relative's?" asked Miles. "Surely, if he intends to evade us for long, he has to take a chance on resupply, on information. Will they turn him in when he surfaces?"

"It's hard to say." Karal turned his hand palm-out. "It's … a hard problem for 'em, m'lord."

"Hm."

How long would Lem Csurik hang around out there in the scrub, anyway? His whole life—his blown-to-bits life—was all here in Silvy Vale. Miles considered the contrast. A few weeks ago, Csurik had been a young man with everything going for him; a home, a wife, a family on the way, happiness; by Silvy Vale standards, comfort and security. His cabin, Miles had not failed to note, though simple, had been kept with love and energy, and so redeemed from the potential squalor of its poverty. Grimmer in the winter, to be sure. Now Csurik was a hunted fugitive, all the little he had torn away in the twinkling of an eye. With nothing to hold him, would he run away and keep running? With nothing to run to, would he linger near the ruins of his life?

The police force available to Miles a few hours away in Hassadar was an itch in his mind. Was it not time to call them in, before he fumbled this into a worse mess? But … if he were meant to solve this by a show of force, why hadn't the Count let him come by aircar on the first day? Miles regretted that two-and-a-half-day ride. It had sapped his forward momentum, slowed him down to Silvy Vale's walking pace, tangled him with time to doubt. Had the Count foreseen it? What did he know that Miles didn't? What *could* he know? Dammit, this test didn't need to be made harder by artificial stumbling blocks, it was bad enough all on its own. *He wants me to be clever*, Miles thought morosely. *Worse, he wants me to be seen to be clever, by everyone here*. He prayed he was not about to be spectacularly stupid instead.

"Very well, Speaker Karal. You've done all you can for today. Knock off for the night. Call your men off too. You're not likely to find anything in the dark."

Pym held up his scanner, clearly about to volunteer its use, but Miles waved him down. Pym's brows rose, editorially. Miles shook his head.

Karal needed no further urging. He dispatched Alex to call off the night search with torches. He remained wary of Miles. Perhaps Miles puzzled him as much as he puzzled Miles? Dourly, Miles hoped so.

Miles was not sure at what point the long summer evening segued into a party. After supper the men began to drift in, Karal's cronies, Silvy Vale's elders. Some were apparently regulars who shared the evening government news broadcasts on Karal's audio set. Too many names, and Miles daren't forget a one. A group of amateur musicians arrived with their homemade mountain instruments, rather breathless, obviously the band tapped for all the major weddings and wakes in Silvy Vale; this all seemed more like a funeral to Miles every minute.

The musicians stood in the middle of the yard and played. Miles's porch-HQ now became his aristocratic box seat. It was hard to get involved with the music when the audience was all so intently watching him. Some songs were serious, some—rather carefully at first—funny. Miles's spontaneity was frequently frozen in mid-laugh by a faint sigh of relief from those around him; his stiffening froze them in turn, self-stymied like two people trying to dodge each other in a corridor.

But one song was so hauntingly beautiful—a lament for lost love—that Miles was struck to the heart. *Elena* .... In that moment, old pain transformed to melancholy, sweet and distant; a sort of healing, or at least the realization that a healing had taken place, unwatched. He almost had the singers stop there, while they were perfect, but feared they might think him displeased. But he remained quiet and inward for a time afterward, scarcely hearing their next offering in the gathering twilight.

At least the piles of food that had arrived all afternoon were thus accounted for. Miles had been afraid Ma Karal and her cronies had expected him to get around that culinary mountain all by himself.

At one point Miles leaned on the rail and glanced down the yard to see Fat Ninny at tether, making more friends. A whole flock of pubescent girls were clustered around him, petting him, brushing his fetlocks, braiding flowers and ribbons in his mane and tail, feeding him tidbits, or just resting their cheeks against his warm silky side. Ninny's eyes were half-closed in smug content.

God, thought Miles in jealousy, *if I had half the sex appeal of that bloody horse I'd have more girlfriends than my cousin Ivan.* Miles considered, very briefly, the pros and cons of making a play for some unattached female. The striding lords of old and all that … no. There were some kinds of stupid he didn't have to be, and that was definitely one of them. The service he had already sworn to one small lady of Silvy Vale was surely all he could bear without breaking; he could feel the strain of it all around him now, like a dangerous pressure in his bones.

He turned to find Speaker Karal presenting a woman to him, far from pubescent; she was perhaps fifty, lean and little, work-worn. She was carefully clothed in an aging best-dress, her graying hair combed back and bound at the nape of her neck. She bit at her lips and cheeks in quick tense motions, half-suppressed in her self-consciousness.

"'S Ma Csurik, m'lord. Lem's mother." Speaker Karal ducked his head and backed away, abandoning Miles without aid or mercy—*Come back, you coward!*

"Ma'am," Miles said. His throat was dry. Karal had set him up, dammit, a public play—no, the other guests were retreating out of earshot too, most of them.

"M'lord," said Ma Csurik. She managed a nervous curtsey.

"Uh … do sit down." With a ruthless jerk of his chin Miles evicted Dr. Dea from his chair and motioned the hill woman into it. He turned his own chair to face hers. Pym stood behind them, silent as a statue, tight as a wire. Did he imagine the old woman was about to whip a needler-pistol from her skirts? No—it was Pym's job to imagine things like that for Miles, so that Miles might free his whole mind for the problem at hand. Pym was almost as much an object of study as Miles himself. Wisely, he'd been holding himself apart, and would doubtless continue to do so till the dirty work was over.

"M'lord," said Ma Csurik again, and stumbled again to silence. Miles could only wait. He prayed she wasn't about to come unglued and weep on his knees or some damn thing. This was excruciating. *Stay strong, woman,* he urged silently.

"Lem, he …"—she swallowed—"I'm sure he didn't kill the babe. There's never been any of that in our family, I swear it! He says he didn't, and I believe him."

"Good," said Miles affably. "Let him come say the same thing to me under fast-penta, and I'll believe him, too."

"Come away, Ma," urged a lean young man who had accompanied her and now stood waiting by the steps, as if ready to bolt into the dark at a motion. "It's no good, can't you see." He glowered at Miles.

She shot the boy a quelling frown—another of her five sons?—and turned back more urgently to Miles, groping for words. "My Lem. He's only twenty, lord."

"*I'm* only twenty, Ma Csurik," Miles felt compelled to point out. There was another brief impasse.

"Look, I'll say it again," Miles burst out impatiently. "And again, and again, till the message penetrates all the way back to its intended recipient. I *cannot* condemn an innocent person. My truth drugs won't let me. Lem can clear himself. He has only to come in. Tell him, will you? Please?"

She went stony, guarded. "I … haven't seen him, m'lord."

"But you might."

She tossed her head. "So? I might not." Her eyes shifted to Pym and away, as if the sight of him burned. The silver Vorkosigan logos embroidered on Pym's collar gleamed in the twilight like animal eyes, moving only with his breathing. Karal was now bringing lighted lamps onto the porch, but keeping his distance still.

"Ma'am," said Miles tightly. "The Count my father has ordered me to investigate the murder of your granddaughter. If your son means so much to you, how can his child mean so little? Was she … your first grandchild?"

Her face was sere. "No, lord. Lem's older sister, she has two. *They're* all right," she added with emphasis.

Miles sighed. "If you truly believe your son is innocent of this crime, you must help me prove it. Or—do you doubt?"

She shifted uneasily. There was doubt in her eyes—she didn't know, blast it. Fast-penta would be useless on her, for sure. As Miles's magic wonder drug, much counted-upon, fast-penta seemed to be having wonderfully little utility in this case so far.

"Come away, Ma," the young man urged again. "It's no good. The mutie lord came up here for a killing. They have to have one. It's a show."

Damn straight, thought Miles acidly. He was a perceptive young lunk, that one.

Ma Csurik let herself be persuaded away by her angry and embarrassed son plucking at her arm. She paused on the steps, though, and shot bitterly over her shoulder, "It's all so easy for you, isn't it?"

My head hurts, thought Miles.

There was worse to come before the evening ended.

The new woman's voice was grating, low and angry. "Don't you talk down to me, Serg Karal. I got a right for one good look at this mutie lord."

She was tall and stringy and tough. *Like her daughter,* Miles thought. She had made no attempt to freshen up. A faint reek of summer sweat hung about her working dress. And how far had she walked? Her gray hair hung in a switch down her back, a few strands escaping the tie. If Ma Csurik's bitterness had been a stabbing pain behind the eyes, this one's rage was a wringing knot in the gut.

She shook off Karal's attempted restraint and stalked up to Miles in the lamplight. "So."

"Uh … this is Ma Mattulich, m'lord," Karal introduced her. "Harra's mother."

Miles rose to his feet, managed a short formal nod. "How do you do, madam." He was very conscious of being a head shorter. She had once been of a height with Harra, Miles estimated, but her aging bones were beginning to pull her down.

She merely stared. She was a gum-leaf chewer, by the faint blackish stains around her mouth. Her jaw worked now on some small bit, tiny chomps, grinding too hard. She studied him openly, without subterfuge or the least hint of apology, taking in his head, his neck, his back, his short and crooked legs. Miles had the unpleasant illusion that she saw right through to all the healed cracks in his brittle bones as well. Miles's chin jerked up twice in the twitchy, nervous-involuntary tic that he was sure made him look spastic, before he controlled it with an effort.

"All right," said Karal roughly, "you've seen. Now come away, for God's sake, Mara." His hand opened in apology to Miles. "Mara, she's been pretty distraught over all this, m'lord. Forgive her."

"Your only grandchild," said Miles to her, in an effort to be kind, though her peculiar anguish repelled kindness with a scraped and bleeding scorn. "I understand your distress, ma'am. But there will be justice for little Raina. That I have sworn."

"How can there be justice *now*?" she raged, thick and low. "It's too late—a world too late—for justice, mutie lordling. What use do I have for your damned justice *now*?"

"Enough, Mara!" Karal insisted. His brows drew down and his lips thinned, and he forced her away and escorted her firmly off his porch.

The last lingering remnant of visitors parted for her with an air of respectful mercy, except for two lean teenagers hanging on the fringes who drew away as if avoiding poison. Miles was forced to revise his mental image of the Brothers Csurik. If those two were another sample, there was no team of huge menacing hill hulks after all. They were a team of skinny menacing hill squirts instead. Not really an improvement; they looked as if they could move as fast as striking ferrets if they had to. Miles's lips curled in frustration.

The evening's entertainments ended finally, thank God, close to midnight. Karal's last cronies marched off into the woods by lantern light. The repaired and re-powered audio set was carried off by its owner with many thanks to Karal. Fortunately it had been a mature and sober crowd, even somber, no drunken brawls or anything. Pym got the Karal boys settled in the tent, took a last patrol around the cabin, and joined Miles and Dea in the loft. The pallets' stuffing had been spiked with fresh scented native herbs, to which Miles hoped devoutly he was not allergic. Ma Karal had wanted to turn her own bedroom over to Miles's exclusive lordly use, exiling herself and her husband to the porch, too, but fortunately Pym had been able to persuade her that putting Miles in the loft, flanked by Dea and himself, was to be preferred from a security standpoint.

Dea and Pym were soon snoring, but sleep eluded Miles. He tossed on his pallet as he turned his ploys of the day, such as they had been, over and over in his mind. Was he being too slow, too careful, too conservative? This wasn't exactly good assault tactics, surprise with a superior force. The view he'd gained of the terrain from Karal's porch tonight had been ambiguous at best.

On the other hand, it did no good to charge off across a swamp, as his fellow cadet and cousin Ivan Vorpatril had demonstrated so memorably once on summer maneuvers. It had taken a heavy hovercab with a crane to crank the six big, strong, healthy, fully field-equipped young men of Ivan's patrol out of the chest-high gooey black mud. Ivan had got his revenge simultaneously, though, when the cadet 'sniper' they had been attacking fell out of his tree and broke his arm while laughing hysterically as they sank slowly and beautifully into the ooze. Ooze that a little guy, with his laser rifle wrapped in his loincloth, could swim across like a frog. The war games umpire had ruled it a draw. Miles rubbed his forearm and grinned in memory, and faded out at last.

Miles awoke abruptly and without transition deep in the night with a sense of something wrong. A faint orange glow shimmered in the blue darkness of the loft. Quietly, so as not to disturb his sleeping companions, he rose on his pallet and peered over the edge into the main room. The glow was coming through the front window.

Miles swung onto the ladder and padded downstairs for a look outdoors. "Pym," he called softly.

Pym shot awake with a snort. "M'lord?" he said, alarmed.

"Come down here. Quietly. Bring your stunner."

Pym was by his side in seconds. He slept in his trousers with his stunner holster and boots by his pillow. "What the hell—?" Pym muttered, looking out too.

The glow was from fire. A pitchy torch, flung to the top of Miles's tent set up in the yard, was burning quietly. Pym lurched toward the door, then controlled his movements as the same realization came to him as had to Miles. Theirs was a Service-issue tent, and its combat-rated synthetic fabric would neither melt nor burn.

Miles wondered if the person who'd heaved the torch had known that. Was this some arcane warning, or a singularly inept attack? If the tent had been ordinary fabric, and Miles in it, the intended result might not have been trivial. Worse with Karal's boys in it—a bursting blossom of flame—Miles shuddered.

Pym loosened his stunner in his holster and stood poised by the front door. "How long?"

"I'm not sure. Could have been burning like that for ten minutes before it woke me."

Pym shook his head, took a slight breath, raised his scanner, and vaulted into the fire-gilded darkness.

"Trouble, m'lord?" Speaker Karal's anxious voice came from his bedroom door.

"Maybe. Wait—" Miles halted him as he plunged for the door. "Pym's running a patrol with a scanner and a stunner. Wait'll he calls the all-clear, I think. Your boys may be safer inside the tent."

Karal came up to the window, caught his breath, and swore.

Pym returned in a few minutes. "There's no one within a kilometer, now," he reported shortly. He helped Karal take the goat bucket and douse the torch. The boys, who had slept through the fire, woke at its quenching.

"I think maybe it was a bad idea to lend them my tent," said Miles from the porch in a choked voice. "I am profoundly sorry, Speaker Karal. I didn't think."

"This should *never* ..."—Karal was spluttering with anger and delayed fright—"this should never have happened, m'lord. I apologize for ... for Silvy Vale." He turned helplessly, peering into the darkness. The night sky, star-flecked, lovely, was threatening now.

The boys, once the facts penetrated their sleepiness, thought it was all just great, and wanted to return to the tent and lie in wait for the next assassin. Ma Karal, shrill and firm, herded them indoors instead and made them bed down in the main room. It was an hour before they stopped complaining at the injustice of it and went back to sleep.

Miles, keyed up nearly to the point of gibbering, did not sleep at all. He lay stiffly on his pallet, listening to Dea, who slept breathing heavily, and Pym, feigning sleep for courtesy and scarcely seeming to breathe at all.

Miles was about to suggest to Pym that they give up and go out on the porch for the rest of the night when the silence was shattered by a shrill squeal, enormously loud, pain-edged, from outside.

"The horses!" Miles spasmed to his feet, heart racing, and beat Pym to the ladder. Pym cut ahead of him by dropping straight over the side of the loft into an elastic crouch, and beat him to the door. There, Pym's trained bodyguard's reflexes compelled him to try to thrust Miles back inside. Miles almost bit him. "Go, dammit! I've got a weapon!"

Pym, good intentions frustrated, swung out the cabin door with Miles on his heels. Halfway down the yard they split to each side as a massive snorting shape loomed out of the darkness and nearly ran them down; the sorrel mare, loose again. Another squeal pierced the night from the lines where the horses were tethered.

"Ninny?" Miles called, panicked. It was Ninny's voice making those noises, the like of which Miles had not heard since the night a shed had burned down at Vorkosigan Surleau with a horse trapped inside. "Ninny!"

Another grunting squeal, and a thunk like someone splitting a watermelon with a mallet. Pym staggered back, inhaling with difficulty, a resonant deep stutter, and tripped to the ground where he lay curled up around himself. Not killed outright, apparently, because between gasps he was managing to swear lividly. Miles dropped to the ground beside him, checked his skull—no, thank God, it had been Pym's chest Ninny's hoof had hit with that alarming sound. The bodyguard only had the wind knocked out of him, maybe a cracked rib. Miles more sensibly ran around to the *front* of the horse lines. "Ninny!"

Fat Ninny was jerking his head against his rope, attempting to rear. He squealed again, his white-rimmed eyes gleaming in the darkness. Miles ran to his head. "Ninny, boy! What is it?" His left hand slid up the rope to Ninny's halter, his right stretched to stroke Ninny's shoulder soothingly. Fat Ninny flinched, but stopped trying to rear, and stood trembling. The horse shook his head. Miles's face and chest were suddenly spattered with something hot and dark and sticky.

"Dea!" Miles yelled. "*Dea*!"

Nobody slept through this uproar. Six people tumbled off the porch and down the yard, and not one of them thought to bring a light … no, the brilliant flare of a cold light sprang from between

Dr. Dea's fingers, and Ma Karal was struggling even now to light a lantern. "Dea, get that damn light over here!" Miles demanded, and stopped to choke his voice back down an octave to its usual carefully cultivated deeper register.

Dea galloped up and thrust the light toward Miles, then gasped, his face draining. "My lord! Are you shot?" In the flare the dark liquid soaking Miles's shirt glowed suddenly scarlet.

"Not me," Miles said, looking down at his chest in horror. A flash of memory turned his stomach over, cold at the vision of another blood-soaked death, that of the late Sergeant Bothari whom Pym had replaced. Would never replace.

Dea spun. "Pym?"

"He's all right," said Miles. A long inhaling wheeze rose from the grass a few meters off, the exhalation punctuated with obscenities. "But he got kicked by the horse. Get your medkit!" Miles peeled Dea's fingers off the cold light, and Dea dashed back to the cabin.

Miles held the light up to Ninny, and swore in a sick whisper. A huge cut, a third of a meter long and of unknown depth, scored Ninny's glossy neck. Blood soaked his coat and runneled down his foreleg. Miles's fingers touched the wound fearfully; his hands spread on either side, trying to push it closed, but the horse's skin was elastic and it pulled apart and bled profusely as Fat Ninny shook his head in pain. Miles grabbed the horse's nose—"Hold still, boy!" Somebody had been going for Ninny's jugular. And had almost made it; Ninny—tame, petted, friendly, trusting Ninny—would not have moved from the touch until the knife bit deep.

Karal was helping Pym to his feet as Dr. Dea returned. Miles waited while Dea checked Pym over, then called, "Here, Dea!"

Zed, looking quite as horrified as Miles, helped to hold Ninny's head as Dea made inspection of the cut. "I took tests," Dea complained *sotto voce* as he worked. "I beat out twenty-six other applicants, for the honor of becoming the Prime Minister's personal physician. I have practiced the procedures of seventy separate possible medical emergencies, from coronary thrombosis to attempted assassination. Nobody—*nobody*—told me my duties would include sewing up a damned horse's neck in the middle of the night in the middle of a howling wilderness ...." But he kept working as he complained, so Miles didn't quash him, but kept gently petting Ninny's nose, and hypnotically rubbing the hidden pattern of his muscles, to soothe and still him. At last Ninny relaxed enough to rest his slobbery chin on Miles's shoulder.

"Do horses get anesthetics?" asked Dea plaintively, holding his medical stunner as if not sure just what to do with it.

"This one does," said Miles stoutly. "You treat him just like a person, Dea. This is the last animal that the Count my grandfather personally trained. He named him. I watched him get born. We trained him together. Grandfather had me pick him up and hold him every day for a week after he was foaled, till he got too big. Horses are creatures of habit, Grandfather said, and take first impressions to heart. Forever after Ninny thought I was bigger than he was."

Dea sighed and made busy with anesthetic stun, cleansing solution, antibiotics, muscle relaxants, and biotic glue. With a surgeon's touch, he shaved the edges of the cut and placed the reinforcing net. Zed held the light anxiously.

"The cut is clean," said Dea, "but it will undergo a lot of flexing—I don't suppose it can very well be immobilized, in this position? No, hardly. This should do. If he were a human, I'd tell him to rest at this point."

"He'll be rested," Miles promised firmly. "Will he be all right now?"

"I suppose so. How the devil should I know?" Dea looked highly aggrieved, but his hand sneaked out to recheck his repairs.

"General Piotr," Miles assured him, "would have been very pleased with your work." Miles could hear him in his head now, snorting, *Damned technocrats. Nothing but horse doctors with a more expensive set of toys.* Grandfather would have loved being proved right. "You, ah … never met my grandfather, did you?"

"Before my time, my lord," said Dea. "I've studied his life and campaigns, of course."

"Of course."

Pym had a hand-light now, and was limping with Karal in a slow spiral around the horse lines, inspecting the ground. Karal's eldest boy had recaptured the sorrel mare and brought her back to re-tether her. Her tether had been torn loose, not cut; had the mysterious attacker's choice of equine victim been random, or calculated?

How calculated? Was Ninny attacked as a mere symbol of his master, or had the person known how passionately Miles loved the animal? Was this vandalism, a political statement, or an act of precisely directed, subtle cruelty?

What have I ever done to you? Miles's thought howled silently to the surrounding darkness.

"They got away, whoever it was," Pym reported. "Out of scanner range before I could breathe again. My apologies, m'lord. They don't seem to have dropped anything on the ground."

There had to have been a knife, at least. A knife, its haft gory with horse blood in a pattern of perfect fingerprints, would have been extremely convenient just now. Miles sighed.

Ma Karal drifted up and eyed Dea's medkit, as he cleaned and repacked it. "All that," she muttered under her breath, "for a horse …"

Miles refrained, barely, from leaping to a hot defense of the value of this particular horse. How many people in Silvy Vale had Ma Karal seen suffer and die, in her lifetime, for lack of no more medical technology than what Dea was carrying under his arm just now?

Guarding his horse, Miles watched from the porch as dawn crept over the landscape. He had changed his shirt and washed off. Pym was inside getting his ribs taped. Miles sat with his back to the wall and a stunner on his lap as the night mists slowly grew gray. The valley was a blur, fog-shrouded, the hills darker rolls of fog beyond. Directly overhead, gray thinned to a paling blue. The day would be fine and hot once the fog burned away.

It was surely time now to call out the troops from Hassadar. This was getting just too weird. His bodyguard was half out of commission—true, it was Miles's horse that had rendered him so, not the mystery attacker. But just because the attacks hadn't been fatal didn't mean they hadn't been intended so. Perhaps a third attack would be brought off more expertly. Practice makes perfect.

Miles felt unstrung with nervous exhaustion. How had he let a mere horse become such a handle on his emotions? Bad, that, almost unbalanced—yet Ninny's was surely one of the truly innocent pure souls Miles had ever known. Miles remembered the other innocent in the case then, and shivered in the damp. *It was cruel, lord, something cruel* .... Pym was right, the bushes could be crawling with Csurik assassins right now.

Dammit, the bushes *were* crawling—over there, a movement, a damping wave of branch lashing in recoil from—what? Miles's heart lurched in his chest. He adjusted his stunner to full power, slipped silently off the porch, and began his stalk, crouching low, taking advantage of cover wherever the long grasses of the yard had not been trampled flat by the activities of the last day, and night. Miles froze like a predatory cat as a shape seemed to coalesce out of the mist.

A lean young man, not too tall, dressed in the baggy trousers that seemed to be standard here, stood wearily by the horse lines, staring up the yard at Karal's cabin. He stood so for a full two minutes without moving. Miles held a bead on him with his stunner. If he dared make one move toward Ninny ...

The young man walked back and forth uncertainly, then crouched on his heels, still gazing up the yard. He pulled something from the pocket of his loose jacket—Miles's finger tightened on the trigger—but he only put it to his mouth and bit. An apple. The crunch carried clearly in the damp air, and the faint perfume of its juices. He ate about half, then stopped, seeming to have trouble swallowing. Miles checked the knife at his belt, made sure it was loose in its sheath. Ninny's nostrils widened, and he nickered hopefully, drawing the young man's attention. He rose and walked over to the horse.

The blood pulsed in Miles's ears, louder than any other sound. His grip on the stunner was damp and white-knuckled. The young man fed Ninny his apple. The horse chomped it down, big jaw rippling under his skin, then cocked his hip, dangled one hind hoof, and sighed hugely. If he hadn't seen the man eat off the fruit first Miles might have shot him on the spot. It couldn't be poisoned ... The man made to pet Ninny's neck, then his hand drew back in startlement as he encountered Dea's dressing. Ninny shook his head uneasily. Miles rose slowly and stood waiting. The man scratched Ninny's ears instead, looked up one last time at the cabin, took a deep breath, stepped forward, saw Miles, and stood stock-still.

"Lem Csurik?" said Miles.

A pause, a frozen nod. "Lord Vorkosigan?" said the young man. Miles nodded in turn.

Csurik swallowed. "Vor lord," he quavered, "do you keep your word?"

What a bizarre opening. Miles's brows climbed. Hell, go with it. "Yes. Are you coming in?"

"Yes and no, m'lord."

"Which?"

"A bargain, lord. I must have a bargain, and your word on it."

"If you killed Raina …"

"No, lord. I swear it. I didn't."

"Then you have nothing to fear from me."

Lem Csurik's lips thinned. What the devil could this hill man find ironic? How dare he find irony in Miles's confusion? Irony, but no amusement.

"Oh, lord," breathed Csurik, "I wish that were so. But I have to prove it to Harra. Harra must believe me—you have to make her believe me, lord!"

"You have to make me believe you first. Fortunately, that isn't hard. You come up to the cabin and make that same statement under fast-penta, and I will rule you cleared."

Csurik was shaking his head.

"Why not?" said Miles patiently. That Csurik had turned up at all was strong circumstantial indication of his innocence. Unless he somehow imagined he could beat the drug. Miles would be patient for, oh, three or four seconds at least. Then, by God, he'd stun him, drag him inside, tie him up till he came round, and get to the bottom of this before breakfast.

"The drug—they say you can't hold anything back."

"It would be pretty useless if you could."

Csurik stood silent a moment.

"Are you trying to conceal some lesser crime on your conscience? Is that the bargain you wish to strike? An amnesty? It … might be possible. If it's short of another murder, that is."

"No, lord. I've never killed anybody!"

"Then maybe we can deal. Because if you're innocent, I need to know as soon as possible. Because it means my work isn't finished here."

"That's … that's the trouble, m'lord." Csurik shuffled, then seemed to come to some internal decision and stood sturdily. "I'll come in and risk your drug. And I'll answer anything about me you want to ask. But you have to promise—swear!—you won't ask me about … about anything else. Anybody else."

"Do you know who killed your daughter?"

"Not for sure." Csurik threw his head back defiantly. "I didn't see it. I have guesses."

"I have guesses, too."

"That's as may be, lord. Just so's they don't come from my mouth. That's all I ask."

Miles bolstered his stunner, and rubbed his chin. "Hm." A very slight smile turned one corner of his lip. "I admit, it would be more—elegant—to solve this case by reason and deduction than brute force. Even so tender a force as fast-penta."

Csurik's head lowered. "I don't know elegant, lord. But I don't want it to be from my mouth."

Decision bubbled up in Miles, straightening his spine. Yes. He *knew*, now. He had only to run through the proofs, step by chained step. Just like 5-Space math. "Very well. I swear by my word as Vorkosigan, I shall confine my questions to the facts to which you were an eyewitness. I will not ask you for conjectures about persons or events for which you were not present. There, will that do?"

Csurik bit his lip. "Yes, lord. If you keep your word."

"Try me," suggested Miles. His lips wrinkled back on a vulpine smile, absorbing the implied insult without comment.

Csurik climbed the yard beside Miles as if to an executioner's block. Their entrance created a tableau of astonishment among Karal and his family, clustered around their wooden table where Dea was treating Pym. Pym and Dea looked rather blanker, till Miles made introduction: "Dr. Dea, get out your fast-penta. Here's Lem Csurik come to talk with us."

Miles steered Lem to a chair. The hill man sat with his hands clenched. Pym, a red and purpling bruise showing at the edges of the white tape circling his chest, took up his stunner and stepped back.

Dr. Dea muttered under his breath to Miles as he got out the hypospray. "How'd you *do* that?"

Miles's hand brushed his pocket. He pulled out a sugar cube and held it up, and grinned through the C of his thumb and finger. Dea snorted, but pursed his lips with reluctant respect.

Lem flinched as the hypospray hissed on his arm, as if he expected it to hurt.

"Count backwards from ten," Dea instructed. By the time Lem reached three, he had relaxed; at zero, he giggled.

"Karal, Ma Karal, Pym, gather round," said Miles. "You are my witnesses. Boys, stay back and stay quiet. No interruptions, please."

Miles ran through the preliminaries, half a dozen questions designed to set up a rhythm and kill time while the fast-penta took full effect. Lem Csurik grinned foolishly, lolling in his chair, and answered them all with sunny goodwill. Fast-penta interrogation had been part of Miles's military intelligence course at the Service Academy. The drug seemed to be working exactly as advertised, oddly enough.

"Did you return to your cabin that morning, after you spent the night at your parents?"

"Yes, m'lord." Lem smiled.

"About what time?"

"Midmorning."

Nobody here had a chrono; that was probably as precise an answer as Miles was likely to get. "What did you do when you got there?"

"Called for Harra. She was gone, though. It frightened me that she was gone. Thought she might've run out on me." Lem hiccoughed. "I want my Harra."

"Later. Was the baby asleep?"

"She was. She woke up when I called for Harra. Started crying again. It goes right up your spine."

"What did you do then?"

Lem's eyes widened. "I got no milk. She wanted Harra. There's nothing I could do for her."

"Did you pick her up?"

"No, lord, I let her lay. There was nothing I could do for her. Harra, she'd hardly let me touch her, she was that nervous about her. Told me I'd drop her or something."

"You didn't shake her, to stop her screaming?"

"No, lord, I let her lay. I left to look down the path for Harra."

"Then where did you go?"

Lem blinked. "My sister's. I'd promised to help haul wood for a new cabin. Bella—m'other sister—is getting married, y'see, and—"

He was beginning to wander, as was normal for this drug. "Stop," said Miles. Lem fell silent obediently, swaying slightly in his chair. Miles considered his next question carefully. He was approaching the fine line, here. "Did you meet anyone on the path? Answer yes or no."

"Yes."

Dea was getting excited. "Who? Ask him who!"

Miles held up his hand. "You can administer the antagonist now, Dr. Dea."

"Aren't you going to ask him? It could be vital!"

"I can't. I gave my word. Administer the antagonist now, Doctor!"

Fortunately, the confusion of two interrogators stopped Lem's mumbled willing reply to Dea's question. Dea, bewildered, pressed his hypospray against Lem's arm. Lem's eyes, half-closed, snapped open within seconds. He sat up straight and rubbed his arm, and his face.

"Who did you meet on the path?" Dea asked him directly.

Lem's lips pressed tight; he looked for rescue to Miles.

Dea looked too. "Why won't you ask him?"

"Because I don't need to," said Miles. "I know precisely who Lem met on the path, and why he went on and not back. It was Raina's murderer. As I shall shortly prove. And—witness this, Karal, Ma Karal—that information did not come from Lem's mouth. Confirm!"

Karal nodded slowly. "I … see, m'lord. That was … very good of you."

Miles gave him a direct stare, his mouth set in a tight smile. "And when is a mystery no mystery at all?"

Karal reddened, not replying for a moment. Then he said, "You may as well keep on like you're going, m'lord. There's no stopping you now, I suppose."

"No."

✧ ✧ ✧

Miles sent runners to collect the witnesses, Ma Karal in one direction, Zed in a second, Speaker Karal and his eldest in a third. He had Lem wait with Pym, Dea, and himself. Having the shortest distance to cover, Ma Karal arrived back first, with Ma Csurik and two of her sons in tow.

His mother fell on Lem, embracing him and then looking fearfully over her shoulder at Miles. The younger brothers hung back, but Pym had already moved between them and the door.

"It's all right, Ma." Lem patted her on the back. "Or … anyway, I'm all right. I'm clear. Lord Vorkosigan believes me."

She glowered at Miles, still holding Lem's arm. "You didn't let the mutie lord give you that poison drug, did you?"

"Not poison," Miles denied. "In fact, the drug may have saved his life. That damn near makes it a medicine, I'd say. However." He turned toward Lem's two younger brothers, folding his arms sternly. "I would like to know which of you young morons threw the torch on my tent last night?"

The younger one whitened; the elder, hotly indignant, noticed his brother's expression and cut his denial off in midsyllable. "You didn't!" he hissed in horror.

"Nobody," said the white one. "Nobody did."

Miles raised his eyebrows. There followed a short, choked silence.

"Well, *nobody* can make his apologies to Speaker and Ma Karal, then," said Miles, "since it was their sons who were sleeping in the tent last night. I and my men were in the loft."

The boy's mouth opened in dismay. The youngest Karal stared at the pale Csurik brother, his age-mate, and whispered importantly, "You, Dono! You idiot, didn't ya know that tent wouldn't burn? It's real Imperial Service issue!"

Miles clasped his hands behind his back, and fixed the Csuriks with a cold eye. "Rather more to the point, it was attempted assassination upon your Count's heir, which carries the same capital charge of treason as an attempt upon the Count himself. Or perhaps Dono didn't think of that?"

Dono was thrown into flummoxed confusion. No need for fast-penta here; the kid couldn't carry off a lie worth a damn. Ma Csurik now had hold of Dono's arm too, without letting go of Lem's;

she looked as frantic as a hen with too many chicks, trying to shelter them from a storm.

"I wasn't trying to kill you, lord!" cried Dono.

"What were you trying to do, then?"

"You'd come to kill Lem. I wanted to … make you go away. Frighten you away. I didn't think anyone would really get hurt—I mean, it was only a tent!"

"You've never seen anything burn down, I take it. Have you, Ma Csurik?"

Lem's mother nodded, lips tight, clearly torn between a desire to protect her son from Miles, and a desire to beat Dono till he bled for his potentially lethal stupidity.

"Well, but for a chance, you could have killed or horribly injured three of your friends. Think on that, please. In the meantime, in view of your youth and ah, apparent mental defectiveness, I shall hold the treason charge. In return, Speaker Karal and your parents shall be responsible for your good behavior in the future, and decide what punishment is appropriate."

Ma Csurik melted with relief and gratitude. Dono looked as if he'd rather have been shot. His brother poked him, and whispered, "Mental defective!" Ma Csurik slapped the taunter on the side of his head, suppressing him effectively.

"What about your horse, m'lord?" asked Pym.

"I … do not suspect them of the business with the horse," Miles replied slowly. "The attempt to fire the tent was plain stupidity. The other was … a different order of calculation altogether."

Zed, who had been permitted to take Pym's horse, returned then with Harra up behind him. Harra entered Speaker Karal's cabin, saw Lem, and stopped with a bitter glare. Lem stood openhanded, his eyes wounded, before her.

"So, lord," Harra said. "You caught him." Her jaw was clenched in joyless triumph.

"Not exactly," said Miles. "He came here and turned himself in. He's made his statement under fast-penta, and cleared himself. Lem did not kill Raina."

Harra turned from side to side. "But I saw he'd been there! He'd left his jacket, and took his good saw and wood planer away with him. I knew he'd been back while I was out! There must be something wrong with your drug!"

Miles shook his head. "The drug worked fine. Your deduction was correct as far as it went; Lem did visit the cabin while you were out. But when he left, Raina was still alive, crying vigorously. It wasn't Lem."

She swayed. "Who, then?"

"I think you know. I think you've been working very hard to deny that knowledge, hence your excessive focus on Lem. As long as you were sure it was Lem, you didn't have to think about the other possibilities."

"But who else would care?" Harra cried. "Who else would bother?"

"Who, indeed?" sighed Miles. He walked to the front window and glanced down the yard. The fog was clearing in the full light of morning. The horses were moving uneasily. "Dr. Dea, would you please get a second dose of fast-penta ready?" Miles turned, pacing back to stand before the fireplace, its coals still banked for the night. The faint heat was pleasant on his back.

Dea was staring around, the hypospray in his hand, clearly wondering to whom to administer it. "My lord?" he queried, brows lowering in demand for explanation.

"Isn't it obvious to you, Doctor?" Miles asked lightly.

"*No*, my lord." His tone was slightly indignant.

"Nor to you, Pym?"

"Not ... entirely, m'lord." Pym's glance, and stunner aim, wavered uncertainly to Harra.

"I suppose it's because neither of you ever met my grandfather," Miles decided. "He died just about a year before you entered my father's service, Pym. He was born at the very end of the Time of Isolation, and lived through every wrenching change this century has dealt to Barrayar. He was called the last of the Old Vor, but really, he was the first of the new. He changed with the times, from the tactics of horse cavalry to that of flyer squadrons, from swords to atomics, and he changed *successfully*. Our present freedom from the Cetagandan Occupation is a measure of how fiercely he could adapt, then throw it all away and adapt again. At the end of his life he was called a conservative, only because so much of Barrayar had streamed past him in the direction he had led, prodded, pushed, and pointed all his life.

"He changed, and adapted, and bent with the wind of the times. Then, in his age—for my father was his youngest and sole surviving son, and did not himself marry till middle-age—in his age, he was hit with me. And he had to change again. And he couldn't.

"He begged for my mother to have an abortion, after they knew more or less what the fetal damage would be. He and my parents were estranged for five years after I was born. They didn't see each other or speak or communicate. Everyone thought my father moved us to the Imperial Residence when he became Regent because he was angling for the throne, but in fact it was because the Count my grandfather denied him the use of Vorkosigan House. Aren't family squabbles jolly fun? Bleeding ulcers run in my family, we give them to each other." Miles strolled back to the window and looked out. Ah, yes. Here it came.

"The reconciliation was gradual, when it became quite clear there would be no other son," Miles went on. "No dramatic denouement. It helped when the medics got me walking. It was essential that I tested out bright. Most important of all, I never let him see me give up."

Nobody had dared interrupt this lordly monologue, but it was clear from several expressions that the point of it was escaping them. Since half the point was to kill time, Miles was not greatly disturbed by their failure to track. Footsteps sounded on the wooden porch outside. Pym moved quietly to cover the door with an unobscured angle of fire.

"Dr. Dea," said Miles, sighting through the window, "would you be so kind as to administer that fast-penta to the first person through the door, as they step in?"

"You're not waiting for a volunteer, my lord?"

"Not this time."

The door swung inward, and Dea stepped forward, raising his hand. The hypospray hissed. Ma Mattulich wheeled to face Dea, the skirts of her work dress swirling around her veined calves, hissing in return—"You dare!" Her arm drew back as if to strike him, but slowed in mid-swing and failed to connect as Dea ducked out of her way. This unbalanced her, and she staggered. Speaker Karal, coming in behind, caught her by the arm and steadied her. "You dare!" she wailed again, then turned to see not only Dea but all the other witnesses waiting: Ma Csurik, Ma Karal, Lem, Harra, Pym. Her shoulders sagged, and then the drug cut in and she just stood, a silly smile fighting with anguish for possession of her harsh face.

The smile made Miles ill, but it was the smile he needed. "Sit her down, Dea, Speaker Karal."

They guided her to the chair lately vacated by Lem Csurik. She was fighting the drug desperately, flashes of resistance melting into flaccid docility. Gradually the docility became ascendant, and she sat draped in the chair, grinning helplessly. Miles sneaked a peek at Harra. She stood white and silent, utterly closed.

For several years after the reconciliation Miles had never been left with his grandfather without his personal bodyguard. Sergeant Bothari had worn the Count's livery, but been loyal to Miles alone, the one man dangerous enough—some said, crazy enough—to stand up to the great General himself. There was no need, Miles decided, to spell out to these fascinated people just what interrupted incident had made his parents think Sergeant Bothari a necessary precaution. Let General Piotr's untarnished reputation serve—Miles, now. As *he* willed. Miles's eyes glinted.

Lem lowered his head. "If I had known—if I had guessed—I wouldn't have left them alone together, m'lord. I thought—Harra's mother would take care of her. I couldn't have—I didn't know *how*—"

Harra did not look at him. Harra did not look at anything.

"Let us conclude this." Miles sighed. Again, he requested formal witness from the crowd in the room, and cautioned against interruptions, which tended to unduly confuse a drugged subject. He moistened his lips and turned to Ma Mattulich.

Again, he began with the standard neutral questions, name, birthdate, parents' names, checkable biographical facts. Ma Mattulich was harder to lull than the cooperative Lem had been, her responses scattered and staccato. Miles controlled his impatience with difficulty. For all its deceptive ease, fast-penta interrogation required skill, skill and patience. He'd come too far to risk a stumble now. He worked his questions up gradually to the first critical ones.

"Were you there, when Raina was born?"

Her voice was low and drifting, dreamy. "The birth came in the night. Lem, he went for Jean the midwife. The midwife's son was supposed to go for me, but he fell back to sleep. I didn't get there till morning, and then it was too late. They'd all seen."

"Seen what?"

"The cat's mouth, the dirty mutation. Monsters in us. Cut them out. Ugly little man." This last, Miles realized, was an aside upon himself. Her attention had hung up on him, hypnotically. "Muties make more muties, they breed faster, overrun … I saw you watching the girls. You want to make mutie babies on clean women, poison us all …"

Time to steer her back to the main issue. "Were you ever alone with the baby after that?"

"No, Jean she hung around. Jean knows me, she knew what I wanted. None of her damn business. And Harra was always there. Harra must not know. Harra must not … why should she get off so soft? The poison must be in her. Must have come from her Da, I lay only with her Da and they were all wrong but the one."

Miles blinked. "What were all wrong?" Across the room Miles saw Speaker Karal's mouth tighten. The headman caught Miles's glance and stared down at his own feet, absenting himself from the proceedings. Lem, his lips parted in absorption, and the rest of the boys were listening with alarm. Harra hadn't moved.

"All my babies," Ma Mattulich said.

Harra looked up sharply at that, her eyes widening.

"Was Harra not your only child?" Miles asked. It was an effort to keep his voice cool, calm; he wanted to shout. He wanted to be gone from here …

"No, of course not. She was my only clean child, I thought. I thought, but the poison must have been hidden in her. I fell on my knees and thanked God when she was born clean, a clean one at last, after so many, so much pain … . I thought I had finally been punished enough. She was such a pretty baby, I thought it was over at last. But she must have been mutie after all, hidden, tricksy, sly …"

"How many," Miles choked, "babies did you have?"

"Four, besides Harra my last."

"And you killed all four of them?" Speaker Karal, Miles saw, gave a slow nod to his feet.

"No!" said Ma Mattulich. Indignation broke through the fast-penta wooze briefly. "Two were born dead already, the first one, and the twisted-up one. The one with too many fingers and toes, and the one with the bulgy head, those I cut. Cut out. My mother, she watched over me to see I did it right. Harra, I made it soft for Harra. I did it for her."

"So you have in fact murdered not one infant, but three?" said Miles frozenly. The younger witnesses in the room, Karal's boys and the Csurik brothers, looked horrified. The older ones, Ma Mattulich's contemporaries, who must have lived through the events with her, looked mortified, sharing her shame. Yes, they all must have known.

"Murdered?" said Ma Mattulich. "No! I cut them out. I had to. I had to do the right thing." Her chin lifted proudly, then drooped. "Killed my babies, to please, to please … I don't know who. And now you call me a murderer? Damn you! What use is your justice to me *now*? I needed it then—where were you then?" Suddenly, shockingly, she burst into tears, which wavered almost instantly into rage. "If mine must die then so must hers! Why should she get off so soft? Spoiled her … I tried my best, I did my best, it's not fair …"

The fast-penta was not keeping up with this … no, it was working, Miles decided, but her emotions were too overwhelming. Upping the dose might level her emotional surges, at some risk of respiratory arrest, but it would not elicit any more complete a confession. Miles's belly was trembling, a reaction he trusted he concealed. It had to be completed now.

"Why did you break Raina's neck, instead of cutting her throat?"

"Harra, she must not know," said Ma Mattulich. "Poor baby. It would look like she just died …"

Miles eyed Lem, Speaker Karal. "It seems a number of others shared your opinion that Harra should not know."

"I didn't want it to be from my mouth," repeated Lem sturdily.

"I wanted to save her double grief, m'lord," said Karal. "She'd had so much …"

Miles met Harra's eyes at that. "I think you all underestimate her. Your excessive tenderness insults both her intelligence and will. She comes from a tough line, that one."

Harra inhaled, controlling her own trembling. She gave Miles a short nod, as if to say *Thank you, little man.* He returned her a slight inclination of the head, *Yes, I understand.*

"I'm not sure yet where justice lies in this case," said Miles, "but this I swear to you, the days of cooperative concealment are over. No more secret crimes in the night. Daylight's here. And speaking of crimes in the night"—he turned back to Ma Mattulich—"*was* it you who tried to cut my horse's throat last night?"

"I tried," said Ma Mattulich, calmer now in a wave of fast-penta mellowness, "but it kept rearing up on me."

"Why my *horse*?" Miles could not keep exasperation from his voice, though a calm, even tone was enjoined upon fast-penta interrogators by the training manual.

"I couldn't get at you," said Ma Mattulich simply.

Miles rubbed his forehead. "Retroactive infanticide by proxy?" he muttered.

"You," said Ma Mattulich, and her loathing came through even the nauseating fast-penta cheer, "*you* are the worst. All I went through, all I did, all the grief, and you come along at the end. A mutie made lord over us all, and all the rules changed, betrayed at the end by an off-worlder woman's weakness. You make it all for *nothing*. Hate you. Dirty mutie …" Her voice trailed off in a drugged mumble.

Miles took a deep breath, looking around the room. The stillness was profound, and no one dared break it.

"I believe," he said, "that concludes my investigation into the facts of this case."

The mystery of Raina's death was solved.

The problem of justice, unfortunately, remained.

Miles took a walk.

The graveyard, though little more than a crude clearing in the woodland, was a place of peace and beauty in the morning light.

The stream burbled endlessly, shifting green shadows and blinding brilliant reflections. The faint breeze that had shredded away the last of the night fog whispered in the trees, and the tiny short-lived creatures that everyone on Barrayar but biologists called bugs sang and twittered in the patches of native scrub.

"Well, Raina," Miles sighed, "and what do I do now?" Pym lingered by the borders of the clearing, giving Miles room. "It's all right," Miles assured the tiny grave. "Pym's caught me talking to dead people before. He may think I'm crazy, but he's far too well trained to say so."

Pym in fact did not look happy, nor altogether well. Miles felt rather guilty for dragging him out; by rights the man should be resting in bed, but Miles had desperately needed this time alone. Pym wasn't just suffering the residual effect of having been kicked by Ninny. He had been silent ever since Miles had extracted the confession from Ma Mattulich. Miles was unsurprised. Pym had steeled himself to play executioner to their imagined hill bully; the substitution of a mad grandmother as his victim had clearly given him pause. He would obey whatever order Miles gave him, though, Miles had no doubt of that.

Miles considered the peculiarities of Barrayaran law as he wandered about the clearing, watching the stream and the light, turning over an occasional rock with the toe of his boot. The fundamental principle was clear; the spirit was to be preferred over the letter, truth over technicalities. Precedent was held subordinate to the judgment of the man on the spot. Alas, the man on the spot was himself. There was no refuge for him in automated rules, no hiding behind *the law says* as if the law were some living overlord with a real Voice. The only voice here was his own.

And who would be served by the death of that half-crazed old woman? Harra? The relationship between mother and daughter had been wounded unto death by this, Miles had seen that in their eyes, yet still Harra had no stomach for matricide. Miles rather preferred it that way; having her standing by his ear crying for bloody revenge would have been enormously distracting just now. The obvious justice made a damn poor reward for Harra's courage in reporting the crime. Raina? Ah. That was more difficult.

"I'd like to lay the old gargoyle right there at your feet, small lady," Miles muttered to her. "Is it your desire? Does it serve you? What *would* serve you?" Was this the great burning he had promised her?

What judgment would reverberate along the entire Dendarii mountain range? Should he indeed sacrifice these people to some larger political statement, regardless of their wants? Or should he forget all that, make his judgment serve only those directly involved? He scooped up a stone and flung it full force into the stream. It vanished invisibly in the rocky bed.

He turned to find Speaker Karal waiting by the edge of the graveyard. Karal ducked his head in greeting and approached cautiously.

"So, m'lord," said Karal.

"Just so," said Miles.

"Have you come to any conclusion?"

"Not really." Miles gazed around. "Anything less than Ma Mattulich's death seems … inadequate justice, and yet … I cannot see who her death would serve."

"Neither could I. That's why I took the position I did in the first place."

"No …" said Miles slowly, "no, you were wrong in that. For one thing, it very nearly got Lem Csurik killed. I was getting ready to pursue him with deadly force at one point. It almost destroyed him with Harra. Truth is better. Slightly better. At least it isn't a fatal error. Surely I can do … something with it."

"I didn't know what to expect of you, at first," admitted Karal.

Miles shook his head. "I meant to make changes. A difference. Now … I don't know."

Speaker Karal's balding forehead wrinkled. "But we are changing."

"Not enough. Not fast enough."

"You're young yet, that's why you don't see how much, how fast. Look at the difference between Harra and her mother. God—look at the difference between Ma Mattulich and *her* mother. *There* was a harridan." Speaker Karal shuddered. "I remember her, all right. And yet, she was not so unusual, in her day. So far from having to make change, I don't think you could stop it if you tried. The minute we finally get a powersat receptor up here, and get on the comnet, the past will be done and over. As soon as the kids see the future—their future—they'll be mad after it. They're already lost to the old ones like Ma Mattulich. The old ones know it, too, don't believe they don't know it. Why d'you think we haven't been able to get at least a small unit up here yet? Not just the cost. The old ones are fighting it. They call it off-planet corruption, but it's really the future they fear."

"There's so much still to be done."

"Oh, yes. We are a desperate people, no lie. But we have hope. I don't think you realize how much you've done, just by coming up here."

"I've done nothing," said Miles bitterly. "Sat around, mostly. And now, I swear, I'm going to end up doing more nothing. And then go home. Hell!"

Speaker Karal pursed his lips, looked at his feet, at the high hills. "You are doing something for us every minute. Mutie lord. Do you think you are invisible?"

Miles grinned wolfishly. "Oh, Karal, I'm a one-man band, I am. I'm a parade."

"As you say, just so. Ordinary people need extraordinary examples. So they can say to themselves, well, if he can do *that*, I can surely do *this*. No excuses."

"No quarter, yes, I know that game. Been playing it all my life."

"I think," said Karal, "Barrayar needs you. To go on being just what you are."

"Barrayar will eat me, if it can."

"Yes," said Karal, his eyes on the horizon, "so it will." His gaze fell to the graves at his feet. "But it swallows us all in the end, doesn't it? You will outlive the old ones."

"Or in the beginning." Miles pointed down. "Don't tell *me* who I'm going to outlive. Tell Raina."

Karal's shoulders slumped. "True. S'truth. Make your judgment, lord. I'll back you."

Miles assembled them all in Karal's yard for his Speaking, the porch now having become his podium. The interior of the cabin would have been impossibly hot and close for this crowd, suffocating with the afternoon sun beating on the roof, though outdoors the light made them squint. They were all here, everyone they could round up, Speaker Karal, Ma Karal, their boys, all the Csuriks, most of the cronies who had attended last night's funereal festivities, men, women, and children. Harra sat apart. Lem kept trying to hold her hand, though from the way she flinched it was clear she didn't want to be touched. Ma Mattulich sat displayed by Miles's side, silent and surly, flanked by Pym and an uncomfortable-looking Deputy Alex.

Miles jerked up his chin, settling his head on the high collar of his dress greens, as polished and formal as Pym's batman's expertise could make him. The Imperial Service uniform that Miles had earned. Did these people know he had earned it, or did they all imagine it a mere gift from his father, nepotism at work? Damn what they thought. He knew. He stood before his people, and gripped the porch rail.

"I have concluded the investigation of the charges laid before the Count's Court by Harra Csurik of the murder of her daughter Raina. By evidence, witness, and her own admission, I find Mara Mattulich guilty of this murder, she having twisted the infant's neck until it broke, and then attempted to conceal that crime. Even when that concealment placed her son-in-law Lem Csurik in mortal danger from false charges. In light of the helplessness of the victim, the cruelty of the method, and the cowardly selfishness of the attempted concealment, I can find no mitigating excuse for the crime.

"In addition, Mara Mattulich by her own admission testifies to two previous infanticides, some twenty years ago, of her own children. These facts shall be announced by Speaker Karal in every corner of Silvy Vale, until every subject has been informed."

He could feel Ma Mattulich's glare boring into his back. *Yes, go on and hate me, old woman. I will bury you yet, and you know it.* He swallowed and continued, the formality of the language a sort of shield before him.

"For this unmitigated crime, the only proper sentence is death. And I so sentence Mara Mattulich. But in light of her age and close relation to the next-most-injured party in the case, Harra Csurik, I choose to hold the actual execution of that sentence. Indefinitely." Out of the corner of his eye Miles saw Pym let out, very carefully and covertly, a sigh of relief. Harra combed at her straw-colored bangs with her fingers and listened intently.

"But she shall be as dead before the law. All her property, even to the clothes on her back, now belongs to her daughter Harra, to dispose of as she wills. Mara Mattulich may not own property, enter contracts, sue for injuries, nor exert her will after death in any testament. She shall not leave Silvy Vale without Harra's permission. Harra shall be given power over her as a parent over a child, or as in senility. In Harra's absence Speaker Karal will be her deputy. Mara Mattulich shall be watched to see she harms no other child.

"Further. She shall die without sacrifice. No one, not Harra nor any other, shall make a burning for her when she goes into the ground at last. As she murdered her future, so her future shall return only death to her spirit. She will die as the childless do, without remembrance."

A low sigh swept the older members of the crowd before Miles. For the first time, Mara Mattulich bent her stiff neck.

Some, Miles knew, would find this only spiritually symbolic. Others would see it as literally lethal, according to the strength of their beliefs. The literal-minded, such as those who saw mutation as a sin to be violently expiated. But even the less superstitious, Miles saw in their faces, found the meaning clear. So.

Miles turned to Ma Mattulich, and lowered his voice. "Every breath you take from this moment on is by my mercy. Every bite of food you eat, by Harra's charity. By charity and mercy—such as you did not give—you shall live. Dead woman."

"Some mercy. Mutie lord." Her growl was low, weary, beaten.

"You get the point," he said through his teeth. He swept her a bow, infinitely ironic, and turned his back on her. "I am the Voice of Count Vorkosigan. This concludes my Speaking."

Miles met Harra and Lem afterward, in Speaker Karal's cabin.

"I have a proposition for you." Miles controlled his nervous pacing and stood before them. "You're free to turn it down, or think about it for a while. I know you're very tired right now." *As are we all.* Had he really been in Silvy Vale only a day and a half? It seemed like a century. His head ached with fatigue. Harra was red-eyed, too. "First of all, you can read and write?"

"Some," Harra admitted. "Speaker Karal taught us some, and Ma Lannier."

"Well, good enough. You wouldn't be starting completely blind. Look. A few years back Hassadar started a teacher's college. It's not very big yet, but it's begun. There are some scholarships. I can swing one your way, if you will agree to live in Hassadar for three years of intense study."

"Me!" said Harra. "I couldn't go to a college! I barely know … any of that stuff."

"Knowledge is what you're supposed to have coming out, not going in. Look, they know what they're dealing with in this district. They have a lot of remedial courses. It's true, you'd have to work harder, to catch up with the town-bred and the lowlanders. But I know you have courage, and I know you have will. The rest is just picking yourself up and ramming into the wall again and again until it falls down. You get a bloody forehead, so what? You can do it, I swear you can."

Lem, sitting beside her, looked worried. He captured her hand again. "Three years?" he said in a small voice. "Gone away?"

"The school stipend isn't that much," said Miles. "But Lem, I understand you have carpenter's skills. There's a building boom going on in Hassadar right now. Hassadar's going to be the next Vorkosigan Vashnoi, I think. I'm certain you could get a job. Between you, you could live."

Lem looked at first relieved, then extremely worried. "But they all use power tools—computers—robots …"

"By no means. And they weren't all born knowing how to use that stuff, either. If they can learn it, you can. Besides, the rich pay well for hand-work, unique one-off items, if the quality's good. I can see you get a start, which is usually the toughest moment. After that you should be able to figure it out all right."

"To leave Silvy Vale …" said Harra in a dismayed tone.

"Only in order to return. That's the other half of the bargain. I can send a com unit up here, a small one with a portable power pack that lasts a year. Somebody'd have to hump down to Vorkosigan Surleau to replace it annually, no big problem. The whole setup wouldn't cost much more than oh, a new lightflyer." Such as the shiny red one Miles had coveted in a dealer's showroom in Vorbarr Sultana, very suitable for a graduation present, he had pointed out to his parents. The credit chit was sitting in the top drawer of his dresser in the lake house at Vorkosigan Surleau right now. "It's not a massive project like installing a powersat receptor for the whole of Silvy Vale or anything. The holovid would pick up the educational satellite broadcasts from the capital; set it up in some central cabin, add a couple of dozen lap-links for the kids, and you've got an instant school. All the children would be required to attend, with Speaker Karal to enforce it, though once they'd discovered the holovid you'd probably have to beat them to make them go home. I, ah"—Miles cleared his throat—"thought you might name it the Raina Csurik Primary School."

"Oh," said Harra, and began to cry for the first time that grueling day. Lem patted her clumsily. She returned the grip of his hand at last.

"I can send a lowlander up here to teach," said Miles. "I'll get one to take a short-term contract, till you're ready to come back. But he or she won't understand Silvy Vale like you do. Wouldn't understand *why*. You—you already know. You know what they can't teach in any lowland college."

Harra scrubbed her eyes, and looked up—not very far up—at him. "You went to the Imperial Academy."

"I did." His chin jerked up.

"Then I," she said shakily, "can manage … Hassadar Teacher's College." The name was awkward in her mouth. At first. "At any rate—I'll try, m'lord."

"I'll bet on you," Miles agreed. "Both of you. Just, ah"—a smile sped across his mouth and vanished—"stand up straight and speak the truth, eh?"

Harra blinked understanding. An answering half-smile lit her tired face, equally briefly. "I will. Little man."

Fat Ninny rode home by air the next morning, in a horse van, along with Pym. Dr. Dea went along with his two patients, and his nemesis the sorrel mare. A replacement bodyguard had been sent with the groom who flew the van from Vorkosigan Surleau, and stayed with Miles to help him ride the remaining two horses back down. Well, Miles thought, he'd been considering a camping trip in the mountains with his cousin Ivan as part of his home leave anyway. The liveried man was the laconic veteran Esterhazy, whom Miles had known most of his life; excellent company for a man who didn't want to talk about it, unlike Ivan you could almost forget he was there. Miles wondered if Esterhazy's assignment had been random chance, or a mercy of the Count's. Esterhazy was good with horses.

They camped overnight by the river of roses. Miles walked up the vale in the evening light, desultorily looking for the spring of it; indeed, the floral barrier did seem to peter out a couple of kilometers upstream, merging into slightly less impassable scrub. Miles plucked a rose, checked to make sure that Esterhazy was nowhere in sight, and bit into it curiously. Clearly, he was not a horse. A cut bunch would probably not survive the trip back as a treat for Ninny. Ninny could settle for oats.

Miles watched the evening shadows flowing up along the backbone of the Dendarii range, high and massive in the distance. How small those mountains looked from space! Little wrinkles on the skin of a globe he could cover with his hand, all their crushing mass made invisible. Which was illusory, distance or nearness? Distance, Miles decided. Distance was a damned lie. Had his father known this? Miles suspected so.

He contemplated his urge to throw all his money, not just a lightflyer's worth, at those mountains; to quit it all and go teach children to read and write, to set up a free clinic, a powersat net, or all of these at once. But Silvy Vale was only one of hundreds of such communities buried in these mountains, one of thousands across the whole of Barrayar. Taxes squeezed from this very district helped maintain the very elite military school he'd just spent—how much of their resources in? How much would he have to give back just to make it even, now? He was himself a planetary resource, his training had made him so, and his feet were set on their path.

What God means you to do, Miles's theist mother claimed, could be deduced from the talents He gave you. The academic honors,

Miles had amassed by sheer brute work. But the war games, outwitting his opponents, staying one step ahead—a necessity, true, he had no margin for error—the war games had been an unholy joy. War had been no game here once, not so long ago. It might be so again. What you did best, that was what was wanted from you. God seemed to be lined up with the Emperor on that point, at least, if no other.

Miles had sworn his officer's oath to the Emperor less than two weeks ago, puffed with pride at his achievement. In his secret mind he had imagined himself keeping that oath through blazing battle, enemy torture, what-have-you, even while sharing cynical cracks afterwards with Ivan about archaic dress swords and the sort of people who insisted on wearing them.

But in the dark of subtler temptations, those which hurt without heroism for consolation, he foresaw, the Emperor would no longer be the symbol of Barrayar in his heart.

Peace to you, small lady, he thought to Raina. *You've won a twisted poor modern knight, to wear your favor on his sleeve. But it's a twisted poor world we were both born into, that rejects us without mercy and ejects us without consultation. At least I won't just tilt at windmills for you. I'll send in sappers to mine the twirling suckers, and blast them into the sky …*

He knew who he served now. And why he could not quit. And why he must not fail.

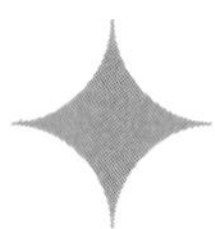

SEVEN VIEWS OF OLDUVAI GORGE

Mike Resnick

Introduction

Shahid (the publisher) asked me to write an introduction explaining how this novella came to be. On one of our trips to Africa we went to Tanzania to see Odovai Gorge and the Nagorno-Nagormo Crater. If you only have a short time to spend in this area of Africa go to the Crater; you will get a great look at how Africa was for most of our hominid ancestors and as well as seeing a great collection of the animals Africa offers tourists.

The gorge wasn't very impressive; if you've been to a desert and seen a rather shallow gorge formed by water runoff, you've seen Odovai Gorge. The little vegetation will be different—not the thorn scrub common to East Africa—but the effect is the same. There is a small museum in Nairobi that contains a lot of small hand tools found at the Gorge; and you can see the whole museum in a few hours if you're interested. If you can only do a short trip, go to the Crater and skip the Gorge; use your imagination to see early hominids in the scenery.

When we got home, Mike wanted to write about the history of East Africa as Science Fiction. so he thought that he'd do a novella about the gorge through time. The first and last section are pure science fiction. There is a short story about halfway through the novella about the Mau-Mau and hunting them. One of our guides was sent to Kenya as a nineteen-year-old soldier; he didn't speak the lingua-franca of East Africa but he learned it leading his local soldiers. The basis of this story was campfire talk and storytelling we heard at night around campfires from our guide and other locals. They reminisced about the good and bad old days; maybe all people do—probably even our hominid ancestors did when they had developed speech.

Mike got the title from a coffee-table book about that classic of Japanese literature and art—"The Seven Views of Mt. Fujiyama." We had bought the book for the art and the poetry and Mike saw it as a great title for his novella since he wanted to do short stories of the Gorge through time. I think the title fits the content of the novella even better than the original title fit the coffee-table book. He worked on the novella for about a month since he was also writing a novel. The question asked at the end of the novella was one of the underlying issues of the novella. Mike doesn't give us his answer but he was well aware that we developed as a species on the African plains trying not to be eaten by all the predators that existed then and the smaller number we have today. We also had to feed the members of our small family units. I find one of the interesting things about hominids is that we always litter; without that litter we'd have a terrible time discovering our past history.

—CAROL RESNICK

The creatures came again last night.

The moon had just slipped behind the clouds when we heard the first rustlings in the grass. Then there was a moment of utter silence, as if they knew we were listening for them, and finally there were the familiar hoots and shrieks as they raced to within fifty meters of us and, still screeching, struck postures of aggression.

They fascinate me, for they never show themselves in the daylight, and yet they manifest none of the features of the true nocturnal animal. Their eyes are not oversized, their ears cannot move independently, they tread very heavily on their feet. They frighten most of the other members of my party, and while I am curious about them, I have yet to absorb one of them and study it.

To tell the truth, I think my use of absorption terrifies my companions more than the creatures do, though there is no reason why it should. Although I am relatively young by my race's standards, I am nevertheless many millennia older than any other member of my party. You would think, given their backgrounds, that they would know that any trait someone of my age possesses must by definition be a survival trait.

Still, it bothers them. Indeed, it *mystifies* them, much as my memory does. Of course, theirs seem very inefficient to me. Imagine having to learn everything one knows in a single lifetime, to be totally ignorant at the moment of birth! Far better to split off from your parent with his knowledge intact in your brain, just as *my* parent's knowledge came to him, and ultimately to me.

But then, that is why we are here: not to compare similarities, but to study differences. And never was there a race so different from all his fellows as Man. He was extinct barely seventeen millennia after he strode boldly out into the galaxy from this, the planet of his birth—but during that brief interval he wrote a chapter in galactic history that will last forever. He claimed the stars for his own, colonized a million worlds, ruled his empire with an iron will. He gave no quarter during his primacy, and he asked for none during his decline and fall. Even now, some forty-eight centuries after his extinction, his accomplishments and his failures still excite the imagination.

Which is why we are on Earth, at the very spot that was said to be Man's true birthplace, the rocky gorge where he first crossed over the evolutionary barrier, saw the stars with fresh eyes, and vowed that they would someday be his.

Our leader is Bellidore, an Elder of the Kragan people, orange-skinned, golden fleeced, with wise, patient ways. Bellidore is well-versed in the behavior of sentient beings, and settles our disputes before we even know that we are engaged in them.

Then there are the Stardust Twins, glittering silver beings who answer to each other's names and finish each other's thoughts. They have worked on seventeen archaeological digs, but even *they* were surprised when Bellidore chose them for this most prestigious of all missions. They behave like life mates, though they display no sexual characteristics—but like all the others, they refuse to have physical contact with me, so I cannot assuage my curiosity.

Also in our party is the Moriteu, who eats the dirt as if it were a delicacy, speaks to no one, and sleeps upside-down while hanging from a branch of a nearby tree. For some reason, the creatures always leave it alone. Perhaps they think it is dead, possibly they know it is asleep and that only the rays of the sun can awaken it. Whatever the reason, we would be lost without it, for only the delicate tendrils that extend from its mouth can excavate the ancient artifacts we have discovered with the proper care.

We have four other species with us: one is an Historian, one an Exobiologist, one an Appraiser of human artifacts, and one a Mystic. (At least, I *assume* she is a Mystic, for I can find no pattern to her approach, but this may be due to my own shortsightedness. After all, what I do seems like magic to my companions and yet it is a rigorously applied science.)

And, finally, there is me. I have no name, for my people do not use names, but for the convenience of the party I have taken the name of He Who Views for the duration of the expedition. This is a double misnomer: I am not a *he*, for my race is not divided by gender; and I am not a viewer, but a Fourth Level Feeler. Still, I could intuit very early in the voyage that "feel" means something very different to my companions than to myself, and out of respect for their sensitivities, I chose a less accurate name.

Every day finds us back at work, examining the various strata. There are many signs that the area once teemed with living things, that early on there was a veritable explosion of life-forms in this place, but very little remains today. There are a few species of insects and birds, some small rodents, and of course the creatures who visit our camp nightly.

Our collection has been growing slowly. It is fascinating to watch my companions perform their tasks, for in many ways they are as much of a mystery to me as my methods are to them. For example, our Exobiologist needs only to glide her tentacle across an object to tell us whether it was once living matter; the Historian, surrounded by its complex equipment, can date any object, carbon based or otherwise, to within a decade of its origin, regardless of its state of preservation; and even the Moriteu is a thing of beauty and fascination as it gently separates the artifacts from the strata where they have rested for so long.

I am very glad I was chosen to come on this mission.

We have been here for two lunar cycles now, and the work goes slowly. The lower strata were thoroughly excavated eons ago (I have such a personal interest in learning about Man that I almost used the word *plundered* rather than *excavated*, so resentful am I at not finding more artifacts), and for reasons as yet unknown there is almost nothing in the more recent strata.

Most of us are pleased with our results, and Bellidore is particularly elated. He says that finding five nearly intact artifacts makes the expedition an unqualified success.

All the others have worked tirelessly since our arrival. Now it is almost time for me to perform my special function, and I am very excited. I know that my findings will be no more important that the others', but perhaps, when we put them all together, we can finally begin to understand what it was that made Man what he was.

"Are you ..." asked the first Stardust Twin.

"... ready?" said the second.

I answered that I was ready, that indeed I had been anxious for this moment.

"May we ..."

"... observe?" they asked.

"If you do not find it distasteful," I replied.

"We are ..."

"... scientists," they said. "There is ..."

"... very little ..."

"... that we cannot view ..."

"... objectively."

I ambulated to the table upon which the artifact rested. It was a stone, or at least that is what it appeared to be to my exterior sensory organs. It was triangular, and the edges showed signs of work.

"How old is this?" I asked.

"Three million ..."

"... five hundred and sixty-one thousand ..."

"... eight hundred and twelve years," answered the Stardust Twins.

"I see," I said.

"It is much ..."

"... the oldest ..."

"... of our finds."

I stared at it for a long time, preparing myself. Then I slowly, carefully, altered my structure and allowed my body to flow over and around the stone, engulfing it, and assimilating its history. I began to feel a delicious warmth as it became one with me, and while all my exterior senses had shut down, I knew that I was undulating and glowing with the thrill of discovery. I became one with the stone, and in that corner of my mind that is set aside for Feeling, I seemed to sense the Earth's moon looming low and ominous just above the horizon …

Enkatai awoke with a start just after dawn and looked up at the moon, which was still high in the sky. After all these weeks it still seemed far too large to hang suspended in the sky, and must surely crash down onto the planet any moment. The nightmare was still strong in her mind, and she tried to imagine the comforting sight of five small, unthreatening moons leapfrogging across the silver sky of her own world. She was able to hold the vision in her mind's eye for only a moment, and then it was lost, replaced by the reality of the huge satellite above her.

Her companion approached her.

"Another dream?" he asked.

"Exactly like the last one," she said uncomfortably. "The moon is visible in the daylight, and then we begin walking down the path …"

He stared at her with sympathy and offered her nourishment. She accepted it gratefully, and looked off across the veldt.

"Just two more days," she sighed, "and then we can leave this awful place."

"It is not such a terrible world," replied Bokatu. "It has many good qualities."

"We have wasted our time here," she said. "It is not fit for colonization."

"No, it is not," he agreed. "Our crops cannot thrive in this soil, and we have problems with the water. But we have learned many things, things that will eventually help us choose the proper world."

"We learned most of them the first week we were here," said Enkatai. "The rest of the time was wasted."

"The ship had other worlds to explore. They could not know we would be able to analyze this one in such a short time."

She shivered in the cool morning air. "I hate this place."

"It will someday be a fine world," said Bokatu. "It awaits only the evolution of the brown monkeys."

Even as he spoke, an enormous baboon, some 350 pounds in weight, heavily muscled, with a shaggy chest and bold, curious eyes, appeared in the distance. Even walking on all fours it was a formidable figure, fully twice as large as the great spotted cats.

"*We* cannot use this world," continued Bokatu, "but someday *his* descendants will spread across it."

"They seem so placid," commented Enkatai.

"They *are* placid," agreed Bokatu, hurling a piece of food at the baboon, which raced forward and picked it up off the ground. It sniffed at it, seemed to consider whether or not to taste it, and finally, after a moment of indecision, put it in its mouth. "But they will dominate this planet. The huge grass-eaters spend too much time feeding, and the predators sleep all the time. No, my choice is the brown monkey. They are fine, strong, intelligent animals. They have already developed thumbs, they possess a strong sense of community, and even the great cats think twice about attacking them. They are virtually without natural predators." He nodded his head, agreeing with himself. "Yes, it is they who will dominate this world in the eons to come."

"No predators?" said Enkatai.

"Oh, I suppose one falls prey to the great cats now and then, but even the cats do not attack when they are with their troop." He looked at the baboon. "That fellow has the strength to tear all but the biggest cat to pieces."

"Then how do you account for what we found at the bottom of the gorge?" she persisted.

"Their size has cost them some degree of agility. It is only natural that one occasionally falls down the slopes to its death."

"Occasionally?" she repeated. "I found seven skulls, each shattered as if from a blow."

"The force of the fall," said Bokatu with a shrug. "Surely you don't think the great cats brained them before killing them?"

"I wasn't thinking of the cats," she replied.

"What, then?"

"The small, tailless monkeys that live in the gorge."

Bokatu allowed himself the luxury of a superior smile. "Have you *looked* at them?" he said. "They are scarcely a quarter the size of the brown monkeys."

"I *have* looked at them," answered Enkatai. "And they, too, have thumbs."

"Thumbs alone are not enough," said Bokatu.

"They live in the shadow of the brown monkeys, and they are still here," she said. "*That* is enough."

"The brown monkeys are eaters of fruits and leaves. Why should they bother the tailless monkeys?"

"They do more than not bother them," said Enkatai. "They avoid them. That hardly seems like a species that will someday spread across the world."

Bokatu shook his head. "The tailless monkeys seem to be at an evolutionary dead end. Too small to hunt game, too large to feed themselves on what they can find in the gorge, too weak to compete with the brown monkeys for better territory. My guess is that they're an earlier, more primitive species, destined for extinction."

"Perhaps," said Enkatai.

"You disagree?"

"There is something about them …"

"What?"

Enkatai shrugged. "I do not know. They make me uneasy. It is something in their eyes, I think—a hint of malevolence."

"You are imagining things," said Bokatu.

"Perhaps," replied Enkatai again.

"I have reports to write today," said Bokatu. "But tomorrow I will prove it to you."

The next morning Bokatu was up with the sun. He prepared their first meal of the day while Enkatai completed her prayers, then performed his own while she ate.

"Now," he announced, "we will go down into the gorge and capture one of the tailless monkeys."

"Why?"

"To show you how easy it is. I may take it back with me as a pet. Or perhaps we shall sacrifice it in the lab and learn more about its life processes."

"I do not *want* a pet, and we are not authorized to kill any animals."

"As you wish," said Bokatu. "We will let it go."

"Then why capture one to begin with?"

"To show you that they are not intelligent, for if they are as bright as you think, I will not be able to capture one." He pulled her to an upright position. "Let us begin."

"This is foolish," she protested. "The ship arrives in midafternoon. Why don't we just wait for it?"

"We will be back in time," he replied confidently. "How long can it take?"

She looked at the clear blue sky, as if trying to urge the ship to appear. The moon was hanging, huge and white, just above the horizon. Finally she turned to him.

"All right, I will come with you—but only if you promise merely to observe them, and not to try to capture one."

"Then you admit I'm right?"

"Saying that you are right or wrong has nothing to do with the truth of the situation. I *hope* you are right, for the tailless monkeys frighten me. But I do not know you are right, and neither do you."

Bokatu stared at her for a long moment.

"I agree," he said at last.

"You agree that you cannot know?"

"I agree not to capture one," he said. "Let us proceed."

They walked to the edge of the gorge and then began climbing down the steep embankments, steadying themselves by wrapping their limbs around trees and other outgrowths. Suddenly they heard a loud screeching.

"What is that?" asked Bokatu.

"They have seen us," replied Enkatai.

"What makes you think so?"

"I have heard that scream in my dream—and always the moon was just as it appears now."

"Strange," mused Bokatu. "I have heard them many times before, but somehow they seem louder this time."

"Perhaps more of them are here."

"Or perhaps they are more frightened," he said. He glanced above him. "Here is the reason," he said, pointing. "We have company."

She looked up and saw a huge baboon, quite the largest she had yet seen, following them at a distance of perhaps fifty feet. When its eyes met hers it growled and looked away, but made no attempt to move any closer or farther away.

They kept climbing, and whenever they stopped to rest, there was the baboon, its accustomed fifty feet away from them.

"Does *he* look afraid to you?" asked Bokatu. "If these puny little creatures could harm him, would he be following us down into the gorge?"

"There is a thin line between courage and foolishness, and an even thinner line between confidence and overconfidence," replied Enkatai.

"If he is to die here, it will be like all the others," said Bokatu. "He will lose his footing and fall to his death."

"You do not find it unusual that every one of them fell on its head?" she asked mildly.

"They broke every bone in their bodies," he replied. "I don't know why you consider only the heads."

"Because you do not get identical head wounds from different incidents."

"You have an overactive imagination," said Bokatu. He pointed to a small hairy figure that was staring up at them. "Does *that* look like something that could kill our friend here?"

The baboon glared down into the gorge and snarled. The tailless monkey looked up with no show of fear or even interest. Finally it shuffled off into the thick bush.

"You see?" said Bokatu smugly. "One look at the brown monkey and it retreats out of sight."

"It didn't seem frightened to me," noted Enkatai.

"All the more reason to doubt its intelligence."

In another few minutes they reached the spot where the tailless monkey had been. They paused to regain their strength, and then continued to the floor of the gorge.

"Nothing," announced Bokatu, looking around. "My guess is that the one we saw was a sentry, and by now the whole tribe is miles away."

"Observe our companion."

The baboon had reached the floor of the gorge and was tensely testing the wind.

"He hasn't crossed over the evolutionary barrier yet," said Bokatu, amused. "Do you expect him to search for predators with a sensor?"

"No," said Enkatai, watching the baboon. "But if there is no danger, I expect him to relax, and he hasn't done that yet."

"That's probably how he lived long enough to grow this large," said Bokatu, dismissing her remarks. He looked around. "What could they possibly find to eat here?"

"I don't know."

"Perhaps we should capture one and dissect it. The contents of its stomach might tell us a lot about it."

"You promised."

"It would be so simple, though," he persisted. "All we'd have to do would be bait a trap with fruits or nuts."

Suddenly the baboon snarled, and Bokatu and Enkatai turned to locate the source of his anger. There was nothing there, but the baboon became more and more frenzied. Finally it raced back up the gorge.

"What was that all about, I wonder?" mused Bokatu.

"I think we should leave."

"We have half a day before the ship returns."

"I am uneasy here. I walked down a path exactly like this in my dream."

"You are not used to the sunlight," he said. "We will rest inside a cave."

She reluctantly allowed him to lead her to a small cave in the wall of the gorge. Suddenly she stopped and would go no further.

"What is the matter?"

"This cave was in my dream," she said. "Do not go into it."

"You must learn not to let dreams rule your life," said Bokatu. He sniffed the air. "Something smells strange."

"Let us go back. We want nothing to do with this place."

He stuck his head into the cave. "New world, new odors."

"Please, Bokatu!"

"Let me just see what causes that odor," he said, shining his light into the cave. It illuminated a huge pile of bodies, many of them half-eaten, most in various states of decomposition.

"What are they?" he asked, stepping closer.

"Brown monkeys," she replied without looking. "Each with its head staved in."

"This was part of your dream, too?" he asked, suddenly nervous.

She nodded her head. "We must leave this place *now*!"

He walked to the mouth of the cave.

"It seems safe," he announced.

"It is never safe in my dream," she said uneasily.

They left the cave and walked about fifty yards when they came to a bend in the floor of the gorge. As they followed it, they found themselves facing a tailless monkey.

"One of them seems to have stayed behind," said Bokatu. "I'll frighten him away." He picked up a rock and threw it at the monkey, which ducked but held its ground.

Enkatai touched him urgently on the shoulder. "More than one," she said.

He looked up. Two more tailless monkeys were in a tree almost directly overhead. As he stepped aside, he saw four more lumbering toward them out of the bush. Another emerged from a cave, and three more dropped out of nearby trees.

"What have they got in their hands?" he asked nervously.

"You would call them the femur bones of grass-eaters," said Enkatai, with a sick feeling in her thorax. "*They* would call them weapons."

The hairless monkeys spread out in a semicircle, then began approaching them slowly.

"But they're so *puny*!" said Bokatu, backing up until he came to a wall of rock and could go no farther.

"You are a fool," said Enkatai, helplessly trapped in the reality of her dream. "*This* is the race that will dominate this planet. Look into their eyes!"

Bokatu looked, and he saw things, terrifying things, that he had never seen in any being or any animal before. He barely had time to offer a brief prayer for some disaster to befall this race before it could reach the stars, and then a tailless monkey hurled a smooth, polished, triangular stone at his head. It dazed him, and as he fell to the ground, the clubs began pounding down rhythmically on him and Enkatai.

At the top of the gorge, the baboon watched the carnage until it was over, and then raced off toward the vast savannah, where he would be safe, at least temporarily, from the tailless monkeys.

"A weapon," I mused. "It was a *weapon*!"

I was all alone. Sometime during the Feeling, the Stardust Twins had decided that I was one of the few things they could not be objective about, and had returned to their quarters.

I waited until the excitement of discovery had diminished enough for me to control my physical structure. Then I once again took the shape that I presented to my companions, and reported my findings to Bellidore.

"So even then they were aggressors," he said. "Well, it is not surprising. The will to dominate the stars had to have come from somewhere."

"It is surprising that there is no record of any race having landed here in their prehistory," said the Historian.

"It was a survey team, and Earth was of no use to them," I answered. "They doubtless touched down on any number of planets. If there is a record anywhere, it is probably in their archives, stating that Earth showed no promise as a colony world."

"But didn't they wonder what had happened to their team?" asked Bellidore.

"There were many large carnivores in the vicinity," I said. "They probably assumed the team had fallen prey to them. Especially if they searched the area and found nothing."

"Interesting," said Bellidore. "That the weaker of the species should have risen to dominance."

"I think it is easily explained," said the Historian. "*As* the smaller species, they were neither as fast as their prey nor as strong as their predators, so the creation of weapons was perhaps the only way to avoid extinction ... or at least the best way."

"Certainly they displayed the cunning of the predator during their millennia abroad in the galaxy," said Bellidore.

"One does not *stop* being aggressive simply because one invents a weapon," said the Historian. "In fact, it may *add* to one's aggression."

"I shall have to consider that," said Bellidore, looking somewhat unconvinced.

"I have perhaps oversimplified my train of thought for the sake of this discussion," replied the Historian. "Rest assured that I will build a lengthy and rigorous argument when I present my findings to the Academy."

"And what of you, He Who Views?" asked Bellidore. "Have you any observations to add to what you have told us?"

"It is difficult to think of a rock as being the precursor of the sonic rifle and the molecular imploder," I said thoughtfully, "but I believe it to be the case."

"A most interesting species," said Bellidore.

It took almost four hours for my strength to return, for Feeling saps the energy like no other function, drawing equally from the body, the emotions, the mind, and the empathic powers.

The Moriteu, its work done for the day, was hanging upside down from a tree limb, lost in its evening trance, and the Stardust Twins had not made an appearance since I had Felt the stone.

The other party members were busy with their own pursuits, and it seemed an ideal time for me to Feel the next object, which the Historian told me was approximately 23,300 years old.

It was a link of metallic chain, rusted and pitted, and before I assimilated it, I thought I could see a spot where it had been deliberately broken …

His name was Mtepwa, and it seemed to him that he had been wearing a metal collar around his neck since the day he had been born. He knew that couldn't be true, for he had fleeting memories of playing with his brothers and sisters, and of stalking the kudu and the bongo on the tree-covered mountain where he grew up.

But the more he concentrated on those memories, the more vague and imprecise they became, and he knew they must have happened a very long time ago. Sometimes he tried to remember the name of his tribe, but it was lost in the mists of time, as were the names of his parents and siblings.

It was at times like this that Mtepwa felt sorry for himself, but then he would consider his companions' situation, and he felt better, for while they were to be taken in ships and sent to the edge of the world to spend the remainder of their lives as slaves of the Arabs and the Europeans, he himself was the favored servant of his master, Sharif Abdullah, and as such his position was assured.

This was his eighth caravan—or was it his ninth?—from the Interior. They would trade salt and cartridges to the tribal chiefs who would in turn sell them their least productive warriors and women as slaves, and then they would march them out, around the huge lake and across the dry flat savannah. They would circle the mountain that was so old that it had turned white on the top, just like a white-haired old man, and finally out to the coast, where dhows filled the harbor. There they would sell their human booty to the highest bidders, and Sharif Abdullah would purchase another wife and turn half the money over to his aged, feeble father, and they would be off to the Interior again on another quest for black gold.

Abdullah was a good master. He rarely drank—and when he did, he always apologized to Allah at the next opportunity—and he did not beat Mtepwa overly much, and they always had enough to eat, even when the cargo went hungry. He even went so far as to teach Mtepwa how to read, although the only reading matter he carried with him was the Koran.

Mtepwa spent long hours honing his reading skills with the Koran, and somewhere along the way he made a most interesting discovery: the Koran forbade a practitioner of the True Faith to keep another member in bondage.

It was at that moment that Mtepwa made up his mind to convert to Islam. He began questioning Sharif Abdullah incessantly on the finer points of his religion, and made sure that the old man saw him sitting by the fire, hour after hour, reading the Koran.

So enthused was Sharif Abdullah at this development that he frequently invited Mtepwa into his tent at suppertime, and lectured him on the subtleties of the Koran far into the night. Mtepwa was a motivated student, and Sharif Abdullah marveled at his enthusiasm.

Night after night, as lions prowled around their camp in the Serengeti, master and pupil studied the Koran together. And finally the day came when Sharif Abdullah could not longer deny that Mtepwa was indeed a true believer of Islam. It happened as they camped at the Olduvai Gorge, and that very day Sharif Abdullah had his smith remove the collar from Mtepwa's neck, and Mtepwa himself destroyed the chains link by link, hurling them deep into the gorge when he was finished. He kept a single link, which he wore around his neck as a charm.

Mtepwa was now a free man, but knowledgeable in only two areas: the Koran, and slave-trading. So it was only natural that when he looked around for some means to support himself, he settled upon following in Sharif Abdullah's footsteps. He became a junior partner to the old man, and after two more trips to the Interior, he decided that he was ready to go out on his own.

To do that, he required a trained staff—warriors, smiths, cooks, trackers—and the prospect of assembling one from scratch was daunting, so, since his faith was less strong than his mentor's, he simply sneaked into Sharif Abdullah's quarters on the coast one night and slit the old man's throat.

The next day, he marched inland at the head of his own caravan.

He had learned much about the business of slaving, both as a practitioner and a victim, and he put his knowledge to full use. He knew that healthy slaves would bring a better price at market, and so he fed and treated his captives far better than Sharif Abdullah and most other slavers did. On the other hand, he knew which ones were fomenting trouble, and knew it was better to kill them on the spot as an example to the others, than to let any hopes of insurrection spread among the captives.

Because he was thorough, he was equally successful, and soon expanded into ivory trading as well. Within six years he had the biggest slaving and poaching operation in East Africa.

From time to time he ran across European explorers. It was said that he even spent a week with Dr. David Livingstone and left without the missionary ever knowing that he had been playing host to the slaver he most wanted to put out of business.

After America's War Between the States killed his primary market, he took a year off from his operation to go to Asia and the Arabian Peninsula and open up new ones. Upon returning he found that Abdullah's son, Sharif Ibn Jad Mahir, had appropriated all his men and headed inland, intent on carrying on his father's business. Mtepwa, who had become quite wealthy, hired some 500 *askari*, placed them under the command of the notorious ivory poacher Alfred Henry Pym, and sat back to await the results.

Three months later Pym marched some 438 men back to the Tanganyikan coast—276 were slaves that Sharif Ibn Jad Mahir had captured; the remainder were the remnants of Mtepwa's organization, who had gone to work for Sharif Ibn Jad Mahir. Mtepwa sold all 438 of them into slavery and built a new organization, composed of the warriors who had fought for him under Pym's leadership.

Most of the colonial powers were inclined to turn a blind eye to his practices, but the British, who were determined to put an end to slavery, issued a warrant for Mtepwa's arrest. Eventually he tired of continually looking over his shoulder, and moved his headquarters to Mozambique, where the Portuguese were happy to let him set up shop as long as he remembered that colonial palms needed constant greasing.

He was never happy there—he didn't speak Portuguese or any of the local languages—and after nine years he returned to Tanganyika, now the wealthiest black man on the continent.

One day he found among his latest batch of captives a young Acholi boy named Haradi, no more than ten years old, and decided to keep him as a personal servant rather than ship him across the ocean.

Mtepwa had never married. Most of his associates assumed that he had simply never had the time, but as the almost-nightly demands for Haradi to visit him in his tent became common knowledge, they soon revised their opinions. Mtepwa seemed besotted with his servant boy, though—doubtless remembering his own experience—he never taught Haradi to read, and promised a slow and painful death to anyone who spoke of Islam to the boy.

Then one night, after some three years had passed, Mtepwa sent for Haradi. The boy was nowhere to be found. Mtepwa awoke all his warriors and demanded that they search for him, for a leopard had been seen in the vicinity of the camp, and the slaver feared the worst.

They found Haradi an hour later, not in the jaws of a leopard, but in the arms of a young female slave they had taken from the Zaneke tribe. Mtepwa was beside himself with rage, and had the poor girl's arms and legs torn from her body.

Haradi never offered a word of protest, and never tried to defend the girl—not that it would have done any good—but the next morning he was gone, and though Mtepwa and his warriors spent almost a month searching for him, they found no trace of him.

By the end of the month Mtepwa was quite insane with rage and grief. Deciding that life was no longer worth living, he walked up to a pride of lions that were gorging themselves on a topi carcass and, striding into their midst, began cursing them and hitting them with his bare hands. Almost unbelievably, the lions backed away from him, snarling and growling, and disappeared into the thick bush.

The next day he picked up a large stick and began beating a baby elephant with it. That should have precipitated a brutal attack by its mother—but the mother, standing only a few feet away, trumpeted in terror and raced off, the baby following her as best it could.

It was then that Mtepwa decided that he could not die, that somehow the act of dismembering the poor Zanake girl had made him immortal. Since both incidents had occurred within sight of his superstitious followers, they fervently believed him.

Now that he was immortal, he decided that it was time to stop trying to accommodate the Europeans who had invaded his land and kept issuing warrants for his arrest. He sent a runner to the Kenya border and invited the British to meet him in battle. When the appointed day came, and the British did not show up to fight him, he confidently told his warriors that word of his immortality had reached the Europeans and that from that day forth no white men would ever be willing to oppose him. The fact that he was still in German territory, and the British had no legal right to go there, somehow managed to elude him.

He began marching his warriors inland, openly in search of slaves, and he found his share of them in the Congo. He looted villages of their men, their women, and their ivory, and finally, with almost 600 captives and half that many tusks, he finally turned east and began the months-long trek to the coast.

This time the British were waiting for him at the Uganda border, and they had so many armed men there that Mtepwa turned south, not for fear for his own life, but because he could not afford to lose his slaves and his ivory, and he knew that his warriors lacked his invulnerability.

He marched his army down to Lake Tanganyika, then headed east. It took him two weeks to reach the western corridor of the Serengeti, and another ten days to cross it.

One night he made camp at the lip of the Olduvai Gorge, the very place where he had gained his freedom. The fires were lit, a wildebeest was slaughtered and cooked, and as he relaxed after the meal he became aware of a buzzing among his men. Then, from out of the shadows, stepped a strangely familiar figure. It was Haradi, now fifteen years old, and as tall as Mtepwa himself.

Mtepwa stared at him for a long moment, and suddenly all the anger seemed to drain from his face.

"I am very glad to see you again, Haradi," he said.

"I have heard that you cannot be killed," answered the boy, brandishing a spear. "I have come to see if that is true."

"We have no need to fight, you and I," said Mtepwa. "Join me in my tent, and all will be as it was."

"Once I tear your limbs from your body, *then* we will have no reason to fight," responded Haradi. "And even then, you will seem no less repulsive to me than you do now, or than you did all those many years ago."

Mtepwa jumped up, his face a mask of fury. "Do your worst, then!" he cried. "And when you realize that I cannot be harmed, I will do to you as I did to the Zanake girl!"

Haradi made no reply, but hurled his spear at Mtepwa. It went into the slaver's body, and was thrown with such force that the point emerged a good six inches on the other side. Mtepwa stared at Haradi with disbelief, moaned once, and tumbled down the rocky slopes of the gorge.

Haradi looked around at the warriors. "Is there any among you who dispute my right to take Mtepwa's place?" he asked confidently.

A burly Makonde stood up to challenge him, and within thirty seconds Haradi, too, was dead.

The British were waiting for them when they reached Zanzibar. The slaves were freed, the ivory confiscated, the warriors arrested and forced to serve as laborers on the Mombasa/Uganda Railway. Two of them were later killed and eaten by lions in the Tsavo District.

By the time Lieutenant-Colonel J. H. Patterson shot the notorious Man-Eaters of Tsavo, the railway had almost reached the shanty town of Nairobi, and Mtepwa's name was so thoroughly forgotten that it was misspelled in the only history book in which it appeared.

"Amazing!" said the Appraiser. "I knew they enslaved many races throughout the galaxy—but to enslave *themselves*! It is almost beyond belief!"

I had rested from my efforts, and then related the story of Mtepwa.

"All ideas must begin somewhere," said Bellidore placidly. "This one obviously began on Earth."

"It is barbaric!" muttered the Appraiser.

Bellidore turned to me. "Man never attempted to subjugate *your* race, He Who Views. Why was that?"

"We had nothing that he wanted."

"Can you remember the galaxy when Man dominated it?" asked the Appraiser.

"I can remember the galaxy when Man's progenitors killed Bokatu and Enkatai," I replied truthfully.

"Did you ever have any dealings with Man?"

"None. Man had no use for us."

"But did he not destroy profligately things for which he had no use?"

"No," I said. "He took what he wanted, and he destroyed that which threatened him. The rest he ignored."

"Such arrogance!"

"Such practicality," said Bellidore.

"You call genocide on a galactic scale *practical*?" demanded the Appraiser.

"From Man's point of view, it was," answered Bellidore. "It got him what he wanted with a minimum of risk and effort. Consider that one single race, born not five hundred yards from us, at one time ruled an empire of more than a million worlds. Almost every civilized race in the galaxy spoke Terran."

"Upon pain of death."

"That is true," agreed Bellidore. "I did not say Man was an angel. Only that, if he was indeed a devil, he was an efficient one."

It was time for me to assimilate the third artifact, which the Historian and the Appraiser seemed to think was the handle of a knife, but even as I moved off to perform my function, I could not help but listen to the speculation that was taking place.

"Given his bloodlust and his efficiency," said the Appraiser, "I'm surprised that he lived long enough to reach the stars."

"It *is* surprising in a way," agreed Bellidore. "The Historian tells me that Man was not always homogenous, that early in his history there were several variations of the species. He was divided by color, by belief, by territory." He sighed. "Still, he must have learned to live in peace with his fellow man. That much, at least, accrues to his credit."

I reached the artifact with Bellidore's words still in my ears, and began to engulf it …

Mary Leakey pressed against the horn of the Land Rover. Inside the museum, her husband turned to the young uniformed officer.

"I can't think of any instructions to give you," he said. "The museum's not open to the public yet, and we're a good 300 kilometers from Kikuyuland."

"I'm just following my orders, Dr. Leakey," replied the officer.

"Well, I suppose it doesn't hurt to be safe," acknowledged Leakey. "There are a lot of Kikuyu who want me dead even though I spoke up for Kenyatta at his trial." He walked to the door. "If the discoveries at Lake Turkana prove interesting, we could be gone as long as a month. Otherwise, we should be back within ten to twelve days."

"No problem, sir. The museum will still be here when you get back."

"I never doubted it," said Leakey, walking out and joining his wife in the vehicle.

Lieutenant Ian Chelmswood stood in the doorway and watched the Leakeys, accompanied by two military vehicles, start down the red dirt road. Within seconds the car was obscured by dust, and he stepped back into the building and closed the door to avoid being covered by it. The heat was oppressive, and he removed his jacket and holster and laid them neatly across one of the small display cases.

It was strange. All the images he had seen of African wildlife, from the German Schillings' old still photographs to the American Johnson's motion pictures, had led him to believe that East Africa was a wonderland of green grass and clear water. No one had ever mentioned the dust, but that was the one memory of it that he would take home with him.

Well, not quite the only one. He would never forget the morning the alarm had sounded back when he was stationed in Nanyuki. He arrived at the settlers' farm and found the entire family cut to ribbons and all their cattle mutilated, most with their genitals cut off, many missing ears and eyes. But as horrible as that was, the picture he would carry to his grave was the kitten impaled on a dagger and pinned to the mailbox. It was the Mau Mau's signature, just in case anyone thought some madman had run berserk among the cattle and the humans.

Chelmswood didn't understand the politics of it. He didn't know who had started it, who had precipitated the war. It made no difference to him. He was just a soldier, following orders, and if those orders would take him back to Nanyuki so that he could kill the men who had committed those atrocities, so much the better.

But in the meantime, he had pulled what he considered Idiot Duty. There had been a very mild outburst of violence in Arusha, not really Mau Mau but rather a show of support for Kenya's Kikuyu, and his unit had been transferred there. Then the government found out that Professor Leakey, whose scientific finds had made Olduvai Gorge almost a household word among East Africans, had been getting death threats. Over his objections, they had insisted on providing him with bodyguards. Most of the men from Chelmswood's unit would accompany Leakey on his trip to Lake Turkana, but someone had to stay behind to guard the museum, and it was just his bad luck that his name had been atop the duty roster.

It wasn't even a museum, really, not the kind of museum his parents had taken him to see in London. *Those* were museums; this was just a two-room mud-walled structure with perhaps a hundred of Leakey's finds. Ancient arrowheads, some oddly shaped stones that had functioned as prehistoric tools, a couple of bones that obviously weren't from monkeys but that Chelmswood was certain were not from any creature *he* was related to.

Leakey had hung some crudely drawn charts on the wall, charts that showed what he believed to be the evolution of some small, grotesque, apelike beasts into *homo sapiens*. There were photographs, too, showing some of the finds that had been sent on to Nairobi. It seemed that even if this gorge was the birthplace of the race, nobody really wanted to visit it. All the best finds were shipped back to Nairobi and then to the British Museum. In fact, this wasn't a museum at all, decided Chelmswood, but rather a holding area for the better specimens until they could be sent elsewhere.

It was strange to think of life starting here in this gorge. If there was an uglier spot in Africa, he had yet to come across it. And while he didn't accept Genesis or any of that religious nonsense, it bothered him to think that the first human beings to walk the Earth might have been black. He'd hardly had any exposure to blacks when he was growing up in the Cotswolds, but he'd seen enough of what they could do since coming to British East, and he was appalled by their savagery and barbarism.

And what about those crazy Americans, wringing their hands and saying that colonialism had to end? If they had seen what *he'd* seen on that farm in Nanyuki, they'd know that the only thing that was keeping all of East Africa from exploding into an unholy conflagration of blood and butchery was the British presence. Certainly, there were parallels between the Mau Mau and America: both had been colonized by the British and both wanted their independence … but there all similarity ended. The Americans wrote a Declaration outlining their grievances, and then they fielded an army and fought the British *soldiers*. What did chopping up innocent children and pinning cats to mailboxes have in common with that? If he had his way, he'd march in half a million British troops, wipe out every last Kikuyu—except for the good ones, the loyal ones—and solve the problem once and for all.

He wandered over to the cabinet where Leakey kept his beer and pulled out a warm bottle. Safari brand. He opened it and took a long swallow, then made a face. If that's what people drank on safari, he'd have to remember never to go on one.

And yet he knew that someday he *would* go on safari, hopefully before he was mustered out and sent home. Parts of the country were so damned beautiful, dust or no dust, and he liked the thought of sitting beneath a shade tree, cold drink in hand, while his body servant cooled him with a fan made of ostrich feathers and he and his white hunter discussed the day's kills and what they would go out after tomorrow. It wasn't the shooting that was important, they'd both reassure themselves, but rather the thrill of the hunt. Then he'd have a couple of his black boys draw his bath, and he'd bathe and prepare for dinner. Funny how he had fallen into the habit of calling them boys; most of them were far older than he.

But while they weren't boys, they *were* children in need of guidance and civilizing. Take those Maasai, for example; proud, arrogant bastards. They looked great on postcards, but try *dealing* with them. They acted as if they had a direct line to God, that He had told them they were His chosen people. The more Chelmswood thought about it, the more surprised he was that it was the Kikuyu that had begun Mau Mau rather than the Maasai. And come to think of it, he'd notice four or five Maasai *elmorani* hanging around the museum. He'd have to keep an eye on them …

"Excuse, please?" said a high-pitched voice, and Chelmswood turned to see a small skinny black boy, no more than ten years old, standing in the doorway.

"What do you want?" he asked.

"Doctor Mister Leakey, he promise me candy," said the boy, stepping inside the building.

"Go away," said Chelmswood irritably. "We don't have any candy here."

"Yes yes," said the boy, stepping forward. "Every day."

"He gives you candy every day?"

The boy nodded his head and smiled.

"Where does he keep it?"

The boy shrugged. "Maybe in there?" he said, pointing to a cabinet.

Chelmswood walked to the cabinet and opened it. There was nothing in it but four jars containing primitive teeth.

"I don't see any," he said. "You'll have to wait until Dr. Leakey comes back."

Two tears trickled down the boy's cheek. "But Doctor Mister Leakey, he *promise*!"

Chelmswood looked around. "I don't know where it is."

The boy began crying in earnest.

"Be quiet!" snapped Chelmswood. "I'll look for it."

"Maybe next room," suggested the boy.

"Come along," said Chelmswood, walking through the doorway to the adjoining room. He looked around, hands on hips, trying to imagine where Leakey had hidden the candy.

"This place maybe," said the boy, pointing to a closet.

Chelmswood opened the closet. It contained two spades, three picks, and an assortment of small brushes, all of which he assumed were used by the Leakeys for their work.

"Nothing here," he said, closing the door.

He turned to face the boy, but found the room empty.

"Little bugger was lying all along," he muttered. "Probably ran away to save himself a beating."

He walked back into the main room—and found himself facing a well-built black man holding a machete-like *panga* in his right hand.

"What's going on here?" snapped Chelmswood.

"Freedom is going on here, Lieutenant," said the black man in near-perfect English. "I was sent to kill Dr. Leakey, but you will have to do."

"Why are you killing anyone?" demanded Chelmswood. "What did we ever do to the Maasai?"

"I will let the Maasai answer that. Any one of them could take one look at me and tell you than I am Kikuyu—but we are all the same to you British, aren't we?"

Chelmswood reached for his gun and suddenly realized he had left it on a display case.

"You all look like cowardly savages to me!"

"Why? Because we do not meet you in battle?" The black man's face filled with fury. "You take our land away, you forbid us to own weapons, you even make it a crime for us to carry spears—and then you call us savages when we don't march in formation against your guns!" He spat contemptuously on the floor. "We fight you in the only way that is left to us."

"It's a big country, big enough for both races," said Chelmswood.

"If we came to England and took away your best farmland and forced you to work for us, would you think England was big enough for both races?"

"I'm not political," said Chelmswood, edging another step closer to his weapon. "I'm just doing my job."

"And your job is to keep two hundred whites on land that once held a million Kikuyu," said the black man, his face reflecting his hatred.

"There'll be a lot less than a million when *we* get through with you!" hissed Chelmswood, diving for his gun.

Quick as he was, the black man was faster, and with a single swipe of his *panga* he almost severed the Englishman's right hand from his wrist. Chelmswood bellowed in pain, and spun around, presenting his back to the Kikuyu as he reached for the pistol with his other hand.

The *panga* came down again, practically splitting him open, but as he fell he managed to get his fingers around the handle of his pistol and pull the trigger. The bullet struck the black man in the chest, and he, too, collapsed to the floor.

"You've killed me!" moaned Chelmswood. "Why would anyone want to kill me?"

"You have so much and we have so little," whispered the black man. "Why must you have what is ours, too?"

"What did I ever do to you?" asked Chelmswood.

"You came here. That was enough," said the black man. "Filthy English!" He closed his eyes and lay still.

"Bloody nigger!" slurred Chelmswood, and died.

Outside, the four Maasai paid no attention to the tumult within. They let the small Kikuyu boy leave without giving him so much as a glance. The business of inferior races was none of their concern.

"These notions of superiority among members of the same race are very difficult to comprehend," said Bellidore. "Are you *sure* you read the artifact properly, He Who Views?"

"I do not *read* artifacts," I replied. "I *assimilate* them. I become one with them. Everything *they* have experienced, *I* experience." I paused. "There can be no mistake."

"Well, it is difficult to fathom, especially in a species that would one day control most of the galaxy. Did they think *every* race they met was inferior to them?"

"They certainly behaved as if they did," said the Historian. "They seemed to respect only those races that stood up to them—and even then they felt that militarily defeating them was proof of their superiority."

"And yet we know from ancient records that primitive man worshipped non-sentient animals," put in the Exobiologist.

"They must not have survived for any great length of time," suggested the Historian. "If Man treated the races of the galaxy with contempt, how much worse must he have treated the poor creatures with whom he shared his home world?"

"Perhaps he viewed them much the same as he viewed my own race," I offered. "If they had nothing he wanted, if they presented no threat …"

"They would have had something he wanted," said the Exobiologist. "He was a predator. They would have had meat."

"And land," added the Historian. "If even the galaxy was not enough to quench Man's thirst for territory, think how unwilling he would have been to share his own world."

"It is a question I suspect will never be answered," said Bellidore.

"Unless the answer lies in one of the remaining artifacts," agreed the Exobiologist.

I'm sure the remark was not meant to jar me from my lethargy, but it occurred to me that it had been half a day since I had assimilated the knife handle, and I had regained enough of my strength to examine the next artifact.

It was a metal stylus …

February 15, 2103:

Well, we finally got here! The Supermole got us through the tunnel from New York to London in just over four hours. Even so we were twenty minutes late, missed our connection, and had to wait another five hours for the next flight to Khartoum. From there our means of transport got increasingly more primitive—jet planes to Nairobi and Arusha—and then a quick shuttle to our campsite, but we've finally put civilization behind us. I've never seen open spaces like this before; you're barely aware of the skyscrapers of Nyerere, the closest town.

After an orientation speech telling us what to expect and how to behave on safari, we got the afternoon off to meet our traveling companions. I'm the youngest member of the group: a trip like this just costs too much for most people my age to afford. Of course, most people my age don't have an Uncle Reuben who dies and leaves them a ton of money. (Well, it's probably about eight ounces of money, now that the safari is paid for. Ha ha.)

The lodge is quite rustic. They have quaint microwaves for warming our food, although most of us will be eating at the restaurants. I understand the Japanese and Brazilian ones are the most popular, the former for the food—real fish—and the latter for the entertainment. My roommate is Mr. Shiboni, an elderly Japanese gentleman who tells me he has been saving his money for fifteen years to come on this safari. He seems pleasant and good-natured; I hope he can survive the rigors of the trip.

I had really wanted a shower, just to get in the spirit of things, but water is scarce here, and it looks like I'll have to settle for the same old chemical dryshower. I know, I know, it disinfects as well as cleanses, but if I wanted all the comforts of home, I'd have stayed home and saved $150,000.

February 16:

We met our guide today. I don't know why, but he doesn't quite fit my preconception of an African safari guide. I was expecting some grizzled old veteran who had a wealth of stories to tell, who had maybe even seen a civet cat or a duiker before they became extinct. What we got was Kevin Ole Tambake, a young Maasai who can't be 25 years old and dresses in a suit while we all wear our khakis. Still, he's lived here all his life, so I suppose he knows his way around.

And I'll give him this: he's a wonderful storyteller. He spent half an hour telling us myths about how his people used to live in huts called manyattas, *and how their rite of passage to manhood was to kill a lion with a spear. As if the government would let anyone kill an animal!*

We spent the morning driving down into the Ngorongoro Crater. It's a collapsed caldera, *or volcano, that was once taller than Kilimanjaro itself. Kevin says it used to teem with game, though I can't see how, since any game standing atop it when it collapsed would have been instantly killed.*

I think the real reason we went there was just to get the kinks out of our safari vehicle and learn the proper protocol. Probably just as well. The air-conditioning wasn't working right in two of the compartments, the service mechanism couldn't get the temperature right on the iced drinks, and once, when we thought we saw a bird, three of us buzzed Kevin at the same time and jammed his communication line.

In the afternoon we went out to Serengeti. Kevin says it used to extend all the way to the Kenya border, but now it's just a 20-square-mile park adjacent to the Crater. About an hour into the game run we saw a ground squirrel, but he disappeared into a hole before I could adjust my holo camera. Still, he was very impressive. Varying shares of brown, with dark eyes and a fluffy tail. Kevin estimated that he went almost three pounds, and says he hasn't seen one that big since he was a boy.

Just before we returned to camp, Kevin got word on the radio from another driver that they had spotted two starlings nesting in a tree about eight miles north and east of us. The vehicle's computer told us we wouldn't be able to reach it before dark, so Kevin had it lock the spot in its memory and promised us that we'd go there first thing in the morning.

I opted for the Brazilian restaurant, and spent a few pleasant hours listening to the live band. A very nice end to the first full day of safari.

February 17:

We left at dawn in search of the starlings, and though we found the tree where they had been spotted, we never did see them. One of the passengers—I think it was the little man from Burma, though I'm not sure—must have complained, because Kevin soon announced to the entire party that this was a safari, *that there was no guarantee of seeing any particular bird or animal, and that while he would do his best for us, one could never be certain where the game might be.*

And then, just as he was talking, a banded mongoose almost a foot long appeared out of nowhere. It seemed to pay no attention to us, and Kevin announced that we were killing the motor and going into hover mode so the noise wouldn't scare it away.

After a minute or two everyone on the right side of the vehicle had gotten their holographs, and we slowly spun on our axis so that the left side could see him—but the movement must have scared him off, because though the maneuver took less than thirty seconds, he was nowhere to be seen when we came to rest again.

Kevin announced that the vehicle had captured the mongoose on its automated holos, and copies would be made available to anyone who had missed their holo opportunity.

We were feeling great—the right side of the vehicle, anyway—when we stopped for lunch, and during our afternoon game run we saw three yellow weaver birds building their spherical nests in a tree. Kevin let us out, warning us not to approach closer than thirty yards, and we spent almost an hour watching and holographing them.

All in all, a very satisfying day.

February 18:

Today we left camp about an hour after sunrise, and went to a new location: Olduvai Gorge.

Kevin announced that we would spend our last two days here, that with the encroachment of the cities and farms on all the flat land, the remaining big game was pretty much confined to the gulleys and slopes of the gorge.

No vehicle, not even our specially equipped one, was capable of navigating its way through the gorge, so we all got out and began walking in single file behind Kevin.

Most of us found it very difficult to keep up with Kevin. He clambered up and down the rocks as if he'd been doing it all his life, whereas I can't remember the last time I saw a stair that didn't move when I stood on it. We had trekked for perhaps half an hour when I heard one of the men at the back of our strung-out party give a cry and point to a spot at the bottom of the gorge, and we all looked and saw something racing away at phenomenal speed.

"Another squirrel?" I asked.

Kevin just smiled.

The man behind me said he thought it was a mongoose.

"What you saw," said Kevin, "was a dik-dik, the last surviving African antelope."

"How big was it?" asked a woman.

"About average size," said Kevin. "Perhaps ten inches at the shoulder."

Imagine anything ten inches high being called average!

Kevin explained that dik-diks were very territorial, and that this one wouldn't stray far from his home area. Which meant that if we were patient and quiet—and lucky—we'd be able to spot him again.

I asked Kevin how many dik-diks lived in the gorge, and he scratched his head and considered it for a moment and then guessed that there might be as many as ten. (And Yellowstone has only nineteen rabbits left! Is it any wonder that all the serious animal buffs come to Africa?)

We kept walking for another hour, and then broke for lunch, while Kevin gave us the history of the place, telling us all about Dr. Leakey's finds. There were probably still more skeletons to be dug up, he guessed, but the government didn't want to frighten any animals away from what had become their last refuge, so the bones would have to wait for some future generation to unearth them. Roughly translated, that meant that Tanzania wasn't going to give up the revenues from 300 tourists a week and turn over the crown jewel in their park system to a bunch of anthropologists. I can't say that I blame them.

Other parties had begun pouring into the gorge, and I think the entire safari population must have totaled almost 70 by the time lunch was over. The guides each seemed to have "their" areas marked out, and I noticed that rarely did we get within a quarter mile of any other parties.

Kevin asked us if we wanted to sit in the shade until the heat of the day had passed, but since this was our next-to-last day on safari we voted overwhelmingly to proceed as soon as we were through eating.

It couldn't have been ten minutes later that the disaster occurred. We were clambering down a steep slope in single file, Kevin in the lead as usual, and me right behind him, when I heard a grunt and then a surprised yell, and I looked back to see Mr. Shiboni tumbling down the path. Evidently he'd lost his footing, and we could hear the bones in his leg snap as he hurtled toward us.

Kevin positioned himself to stop him, and almost got knocked down the gorge himself before he finally stopped poor Mr. Shiboni. Then he knelt down next to the old gentleman to tend to his broken leg—but as he did so his keen eyes spotted something we all had missed, and suddenly he was bounding up the slopes like a monkey. He stopped where Mr. Shiboni had initially stumbled, squatted down, and examined something. Then, looking like Death itself, he picked up the object and brought it back down the path.

It was a dead lizard, fully grown, almost eight inches long, and smashed flat by Mr. Shiboni. It was impossible to say whether his fall was caused by stepping on it, or whether it simply couldn't get out of the way once he began tumbling … but it made no difference: he was responsible for the death of an animal in a National Park.

I tried to remember the release we had signed, giving the Park System permission to instantly withdraw money from our accounts should we destroy an animal for any reason, even self-protection. I knew that the absolute minimum penalty was $50,000, but I think that was for two of the more common birds, and that ugaama and gecko lizards were in the $70,000 range.

Kevin held the lizard up for all of us to see, and told us that should legal action ensue, we were all witnesses to what had happened.

Mr. Shiboni groaned in pain, and Kevin said that there was no sense wasting the lizard, so he gave it to me to hold while he splinted Mr. Shiboni's leg and summoned the paramedics on the radio.

I began examining the little lizard. Its feet were finely shaped, its tail long and elegant, but it was the colors that made the most lasting impression on me: a reddish head, a blue body, and grey legs, the color growing lighter as it reached the claws. A beautiful, beautiful thing, even in death.

After the paramedics had taken Mr. Shiboni back to the lodge, Kevin spent the next hour showing us how the ugaama lizard functioned: how its eyes could see in two directions at once, how its claws allowed it to hang upside down from any uneven surface, and how efficiently its jaws could crack the carapaces of the insects it caught. Finally, in view of the tragedy, and also because he wanted to check on Mr. Shiboni's condition, Kevin suggested that we call it a day.

None of us objected—we knew Kevin would have hours of extra work, writing up the incident and convincing the Park Department that his safari company was not responsible for it—but still we felt cheated, since there was only one day left. I think Kevin knew it, because just before we reached the lodge he promised us a special treat tomorrow.

I've been awake half the night wondering what it could be? Can he possibly know where the other dik-diks are? Or could the legends of a last flamingo possibly be true?

February 19:

We were all excited when we climbed aboard the vehicle this morning. Everyone kept asking Kevin what his "special treat" was, but he merely smiled and kept changing the subject. Finally we reached Olduvai Gorge and began walking, only this time we seemed to be going to a specific location, and Kevin hardly stopped to try to spot the dik-dik.

We climbed down twisting, winding paths, tripping over tree roots, cutting our arms and legs on thorn bushes, but nobody objected, for Kevin seemed so confident of his surprise that all these hardships were forgotten.

Finally we reached the bottom of the gorge and began walking along a flat winding path. Still, by the time we were ready to stop for lunch, we hadn't seen a thing. As we sat beneath the shade of an acacia tree, eating, Kevin pulled out his radio and conversed with the other guides. One group had seen three dik-diks, and another had found a lilac-breasted roller's nest with two hatchlings in it. Kevin is very competitive, and ordinarily news like that would have had him urging everyone to finish eating quickly so that we would not return to the lodge having seen less than everyone else, but this time he just smiled and told the other guides that we had seen nothing on the floor of the gorge and that the game seemed to have moved out, perhaps in search of water.

Then, when lunch was over, Kevin walked about 50 yards away, disappeared into a cave, and emerged a moment later with a small wooden cage. There was a little brown bird in it, and while I was thrilled to be able to see it close up, I felt somehow disappointed that this was to be the special treat.

"Have you ever seen a honey guide?" he asked.

We all admitted that we hadn't, and he explained that that was the name of the small brown bird.

I asked why it was called that, since it obviously didn't produce honey, and seemed incapable of replacing Kevin as our guide, and he smiled again.

"Do you see that tree?" he asked, pointing to a tree perhaps 75 yards away. There was a huge beehive on a low-hanging branch.

"Yes," I said.

"Then watch," he said, opening the cage and releasing the bird. It stood still for a moment, then fluttered its wings and took off in the direction of the tree.

"He is making sure there is honey there," explained Kevin, pointing to the bird as it circled the hive.

"Where is he going now?" I asked, as the bird suddenly flew down the river bed.

"To find his partner."

"Partner?" I asked, confused.

"Wait and see," said Kevin, sitting down with his back propped against a large rock.

We all followed suit and sat in the shade, our binoculars and holo cameras trained on the tree. After almost an hour nothing had happened, and some of us were getting restless, when Kevin tensed and pointed up the river bed.

"There!" he whispered.

I looked in the direction he was pointing, and there, following the bird, which was flying just ahead of him and chirping frantically, was an enormous black-and-white animal, the largest I have ever seen.

"What is it?" I whispered.

"A honey badger," answered Kevin softly. "They were thought to be extinct twenty years ago, but a mated pair took sanctuary in Olduvai. This is the fourth generation to be born here."

"Is he going to eat the bird?" asked one of the party.

"No," whispered Kevin. "The bird will lead him to the honey, and after he has pulled down the nest and eaten his fill, he will leave some for the bird."

And it was just as Kevin said. The honey badger climbed the bole of the tree and knocked off the beehive with a forepaw, then climbed back down and broke it apart, oblivious to the stings of the bees. We caught the whole fantastic scene on our holos, and when he was done he did indeed leave some honey for the honey guide.

Later, while Kevin was recapturing the bird and putting it back in its cage, the rest of us discussed what we had seen. I thought the honey badger must have weighed 45 pounds, though less excitable members of the party put its weight at closer to 36 or 37. Whichever it was, the creature was enormous. The discussion then shifted to how big a tip to leave for Kevin, for he had certainly earned one.

As I write this final entry in my safari diary, I am still trembling with the excitement that can only come from encountering big game in the wild. Prior to this afternoon, I had some doubts about the safari—I felt it was overpriced, or that perhaps my expectations had been too high—but now I know that it was worth every penny, and I have a feeling that I am leaving some part of me behind here, and that I will never be truly content until I return to this last bastion of the wilderness.

The camp was abuzz with excitement. Just when we were sure that there were no more treasures to unearth, the Stardust Twins had found three small pieces of bone, attached together with a wire—obviously a human artifact.

"But the dates are wrong," said the Historian, after examining the bones thoroughly with its equipment. "This is a primitive piece of jewelry—for the adornment of savages, one might say—and yet the bones and wire both date from centuries after Man discovered space travel."

"Do you …"

"… deny that we …"

"… found it in the …"

… gorge?" demanded the Twins.

"I believe you," said the Historian. "I simply state that it seems to be an anachronism."

"It is our find, and …"

"… it will bear our name."

"No one is denying your right of discovery," said Bellidore. "It is simply that you have presented us with a mystery."

"Give it to …"

"… He Who Views, and he …"

"… will solve the mystery."

"I will do my best," I said. "But it has not been long enough since I assimilated the stylus. I must rest and regain my strength."

"That is …"

"… acceptable."

We let the Moriteu go about brushing and cleaning the artifact, while we speculated on why a primitive fetish should exist in the starfaring age. Finally the Exobiologist got to her feet.

"I am going back into the gorge," she announced. "If the Stardust Twins could find this, perhaps there are other things we have overlooked. After all, it is an enormous area." She paused and looked at the rest of us. "Would anyone care to come with me?"

It was nearing the end of the day, and no one volunteered, and finally the Exobiologist turned and began walking toward the path that led down into the depths of Olduvai Gorge.

It was dark when I finally felt strong enough to assimilate the jewelry. I spread my essence about the bones and the wire and soon became one with them …

His name was Joseph Meromo, and he could live with the money but not the guilt.

It had begun with the communication from Brussels, and the veiled suggestion from the head of the multinational conglomerate headquartered there. They had a certain commodity to get rid of. They had no place to get rid of it. Could Tanzania help?

Meromo had told them he would look into it, but he doubted that his government could be of use.

Just *try*, came the reply.

In fact, more than the reply came. The next day a private courier delivered a huge wad of large-denomination bills, with a polite note thanking Meromo for his efforts on their behalf.

Meromo knew a bribe when he saw one—he'd certainly taken enough in his career—but he'd never seen one remotely the size of this one. And not even for helping them, but merely for being willing to explore possibilities.

Well, he had thought, why not? What could they conceivably have? A couple of containers of toxic waste? A few plutonium rods? You bury them deep enough in the earth and no one would ever know or care. Wasn't that what the Western countries did?

Of course, there was the Denver Disaster, and that little accident that made the Thames undrinkable for almost a century, but the only reason they popped so quickly to mind is because they were the *exceptions*, not the rule. There were thousands of dumping sites around the world, and ninety-nine percent of them caused no problems at all.

Meromo had his computer cast a holographic map of Tanzania above his desk. He looked at it, frowned, added topographical features, then began studying it in earnest.

If he decided to help them dump the stuff, whatever it was—and he told himself that he was still uncommitted—where would be the best place to dispose of it?

Off the coast? No, the fishermen would pull it up two minutes later, take it to the press, and raise enough hell to get him fired, and possibly even cause the rest of the government to resign. The party really couldn't handle any more scandals this year.

The Selous Province? Maybe five centuries ago, when it was the last wilderness on the continent, but not now, not with a thriving, semiautonomous city-state of fifty-two million people where once there had been nothing but elephants and almost-impenetrable thorn bush.

Lake Victoria? No. Same problem with the fishermen.

Dar es Salaam? It was a possibility. Close enough to the coast to make transport easy, practically deserted since Dodoma had become the new capital of the country.

But Dar es Salaam had been hit by an earthquake twenty years ago, when Meromo was still a boy, and he couldn't take the chance of another one exposing or breaking open whatever it was that he planned to hide.

He continued going over the map: Gombe, Ruaha, Iringa, Mbeya, Mtwara, Tarengire, Olduvai …

He stopped and stared at Olduvai, then called up all available data.

Almost a mile deep. That was in its favor. No animals left. Better still. No settlements on its steep slopes. Only a handful of Maasai still living in the area, no more than two dozen families, and they were too arrogant to pay any attention to what the government was doing. Of that Meromo was sure: he himself was a Maasai.

So he strung it out for as long as he could, collected cash gifts for almost two years, and finally gave them a delivery date.

Meromo stared out the window of his 34th floor office, past the bustling city of Dodoma, off to the east, to where he imagined Olduvai Gorge was.

It had seemed so simple. Yes, he was paid a lot of money, a disproportionate amount—but these multinationals had money to burn. It was just supposed to be a few dozen plutonium rods, or so he had thought. How was he to know that they were speaking of forty-two *tons* of nuclear waste?

There was no returning the money. Even if he wanted to, he could hardly expect them to come back and pull all that deadly material back out of the ground. Probably it was safe, probably no one would ever know …

But it haunted his days, and even worse, it began haunting his nights as well, appearing in various guises in his dreams. Sometimes it was as carefully sealed containers, sometimes it was as ticking bombs, sometimes a disaster had already occurred and all he could see were the charred bodies of Maasai children spread across the lip of the gorge.

For almost eight months he fought his devils alone, but eventually he realized that he must have help. The dreams not only haunted him at night, but invaded the day as well. He would be sitting at a staff meeting, and suddenly he would imagine he was sitting among the emaciated, sore-covered bodies of the Olduvai Maasai. He would be reading a book, and the words seemed to change and he would be reading that Joseph Meromo had been sentenced to death for his greed. He would watch a holo of the Titanic disaster, and suddenly he was viewing some variation of the Olduvai Disaster.

Finally he went to a psychiatrist, and because he was a Maasai, he choose a Maasai psychiatrist. Fearing the doctor's contempt, Meromo would not state explicitly what was causing the nightmares and intrusions, and after almost half a year's worth of futile attempts to cure him, the psychiatrist announced that he could do no more.

"Then am I to be cursed with these dreams forever?" asked Meromo.

"Perhaps not," said the psychiatrist. "*I* cannot help you, but just possibly there is one man who can."

He rummaged through his desk and came up with a small white card. On it was written a single word: MULEWO.

"This is his business card," said the psychiatrist. "Take it."

"There is no address on it, no means of communicating with him," said Meromo. "How will I contact him?"

"He will contact you."

"You will give him my name?"

The psychiatrist shook his head. "I will not have to. Just keep the card on your person. He will know you require his services."

Meromo felt like he was being made the butt of some joke he didn't understand, but he dutifully put the card in his pocket and soon forgot about it.

Two weeks later, as he was drinking at a bar, putting off going home to sleep as long as he could, a small woman approached him.

"Are you Joseph Meromo?" she asked.

"Yes."

"Please follow me."

"Why?" he asked suspiciously.

"You have business with Mulewo, do you not?" she said.

Meromo fell into step behind her, at least as much to avoid going home as from any belief that this mysterious man with no first name could help him. They went out to the street, turned left, walked in silence for three blocks, and turned right, coming to a halt at the front door to a steel-and-glass skyscraper.

"The 63rd floor," she said. "He is expecting you."

"You're not coming with me?" asked Meromo.

She shook her head. "My job is done." She turned and walked off into the night.

Meromo looked up at the top of the building. It seemed residential. He considered his options, finally shrugged, and walked into the lobby.

"You're here for Mulewo," said the doorman. It was not a question. "Go to the elevator on the left."

Meromo did as he was told. The elevator was paneled with an oiled wood, and smelled fresh and sweet. It operated on voice command and quickly took him to the 63rd floor. When he emerged he found himself in an elegantly decorated corridor, with ebony wainscoting and discreetly placed mirrors. He walked past three unmarked doors, wondering how he was supposed to know which apartment belonged to Mulewo, and finally came to one that was partially open.

"Come in, Joseph Meromo," said a hoarse voice from within.

Meromo opened the door the rest of the way, stepped into the apartment, and blinked.

Sitting on a torn rug was an old man, wearing nothing but a red cloth gathered at the shoulder. The walls were covered by reed matting, and a noxious-smelling caldron bubbled in the fireplace. A torch provided the only illumination.

"What *is* this?" asked Meromo, ready to step back into the corridor if the old man appeared as irrational as his surroundings.

"Come sit across from me, Joseph Meromo," said the old man. "Surely this is less frightening than your nightmares."

"What do you know about my nightmares?" demanded Meromo.

"I know why you have them. I know what lies buried at the bottom of Olduvai Gorge."

Meromo shut the door quickly.

"Who told you?"

"No one told me. I have peered into your dreams, and sifted through them until I found the truth. Come sit."

Meromo walked to where the old man indicated and sat down carefully, trying not to get too much dirt on his freshly pressed outfit.

"Are you Mulewo?" he asked.

The old man nodded. "I am Mulewo."

"How do you know these things about me?"

"I am a *laibon*," said Mulewo.

"A witch doctor?"

"It is a dying art," answered Mulewo. "I am the last practitioner."

"I thought *laibons* cast spells and created curses."

"They also remove curses—and your nights, and even your days, are cursed, are they not?"

"You seem to know all about it."

"I know that you have done a wicked thing, and that you are haunted not only by the ghost of it, but by the ghosts of the future as well."

"And you can end the dreams?"

"That is why I have summoned you here."

"But if I did such a terrible thing, why do you *want* to help me?"

"I do not make moral judgments. I am here only to help the Maasai."

"And what about the Maasai who live by the gorge?" asked Meromo. "The ones who haunt my dreams?"

"When *they* ask for help, then I will help them."

"Can you cause the material that's buried there to vanish?"

Mulewo shook his head. "I cannot undo what has been done. I cannot even assuage your guilt, for it is a just guilt. All I can do is banish it from your dreams."

"I'll settle for that," said Meromo.

There was an uneasy silence.

"What do I do now?" asked Meromo.

"Bring me a tribute befitting the magnitude of the service I shall perform."

"I can write you a check right now, or have money transferred from my account to your own."

"I have more money than I need. I must have a tribute."

"But—"

"Bring it back tomorrow night," said Mulewo.

Meromo stared at the old *laibon* for a long minute, then got up and left without another word.

He called in sick the next morning, then went to two of Dodoma's better antique shops. Finally he found what he was looking for, charged it to his personal account, and took it home with him. He was afraid to nap before dinner, so he simply read a book all afternoon, then ate a hasty meal and returned to Mulewo's apartment.

"What have you brought me?" asked Mulewo.

Meromo laid the package down in front of the old man. "A headdress made from the skin of a lion," he answered. "They told me it was worn by Sendayo himself, the greatest of all *laibons*."

"It was not," said Mulewo, without unwrapping the package. "But it is a sufficient tribute nonetheless." He reached beneath his red cloth and withdrew a small necklace, holding it out for Meromo.

"What is this for?" asked Meromo, examining the necklace. It was made of small bones that had been strung together.

"You must wear it tonight when you go to sleep," explained the old man. "It will take all your visions unto itself. Then, tomorrow, you must go to Olduvai Gorge and throw it down to the bottom, so that the visions may lay side by side with the reality."

"And that's all?"

"That is all."

Meromo went back to his apartment, donned the necklace, and went to sleep. That night his dreams were worse than they had ever been before.

In the morning he put the necklace into a pocket and had a government plane fly him to Arusha. From there he rented a ground vehicle, and two hours later he was standing on the edge of the gorge. There was no sign of the buried material.

He took the necklace in his hand and hurled it far out over the lip of the gorge.

His nightmares vanished that night.

One-hundred thirty-four years later, mighty Kilimanjaro shuddered as the long-dormant volcano within it came briefly to life.

One hundred miles away, the ground shifted on the floor of Olduvai Gorge, and three of the lead-lined containers broke open.

Joseph Meromo was long dead by that time; and, unfortunately, there were no *laibons* remaining to aid those people who were now compelled to live Meromo's nightmares.

✧ ✧ ✧

I had examined the necklace in my own quarters, and when I came out to report my findings, I discovered that the entire camp was in a tumultuous state.

"What has happened?" I asked Bellidore.

"The Exobiologist has not returned from the gorge," he said.

"How long has she been gone?"

"She left at sunset last night. It is now morning, and she has not returned or attempted to use her communicator."

"We fear …

"… that she might …"

"… have fallen and …"

"… become immobile. Or perhaps even …"

"… unconscious …" said the Stardust Twins.

"I have sent the Historian and the Appraiser to look for her," said Bellidore.

"I can help, too," I offered.

"No, you have the last artifact to examine," he said. "When the Moriteu awakens, I will send it as well."

"What about the Mystic?" I asked.

Bellidore looked at the Mystic and sighed. "She has not said a word since landing on this world. In truth, I do not understand her function. At any rate, I do not know how to communicate with her."

The Stardust Twins kicked at the earth together, sending up a pair of reddish dust clouds.

"It seems ridiculous …" said one.

"… that we can find the tiniest artifact …" said the other.

"… but we cannot find …

"… an entire exobiologist."

"Why do you not help search for it?" I asked.

"They get vertigo," explained Bellidore.

"We searched …"

"… the entire camp," they added defensively.

"I can put off assimilating the last piece until tomorrow, and help with the search," I volunteered.

"No," replied Bellidore. "I have sent for the ship. We will leave tomorrow, and I want all of our major finds examined by then. It is *my* job to find the Exobiologist; it is *yours* to read the history of the last artifact."

"If that is your desire," I said. "Where is it?"

He led me to a table where the Historian and the Appraiser had been examining it.

"Even *I* know what this is," said Bellidore. "An unspent cartridge." He paused. "Along with the fact that we have found no human artifacts on any higher strata, I would say this in itself is unique: a bullet that a man chose *not* to fire."

"When you state it in those terms, it *does* arouse the curiosity," I acknowledged.

"Are you …"

"… going to examine it …"

"… now?" asked the Stardust Twins apprehensively.

"Yes, I am," I said.

"Wait!" they shouted in unison.

I paused above the cartridge while they began backing away.

"We mean …"

"… no disrespect …"

"… but watching you examine artifacts …"

"… is too unsettling."

And with that, they raced off to hide behind some of the camp structures.

"What about you?" I asked Bellidore. "Would you like me to wait until you leave?"

"Not at all," he replied. "I find diversity fascinating. With your permission, I would like to stay and observe."

"As you wish," I said, allowing my body to melt around the cartridge until it had become a part of myself, and its history became my own history, as clear and precise as if it had all occurred yesterday …

"They are coming!"

Thomas Naikosiai looked across the table at his wife.

"Was there ever any doubt that they would?"

"This was foolish, Thomas!" she snapped. "They will force us to leave, and because we made no preparations, we will have to leave all our possessions behind."

"Nobody is leaving," said Naikosiai.

He stood up and walked to the closet. "You stay here," he said, donning his long coat and his mask. "I will meet them outside."

"That is both rude and cruel, to make them stand out there when they have come all this way."

"They were not invited," said Naikosiai. He reached deep into the closet and grabbed the rifle that leaned up against the back wall, then closed the closet, walked through the airlock and emerged on the front porch.

Six men, all wearing protective clothing and masks to filter the air, confronted him.

"It is time, Thomas," said the tallest of them.

"Time for *you*, perhaps," said Naikosiai, holding the rifle casually across his chest..

"Time for all of us," answered the tall man.

"I am not going anywhere. This is my home. I will not leave it."

"It is a pustule of decay and contamination, as is this whole country," came the answer. "We are all leaving."

Naikosiai shook his head. "My father was born on this land, and his father, and his father's father. *You* may run from danger, if you wish; I will stay and fight it."

"How can you make a stand against radiation?" demanded the tall man. "Can you put a bullet through it? How can you fight air that is no longer safe to breathe?"

"Go away," said Naikosiai, who had no answer to that, other than the conviction that he would never leave his home. "I do not demand that you stay. Do not demand that I leave."

"It is for your own good, Naikosiai," urged another. "If you care nothing for your own life, think of your wife's. How much longer can she breathe the air?"

"Long enough."

"Why not let *her* decide?"

"*I* speak for our family."

An older man stepped forward. "She is *my* daughter, Thomas," he said severely. "I will not allow you to condemn her to the life you have chosen for yourself. Nor will I let my grandchildren remain here."

The old man took another step toward the porch, and suddenly the rifle was pointing at him.

"That's far enough," said Naikosiai.

"They are Maasai," said the old man stubbornly. "They must come with the other Maasai to our new world."

"You are not Maasai," said Naikosiai contemptuously. "Maasai did not leave their ancestral lands when the rinderpest destroyed their herds, or when the white man came, or when the governments sold off their lands. Maasai never surrender. *I* am the last Maasai."

"Be reasonable, Thomas. How can you not surrender to a world that is no longer safe for people to live on? Come with us to New Kilimanjaro."

"The Maasai do not run from danger," said Naikosiai.

"I tell you, Thomas Naikosiai," said the old man, "that I cannot allow you to condemn my daughter and my grandchildren to live in this hellhole. The last ship leaves tomorrow morning. They will be on it."

"They will stay with me, to build a new Maasai nation."

The six men whispered among themselves, and then their leader looked up at Naikosiai.

"You are making a terrible mistake, Thomas," he said. "If you change your mind, there is room for you on the ship."

They all turned to go, but the old man stopped and turned to Naikosiai.

"I will be back for my daughter," he said.

Naikosiai gestured with his rifle. "I will be waiting for you."

The old man turned and walked off with the others, and Naikosiai went back into his house through the airlock. The tile floor smelled of disinfectant, and the sight of the television set offended his eyes, as always. His wife was waiting for him in the kitchen, amid the dozens of gadgets she had purchased over the years.

"How can you speak with such disrespect to the Elders!" she demanded. "You have disgraced us."

"No!" he snapped. "*They* have disgraced us, by leaving!"

"Thomas, you cannot grow anything in the fields. The animals have all died. You cannot even breathe the air without a filtering mask. *Why* do you insist on staying?"

"This is our ancestral land. We will not leave it."

"But all the others—"

"They can do as they please," he interrupted. "En-kai will judge them, as He judges us all. I am not afraid to meet my creator."

"But why must you meet him so soon?" she persisted. "You have seen the tapes and disks of New Kilimanjaro. It is a beautiful world, green and gold and filled with rivers and lakes."

"Once Earth was green and gold and filled with rivers and lakes," said Naikosiai. "They ruined this world. They will ruin the next one."

"Even if they do, we will be long dead," she said. "I want to go."

"We've been through all this before."

"And it always ends with an order rather than an agreement," she said. Her expression softened. "Thomas, just once before I die, I want to see water that you can drink without adding chemicals to it. I want to see antelope grazing on long green grasses. I want to walk outside without having to protect myself from the very air I breathe."

"It's settled."

She shook her head. "I love you, Thomas, but I cannot stay here, and I cannot let our children stay here."

"No one is taking my children from me!" he yelled.

"Just because you care nothing for *your* future, I cannot permit you to deny our sons *their* future."

"Their future is here, where the Maasai have always lived."

"Please come with us, Papa," said a small voice behind him, and Naikosiai turned to see his two sons, eight and five, standing in the doorway to their bedroom, staring at him.

"What have you been saying to them?" demanded Naikosiai suspiciously.

"The truth," said his wife.

He turned to the two boys. "Come here," he said, and they trudged across the room to him.

"What are you?" he asked.

"Boys," said the younger child.

"What *else*?"

"Maasai," said the older.

"That is right," said Naikosiai. "You come from a race of giants. There was a time when, if you climbed to the very top of Kilimanjaro, all the land you could see in every direction belonged to us."

"But that was long ago," said the older boy.

"Someday it will be ours again," said Naikosiai. "You must remember who you are, my son. You are the descendant of Leeyo, who killed 100 lions with just his spear; of Nelion, who waged war against the whites and drove them from the Rift; of Sendayo, the greatest of all the *laibons*. Once the Kikuyu and the Wakamba and the Lumbwa trembled in fear at the very mention of the word Maasai. This is your heritage; do not turn your back on it."

"But the Kikuyu and the other tribes have all left."

"What difference does that make to the Maasai? We did not make a stand only against the Kikuyu and the Wakamba, but against *all* men who would have us change our ways. Even after the Europeans conquered Kenya and Tanganyika, they never conquered the Maasai. When Independence came, and all the other tribes moved to cities and wore suits and aped the Europeans, we remained as we had always been. We wore what we chose and we lived where we chose, for we were proud to be Maasai. Does that not *mean* something to you?"

"Will we not still be Maasai if we go to the new world?" asked the older boy.

"No," said Naikosiai firmly. "There is a bond between the Maasai and the land. We define it, and it defines us. It is what we have always fought for and always defended."

"But it is diseased now," said the boy.

"If I were sick, would you leave me?" asked Naikosiai.

"No, Papa."

"And just as you would not leave me in my illness, so we will not leave the land in *its* illness. When you love something, when it is a part of what you are, you do not leave it simply because it becomes sick. You stay, and you fight even harder to cure it than you fought to win it."

"But—"

"Trust me," said Naikosiai. "Have I ever misled you?"

"No, Papa."

"I am not misleading you now. We are En-kai's chosen people. We live on the ground He has given us. Don't you see that we *must* remain here, that we must keep our covenant with En-kai?"

"But I will never see my friends again!" wailed his younger son.

"You will make new friends."

"Where?" cried the boy. "Everyone is gone!"

"Stop that at once!" said Naikosiai harshly. "Maasai do not cry."

The boy continued sobbing, and Naikosiai looked up at his wife. "This is *your* doing," he said. "You have spoiled him."

She stared unblinking into his eyes. "Five-year-old boys are allowed to cry."

"Not Maasai boys," he answered.

"Then he is no longer Maasai, and you can have no objection to his coming with me."

"I want to go too!" said the eight-year-old, and suddenly he, too, forced some tears down his face.

Thomas Naikosiai looked at his wife and his children—really *looked* at them—and realized that he did not know them at all. This was not the quiet maiden, raised in the traditions of his people, that he had married nine years ago. These soft sobbing boys were not the successors of Leeyo and Nelion.

He walked to the door and opened it.

"Go to the new world with the rest of the black Europeans," he growled.

"Will you come with us?" asked his oldest son.

Naikosiai turned to his wife. "I divorce you," he said coldly. "All that was between us is no more."

He walked over to his two sons. "I disown you. I am no longer your father, you are no longer my sons. Now go!"

His wife puts coats and masks on both of the boys, then donned her own.

"I will send some men for my things before morning," she said.

"If any man comes onto my property, I will kill him," said Naikosiai.

She stared at him, a look of pure hatred. Then she took the children by the hands and led them out of the house and down the long road to where the ship awaited them.

Naikosiai paced the house for a few minutes, filled with nervous rage. Finally he went to the closet, donned his coat and mask, pulled out his rifle, and walked through the airlock to the front of his house.

Visibility was poor, as always, and he went out to the road to see if anyone was coming.

There was no sign of any movement. He was almost disappointed. He planned to show them how a Maasai protected what was his.

And suddenly he realized that this was *not* how a Maasai protected his own. He walked to the edge of the gorge, opened the bolt, and threw his cartridges into the void one by one. Then he held the rifle over his head and hurled it after them. The coat came next, then the mask, and finally his clothes and shoes.

He went back into the house and pulled out that special trunk that held the memorabilia of a lifetime. In it he found what he was looking for: a simple piece of red cloth. He attached it at his shoulder.

Then he went into the bathroom, looking among his wife's cosmetics. It took almost half an hour to hit upon the right combinations, but when he emerged his hair was red, as if smeared with clay.

He stopped by the fireplace and pulled down the spear that hung there. Family tradition had it that the spear had once been used by Nelion himself; he wasn't sure he believed it, but it was definitely a Maasai spear, blooded many times in battle and hunts during centuries past.

Naikosiai walked out the door and positioned himself in front of his house—his *manyatta*. He planted his bare feet on the diseased ground, placed the butt of his spear next to his right foot, and stood at attention. Whatever came down the road next—a band of black Europeans hoping to rob him of his possessions, a lion out of history, a band of Nandi or Lumbwa come to slay the enemy of their blood, they would find him ready.

They returned just after sunrise the next morning, hoping to convince him to emigrate to New Kilimanjaro. What they found was the last Maasai, his lungs burst from the pollution, his dead eyes staring proudly out across the vanished savannah at some enemy only he could see.

I released the cartridge, my strength nearly gone, my emotions drained.

So that was how it had ended for Man on earth, probably less than a mile from where it had begun. So bold and so foolish, so moral and so savage. I had hoped the last artifact would prove to be the final piece of the puzzle, but instead it merely added to the mystery of this most contentious and fascinating race.

Nothing was beyond their ability to achieve. One got the feeling that the day the first primitive man looked up and saw the stars, the galaxy's days as a haven of peace and freedom were numbered. And yet they came out to the stars not just with their lusts and their hatred and their fears, but with their technology and their medicine, their heroes as well as their villains. Most of the races of the galaxy had been painted by the Creator in pastels; Men were primaries.

I had much to think about as I went off to my quarters to renew my strength. I do not know how long I lay, somnolent and unmoving, recovering my energy, but it must have been a long time, for night had come and gone before I felt prepared to rejoin the party.

As I emerged from my quarters and walked to the center of camp, I heard a yell from the direction of the gorge, and a moment later the Appraiser appeared, a large sterile bag balanced atop an air trolley.

"What have you found?" asked Bellidore, and suddenly I remembered that the Exobiologist was missing.

"I am almost afraid to guess," replied the Appraiser, laying the bag on the table.

All the members of the party gathered around as he began withdrawing items: a blood-stained communicator, bent out of shape; the floating shade, now broken, that the Exobiologist used to protect her head from the rays of the sun; a torn piece of clothing; and finally, a single gleaming white bone.

The instant the bone was placed on the table, the Mystic began screaming. We were all shocked into momentary immobility, not only because of the suddenness of her reaction, but because it was the first sign of life she had shown since joining our party. She continued to stare at the bone and scream, and finally, before we could question her or remove the bone from her sight, she collapsed.

"I don't suppose there can be much doubt about what happened," said Bellidore. "The creatures caught up with the Exobiologist somewhere on her way down the gorge and killed her."

"Probably ate …"

"… her too," said the Stardust Twins.

"I am glad we are leaving today," continued Bellidore. "Even after all these millennia, the spirit of Man continues to corrupt and degrade this world. Those lumbering creatures can't possibly be predators: there are no meat animals left on Earth. But given the opportunity, they fell upon the Exobiologist and consumed her flesh. I have this uneasy feeling that if we stayed much longer, we, too, would become corrupted by this world's barbaric heritage."

The Mystic regained consciousness and began screaming again, and the Stardust Twins gently escorted her back to her quarters, where she was given a sedative.

"I suppose we might as well make it official," said Bellidore. He turned to the Historian. "Would you please check the bone with your instruments and make sure that this is the remains of the Exobiologist?"

The Historian stared at the bone, horror-stricken. "She was my *friend*!" it said at last. "I cannot touch it as if it were just another artifact."

"We must know for sure," said Bellidore. "If it is not part of the Exobiologist, then there is a chance, however slim, that your friend might still be alive."

The Historian reached out tentatively for the bone, then jerked its hand away. "I can't!"

Finally Bellidore turned to me.

"He Who Views," he said. "Have you the strength to examine it?"

"Yes," I answered.

They all moved back to give me room, and I allowed my mass to slowly spread over the bone and engulf it. I assimilated its history and ingested its emotional residue, and finally I withdrew from it.

"It is the Exobiologist," I said.

"What are the funeral customs of her race?" asked Bellidore.

"Cremation," said the Appraiser.

"Then we shall build a fire and incinerate what remains of our friend, and we will each offer a prayer to send her soul along the Eternal Path."

And that is what we did.

The ship came later that day, and took us off the planet, and it is only now, safely removed from its influence, that I can reconstruct what I learned on that last morning.

I lied to Bellidore—to the entire party—for once I made my discovery I knew that my primary duty was to get them away from Earth as quickly as possible. Had I told them the truth, one or more of them would have wanted to remain behind, for they are scientists with curious, probing minds, and I would never be able to convince them that a curious, probing mind is no match for what I found in my seventh and final view of Olduvai Gorge.

The bone was *not* a part of the Exobiologist. The Historian, or even the Moriteu, would have known that had they not been too horrified to examine it. It was the tibia of a *man*.

Man has been extinct for five thousand years, at least as we citizens of the galaxy have come to understand him. But those lumbering, ungainly creatures of the night, who seemed so attracted to our campfires, are what Man has become. Even the pollution and radiation he spread across his own planet could not kill him off. It merely changed him to the extent that we were no longer able to recognize him.

I could have told them the simple facts, I suppose: that a tribe of these pseudo-Men stalked the Exobiologist down the gorge, then attacked and killed and, yes, ate her. Predators are not unknown throughout the worlds of the galaxy.

But as I became one with the tibia, as I felt it crashing down again and again upon our companion's head and shoulders, I felt a sense of power, of exultation I had never experienced before. I suddenly seemed to see the world through the eyes of the bone's possessor. I saw how he had killed his own companion to create the weapon, I saw how he planned to plunder the bodies of the old and the infirm for more weapons, I saw visions of conquest against other tribes living near the gorge.

And finally, at the moment of triumph, he and I looked up at the sky, and we knew that someday all that we could see would be ours.

And this is the knowledge that I have lived with for two days. I do not know who to share it with, for it is patently immoral to exterminate a race simply because of the vastness of its dreams or the ruthlessness of its ambition.

But this is a race that refuses to die, and somehow I must warn the rest of us, who have lived in harmony for almost five millennia.

It's not over.

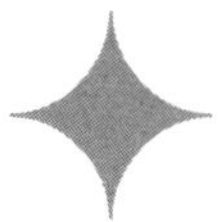

BEGGARS in SPAIN

Nancy Kress

Introduction

Inspiration for stories can spring from many sources, and frequently a writer has no idea where a given story comes from. A piece of it just arrives on the front porch of the mind, like an unordered package from Amazon. With "Beggars in Spain," however, I knew exactly who the mailers were. There were two of them: jealousy and Bruce Sterling.

All my life I have been jealous of people who need only six—or even five—hours of sleep night after night and can still function. I need eight hours in order to remember my name, and I resent it. Those short-sleepers get more *life* than I do. And since a writer's response to any strong emotion is to write about it, I tried for years to write a story about people genetically engineered to not need any sleep. The writing did not go well.

My first effort, near the start of my career, was rejected by every editor of every magazine. Robert Silverberg rejected it twice; I didn't know that he had changed editorial chairs and so I sent it to him at his new job. He replied, "I didn't like this the first time and I still don't." Years later, I tried to write the story—same idea, different characters and setting—and this time it was so bad I never sent it out again. I shelved the idea for another five years.

Enter Bruce Sterling, who was another writer at a workshop for pros that I attended many years during the 1980s and '90s. Sycamore Hill, run by John Kessel, was held on the North Carolina

State campus. For a week, seventeen pros critiqued each other's manuscripts, argued about science fiction, and drank a lot of alcohol. One year I had brought a novelette that I knew was not very good, but I'd run out of time. I knew that my critique session would be rough.

The roughest was Bruce. A fabulous writer himself, he had strong ideas about what makes SF work, and one of those ideas was that if you were going to create a society, it ought to make economic sense. He pointed out, acidly, that mine did not: "You've taken tropes from '60s and '70s science fiction and stuck them together, and I can't tell how this extraterrestrial human colony actually runs. Who holds power? Where do the resources come from? Who is funding this enterprise and why?" I took notes, brought them home, licked my wounds, and thought *Damn it, he's right.*

I started to think seriously about money. Two books stood out in my mind because they are at opposite poles of economic philosophy: Ayn Rand's *Objectivism*, which is basically every-person-for-themself, and Ursula K. Le Guin's *The Dispossessed*, in which nobody owns anything because all resources are shared freely. Neither fully satisfied me. The Rand is cold to the point of cruelty. The Le Guin—despite being my favorite SF novel of all time—requires more faith in human nature than I can muster. The question that came out of my pondering was this: What do the haves owe the have-nots?

Combined with the genmod, non-sleeping thing, the pieces came together and I wrote "Beggars in Spain" in two weeks. The sleep science in the story is not fully developed; I was not yet a hard-SF writer. I could do better now. However, the economics make sense.

Thank you, Bruce.

But I still need too much sleep.

—NANCY KRESS

One

They sat stiffly on his antique Eames chairs, two people who didn't want to be here, or one person who didn't want to and one who resented the other's reluctance. Dr. Ong had seen this before. Within two minutes he was sure: the woman was the silently furious resister. She would lose. The man would pay for it later, in little ways, for a long time.

"I presume you've performed the necessary credit checks already," Roger Camden said pleasantly, "so let's get right on to details, shall we, Doctor?"

"Certainly," Ong said. "Why don't we start by your telling me all the genetic modifications you're interested in for the baby."

The woman shifted suddenly on her chair. She was in her late twenties—clearly a second wife—but already had a faded look, as if keeping up with Roger Camden was wearing her out. Ong could easily believe that. Mrs. Camden's hair was brown, her eyes were brown, her skin had a brown tinge that might have been pretty if her cheeks had had any color. She wore a brown coat, neither fashionable nor cheap, and shoes that looked vaguely orthopedic. Ong glanced at his records for her name: Elizabeth. He would bet people forgot it often.

Next to her, Roger Camden radiated nervous vitality, a man in late middle age whose bullet-shaped head did not match his careful haircut and Italian-silk business suit. Ong did not need to consult his file to recall anything about Camden. A caricature of the bullet-shaped head had been the leading graphic for yesterday's online edition of the *Wall Street Journal*: Camden had led a major coup in cross-border data-atoll investment. Ong was not sure what cross-border data-atoll investment was.

"A girl," Elizabeth Camden said. Ong hadn't expected her to speak first. Her voice was another surprise: upper-class British. "Blonde. Green eyes. Tall. Slender."

Ong smiled. "Appearance factors are the easiest to achieve, as I'm sure you already know. But all we can do about slenderness is give her a genetic disposition in that direction. How you feed the child will naturally—"

"Yes, yes," Roger Camden said, "that's obvious. Now: intelligence. *High* intelligence. And a sense of daring."

"I'm sorry, Mr. Camden, personality factors are not yet understood well enough to allow genet—"

"Just testing," Camden said, with a smile that Ong thought was probably supposed to be lighthearted.

Elizabeth Camden said, "Musical ability."

"Again, Mrs. Camden, a disposition to be musical is all we can guarantee."

"Good enough," Camden said. "The full array of corrections for any potential gene-linked health problem, of course."

"Of course," Dr. Ong said. Neither client spoke. So far theirs was a fairly modest list, given Camden's money; most clients had to be argued out of contradictory genetic tendencies, alteration overload, or unrealistic expectations. Ong waited. Tension prickled in the room like heat.

"And," Camden said, "no need to sleep."

Elizabeth Camden jerked her head sideways to look out the window.

Ong picked up a paper magnet from his desk. He made his voice pleasant. "May I ask how you learned whether that genetic-modification program exists?"

Camden grinned. "You're not denying it exists. I give you full credit for that, Doctor."

Ong held his temper. "May I ask how you learned whether the program exists?"

Camden reached into an inner pocket of his suit. The silk crinkled and pulled; body and suit came from different classes. Camden was, Ong remembered, a Yagaiist, a personal friend of Kenzo Yagai himself. Camden handed Ong hard copy: program specifications.

"Don't bother hunting down the security leak in your data banks, Doctor. You won't find it. But if it's any consolation, neither will anybody else. Now." He leaned forward suddenly. His tone changed. "I know that you've created twenty children who don't need to sleep at all, that so far nineteen are healthy, intelligent, and psychologically normal. In fact, they're better than normal; they're all unusually precocious. The oldest is already four years old and can read in two languages. I know you're thinking of offering this genetic modification on the open market in a few years. All I want is a chance to buy it for my daughter now. At whatever price you name."

Ong stood. "I can't possibly discuss this with you unilaterally, Mr. Camden. Neither the theft of our data—"

"Which wasn't a theft—your system developed a spontaneous bubble regurgitation into a public gate. You'd have a hell of a time proving otherwise—"

"—*nor* the offer to purchase this particular genetic modification lie in my sole area of authority. Both have to be discussed with the Institute's board of directors."

"By all means, by all means. When can I talk to them, too?"

"You?"

Camden, still seated, looked up at him. It occurred to Ong that there were few men who could look so confident eighteen inches below eye level. "Certainly. I'd like the chance to present my offer to whoever has the actual authority to accept it. That's only good business."

"This isn't solely a business transaction, Mr. Camden."

"It isn't solely pure scientific research, either," Camden retorted. "You're a for-profit corporation here. *With* certain tax breaks available only to firms meeting certain fair-practice laws."

For a minute Ong couldn't think what Camden meant. "Fair-practice laws ..."

"... are designed to protect minorities who are suppliers. I know it hasn't ever been tested in the case of customers, except for redlining in Y-energy installations. But it could be tested,

Dr. Ong. Minorities are entitled to the same product offerings as non-minorities. I know the Institute would not welcome a court case, Doctor. None of your twenty genetic beta-test families is either Black or Jewish!"

"A court … but you're not Black *or* Jewish!"

"I'm a different minority. Polish-American. The name was Kaminsky." Camden finally stood. And smiled warmly. "Look, it is preposterous. You know that, and I know that, and we both know what a grand time journalists would have with it anyway. And you know that I don't want to sue you with a preposterous case just to use the threat of premature and adverse publicity to get what I want. I don't want to make threats at all, believe me I don't. I just want this marvelous advancement you've come up with for my daughter." His face changed, to an expression Ong wouldn't have believed possible on those particular features: wistfulness. "Doctor, do you know how much more I could have accomplished if I hadn't had to *sleep* all my life?"

Elizabeth Camden said harshly, "You hardly sleep now."

Camden looked down at her as if he had forgotten she was there. "Well, no, my dear, not now. But when I was young … college, I might have been able to finish college and still support … . Well. None of that matters now. What matters, Doctor, is that you and I and your board come to an agreement."

"Mr. Camden, please leave my office now."

"You mean before you lose your temper at my presumptuousness? You wouldn't be the first. I'll expect to have a meeting set up by the end of next week, whenever and wherever you say, of course. Just let my personal secretary, Diane Clavers, know the details. Anytime that's best for you."

Ong did not accompany them to the door. Pressure throbbed behind his temples. In the doorway Elizabeth Camden turned. "What happened to the twentieth one?"

"What?"

"The twentieth baby. My husband said nineteen of them are healthy and normal. What happened to the twentieth?"

The pressure grew stronger, hotter. Ong knew that he should not answer; that Camden probably already knew the answer even if his wife didn't; that he, Ong, was going to answer anyway; that he would regret the lack of self-control, bitterly, later.

"The twentieth baby is dead. His parents turned out to be unstable. They separated during the pregnancy, and his mother could not bear the twenty-four-hour crying of a baby who never sleeps."

Elizabeth Camden's eyes widened. "She killed it?"

"By mistake," Camden said shortly. "Shook the little thing too hard." He frowned at Ong. "Nurses, Doctor. In shifts. You should have picked only parents wealthy enough to afford nurses in shifts."

"That's horrible!" Mrs. Camden burst out, and Ong could not tell if she meant the child's death, the lack of nurses, or the Institute's carelessness. Ong closed his eyes.

When they had gone, he took ten milligrams of cyclobenzaprine-III. For his back—it was solely for his back. The old injury was hurting again. Afterward he stood for a long time at the window, still holding the paper magnet, feeling the pressure recede from his temples, feeling himself calm down. Below him Lake Michigan lapped peacefully at the shore; the police had driven away the homeless in another raid just last night, and they hadn't yet had time to return. Only their debris remained, thrown into the bushes of the lakeshore park: tattered blankets, newspapers, plastic bags like pathetic trampled standards. It was illegal to sleep in the park, illegal to enter it without a resident's permit, illegal to be homeless and without a residence. As Ong watched, uniformed park attendants began methodically spearing newspapers and shoving them into clean self-propelled receptacles.

Ong picked up the phone to call the chairman of Biotech Institute's board of directors.

Four men and three women sat around the polished mahogany table of the conference room. *Doctor, lawyer, Indian chief,* thought Susan Melling, looking from Ong to Sullivan to Camden. She smiled. Ong caught the smile and looked frosty. Pompous ass. Judy Sullivan, the Institute lawyer, turned to speak in a low voice to Camden's lawyer, a thin nervous man with the look of being owned.

The owner, Roger Camden, the Indian chief himself, was the happiest-looking person in the room. The lethal little man—what did it take to become that rich, starting from nothing? She, Susan, would certainly never know—radiated excitement. He beamed, he glowed, so unlike the usual parents-to-be that Susan was intrigued. Usually the prospective daddies and mommies—especially the daddies—sat there looking as if they were at a corporate merger. Camden looked as if he were at a birthday party.

Which, of course, he was. Susan grinned at him, and was pleased when he grinned back. Wolfish, but with a sort of delight that could only be called innocent—what would he be like in bed? Ong frowned majestically and rose to speak.

"Ladies and gentlemen, I think we're ready to start. Perhaps introductions are in order. Mr. Roger Camden, Mrs. Camden, are of course our clients. Mr. John Jaworski, Mr. Camden's lawyer. Mr. Camden, this is Judith Sullivan, the Institute's head of Legal; Samuel Krenshaw, representing Institute Director Dr. Brad Marsteiner, who unfortunately couldn't be here today; and Dr. Susan Melling, who developed the genetic modification affecting sleep. A few legal points of interest to both parties—"

"Forget the contracts for a minute," Camden interrupted. "Let's talk about the sleep thing. I'd like to ask a few questions."

Susan said, "What would you like to know?" Camden's eyes were very blue in his blunt-featured face; he wasn't what she had expected. Mrs. Camden, who apparently lacked both a first name and a lawyer, since Jaworski had been introduced as her husband's but not hers, looked either sullen or scared, it was difficult to tell which.

Ong said sourly, "Then perhaps we should start with a short presentation by Dr. Melling."

Susan would have preferred a Q&A, to see what Camden would ask. But she had annoyed Ong enough for one session. Obediently she rose.

"Let me start with a brief description of sleep. Researchers have known for a long time that there are actually three kinds of sleep. One is 'slow-wave sleep,' characterized on an EEG by delta waves. One is 'rapid-eye-movement sleep,' or REM sleep, which is much lighter sleep and contains most dreaming. Together these two make up 'core sleep.' The third type of sleep is 'optional sleep,' so-called because people seem to get along without it with no ill effects, and some short sleepers don't do it at all, sleeping naturally only three or four hours a night."

"That's me," Camden said. "I trained myself into it. Couldn't everybody do that?"

Apparently they were going to have a Q&A after all. "No. The actual sleep mechanism has some flexibility, but not the same amount for every person. The raphe nuclei on the brain stem—"

Ong said, "I don't think we need that level of detail, Susan. Let's stick to basics."

Camden said, "The raphe nuclei regulate the balance among neurotransmitters and peptides that leads to a pressure to sleep, don't they?"

Susan couldn't help it; she grinned. Camden, the laser-sharp ruthless financier, sat trying to look solemn, a third-grader waiting to have his homework praised. Ong looked sour. Mrs. Camden looked away, out the window.

"Yes, that's correct, Mr. Camden. You've done your research."

Camden said, "This is my *daughter*," and Susan caught her breath. When was the last time she had heard that note of reverence in anyone's voice? But no one in the room seemed to notice.

"Well, then," Susan said, "you already know that the reason people sleep is because a pressure to sleep builds up in the brain. Over the past twenty years, research has determined that's the *only* reason. Neither slow-wave sleep nor REM sleep serve functions that can't be carried on while the body and brain are awake. A lot goes on during sleep, but it can go on during wakefulness just as well, if other hormonal adjustments are made.

"Sleep served an important evolutionary function. Once Clem Pre-Mammal was done filling his stomach and squirting his sperm around, sleep kept him immobile and away from predators. Sleep was an aid to survival. But now it's a leftover mechanism, a vestige like the appendix. It switches on every night, but the need is gone. So we turn off the switch at its source, in the genes."

Ong winced. He hated it when she oversimplified like that. Or maybe it was the lightheartedness he hated. If Marsteiner were making this presentation, there'd be no Clem Pre-Mammal.

Camden said, "What about the need to dream?"

"Not necessary. A leftover bombardment of the cortex to keep it on semi-alert in case a predator attacked during sleep. Wakefulness does that better."

"Why not have wakefulness instead then? From the start of the evolution?"

He was testing her. Susan gave him a full, lavish smile, enjoying his brass. "I told you. Safety from predators. But when a modern predator attacks—say, a cross-border data-atoll investor—it's safer to be awake."

Camden shot at her, "What about the high percentage of REM sleep in fetuses and babies?"

"Still an evolutionary hangover. Cerebrum develops perfectly well without it."

"What about neural repair during slow-wave sleep?"

"That does go on. But it can go on during wakefulness, if the DNA is programmed to do so. No loss of neural efficiency, as far as we know."

"What about the release of human growth enzyme in such large concentrations during slow-wave sleep?"

Susan looked at him admiringly. "Goes on without the sleep. Genetic adjustments tie it to other changes in the pineal gland."

"What about the—"

"The *side effects*?" Mrs. Camden said. Her mouth turned down. "What about the bloody side effects?"

Susan turned to Elizabeth Camden. She had forgotten she was there. The younger woman stared at Susan, mouth turned down at the corners.

"I'm glad you asked that, Mrs. Camden. Because there are side effects." Susan paused; she was enjoying herself. "Compared to their age mates, the nonsleep children—who have *not* had IQ genetic manipulation—are more intelligent, better at problem-solving, and more joyous."

Camden took out a cigarette. The archaic, filthy habit surprised Susan. Then she saw that it was deliberate: Roger Camden was drawing attention to an ostentatious display to draw attention away from what he was feeling. His cigarette lighter was gold, monogrammed, innocently gaudy.

"Let me explain," Susan said. "REM sleep bombards the cerebral cortex with random neural firings from the brain stem; dreaming occurs because the poor besieged cortex tries so hard to make sense of the activated images and memories. It spends a lot of energy doing that. Without that energy expenditure, nonsleep cerebrums save the wear-and-tear and do better at coordinating real-life input. Thus, greater intelligence and problem-solving.

"Also, doctors have known for sixty years that antidepressants, which lift the mood of depressed patients, also suppress REM sleep entirely. What they have proved in the past ten years is that the reverse is equally true: suppress REM sleep and people don't *get* depressed. The nonsleep kids are cheerful, outgoing ... *joyous*. There's no other word for it."

"At what cost?" Mrs. Camden said. She held her neck rigid, but the corners of her jaw worked.

"No cost. No negative side effects at all."

"So far," Mrs. Camden shot back.

Susan shrugged. "So far."

"They're only four years old! At the most!"

Ong and Krenshaw were studying her closely. Susan saw the moment the Camden woman realized it; she sank back into her chair, drawing her fur coat around her, her face blank.

Camden did not look at his wife. He blew a cloud of cigarette smoke. "Everything has costs, Dr. Melling."

She liked the way he said her name. "Ordinarily, yes. Especially in genetic modification. But we honestly have not been able to find any here, despite looking." She smiled directly into Camden's eyes. "Is it too much to believe that just once the universe has given us something wholly good, wholly a step forward, wholly beneficial? Without hidden penalties?"

"Not the universe. The intelligence of people like you," Camden said, surprising Susan more than anything else that had gone before. His eyes held hers. She felt her chest tighten.

"I think," Dr. Ong said dryly, "that the philosophy of the universe may be beyond our concerns here. Mr. Camden, if you have no further medical questions, perhaps we can return to the legal points Ms. Sullivan and Mr. Jaworski have raised. Thank you, Dr. Melling."

Susan nodded. She didn't look again at Camden. But she knew what he said, how he looked, that he was there.

The house was about what she had expected, a huge mock-Tudor on Lake Michigan north of Chicago. The land was heavily wooded between the gate and the house, open between the house and the surging water. Patches of snow dotted the dormant grass. Biotech had been working with the Camdens for four months, but this was the first time Susan had driven to their home.

As she walked toward the house another car drove up behind her. No, a truck, continuing around the curved driveway to a service entry at the side of the house. One man rang the service bell; a second began to unload a plastic-wrapped playpen from the back of the truck. White, with pink and yellow bunnies. Susan briefly closed her eyes.

Camden opened the door himself. She could see his effort not to look worried. "You didn't have to drive out, Susan; I'd have come into the city!"

"No, I didn't want you to do that, Roger. Mrs. Camden is here?"

"In the living room." Camden led her into a large room with a stone fireplace, English country-house furniture, and prints of dogs or boats, all hung eighteen inches too high; Elizabeth Camden must have done the decorating. She did not rise from her wing chair as Susan entered.

"Let me be concise and fast," Susan said, "I don't want to make this any more drawn-out for you than I have to. We have all the amniocentesis, ultrasound, and Langston test results. The fetus is fine, developing normally for two weeks, no problems with the implant on the uterine wall. But a complication has developed."

"What?" Camden said. He took out a cigarette, looked at his wife, and put it back unlit.

Susan said quietly, "Mrs. Camden, by sheer chance both your ovaries released eggs last month. We removed one for the gene surgery. By more sheer chance the second was fertilized and implanted. You're carrying two fetuses."

Elizabeth Camden grew still. "Twins?"

"No," Susan said. Then she realized what she had said. "I mean, yes. They're twins, but non-identical. Only one has been genetically altered. The other will be no more similar to her than any two siblings. It's a so-called normal baby. And I know you didn't want a so-called normal baby."

Camden said, "No. I didn't."

Elizabeth Camden said, "I did."

Camden shot her a fierce look that Susan couldn't read. He took out the cigarette again, and lit it. His face was in profile to Susan, and he was thinking intently; she doubted he knew the cigarette was there, or that he was lighting it. "Is the baby being affected by the other one's being there?"

"No," Susan said. "No, of course not. They're just … coexisting."

"Can you abort it?"

"Not without aborting both of them. Removing the unaltered fetus would cause changes in the uterine lining that would probably lead to a spontaneous miscarriage of the other." She drew a deep breath. "There's that option, of course. We can start the whole process over again. But as I told you at the time, you were very lucky to have the *in vitro* fertilization take on only the second try. Some couples take eight or ten tries. If we started all over, the process could be a lengthy one."

Camden said, "Is the presence of this second fetus harming my daughter? Taking away nutrients or anything? Or will it change anything for her later on in the pregnancy?"

"No. Except that there is a chance of premature birth. Two fetuses take up a lot more room in the womb, and if it gets too crowded, birth can be premature. But the—"

"How premature? Enough to threaten survival?"

"Most probably not."

Camden went on smoking. A man appeared at the door. "Sir, London calling. James Kendall for Mr. Yagai."

"I'll take it." Camden rose. Susan watched him study his wife's face. When he spoke, it was to her. "All right, Elizabeth. All right." He left the room.

For a long moment the two women sat in silence. Susan was aware of the disappointment; this was not the Camden she had expected to see. She became aware of Elizabeth Camden watching her with amusement.

"Oh, yes, Doctor. He's like that."

Susan said nothing.

"Completely overbearing. But not this time." She laughed softly, with excitement. "Two. Do you … do you know what sex the other one is?"

"Both fetuses are female."

"I wanted a girl, you know. And now I'll have one."

"Then you'll go ahead with the pregnancy."

"Oh, yes. Thank you for coming, Doctor."

She was dismissed. No one saw her out. But as she was getting into her car, Camden rushed out of the house, coatless. "Susan! I wanted to thank you. For coming all the way out here to tell us yourself."

"You already thanked me."

"Yes. Well. You're sure the second fetus is no threat to my daughter?"

Susan said deliberately, "Nor is the genetically altered fetus a threat to the naturally conceived one."

He smiled. His voice was low and wistful. "And you think that should matter to me just as much. But it doesn't. And why should I fake what I feel? Especially to you?"

Susan opened her car door. She wasn't ready for this, or she had changed her mind, or something. But then Camden leaned over to close the door, and his manner held no trace of flirtatiousness, no smarmy ingratiation. "I better order a second playpen."

"Yes."

"And a second car seat."

"Yes."

"But not a second night-shift nurse."

"That's up to you."

"And you." Abruptly he leaned over and kissed her, a kiss so polite and respectful that Susan was shocked. Neither lust nor conquest would have shocked her; this did. Camden didn't give her a chance to react; he closed the car door and turned back toward the house. Susan drove toward the gate, her hands shaky on the wheel until amusement replaced shock: It *had* been a deliberate, blatant, respectful kiss, an engineered enigma. And nothing else could have guaranteed so well that there would have to be another.

She wondered what the Camdens would name their daughters.

Dr. Ong strode the hospital corridor, which had been dimmed to half-light. From the nurse's station in Maternity a nurse stepped forward as if to stop him—it was the middle of the night, long past visiting hours—got a good look at his face, and faded back into her station. Around a corner was the viewing glass to the nursery. To Ong's annoyance, Susan Melling stood pressed against the glass. To his further annoyance, she was crying.

Ong realized that he had never liked the woman. Maybe not any women. Even those with superior minds could not seem to refrain from being made damn fools by their emotions.

"Look," Susan said, laughing a little, swiping at her face. "Doctor—*look*."

Behind the glass Roger Camden, gowned and masked, was holding up a baby in a white undershirt and pink blanket. Camden's blue eyes—theatrically blue—a man really should not have such garish eyes—glowed. The baby's head was covered with blond fuzz; it had wide eyes and pink skin. Camden's eyes above the mask said that no other child had ever had these attributes.

Ong said, "An uncomplicated birth?"

"Yes," Susan Melling sobbed. "Perfectly straightforward. Elizabeth is fine. She's asleep. Isn't she beautiful? He has the most adventurous spirit I've ever known." She wiped her nose on her sleeve; Ong realized that she was drunk. "Did I ever tell you that I was engaged once? Fifteen years ago, in med school? I broke it off because he grew to seem so ordinary, so boring. Oh, God, I shouldn't be telling you all this. I'm sorry. I'm sorry."

Ong moved away from her. Behind the glass Roger Camden laid the baby in a small wheeled crib. The nameplate said BABY GIRL CAMDEN #1. 5.9 POUNDS. A night nurse watched indulgently.

Ong did not wait to see Camden emerge from the nursery or to hear Susan Melling say to him whatever she was going to say.

Ong went to have the OB paged. Melling's report was not, under the circumstances, to be trusted. A perfect, unprecedented chance to record every detail of gene alteration with a non-altered control, and Melling was more interested in her own sloppy emotions. Ong would obviously have to do the report himself, after talking to the OB. He was hungry for every detail. And not just about the pink-cheeked baby in Camden's arms. He wanted to know everything about the birth of the child in the other glass-sided crib: BABY GIRL CAMDEN #2. 5.1 POUNDS. The dark-haired baby with the mottled red features, lying scrunched down in her pink blanket, asleep.

Two

Leisha's earliest memory was flowing lines that were not there. She knew they were not there because when she reached out her fist to touch them, her fist was empty. Later she realized that the flowing lines were light: sunshine slanting in bars between curtains in her room, between the wooden blinds in the dining room, between the crisscross lattices in the conservatory. The day she realized the golden flow was light she laughed out loud with the sheer joy of discovery, and Daddy turned from putting flowers in pots and smiled at her.

The whole house was full of light. Light bounded off the lake, streamed across the high white ceilings, puddled on the shining wooden floors. She and Alice moved continually through light, and sometimes Leisha would stop and tip back her head and let it flow over her face. She could feel it, like water.

The best light, of course, was in the conservatory. That's where Daddy liked to be when he was home from making money. Daddy potted plants and watered trees, humming, and Leisha and Alice ran between the wooden tables of flowers with their wonderful earthy smells, running from the dark side of the conservatory where the big purple flowers grew to the sunshine side with sprays of yellow flowers, running back and forth, in and out of the light. "Growth," Daddy said to her, "flowers all fulfilling their promise.

Alice, be careful! You almost knocked over that orchid!" Alice, obedient, would stop running for a while. Daddy never told Leisha to stop running.

After a while the light would go away. Alice and Leisha would have their baths, and then Alice would get quiet, or cranky. She wouldn't play nice with Leisha, even when Leisha let her choose the game or even have all the best dolls. Then Nanny would take Alice to bed, and Leisha would talk with Daddy some more until Daddy said he had to work in his study with the papers that made money. Leisha always felt a moment of regret that he had to go do that, but the moment never lasted very long because Mamselle would arrive and start Leisha's lessons, which she liked. Learning things was so interesting! She could already sing twenty songs and write all the letters in the alphabet and count to fifty. And by the time lessons were done, the light had come back, and it was time for breakfast.

Breakfast was the only time Leisha didn't like. Daddy had gone to the office, and Leisha and Alice had breakfast with Mommy in the big dining room. Mommy sat in a red robe, which Leisha liked, and she didn't smell funny or talk funny the way she would later in the day, but still breakfast wasn't fun. Mommy always started with The Question.

"Alice, sweetheart, how did you sleep?"

"Fine, Mommy."

"Did you have any nice dreams?"

For a long time Alice said no. Then one day she said, "I dreamed about a horse. I was riding him." Mommy clapped her hands and kissed Alice and gave her an extra sticky bun. After that Alice always had a dream to tell Mommy.

Once Leisha said, "I had a dream, too. I dreamed light was coming in the window and it wrapped all around me like a blanket and then it kissed me on my eyes."

Mommy put down her coffee cup so hard that coffee sloshed out of it. "Don't lie to me, Leisha. You did not have a dream."

"Yes, I did," Leisha said.

"Only children who sleep can have dreams. Don't lie to me. You did not have a dream."

"Yes I did! I did!" Leisha shouted. She could see it, almost: the light streaming in the window and wrapping around her like a golden blanket.

"I will not tolerate a child who is a liar! Do you hear me, Leisha—I won't tolerate it!"

"You're a liar!" Leisha shouted, knowing the words weren't true, hating herself because they weren't true but hating Mommy more and that was wrong, too, and there sat Alice stiff and frozen with her eyes wide, Alice was scared and it was Leisha's fault.

Mommy called sharply, "Nanny! Nanny! Take Leisha to her room at once. She can't sit with civilized people if she can't refrain from telling lies!"

Leisha started to cry. Nanny carried her out of the room. Leisha hadn't even had her breakfast. But she didn't care about that; all she could see while she cried was Alice's eyes, scared like that, reflecting broken bits of light.

But Leisha didn't cry long. Nanny read her a story, and then played Data Jump with her, and then Alice came up and Nanny drove them both into Chicago to the zoo where there were wonderful animals to see, animals Leisha could not have dreamed—nor Alice *either*. And by the time they came back Mommy had gone to her room and Leisha knew that she would stay there with the glasses of funny-smelling stuff the rest of the day and Leisha would not have to see her.

But that night, she went to her mother's room.

"I have to go to the bathroom," she told Mamselle. Mamselle said, "Do you need any help?" maybe because Alice still needed help in the bathroom. But Leisha didn't, and she thanked Mamselle. Then she sat on the toilet for a minute even though nothing came, so that what she had told Mamselle wouldn't be a lie.

Leisha tiptoed down the hall. She went first into Alice's room. A little light in a wall socket burned near the crib. There was no crib in Leisha's room. Leisha looked at her sister through the bars. Alice lay on her side with her eyes closed. The lids of the eyes fluttered quickly, like curtains blowing in the wind. Alice's chin and neck looked loose.

Leisha closed the door very carefully and went to her parents' room.

They didn't sleep in a crib but in a huge enormous bed, with enough room between them for more people. Mommy's eyelids weren't fluttering; she lay on her back making a hrrr-hrrr sound through her nose. The funny smell was strong on her. Leisha backed away and tiptoed over to Daddy. He looked like Alice, except that his neck and chin looked even looser, folds of skin collapsed like the tent that had fallen down in the backyard. It scared Leisha to see him like that. Then Daddy's eyes flew open so suddenly that Leisha screamed.

Daddy rolled out of bed and picked her up, looking quickly at Mommy. But she didn't move. Daddy was wearing only his underpants. He carried Leisha out into the hall, where Mamselle came rushing up saying, "Oh, Sir, I'm sorry, she just said she was going to the bathroom—"

"It's all right," Daddy said. "I'll take her with me."

"No!" Leisha screamed, because Daddy was only in his underpants and his neck had looked all funny and the room smelled bad because of Mommy. But Daddy carried her into the conservatory, set her down on a bench, wrapped himself in a piece of green plastic that was supposed to cover up plants, and sat down next to her.

"Now, what happened, Leisha? What were you doing?"

Leisha didn't answer.

"You were looking at people sleeping, weren't you?" Daddy said, and because his voice was softer Leisha mumbled, "Yes." She immediately felt better; it felt good not to lie.

"You were looking at people sleeping because you don't sleep and you were curious, weren't you? Like Curious George in your book?"

"Yes," Leisha said. "I thought you said you made money in your study all night!"

Daddy smiled. "Not all night. Some of it. But then I sleep, although not very much." He took Leisha on his lap. "I don't need much sleep, so I get a lot more done at night than most people. Different people need different amounts of sleep. And a few, a very few, are like you. You don't need any."

"Why not?"

"Because you're special. Better than other people. Before you were born, I had some doctors help make you that way."

"Why?"

"So you could do anything you want to and make manifest your own individuality."

Leisha twisted in his arms to stare at him; the words meant nothing. Daddy reached over and touched a single flower growing on a tall potted tree. The flower had thick white petals like the cream he put in coffee, and the center was a light pink.

"See, Leisha—this tree made this flower. Because it *can*. Only this tree can make this kind of wonderful flower. That plant hanging up there can't, and those can't either. Only this tree. Therefore the most important thing in the world for this tree to do is grow this flower. The flower is the tree's individuality—that means just *it*, and nothing else—made manifest. Nothing else matters."

"I don't understand, Daddy."

"You will. Someday."

"But I want to understand *now*," Leisha said, and Daddy laughed with pure delight and hugged her. The hug felt good, but Leisha still wanted to understand.

"When you make money, is that your indiv … that thing?"

"Yes," Daddy said happily.

"Then nobody else can make money? Like only that tree can make that flower?"

"Nobody else can make it just the way I do."

"What do you do with the money?"

"I buy things for you. This house, your dresses, Mamselle to teach you, the car to ride in."

"What does the tree do with the flower?"

"Glories in it," Daddy said, which made no sense. "Excellence is what counts, Leisha. Excellence supported by individual effort. And that's *all* that counts."

"I'm cold, Daddy."

"Then I better bring you back to Mamselle."

Leisha didn't move. She touched the flower with one finger. "I want to sleep, Daddy."

"No, you don't, sweetheart. Sleep is just lost time, wasted life. It's a little death."

"Alice sleeps.

"Alice isn't like you."

"Alice isn't special?"

"No. You are."

"Why didn't you make Alice special, too?"

"Alice made herself. I didn't have a chance to make her special."

The whole thing was too hard. Leisha stopped stroking the flower and slipped off Daddy's lap. He smiled at her. "My little questioner. When you grow up, you'll find your own excellence, and it will be a new order, a specialness the world hasn't ever seen before. You might even be like Kenzo Yagai. He made the Yagai generator that powers the world."

"Daddy, you look funny wrapped in the flower plastic." Leisha laughed. Daddy did, too. But then she said, "When I grow up, I'll make my specialness find a way to make Alice special, too," and Daddy stopped laughing.

He took her back to Mamselle, who taught her to write her name, which was so exciting she forgot about the puzzling talk with Daddy. There were six letters, all different, and together they were *her name*. Leisha wrote it over and over, laughing, and Mamselle laughed too. But later, in the morning, Leisha thought again about the talk with Daddy. She thought of it often, turning the unfamiliar words over and over in her mind like small hard stones, but the part she thought about most wasn't a word. It was the frown on Daddy's face when she told him she would use her specialness to make Alice special, too.

Every week Dr. Melling came to see Leisha and Alice, sometimes alone, sometimes with other people. Leisha and Alice both liked Dr. Melling, who laughed a lot and whose eyes were bright and warm. Often Daddy was there, too. Dr. Melling played games with them, first with Alice and Leisha separately and then together. She took their pictures and weighed them. She made them lie down on a table and stuck little metal things to their temples, which sounded scary but wasn't because there were so many machines to watch, all making interesting noises, while they were lying there. Dr. Melling was as good at answering questions as Daddy. Once Leisha said, "Is Dr. Melling a special person? Like Kenzo Yagai?" And Daddy laughed and glanced at Dr. Melling and said, "Oh, yes, indeed."

When Leisha was five she and Alice started school. Daddy's driver took them every day into Chicago. They were in different rooms, which disappointed Leisha. The kids in Leisha's room were all older. But from the first day she adored school, with its fascinating science equipment and electronic drawers full of math puzzlers and other children to find countries on the map with. In half a year she had been moved to yet a different room, where the kids were still older, but they were nonetheless nice to her. Leisha started to learn Japanese. She loved drawing the beautiful characters on thick white paper. "The Sauley School was a good choice," Daddy said.

But Alice didn't like the Sauley School. She wanted to go to school on the same yellow bus as Cook's daughter. She cried and threw her paints on the floor at the Sauley School. Then Mommy came out of her room—Leisha hadn't seen her for a few weeks, although she knew Alice had—and threw some candlesticks from the mantelpiece on the floor. The candlesticks, which were china, broke. Leisha ran to pick up the pieces while Mommy and Daddy screamed at each other in the hall by the big staircase.

"She's my daughter, too! And I say she can go!"

"You don't have the right to say anything about it! A weepy drunk, the most rotten role model possible for both of them … and I thought I was getting a fine English aristocrat!"

"You got what you paid for! Nothing! Not that you ever needed anything from me or anybody else!"

"Stop it!" Leisha cried. "Stop it!" There was silence in the hall. Leisha cut her fingers on the china; blood streamed onto the rug. Daddy rushed in and picked her up. "Stop it," Leisha sobbed, and didn't understand when Daddy said quietly, "*You* stop it, Leisha. Nothing *they* do should touch you at all. You have to be at least that strong."

Leisha buried her head in Daddy's shoulder. Alice transferred to Carl Sandburg Elementary School, riding there on the yellow school bus with Cook's daughter.

A few weeks later Daddy told them that Mommy was going away to a hospital, to stop drinking so much. When Mommy came out, he said, she was going to live somewhere else for a while. She and Daddy were not happy. Leisha and Alice would stay with Daddy and they would visit Mommy sometimes. He told them this very carefully, finding the right words for truth. Truth was very important, Leisha already knew. Truth was being true to yourself, your specialness. Your individuality. An individual respected facts, and so always told the truth.

Mommy—Daddy did not say but Leisha knew—did not respect facts.

"I don't want Mommy to go away," Alice said. She started to cry. Leisha thought Daddy would pick Alice up, but he didn't. He just stood there looking at them both.

Leisha put her arms around Alice. "It's all right, Alice. It's all right! We'll make it all right! I'll play with you all the time we're not in school so you don't miss Mommy!"

Alice clung to Leisha. Leisha turned her head so she didn't have to see Daddy's face.

Three

Kenzo Yagai was coming to the United States to lecture. The title of his talk, which he would give in New York, Los Angeles, and Chicago, with a repeat in Washington as a special address to Congress, was "The Further Political Implications of Inexpensive Power." Leisha Camden, eleven years old, was going to have a private introduction after the Chicago talk, arranged by her father.

She had studied the theory of cold fusion at school, and her global studies teacher had traced the changes in the world resulting from Yagai's patented, low-cost applications of what had, until him, been unworkable theory: the rising prosperity of the Third World; the death throes of the old communistic systems; the decline of the oil states; the renewed economic power of the United States. Her study group had written a news script, filmed with the school's professional-quality equipment, about how a 1985 American family lived with expensive energy costs and a belief in tax-supported help, while a 2019 family lived with cheap energy and a belief in the contract as the basis of civilization. Parts of her own research puzzled Leisha.

"Japan thinks Kenzo Yagai was a traitor to his own country," she said to Daddy at supper.

"No," Camden said, "*some* Japanese think that. Watch out for generalizations, Leisha. Yagai patented and licensed Y-energy in the United States because here there were at least the dying embers of individual enterprise. Because of his invention, our entire country has slowly swung back toward an individual meritocracy, and Japan has slowly been forced to follow."

"Your father held that belief all along," Susan said. "Eat your peas, Leisha." Leisha ate her peas. Susan and Daddy had only been married less than a year; it still felt a little strange to have her there. But nice. Daddy said Susan was a valuable addition to their household: intelligent, motivated, and cheerful. Like Leisha herself.

"Remember, Leisha," Camden said, "a man's worth to society and to himself doesn't rest on what he thinks other people should do or be or feel, but on himself. On what he can actually do, and do well. People trade what they do well, and everyone benefits. The basic tool of civilization is the contract. Contracts are voluntary and mutually beneficial. As opposed to coercion, which is wrong."

"The strong have no right to take anything from the weak by force," Susan said. "Alice, eat your peas, too, honey."

"Nor the weak to take anything by force from the strong," Camden said. "That's the basis of what you'll hear Kenzo Yagai discuss tonight, Leisha."

Alice said, "I don't like peas."

Camden said, "Your body does. They're good for you."

Alice smiled. Leisha felt her heart lift; Alice didn't smile much at dinner anymore. "My body doesn't have a contract with the peas."

Camden said, a little impatiently, "Yes, it does. Your body benefits from them. Now eat."

Alice's smile vanished. Leisha looked down at her plate. Suddenly she saw a way out. "No, Daddy, look—Alice's body benefits, but the peas don't! It's not a mutually beneficial consideration, so there's no contract! Alice is right!"

Camden let out a shout of laughter. To Susan he said, "Eleven years old ... *eleven*." Even Alice smiled, and Leisha waved her spoon triumphantly, light glinting off the bowl and dancing silver on the opposite wall.

But even so, Alice did not want to go hear Kenzo Yagai. She was going to sleep over at her friend Julie's house; they were going to curl their hair together. More surprisingly, Susan wasn't coming either. She and Daddy looked at each other a little funny at the front door, Leisha thought, but Leisha was too excited to think about this. She was going to hear *Kenzo Yagai.*

Yagai was a small man, dark and slim. Leisha liked his accent. She liked, too, something about him that took her a while to name. "Daddy," she whispered in the half-darkness of the auditorium, "he's a joyful man."

Daddy hugged her in the darkness.

Yagai spoke about spirituality and economics. "A man's spirituality, which is only his dignity as a man, rests on his own efforts. Dignity and worth are not automatically conferred by aristocratic birth; we have only to look at history to see that. Dignity and worth are not automatically conferred by inherited wealth. A great heir may be a thief, a wastrel, cruel, an exploiter, a person who leaves the world much poorer than he found it. Nor are dignity and worth automatically conferred by existence itself. A mass murderer exists, but is of negative worth to his society and possesses no dignity in his lust to kill.

"No, the only dignity, the only spirituality, rests on what a man can achieve with his own efforts. To rob a man of the chance to achieve, and to trade what he achieves with others, is to rob him of his spiritual dignity as a man. This is why communism has failed in our time. *All* coercion—all force to take from a man his own efforts to achieve—causes spiritual damage and weakens a society. Conscription, theft, fraud, violence, welfare, lack of legislative representation—*all* rob a man of his chance to choose, to achieve on his own, to trade the results of his achievement with others. Coercion is a cheat. It produces nothing new. Only freedom—the freedom to achieve, the freedom to trade freely the results of achievement—creates the environment proper to the dignity and spirituality of man."

Leisha applauded so hard her hands hurt. Going backstage with Daddy, she thought she could hardly breathe. Kenzo Yagai!

But backstage was more crowded than she had expected. There were cameras everywhere. Daddy said, "Mr. Yagai, may I present my daughter Leisha," and the cameras moved in close and fast—on *her*. A Japanese man whispered something in Kenzo Yagai's ear, and he looked more closely at Leisha. "Ah, yes."

"Look over here, Leisha," someone called, and she did. A robot camera zoomed so close to her face that Leisha stepped back, startled. Daddy spoke very sharply to someone, then to someone else. The cameras didn't move. A woman suddenly knelt in front of Leisha and thrust a microphone at her. "What does it feel like to never sleep, Leisha?"

"What?"

Someone laughed. The laugh was not kind. "Breeding geniuses . . ."

Leisha felt a hand on her shoulder. Kenzo Yagai gripped her very firmly, and pulled her away from the cameras. Immediately, as if by magic, a line of Japanese men formed behind Yagai, parting only to let Daddy through. Behind the line, the three of them moved into a dressing room, and Kenzo Yagai shut the door.

"You must not let them bother you, Leisha," he said in his wonderful accent. "Not ever. There is an old Asian proverb: 'The dogs bark but the caravan moves on.' You must never let your individual caravan be slowed by the barking of rude or envious dogs."

"I won't," Leisha breathed, not sure yet what the words really meant, knowing there was time later to sort them out, to talk about them with Daddy. For now she was dazzled by Kenzo Yagai, the actual man himself who was changing the world without force, without guns, by trading his special individual efforts. "We study your philosophy at my school, Mr. Yagai."

Kenzo Yagai looked at Daddy. Daddy said, "A private school. But Leisha's sister also studies it, although cursorily, in the public system. Slowly, Kenzo, but it comes. It comes." Leisha noticed that he did not say why Alice was not here tonight with them.

Back home, Leisha sat in her room for hours, thinking over everything that had happened. When Alice came home from Julie's the next morning, Leisha rushed toward her. But Alice seemed angry about something.

"Alice—what is it?"

"Don't you think I have enough to put up with at school already?" Alice shouted. "Everybody knows, but at least when you stayed quiet it didn't matter too much! They'd stopped teasing me! Why did you have to do it?"

"Do what?" Leisha said, bewildered.

Alice threw something at her: a hard-copy morning paper, on newsprint flimsier than the Camden systems used. The paper dropped open at Leisha's feet. She stared at her own picture, three columns wide, with Kenzo Yagai. The headline said, "Yagai and the Future: Room For the Rest of Us? Y-Energy Inventor Confers with 'Sleep-Free' Daughter of Mega-Financier Roger Camden."

Alice kicked the paper. "It was on TV last night too—on *TV*. I work hard not to look stuck-up or creepy, and you go and do this! Now Julie probably won't even invite me to her slumber party next week!" She rushed up the broad curving stairs to her room.

Leisha looked down at the paper. She heard Kenzo Yagai's voice in her head: *The dogs bark but the caravan moves on*. She looked at the empty stairs. Aloud she said, "Alice—your hair looks really pretty curled like that."

Four

I want to meet the rest of them," Leisha said. "Why have you kept them from me this long?"

"I haven't kept them from you at all," Camden said. "Not offering is not the same as denial. Why shouldn't you be the one to do the asking? You're the one who now wants it."

Leisha looked at him. She was fifteen, in her last year at the Sauley School. "Why didn't you offer?"

"Why should I?"

"I don't know," Leisha said. "But you gave me everything else."

"Including the freedom to ask for what you want."

Leisha looked for the contradiction, and found it. "Most things that you provided for my education I didn't ask for, because I didn't know enough to ask and you as the adult did. But you've never offered the opportunity for me to meet any of the other sleepless mutants—"

"Don't use that word," Camden said sharply.

"—so you must either think it was not essential to my education or else you had another motive for not wanting me to meet them."

"Wrong," Camden said. "There's a third possibility. That I think meeting them is essential to your education, that I do want you to, but this issue provided a chance to further the education of your self-initiative by waiting for *you* to ask."

"All right," Leisha said, a little defiantly; there seemed to be a lot of defiance between them lately, for no good reason. She squared her shoulders. Her new breasts thrust forward. "I'm asking. How many of the Sleepless are there, who are they, and where are they?"

Camden said, "If you're using that term—'the Sleepless'—you've already done some reading on your own. So you probably know that there are 1,082 of you so far in the United States, more in foreign countries, most of them in major metropolitan areas. Seventy-nine are in Chicago, most of them still small children. Only nineteen anywhere are older than you."

Leisha didn't deny reading any of this. Camden leaned forward in his study chair to peer at her. Leisha wondered if he needed glasses. His hair was completely gray now, sparse and stiff, like lonely broom straws. The *Wall Street Journal* listed him among the hundred richest men in America; *Women's Wear Daily* pointed out that he was the only billionaire in the country who did not move in the society of international parties, charity balls, and social secretaries. Camden's jet ferried him to business meetings around the world, to the chairmanship of the Yagai Economics Institute, and to very little else. Over the years he had grown richer, more reclusive, and more cerebral. Leisha felt a rush of her old affection.

She threw herself sideways into a leather chair, her long slim legs dangling over the arm. Absently she scratched a mosquito bite on her thigh. "Well, then, I'd like to meet Richard Keller." He lived in Chicago and was the beta-test Sleepless closest to her own age. He was seventeen.

"Why ask me? Why not just go?"

Leisha thought there was a note of impatience in his voice. He liked her to explore things first, then report on them to him later. Both parts were important.

Leisha laughed. "You know what, Daddy? You're predictable."

Camden laughed, too. In the middle of the laugh Susan came in. "He certainly is not. Roger, what about that meeting in Buenos Aires on Thursday? Is it on or off?" When he didn't answer, her voice grew shriller. "Roger? I'm talking to you!"

Leisha averted her eyes. Two years ago Susan had finally left genetic research to run Camden's house and schedule; before that she had tried hard to do both. Since she had left Biotech, it seemed to Leisha, Susan had changed. Her voice was tighter. She was more insistent that Cook and the gardener follow her directions exactly, without deviation. Her blond braids had become stiff sculptured waves of platinum.

"It's on," Roger said.

"Well, thanks for at least answering. Am I going?"

"If you like."

"I like."

Susan left the room. Leisha rose and stretched. Her long legs rose on tiptoe. It felt good to reach, to stretch, to feel sunlight from the wide windows wash over her face. She smiled at her father, and found him watching her with an unexpected expression.

"Leisha—"

"What?"

"See Keller. But be careful."

"Of what?"

But Camden wouldn't answer.

The voice on the phone had been noncommittal. "Leisha Camden? Yes, I know who you are. Three o'clock on Thursday?" The house was modest; a thirty-year-old colonial on a quiet suburban street where small children on bicycles could be watched from the front window. Few roofs had more than one Y-energy cell. The trees, huge old sugar maples, were beautiful.

"Come in," Richard Keller said.

He was no taller than she, stocky, with a bad case of acne. Probably no genetic alterations except sleep, Leisha guessed. He had thick dark hair, a low forehead, and bushy black brows. Before he closed the door Leisha saw him stare at her car and driver, parked in the driveway next to a rusty ten-speed bike.

"I can't drive yet," she said. "I'm still fifteen."

"It's easy to learn," Richard said. "So, you want to tell me why you're here?"

Leisha liked his directness. "To meet some other Sleepless."

"You mean you never have? Not any of us?"

"You mean the rest of you know each other?" She hadn't expected that.

"Come to my room, Leisha."

She followed him to the back of the house. No one else seemed to be home. His room was large and airy, filled with computers and filing cabinets. A rowing machine sat in one corner. It looked like a shabbier version of the room of any bright classmate at the Sauley School, except there was more space without a bed. She walked over to the computer screen.

"Hey—you working on Boesc equations?"

"On an application of them."

"To what?"

"Fish migration patterns."

Leisha smiled. "Yeah, that would work. I never thought of that." Richard seemed not to know what to do with her smile. He looked at the wall, then at her chin. "You interested in Gaea patterns? In the environment?"

"Well, no," Leisha confessed. "Not particularly. I'm going to study politics at Harvard. Pre-law. But of course we had Gaea patterns at school."

Richard's gaze finally came unstuck from her face. He ran a hand through his dark hair. "Sit down, if you want."

Leisha sat, looking appreciatively at the wall posters, shifting green on blue, like ocean currents. "I like those. Did you program them yourself?"

"You're not at all what I pictured," Richard said.

"How did you picture me?"

He didn't hesitate. "Stuck-up. Superior. Shallow, despite your IQ."

She was more hurt than she had expected to be.

Richard blurted. "You're one of only two Sleepless who're really rich. You and Jennifer Sharifi. But you already know that."

"No, I don't. I've never checked."

He took the chair beside her, stretching his stocky legs straight in front of him, in a slouch that had nothing to do with relaxation. "It makes sense, really. Rich people don't have their children genetically modified to be superior—they think any offspring of theirs is already superior. By their values. And poor people can't afford it. We Sleepless are upper-middle class, no more. Children of professors, scientists, people who value brains and time."

"My father values brains and time," Leisha said. "He's the biggest supporter of Kenzo Yagai."

"Oh, Leisha, do you think I don't already know that? Are you flashing me or what?"

Leisha said with great deliberateness, "I'm *talking* to you." But the next minute she could feel the hurt break through on her face.

"I'm sorry," Richard muttered. He shot off his chair and paced to the computer and back. "I *am* sorry. But I don't ... I don't understand what you're doing here."

"I'm lonely," Leisha said, astonished at herself. She looked up at him. "It's true. I'm lonely. I am. I have friends and Daddy and Alice. But no one really knows, really understands—what? I don't know what I'm saying."

Richard smiled. The smile changed his whole face, opened up its dark planes to the light. "I do. Oh, do I. What do you do when they say, 'I had such a dream last night?'"

"Yes!" Leisha said. "But that's even really minor. It's when I say, 'I'll look that up for you tonight' and they get that funny look on their face that means, 'She'll do it while I'm asleep.'"

"But that's even really minor," Richard said. "It's when you're playing basketball in the gym after supper and then you go to the diner for food and then you say, 'Let's have a walk by the lake,' and they say, 'I'm really tired. I'm going home to bed now.'"

"But that's really minor," Leisha said, jumping up. "It's when you really are absorbed by the movie and then you get the point and it's so goddamn beautiful you leap up and say, 'Yes! Yes!' and Susan says, 'Leisha, really, you'd think nobody but you ever enjoyed anything before.'"

"Who's Susan?" Richard said.

The mood was broken. But not really; Leisha could say, "My stepmother," without much discomfort over what Susan had promised to be and what she had become. Richard stood inches from her, smiling that joyous smile, understanding, and suddenly relief washed over Leisha so strong that she walked straight over to him and put her arms around his neck, only tightening them when she felt his startled jerk. She started to sob—she, Leisha, who never cried.

"Hey," Richard said. "Hey."

"Brilliant," Leisha said, laughing. "Brilliant remark."

She could feel his embarrassed smile. "Wanta see my fish migration curves instead?"

"No," Leisha sobbed, and he went on holding her, patting her back awkwardly, telling her without words that she was home.

Camden waited up for her, although it was past midnight. He had been smoking heavily. Through the blue air he said quietly, "Did you have a good time, Leisha?"

"Yes."

"I'm glad," he said, and put out his last cigarette, and climbed the stairs—slowly, stiffly, he was nearly seventy now—to bed.

They went everywhere together for nearly a year: swimming, dancing, the museums, the theater, the library. Richard introduced her to the others, a group of twelve kids between fourteen and nineteen, all of them intelligent and eager. All Sleepless.

Leisha learned.

Tony Indivino's parents, like her own, had divorced. But Tony, fourteen, lived with his mother, who had not particularly wanted a Sleepless child, while his father, who had, acquired a red sports car and a young girlfriend who designed ergonomic chairs in Paris. Tony was not allowed to tell anyone—relatives, schoolmates—that he was Sleepless. "They'll think you're a freak," his mother said, eyes averted from her son's face. The one time Tony disobeyed her and told a friend that he never slept, his mother beat him. Then she moved the family to a new neighborhood. He was nine years old.

Jeanine Carter, almost as long-legged and slim as Leisha, was training for the Olympics in ice skating. She practiced twelve hours a day, hours no Sleeper still in high school could ever have. So far the newspapers had not picked up the story. Jeanine was afraid that if they did, they would somehow not let her compete.

Jack Bellingham, like Leisha, would start college in September. Unlike Leisha, he had already started his career. The practice of law had to wait for law school; the practice of investing required only money. Jack didn't have much, but his precise financial analyses parlayed six hundred dollars saved from summer jobs to three thousand dollars through stock-market investing, then to ten thousand dollars, and then he had enough to qualify for information-fund speculation. Jack was fifteen, not old enough to make legal investments; the transactions were all in the name of Kevin Baker, the oldest of the Sleepless, who lived in Austin. Jack told Leisha, "When I hit eighty-four percent profit over two consecutive quarters, the data analysts logged onto me. Just sniffing. Well, that's their job, even when the overall amounts are actually small. It's the patterns they care about. If they take the trouble to cross-reference data banks and come up with the fact that Kevin is a Sleepless, will they try to stop us from investing somehow?"

"That's paranoid," Leisha said.

"No, it's not," Jeanine said. "Leisha, you don't *know*."

"You mean because I've been protected by my father's money and caring," Leisha said. No one grimaced; all of them confronted ideas openly, without shadowy allusions. Without dreams.

"Yes," Jeanine said. "Your father sounds terrific. And he raised you to think that achievement should not be fettered—Jesus Christ, he's a Yagaiist. Well, good. We're glad for you." She said it without sarcasm. Leisha nodded. "But the world isn't always like that. They hate us."

"That's too strong," Carol said. "Not hate."

"Well, maybe," Jeanine said. "But they're different from us. We're better, and they naturally resent that."

"I don't see what's natural about it," Tony said. "Why shouldn't it be just as natural to admire what's better? We do. Does any one of us resent Kenzo Yagai for his genius? Or Nelson Wade, the physicist? Or Catherine Raduski?"

"We don't resent them because we *are* better," Richard said. "Q.E.D."

"What we should do is have our own society," Tony said. "Why should we allow their regulations to restrict our natural, honest achievements? Why should Jeanine be barred from skating against them and Jack from investing on their same terms just because we're Sleepless? Some of them are brighter than others of them. Some have greater persistence. Well, we have greater concentration, more biochemical stability, and more time. All men are not created equal."

"Be fair, Jack—no one has been barred from anything yet," Jeanine said.

"But we will be."

"*Wait*," Leisha said. She was deeply troubled by the conversation. "I mean, yes, in many ways we're better. But you quoted out of context, Tony. The Declaration of Independence doesn't say all men are created equal in ability. It's talking about rights and power; it means that all are created equal *under the law*. We have no more right to a separate society or to being free of society's restrictions than anyone else does. There's no other way to freely trade one's efforts, unless the same contractual rules apply to all."

"Spoken like a true Yagaiist," Richard said, squeezing her hand.

"That's enough intellectual discussion for me," Carol said, laughing. "We've been at this for hours. We're at the beach, for Chrissake. Who wants to swim with me?"

"I do," Jeanine said. "Come on, Jack."

All of them rose, brushing sand off their suits, discarding sunglasses. Richard pulled Leisha to her feet. But just before they ran into the water, Tony put his skinny hand on her arm. "One more question, Leisha. Just to think about. If we achieve better than most other people, and if we trade with the Sleepers when it's mutually beneficial, making no distinction there between the strong and the weak—what obligation do we have to those so weak they don't have anything to trade with us? We're already going to give more than we get; do we have to do it when we get nothing at all? Do we have to take care of their deformed and handicapped and sick and lazy and shiftless with the products of our work?"

"Do the Sleepers have to?" Leisha countered.

"Kenzo Yagai would say no. He's a Sleeper."

"He would say they would receive the benefits of contractual trade even if they aren't direct parties to the contract. The whole world is better fed and healthier because of Y-energy."

"Come on!" Jeanine yelled. "Leisha, they're ducking me! Jack, you stop that! Leisha, help me!"

Leisha laughed. Just before she grabbed for Jeanine, she caught the look on Richard's face, and on Tony's: Richard frankly lustful, Tony angry. At her. But why? What had she done, except argue in favor of dignity and trade?

Then Jack threw water on her, and Carol pushed Jack into the warm spray, and Richard was there with his arms around her, laughing.

When she got the water out of her eyes, Tony was gone.

Midnight. "Okay," Carol said. "Who's first?"

The six teenagers in the brambly clearing looked at each other. A Y-lamp, kept on low for atmosphere, cast weird shadows across their faces and over their bare legs. Around the clearing Roger Camden's trees stood thick and dark, a wall between them and the closest of the estate's outbuildings. It was very hot. August air hung heavy, sullen. They had voted against bringing an air-conditioned Y-field because this was a return to the primitive, the dangerous; let it be primitive.

Six pairs of eyes stared at the glass in Carol's hand.

"Come *on*," she said. "Who wants to drink up?" Her voice was jaunty, theatrically hard. "It was difficult enough to get this."

"How *did* you get it?" said Richard, the group member—except for Tony—with the least influential family contacts, the least money. "In a drinkable form like that?"

"Jennifer got it," Carol said, and five sets of eyes shifted to Jennifer Sharifi, who two weeks into her visit with Carol's family was confusing them all. She was the American-born daughter of a Hollywood movie star and an Arab prince who had wanted to found a Sleepless dynasty. The movie star was an aging drug addict; the prince, who had taken his fortune out of oil and put it into Y-energy when Kenzo Yagai was still licensing his first patents, was dead. Jennifer Sharifi was richer than Leisha would someday be, and infinitely more sophisticated about procuring things. The glass held interleukin-1, an immune-system booster, one of many substances which as a side effect induced the brain to swift and deep sleep.

Leisha stared at the glass. A warm feeling crept through her lower belly, not unlike the feeling when she and Richard made love. She caught Jennifer watching her, and flushed.

Jennifer disturbed her. Not for the obvious reasons she disturbed Tony and Richard and Jack: the long black hair, the tall, slim body in shorts and halter. Jennifer didn't laugh. Leisha had never met a Sleepless who didn't laugh, nor one who said so little, with such deliberate casualness. Leisha found herself speculating on what Jennifer Sharifi wasn't saying. It was an odd sensation to feel toward another Sleepless.

Tony said to Carol, "Give it to me!"

Carol handed him the glass. "Remember, you only need a little sip."

Tony raised the glass to his mouth, stopped, and looked at them over the rim from his fierce eyes. He drank.

Carol took back the glass. They all watched Tony. Within a minute he lay on the rough ground; within two, his eyes closed in sleep.

It wasn't like seeing parents sleep, siblings, friends. It was Tony. They looked away, avoided each other's eyes. Leisha felt the warmth between her legs tug and tingle, faintly obscene. She didn't took at Jennifer.

When it was Leisha's turn, she drank slowly, then passed the glass to Richard. Her head turned heavy, as if it were being stuffed with damp rags. The trees at the edge of the clearing blurred. The portable lamp blurred, too. It wasn't bright and clean anymore but squishy, blobby; if she touched it, it would smear. Then darkness swooped over her brain, taking it away: *taking away her mind*. "Daddy!" She tried to call, to clutch for him, but then the darkness obliterated her.

Afterward, they all had headaches. Dragging themselves back through the woods in the thin morning light was torture, compounded by an odd shame. They didn't touch each other. Leisha walked as far away from Richard as she could.

Jennifer was the only one who spoke. "So now we know," she said, and her voice held a strange satisfaction.

It was a whole day before the throbbing left the base of Leisha's skull, or the nausea her stomach. She sat alone in her room, waiting for the misery to pass, and despite the heat, her whole body shivered.

There had not even been any dreams.

"I want you to come with me tonight," Leisha said, for the tenth or twelfth time. "We both leave for college in just two days; this is the last chance. I really want you to meet Richard."

Alice lay on her stomach across her bed. Her hair, brown and lusterless, fell around her face. She wore an expensive yellow jumpsuit, silk by Ann Patterson, which rucked up around her knees.

"Why? What do you care if I meet Richard or not?"

"Because you're my sister," Leisha said. She knew better than to say "my twin." Nothing got Alice angry faster.

"I don't want to." The next moment Alice's face changed. "Oh, I'm sorry, Leisha—I didn't mean to sound so snotty. But … but I don't want to."

"It won't be all of them. Just Richard. And just for an hour or so. Then you can come back here and pack for Northwestern."

"I'm not going to Northwestern."

Leisha stared at her.

Alice said, "I'm pregnant."

Leisha sat on the bed. Alice rolled onto her back, brushed the hair out of her eyes, and laughed. Leisha's ears closed against the sound. "Look at you," Alice said. "You'd think it was *you* who was pregnant. But you never would be, would you, Leisha? Not until it was the proper time. Not you."

"How?" Leisha said. "We both had our caps put in …"

"I had the cap removed," Alice said.

"You wanted to get pregnant?"

"Damn flash I did. And there's not a thing Daddy can do about it. Except, of course, cut off all credit completely, but I don't think he'll do that, do you?" She laughed again. "Even to me?"

"But Alice … why? Not just to anger Daddy!"

"No," Alice said. "Although you would think of that, wouldn't you? Because I want something to love. Something of my *own*. Something that has nothing to do with this house."

Leisha thought of herself and Alice running through the conservatory, years ago, her and Alice, darting in and out of the sunlight. "It hasn't been so bad growing up in this house."

"Leisha, you're stupid. I don't know how anyone so smart can be so stupid. Get out of my room! Get out!"

"But Alice—a *baby*—"

"Get out!" Alice shrieked. "Go to Harvard! Go be successful! Just get out!"

Leisha jerked off the bed. "Gladly! You're irrational, Alice. You don't think ahead, you don't plan, a *baby*—" But she could never sustain anger. It dribbled away, leaving her mind empty. She looked at Alice, who suddenly put out her arms. Leisha went into them.

"You're the baby," Alice said wonderingly. "You *are*. You're so … I don't know what. You're a baby."

Leisha said nothing. Alice's arms felt warm, felt whole, felt like two children running in and out of sunlight. "I'll help you, Alice. If Daddy won't."

Alice abruptly pushed her away. "I don't need your help."

Alice stood. Leisha rubbed her empty arms, fingertips scraping across opposite elbows. Alice kicked the empty, open trunk in which she was supposed to pack for Northwestern, and then abruptly smiled a smile that made Leisha look away. She braced herself for more abuse. But what Alice said, very softly, was, "Have a good time at Harvard."

Five

She loved it.

From the first sight of Massachusetts Hall, older than the United States by a half century, Leisha felt something that had been missing in Chicago: Age. Roots. Tradition. She touched the bricks of Widener Library, the glass cases in the Peabody Museum, as if they were the grail. She had never been particularly sensitive to myth or drama; the anguish of Juliet seemed to her artificial, that of Willy Loman merely wasteful. Only King Arthur, struggling to create a better social order, had interested her. But now, walking under the huge autumn trees, she suddenly caught a glimpse of a force that could span generations, fortunes left to endow learning and achievement the benefactors would never see, individual effort spanning and shaping centuries to come. She stopped, and looked at the sky through the leaves, at the buildings solid with purpose. At such moments she thought of Camden, bending the will of an entire genetic research institute to create her in the image he wanted.

Within a month, she had forgotten all such mega-musings.

The work load was incredible, even for her. The Sauley School had encouraged individual exploration at her own pace; Harvard knew what it wanted from her, at its pace. In the past twenty years, under the academic leadership of a man who in his youth had watched Japanese economic domination with dismay, Harvard had become the controversial leader of a return to hard-edged learning of facts, theories, applications, problem-solving, and intellectual efficiency. The school accepted one of every two hundred applicants from around the world. The daughter of England's prime minister had flunked out her first year and been sent home.

Leisha had a single room in a new dormitory, the dorm because she had spent so many years isolated in Chicago and was hungry for people, the single so she would not disturb anyone else when she worked all night. Her second day a boy from down the hall sauntered in and perched on the edge of her desk.

"So you're Leisha Camden."

"Yes."

"Sixteen years old."

"Almost seventeen."

"Going to outperform us all, I understand, without even trying."

Leisha's smile faded. The boy stared at her from under lowered downy brows. He was smiling, his eyes sharp. From Richard and Tony and the others Leisha had learned to recognize the anger that presents itself as contempt.

"Yes," Leisha said coolly, "I am."

"Are you sure? With your pretty little-girl hair and your mutant little-girl brain?"

"Oh, leave her alone, Hannaway," said another voice. A tall blond boy, so thin his ribs looked like ripples in brown sand, stood in jeans and bare feet, drying his wet hair. "Don't you ever get tired of walking around being an asshole?"

"Do you?" Hannaway said. He heaved himself off the desk and started toward the door. The blond moved out of his way. Leisha moved into it.

"The reason I'm going to do better than you," she said evenly, "is because I have certain advantages you don't. Including sleeplessness. And then after I outperform you, I'll be glad to help you study for your tests so that you can pass, too."

The blond, drying his ears, laughed. But Hannaway stood still, and into his eyes came an expression that made Leisha back away. He pushed past her and stormed out.

"Nice going, Camden," the blond said. "He deserved that."

"But I meant it," Leisha said. "I will help him study."

The blond lowered his towel and stared. "You did, didn't you? You meant it."

"Yes! Why does everybody keep questioning that?"

"Well," the boy said, "*I* don't. You can help me if I get into trouble." Suddenly he smiled. "But I won't."

"Why not?"

"Because I'm just as good at anything as you are, Leisha Camden."

She studied him. "You're not one of us. Not Sleepless."

"Don't have to be. I know what I can do. Do, be, create, trade."

She said, delighted, "You're a Yagaiist!"

"Of course." He held out his hand. "Stewart Sutter. How about a fish burger in the Yard?"

"Great," Leisha said. They walked out together, talking excitedly. When people stared at her, she tried not to notice. She was here. At Harvard. With space ahead of her, time, to learn, and with people like Stewart Sutter who accepted and challenged her.

All the hours he was awake.

She became totally absorbed in her class work. Roger Camden drove up once, walking the campus with her, listening, smiling. He was more at home than Leisha would have expected: he knew Stewart Sutter's father and Kate Addams's grandfather. They talked about Harvard, business, Harvard, the Yagai Economics Institute, Harvard. "How's Alice?" Leisha asked once, but Camden said he didn't know; she had moved out and did not want to see him. He made her an allowance through his attorney. While he said this, his face remained serene.

Leisha went to the Homecoming Ball with Stewart, who was also majoring in pre-law but was two years ahead of Leisha. She took a weekend trip to Paris with Kate Addams and two other girlfriends, taking the Conçorde III. She had a fight with Stewart over whether the metaphor of superconductivity could apply to Yagaiism, a stupid fight they both knew was stupid but had anyway, and afterward they became lovers. After the fumbling sexual explorations with Richard, Stewart was deft, experienced, smiling faintly as he taught her how to have an orgasm both by herself and with him. Leisha was dazzled. "It's so *joyful*," she said, and Stewart looked at her with a tenderness she knew was part disturbance but didn't know why.

At mid-semester she had the highest grades in the freshman class. She got every answer right on every single question on her midterms. She and Stewart went out for a beer to celebrate, and when they came back Leisha's room had been destroyed. The computer was smashed, the data banks wiped, hard copies and books smoldered in a metal wastebasket. Her clothes were ripped to pieces, her desk and bureau hacked apart. The only thing untouched, pristine, was the bed.

Stewart said, "There's no way this could have been done in silence. Everyone on the floor—hell, on the floor *below*—had to know. Someone will talk to the police." No one did. Leisha sat on the edge of the bed, dazed, and looked at the remnants of her Homecoming gown. The next day Dave Hannaway gave her a long, wide smile.

Camden flew east, taut with rage. He rented her an apartment in Cambridge with E-lock security and a bodyguard named Toshio. After he left, Leisha fired the bodyguard but kept the apartment. It gave her and Stewart more privacy, which they used to endlessly discuss the situation. It was Leisha who argued that it was an aberration, an immaturity.

"There have always been haters, Stewart. Hate Jews, hate Blacks, hate immigrants, hate Yagaiists who have more initiative and dignity than you do. I'm just the latest object of hatred. It's not new, it's not remarkable. It doesn't mean any basic kind of schism between the Sleepless and Sleepers."

Stewart sat up in bed and reached for the sandwiches on the night stand. "Doesn't it? Leisha, you're a different kind of person entirely. More evolutionarily fit, not only to survive but to prevail. Those other objects of hatred you cite—they were all powerless in their societies. They occupied *inferior* positions. You, on the other hand—all three Sleepless in Harvard Law are on the *Law Review*. All of them. Kevin Baker, your oldest, has already founded a successful bio-interface software firm and is making money, a lot of it. Every Sleepless is making superb grades, none has psychological problems, all are healthy, and most of you aren't even adults yet. How much hatred do you think you're going to encounter once you hit the high-stakes world of finance and business and scarce endowed chairs and national politics?"

"Give me a sandwich," Leisha said. "Here's my evidence you're wrong: you yourself. Kenzo Yagai. Kate Addams. Professor Lane. My father. Every Sleeper who inhabits the world of fair trade and mutually beneficial contracts. And that's most of you, or at least most of you who are worth considering. You believe that competition among the most capable leads to the most beneficial trades for everyone, strong and weak. Sleepless are making real and concrete contributions to society, in a lot of fields. That has to outweigh the discomfort we cause. We're *valuable* to you. You know that."

Stewart brushed crumbs off the sheets. "Yes. I do. Yagaiists do."

"Yagaiists run the business and financial and academic worlds. Or they will. In a meritocracy, they *should*. You underestimate the majority of people, Stew. Ethics aren't confined to the ones out front."

"I hope you're right," Stewart said. "Because, you know, I'm in love with you."

Leisha put down her sandwich.

"Joy," Stewart mumbled into her breasts, "you are joy."

When Leisha went home for Thanksgiving, she told Richard about Stewart. He listened tight-lipped.

"A Sleeper."

"A *person*," Leisha said. "A good, intelligent, achieving person!"

"Do you know what your good intelligent achieving Sleepers have done, Leisha? Jeanine has been barred from Olympic skating. 'Genetic alteration, analogous to steroid abuse to create an unsportsmanlike advantage.' Chris Devereaux has left Stanford. They trashed his laboratory, destroyed two years' work in memory-formation proteins. Kevin Baker's software company is fighting a nasty advertising campaign, all underground of course, about kids using software designed by nonhuman minds. Corruption, mental slavery, satanic influences: the whole bag of witch-hunt tricks. Wake up, Leisha!"

They both heard his words. Minutes dragged by. Richard stood like a boxer; forward on the balls of his feet, teeth clenched. Finally he said, very quietly, "Do you love him?"

"Yes," Leisha said. "I'm sorry."

"Your choice," Richard said coldly. "What do you do while he's asleep? Watch?"

"You make it sound like a perversion!"

Richard said nothing. Leisha drew a deep breath. She spoke rapidly but calmly, a controlled rush: "While Stewart is asleep I work. The same as you do. Richard—don't do this. I didn't mean to hurt you. And I don't want to lose the group. I believe the Sleepers are the same species as we are. Are you going to punish me for that? Are you going to *add* to the hatred? Are you going to tell me that I can't belong to a wider world that includes all honest, worthwhile people whether they sleep or not? Are you going to tell me that the most important division is by genetics and not by economic spirituality? Are you going to force me into an artificial choice, us or them?"

Richard picked up a bracelet. Leisha recognized it; she had given it to him in the summer. His voice was quiet. "No. It's not a choice." He played with the gold links a minute, then looked at her. "Not yet."

By spring break, Camden walked more slowly. He took medicine for his blood pressure, his heart. He and Susan, he told Leisha, were getting a divorce. "She changed, Leisha, after I married her. You saw that. She was independent and productive and happy, and then after a few years she stopped all that and became a shrew. A whining shrew." He shook his head in genuine bewilderment. "You saw the change."

Leisha had. A memory came to her: Susan leading her and Alice in "games" that were actually controlled cerebral-performance tests, Susan's braids dancing around her sparkling eyes. Alice had loved Susan then, as much as Leisha had.

"Dad, I want Alice's address."

"I told you up at Harvard, I don't have it," Camden said. He shifted in his chair, the impatient gesture of a body that never expected to wear out. In January Kenzo Yagai had died of pancreatic cancer; Camden had taken the news hard. "I make her allowance through an attorney. By her choice."

"Then I want the address of the attorney."

The attorney, a quenched-looking man named John Jaworski, refused to tell Leisha where Alice was. "She doesn't want to be found, Ms. Camden. She wanted a complete break."

"Not from me," Leisha said.

"Yes," Jaworski said, and something flickered in his eyes, something she had last seen in Dave Hannaway's face.

She flew to Austin before returning to Boston, making her a day late for classes. Kevin Baker saw her instantly, canceling a meeting with IBM. She told him what she needed, and he set his best datanet people on it, without telling them why. Within two hours she had Alice's address from Jaworski's electronic files. It was the first time, she realized, that she had ever turned to one of the Sleepless for help, and it had been given instantly. Without trade.

Alice was in Pennsylvania. The next weekend Leisha rented a hover car and driver—she had learned to drive, but only ground cars as yet—and went to High Ridge, in the Appalachian Mountains.

It was an isolated hamlet, twenty-five miles from the nearest hospital. Alice lived with a man named Ed, a silent carpenter twenty years older than she, in a cabin in the woods. The cabin had water and electricity but no newsnet. In the early spring light the earth was raw and bare, slashed with icy gullies. Alice and Ed apparently worked at nothing. Alice was eight months pregnant.

"I didn't want you here," she said to Leisha. "So why are you?"

"Because you're my sister."

"God, look at you. Is that what they're wearing at Harvard? Boots like that? When did you become fashionable, Leisha? You were always too busy being intellectual to care."

"What's this all about, Alice? Why here? What are you doing?"

"Living," Alice said. "Away from dear Daddy, away from Chicago, away from drunken, broken Susan—did you know she drinks? Just like Mom. He does that to people. But not to me. I got out. I wonder if you ever will."

"Got out? To *this*?"

"I'm happy," Alice said angrily. "Isn't that what it's supposed to be about? Isn't that the aim of your great Kenzo Yagai—happiness through individual effort?"

Leisha thought of saying that Alice was making no efforts that she could see. She didn't say it. A chicken ran through the yard of the cabin. Behind, the mountains rose in layer upon layer of blue haze. Leisha thought what this place must have been like in winter cut off from the world where people strived toward goals, learned, changed.

"I'm glad you're happy, Alice."

"Are you?"

"Yes."

"Then I'm glad, too," Alice said, almost defiantly. The next moment she abruptly hugged Leisha, fiercely, the huge, hard mound of her belly crushed between them. Alice's hair smelled sweet, like fresh grass in sunlight.

"I'll come see you again, Alice."

"Don't," Alice said.

Six

Sleepless Mutie Begs for Reversal of Gene Tampering," screamed the headline in the Food Mart. "'Please Let Me Sleep Like Real People!' Child Pleads."

Leisha typed in her credit number and pressed the news kiosk for a printout, although ordinarily she ignored the electronic tabloids. The headline went on circling the kiosk. A Food Mart employee stopped stacking boxes on shelves and watched her. Bruce, Leisha's bodyguard, watched the employee.

She was twenty-two, in her final year at Harvard Law, editor of the *Law Review*, clearly first in her graduating class. The closest three contenders were Jonathan Cocchiara, Len Carter, and Martha Wentz. All Sleepless.

In her apartment she skimmed the printout. Then she accessed the Groupnet run from Austin. The files had more news stories about the child, with comments from other Sleepless, but before she could call them up Kevin Baker came online himself, on voice.

"Leisha. I'm glad you called. I was going to call you."

"What's the situation with this Stella Bevington, Kev? Has anybody checked it out?"

"Randy Davies. He's from Chicago but I don't think you've met him; he's still in high school. He's in Park Ridge, Stella's in Skokie. Her parents wouldn't talk to him—they were pretty abusive, in fact—but he got to see Stella face-to-face anyway. It doesn't look like an abuse case, just the usual stupidity: parents wanted a genius child, scrimped and saved, and now they can't handle that she *is* one. They scream at her to sleep, get emotionally abusive when she contradicts them, but so far no violence."

"Is the emotional abuse actionable?"

"I don't think we want to move on it yet. Two of us will keep in close touch with Stella—she does have a modem, and she hasn't told her parents about the net—and Randy will drive out weekly."

Leisha bit her lip. "A tabloid shitpiece said she's seven years old."

"Yes."

"Maybe she shouldn't be left there. I'm an Illinois resident, I can file an abuse grievance from here if Candy's got too much in her briefcase...." *Seven years old.*

"No. Let it sit a while. Stella will probably be all right. You know that."

She did. Nearly all of the Sleepless stayed all right, no matter how much opposition came from the stupid segment of society. And it was only the stupid segment, Leisha argued, a small if vocal minority. Most people could, and would, adjust to the growing presence of the Sleepless, when it became clear that that presence included not only growing power but growing benefits to the country as a whole.

Kevin Baker, now twenty-six, had made a fortune in microchips so revolutionary that Artificial Intelligence, once a debated dream, was yearly closer to reality. Carolyn Rizzolo had won the Pulitzer Prize in drama for her play *Morning Light*. She was twenty-four. Jeremy Robinson had done significant work in superconductivity applications while still a graduate student at Stanford. William Thaine, *Law Review* editor when Leisha first came to Harvard, was now in private practice. He had never lost a case. He was twenty-six, and the cases were becoming important. His clients valued his ability more than his age.

But not everyone reacted that way.

Kevin Baker and Richard Keller had started the datanet that bound the Sleepless into a tight group, constantly aware of each other's personal fights. Leisha Camden financed the legal battles, the educational costs of Sleepless whose parents were unable to meet them, the support of children in emotionally bad situations. Rhonda Lavelier got herself licensed as a foster mother in California, and whenever possible the Group maneuvered to have young Sleepless who were removed from their homes assigned to Rhonda. The Group now had three licensed lawyers; within the next year it would gain four more, licensed to practice in five different states.

The one time they had not been able to remove an abused Sleepless child legally, they kidnapped him.

Timmy DeMarzo, four years old. Leisha had been opposed to the action. She had argued the case morally and pragmatically—to her they were the same thing—thus: If they believed in their society, in its fundamental laws and in their ability to belong to it as free-trading productive individuals, they must remain bound by the society's contractual laws. The Sleepless were, for the most part, Yagaiists. They should already know this. And if the FBI caught them, the courts and press would crucify them.

They were not caught.

Timmy DeMarzo—not even old enough to call for help on the datanet, they had learned of the situation through the automatic police record scan Kevin maintained through his company—was stolen from his own back yard in Wichita. He had lived the last year in an isolated trailer in North Dakota; no place was too isolated for a modem. He was cared for by a legally irreproachable foster mother who had lived there all her life. The foster mother was second cousin to a Sleepless, a broad cheerful woman with a much better brain than her appearance indicated. She was a Yagaiist. No record of the child's existence appeared in any data bank: not the IRS's, not any school's, not even the local grocery store's computerized checkout slips. Food specifically for the child was shipped in monthly on a truck owned by a Sleepless in State College, Pennsylvania. Ten of the Group knew about the kidnapping, out of the total 3,428 Sleepless born in the United States. Of those, 2,691 were part of the Group via the net. An additional 701 were as yet too young to use a modem. Only thirty-six Sleepless, for whatever reason, were not part of the Group.

The kidnapping had been arranged by Tony Indivino.

"It's Tony I wanted to talk to you about," Kevin said to Leisha. "He's started again. This time he means it. He's buying land."

She folded the tabloid very small and laid it carefully on the table. "Where?"

"Allegheny Mountains. In southern New York State. A lot of land. He's putting in the roads now. In the spring, the first buildings."

"Jennifer Sharifi still financing it?" It had been six years since the interleukin-1 drinking in the woods, but the evening remained vivid to Leisha. So did Jennifer Sharifi.

"Yes. She's got the money to do it. Tony's starting to get a following, Leisha."

"I know."

"Call him."

"I will. Keep me informed about Stella."

She worked until midnight at the *Law Review*, then until 4:00 A.M. preparing her classes. From four to five she handled legal matters for the Group. At 5:00 A.M. she called Tony, still in Chicago. He had finished high school, done one semester at Northwestern, and at Christmas vacation had finally exploded at his mother for forcing him to live as a Sleeper. The explosion, it seemed to Leisha, had never ended.

"Tony? Leisha."

"The answers are yes, yes, no, and go to hell."

Leisha gritted her teeth. "Fine. Now tell me the questions."

"Are you really serious about the Sleepless withdrawing into their own self-sufficient society? Is Jennifer Sharifi willing to finance a project the size of building a small city? Don't you think that's a cheat of all that can be accomplished by patient integration of the Group into the mainstream? And what about the contradictions of living in an armed restricted city and still trading with the Outside?"

"I would never tell *you* to go to hell."

"Hooray for you," Tony said. After a moment he added, "I'm sorry. That sounds like one of *them*."

"It's wrong for us, Tony."

"Thanks for not saying I couldn't pull it off."

She wondered if he could. "We're not a separate species, Tony."

"Tell that to the Sleepers."

"You exaggerate. There are haters out there, there are *always* haters, but to give up …"

"We're not giving up. Whatever we create can be freely traded: software, hardware, novels, information, theories, legal counsel. We can travel in and out. But we'll have a safe place to return *to*. Without the leeches who think we owe them blood because we're better than they are."

"It isn't a matter of owing."

"Really?" Tony said. "Let's have this out, Leisha. All the way. You're a Yagaiist—what do you believe in?"

"Tony …"

"*Do it*," Tony said, and in his voice she heard the fourteen-year-old she had been introduced to by Richard. Simultaneously, she saw her father's face: not as he was now, since the bypass, but as he had been when she was a little girl, holding her on his lap to explain that she was special.

"I believe in voluntary trade that is mutually beneficial. That spiritual dignity comes from supporting one's life through one's own efforts, and from trading the results of those efforts in mutual cooperation throughout the society. That the symbol of this is the contract. And that we need each other for the fullest, most beneficial trade."

"Fine," Tony bit off. "Now what about the beggars in Spain?"

"The what?"

"You walk down a street in a poor country like Spain and you see a beggar. Do you give him a dollar?"

"Probably."

"Why? He's trading nothing with you. He has nothing to trade."

"I know. Out of kindness. Compassion."

"You see six beggars. Do you give them all a dollar?"

"Probably," Leisha said.

"You would. You see a hundred beggars and you haven't got Leisha Camden's money. Do you give them each a dollar?"

"No."

"Why not?"

Leisha reached for patience. Few people could make her want to cut off a comlink; Tony was one of them. "Too draining on my own resources. My life has first claim on the resources I earn."

"All right. Now consider this. At Biotech Institute—where you and I began, dear pseudo-sister—Dr. Melling has just yesterday—"

"*Who?*"

"Dr. Susan Melling. Oh, God, I completely forgot she used to be married to your father!"

"I lost track of her," Leisha said. "I didn't realize she'd gone back to research. Alice once said … never mind. What's going on at Biotech?"

"Two crucial items, just released. Carla Dutcher has had first-month fetal genetic analysis. Sleeplessness is a dominant gene. The next generation of the Group won't sleep either."

"We all knew that," Leisha said. Carla Dutcher was the world's first pregnant Sleepless. Her husband was a Sleeper. "The whole world expected that."

"But the press will have a field day with it anyway. Just watch. Muties Breed! New Race Set to Dominate Next Generation of Children!"

Leisha didn't deny it. "And the second item?"

"It's sad, Leisha. We've just had our first death."

Her stomach tightened. "Who?"

"Bernie Kuhn. Seattle." She didn't know him. "A car accident. It looks pretty straightforward; he lost control on a steep curve when his brakes failed. He had only been driving a few months. He was seventeen. But the significance here is that his parents have donated his brain and body to Biotech, in conjunction with the pathology department at the Chicago Medical School. They're going to take him apart to get the first good look at what prolonged sleeplessness does to the body and brain."

"They should," Leisha said. "That poor kid. But what are you so afraid they'll find?"

"I don't know. I'm not a doctor. But whatever it is, if the haters can use it against us, they will."

"You're paranoid, Tony."

"Impossible. The Sleepless have personalities calmer and more reality-oriented than the norm. Don't you read the literature?"

"Tony—"

"What if you walk down that street in Spain and a hundred beggars each want a dollar and you say no and they have nothing to trade you but they're so rotten with anger about what you have that they knock you down and grab it and then beat you out of sheer envy and despair?"

Leisha didn't answer.

"Are you going to say that's not a human scenario, Leisha? That it never happens?"

"It happens," Leisha said evenly. "But not all that often."

"Bullshit. Read more history. Read more *newspapers*. But the point is: What do you owe the beggars then? What does a good Yagaiist who believes in mutually beneficial contracts do with people who have nothing to trade and can only take?"

"You're not—"

"*What*, Leisha? In the most objective terms you can manage, what do we owe the grasping and nonproductive needy?"

"What I said originally. Kindness. Compassion."

"Even if they don't trade it back? Why?"

"Because …" She stopped.

"Why? Why do law-abiding and productive human beings owe anything to those who neither produce very much nor abide by just laws? What philosophical or economic or spiritual justification is there for owing them anything? Be as honest as I know you are."

Leisha put her head between her knees. The question gaped beneath her, but she didn't try to evade it. "I don't know. I just know we do."

"*Why?*"

She didn't answer. After a moment, Tony did. The intellectual challenge was gone from his voice. He said, almost tenderly, "Come down in the spring and see the site for Sanctuary. The buildings will be going up then."

"No," Leisha said.

"I'd like you to."

"No. Armed retreat is not the way."

Tony said, "The beggars are getting nastier, Leisha. As the Sleepless grow richer. And I don't mean in money."

"Tony—" she said, and stopped. She couldn't think what to say.

"Don't walk down too many streets armed with just the memory of Kenzo Yagai."

✧ ✧ ✧

In March, a bitterly cold March with wind whipping down the Charles River, Richard Keller came to Cambridge. Leisha had not seen him for three years. He didn't send her word on the Groupnet that he was coming. She hurried up the walk to her townhouse, muffled to the eyes in a red wool scarf against the snowy cold, and he stood there blocking the doorway. Behind Leisha, her bodyguard tensed.

"Richard! Bruce, it's all right, this is an old friend."

"Hello, Leisha."

He was heavier, sturdier-looking, with a breadth of shoulder she didn't recognize. But the face was Richard's, older but unchanged: dark low brows, unruly dark hair. He had grown a beard.

"You look beautiful," he said.

Inside, she handed him a cup of coffee. "Are you here on business?" From the Groupnet she knew that he had finished his master's and had done outstanding work in marine biology in the Caribbean but had left that a year ago and disappeared from the net.

"No. Pleasure." He smiled suddenly, the old smile that opened up his dark face. "I almost forgot about that for a long time. Contentment, yes. We're all good at the contentment that comes from sustained work. But pleasure? Whim? Caprice? When was the last time you did something silly, Leisha?"

She smiled. "I ate cotton candy in the shower."

"Really? Why?"

"To see if it would dissolve in gooey pink patterns."

"Did it?"

"Yes. Lovely ones."

"And that was your last silly thing? When was it?"

"Last summer," Leisha said, and laughed.

"Well, mine is sooner than that. It's now. I'm in Boston for no other reason than the spontaneous pleasure of seeing you."

Leisha stopped laughing. "That's an intense tone for a spontaneous pleasure, Richard."

"Yup," he said, intensely. She laughed again. He didn't.

"I've been in India, Leisha. And China and Africa. Thinking, mostly. Watching. First I traveled like a Sleeper, attracting no attention. Then I set out to meet the Sleepless in India and China. There are a few, you know, whose parents were willing to come here for the operation. They pretty much are accepted and left alone. I tried to figure out why desperately poor countries—by our standards anyway; over there Y-energy is mostly available only in big cities—don't have any trouble accepting the superiority of Sleepless, whereas Americans, with more prosperity than any time in history, build in resentment more and more."

Leisha said, "Did you figure it out?"

"No. But I figured out something else, watching all those communes and villages and *kampongs*. We are too individualistic."

Disappointment swept Leisha. She saw her father's face: *Excellence is what counts, Leisha. Excellence supported by individual effort....* She reached for Richard's cup. "More coffee?"

He caught her wrist and looked up into her face. "Don't misunderstand me, Leisha. I'm not talking about work. We are too much individuals in the rest of our lives. Too emotionally rational. Too much alone. Isolation kills more than the free flow of ideas. It kills joy."

He didn't let go of her wrist. She looked down into his eyes, into depths she hadn't seen before. It was the feeling of looking into a mineshaft, both giddy and frightening, knowing that at the bottom might be gold or darkness. Or both.

Richard said softly, "Stewart?"

"Over long ago. An undergraduate thing." Her voice didn't sound like her own.

"Kevin?"

"No, never—we're just friends."

"I wasn't sure. Anyone?"

"No."

He let go of her wrist. Leisha peered at him timidly. He suddenly laughed. "Joy, Leisha." An echo sounded in her mind, but she couldn't place it, and then it was gone and she laughed too, a laugh airy and frothy and pink cotton candy in summer.

"Come home, Leisha. He's had another heart attack."

Susan Melling's voice on the phone was tired. Leisha said, "How bad?"

"The doctors aren't sure. Or say they're not sure. He wants to see you. Can you leave your studies?"

It was May, the last push toward her finals. The *Law Review* proofs were behind schedule. Richard had started a new business, marine consulting to Boston fishermen plagued with sudden inexplicable shifts in ocean currents, and was working twenty hours a day. "I'll come," Leisha said.

Chicago was colder than Boston. The trees were half-budded. On Lake Michigan, filling the huge east windows of her father's house, whitecaps tossed up cold spray. Leisha saw that Susan was living in the house; her brushes were on Camden's dresser, her journals on the credenza in the foyer.

"Leisha," Camden said. He looked old. Grey skin, sunken cheeks, the fretful and bewildered look of men who accepted potency like air, indivisible from their lives. In the corner of the room, on a small eighteenth-century slipper chair, sat a short, stocky woman with brown braids.

"*Alice*."

"Hello, Leisha."

"*Alice*. I've looked for you …" The wrong thing to say. Leisha had looked, but not very hard, deterred by the knowledge that Alice had not wanted to be found. "How are you?"

"I'm fine," Alice said. She seemed remote, gentle, unlike the angry Alice of six years ago in the raw Pennsylvania hills. Camden moved painfully on the bed. He looked at Leisha with eyes which, she saw, were undimmed in their blue brightness.

"I asked Alice to come. And Susan. Susan came a while ago. I'm dying, Leisha."

No one contradicted him. Leisha, knowing his respect for facts, remained silent. Love hurt her chest.

"John Jaworski has my will. None of you can break it. But I wanted to tell you myself what's in it. The past few years I've been selling, liquidating. Most of my holdings are accessible now. I've left a tenth to Alice, a tenth to Susan, a tenth to Elizabeth, and the rest to you, Leisha, because you're the only one with the individual ability to use the money to its full potential for achievement."

Leisha looked wildly at Alice, who gazed back with her strange remote calm. "Elizabeth? My … mother? Is alive?"

"Yes," Camden said.

"You told me she was dead! Years and years ago!"

"Yes. I thought it was better for you that way. She didn't like what you were, was jealous of what you could become. And she had nothing to give you. She would only have caused you emotional harm."

Beggars in Spain …

"That was wrong, Daddy. You were *wrong*. She's my mother …" She couldn't finish the sentence.

Camden didn't flinch. "I don't think I was. But you're an adult now. You can see her if you wish."

He went on looking at her with his bright, sunken eyes, while around Leisha the air heaved and snapped. Her father had lied to her. Susan watched her closely, a small smile on her lips. Was she glad to see Camden fall in his daughter's estimation? Had she all along been that jealous of their relationship, of Leisha …?

She was thinking like Tony.

The thought steadied her a little. But she went on staring at Camden, who went on staring back implacably, unbudged, a man positive even on his deathbed that he was right.

Alice's hand was on her elbow, Alice's voice so soft that no one but Leisha could hear. "He's done talking now, Leisha. And after a while you'll be all right."

Alice had left her son in California with her husband of two years, Beck Watrous, a building contractor she had met while waiting on tables in a resort on the Artificial Islands. Beck had adopted Jordan, Alice's son.

"Before Beck there was a real bad time," Alice said in her remote voice. "You know, when I was carrying Jordan I actually used to dream that he would be Sleepless? Like you. Every night I'd dream that, and every morning I'd wake up and have morning sickness with a baby that was only going to be a stupid nothing like me. I stayed with Ed—in the Appalachian Mountains, remember? You came to see me there once—for two more years. When he beat me, I was glad. I wished Daddy could see. At least Ed was touching me."

Leisha made a sound in her throat.

"I finally left because I was afraid for Jordan. I went to California, did nothing but eat for a year. I got up to 190 pounds." Alice was, Leisha estimated, five foot four. "Then I came home to see Mother."

"You didn't tell me," Leisha said. "You knew she was alive and you didn't tell me."

"She's in a drying-out tank half the time," Alice said, with brutal simplicity. "She wouldn't see you if you wanted to. But she saw me, and she fell slobbering all over me as her 'real' daughter, and she threw up on my dress. And I backed away from her and looked at the dress and knew it *should* be thrown up on, it was so ugly. Deliberately ugly. She started screaming how Dad had ruined her life, ruined mine, all for you. And do you know what I did?"

"What?" Leisha said. Her voice was shaky.

"I flew home, burned all my clothes, got a job, started college, lost fifty pounds, and put Jordan in play therapy."

The sisters sat silent. Beyond the window the lake was dark, unlit by moon or stars. It was Leisha who suddenly shook, and Alice who patted her shoulder.

"Tell me ..." Leisha couldn't think what she wanted to be told, except that she wanted to hear Alice's voice in the gloom, Alice's voice as it was now, gentle and remote, without damage any more from the damaging fact of Leisha's existence. Her very existence as damage. "Tell me about Jordan. He's five now? What's he like?"

Alice turned her head to look levelly into Leisha's eyes. "He's a happy, ordinary little boy. Completely ordinary."

Camden died a week later. After the funeral, Leisha tried to see her mother at the Brookfield Drug and Alcohol Abuse Center. Elizabeth Camden, she was told, saw no one except her only child, Alice Camden Watrous.

Susan Melling, dressed in black, drove Leisha to the airport. Susan talked deftly, determinedly, about Leisha's studies, about Harvard, about the *Law Review*. Leisha answered in monosyllables, but Susan persisted, asking questions, quietly insisting on answers: When would Leisha take her bar exams? Where was she interviewing for jobs? Gradually Leisha began to lose the numbness she had felt since her father's casket was lowered into the ground. She realized that Susan's persistent questioning was a kindness.

"He sacrificed a lot of people," Leisha said suddenly.

"Not me," Susan said. "Only for a while there, when I gave up my work to do his. Roger didn't respect sacrifice much."

"Was he wrong?" Leisha said. The question came out with a kind of desperateness she hadn't intended.

Susan smiled sadly. "No. He wasn't wrong. I should never have left my research. It took me a long time to come back to myself after that."

He does that to people, Leisha heard inside her head. Susan? Or Alice? She couldn't, for once, remember clearly. She saw her father in the old conservatory, now empty, potting and repotting the exotic flowers he had loved.

She was tired. It was muscle fatigue from stress, she knew; twenty minutes of rest would restore her. Her eyes burned from unaccustomed tears. She leaned her head back against the car seat and closed her eyes.

Susan pulled the car into the airport parking lot and turned off the ignition. "There's something I want to tell you, Leisha."

Leisha opened her eyes. "About the will?"

Susan smiled tightly. "No. You really don't have any problems with how he divided the estate, do you? It seems reasonable to you. But that's not it. The research team from Biotech and Chicago Medical has finished its analysis of Bernie Kuhn's brain."

Leisha turned to face Susan. She was startled by the complexity of Susan's expression. It held determination, and satisfaction, and anger, and something else Leisha could not name.

Susan said, "We're going to publish next week, in the *New England Journal of Medicine*. Security has been unbelievably restricted—no leaks to the popular press. But I want to tell you now, myself, what we found. So you'll be prepared."

"Go on," Leisha said. Her chest felt tight.

"Do you remember when you and the other Sleepless kids took interleukin-1 to see what sleep was like? When you were sixteen?"

"How did you know about that?"

"You kids were watched a lot more closely than you think. Remember the headache you got?"

"Yes." She and Richard and Tony and Carol and Brad and Jeanine … no, not Jeanine. Jennifer. It had been Jennifer in the woods with them.

"Interleukin-1 is what I want to talk about. At least partly. It's one of a whole group of substances that boost the immune system. They stimulate the production of antibodies, the activity of white blood cells, and a host of other immuno-enhancements. Normal people have surges of IL-1 released during the slow-wave phases of sleep. That means that they were getting boosts to the immune system during sleep. One of the questions we researchers asked ourselves twenty-eight years ago was: will Sleepless kids who don't get those surges of IL-1 get sick more often?"

"I've never been sick," Leisha said.

"Yes, you have. Chicken pox and three minor colds by the end of your fourth year," Susan said precisely. "But in general you were all a very healthy lot. So we researchers were left with the alternate theory of sleep-driven immuno-enhancement: that the burst of immune activity existed as a counterpart to a greater vulnerability of the body in sleep to disease, probably in some way connected to the fluctuations in body temperature during REM sleep. In other words, sleep *caused* the immune vulnerability that endogenous pyrogens like IL-1 counteracted. Sleep was the problem, immune-system enhancements were the solution. Without sleep, there would be no problem. Are you following this?"

"Yes."

"Of course you are. Stupid question." Susan brushed her hair off her face. It was going gray at the temples. There was a tiny brown age spot beneath her right ear.

"Over the years we collected thousands, maybe hundreds of thousands, of Single Photon Emission Topography scans of you kids' brains, plus endless EEGs, samples of cerebrospinal fluid, and all the rest of it. But we couldn't really see inside your brains, really know what's going on in there. Until Bernie Kuhn hit that embankment."

"Susan," Leisha said, "give it to me straight. Without more buildup."

"You're not going to age."

"What?"

"Oh, cosmetically, a little—sagging due to gravity, maybe. But the absence of sleep peptides and all the rest of it affects the immune and tissue-restoration systems in ways we don't understand. Bernie Kuhn had a perfect liver. Perfect lungs, perfect heart, perfect lymph nodes, perfect pancreas, perfect medulla oblongata. Not just healthy, or young—*perfect*. There's a tissue regeneration enhancement that clearly derives from the operation of the immune system but is radically different from anything we ever suspected. Organs show no wear and tear, not even the minimal amount expected in a seventeen-year-old. They just repair themselves, perfectly, on and on ... and on."

"For how long?" Leisha whispered.

"Who the hell knows? Bernie Kuhn was young. Maybe there's some compensatory mechanism that cuts in at some point and you'll all just collapse, like an entire fucking gallery of Dorian Grays. But I don't think so. Neither do I think it can go on forever; no tissue regeneration can do that. But a long, long time."

Leisha stared at the blurred reflections in the car windshield. She saw her father's face against the blue satin of his casket, banked with white roses. His heart, unregenerated, had given out.

Susan said, "The future is all speculative at this point. We know that the peptide structures that build up the pressure to sleep in normal people resemble the components of bacterial cell walls. Maybe there's a connection between sleep and pathogen receptivity. We don't know. But ignorance never stopped the tabloids. I wanted to prepare you because you're going to get called supermen, *homo perfectus*, who-all-knows what. Immortal."

The two women sat in silence. Finally Leisha said, "I'm going to tell the others. On our datanet. Don't worry about the security. Kevin Baker designed Groupnet; nobody knows anything we don't want them to."

"You're that well organized already?"

"Yes."

Susan's mouth worked. She looked away from Leisha. "We better go in. You'll miss your flight."

"Susan …"

"What?"

"Thank you."

"You're welcome," Susan said, and in her voice Leisha heard the thing she had seen before in Susan's expression and had not been able to name: it was longing.

Tissue regeneration. A long, long time, sang the blood in Leisha's ears on the flight to Boston. *Tissue regeneration.* And, eventually: *immortal.* No, not that, she told herself severely. Not that. The blood didn't listen.

"You sure smile a lot," said the man next to her in first class, a business traveler who had not recognized Leisha. "You coming from a big party in Chicago?"

"No. From a funeral."

The man looked shocked, then disgusted. Leisha looked out the window at the ground far below. Rivers like microcircuits, fields like neat index cards. And on the horizon, fluffy white clouds like masses of exotic flowers, blooms in a conservatory filled with light.

The letter was no thicker than any hard-copy mail, but hard-copy mail addressed by hand to either of them was so rare that Richard was nervous. "It might be explosive." Leisha looked at the letter on their hall credenza. MS. LIESHA CAMDEN. Block letters, misspelled.

"It looks like a child's writing," she said.

Richard stood with head lowered, legs braced apart. But his expression was only weary. "Perhaps deliberately like a child's. You'd be more open to a child's writing, they might have figured."

"'They'? Richard, are we getting that paranoid?"

He didn't flinch from the question. "Yes. For the time being."

A week earlier the *New England Journal of Medicine* had published Susan's careful, sober article. An hour later the broadcast and datanet news had exploded in speculation, drama, outrage, and fear. Leisha and Richard, along with all the Sleepless on the Groupnet, had tracked and charted each of four components, looking for a dominant reaction: speculation ("The Sleepless may live for centuries, and this might lead to the following events...."); drama ("If a Sleepless marries only Sleepers, he may have lifetime enough for a dozen brides, and several dozen children, a bewildering blended family...."); outrage ("Tampering with the law of nature has only brought among us unnatural so-called people who will live with the unfair advantage of time: time to accumulate more kin, more power, more property than the rest of us could ever know...."); and fear ("How soon before the Super-race takes over?").

"They're all fear, of one kind or another," Carolyn Rizzolo finally said, and the Groupnet stopped its differentiated tracking.

Leisha was taking the final exams of her last year of law school. Each day comments followed her to the campus, along the corridors and in the classroom; each day she forgot them in the grueling exam sessions, in which all students were reduced to the same status of petitioner to the great university. Afterward, temporarily drained, she walked silently back home to Richard and the Groupnet, aware of the looks of people on the street, aware of her bodyguard Bruce striding between her and them.

"It will calm down," Leisha said. Richard didn't answer.

The town of Salt Springs, Texas, passed a local ordinance that no Sleepless could obtain a liquor license, on the grounds that civil rights statutes were built on the "all men were created equal" clause of the Declaration of Independence, and Sleepless clearly were not covered. There were no Sleepless within a hundred miles of Salt Springs and no one had applied for a new liquor license there for the past ten years, but the story was picked up by United Press and by Datanet News, and within twenty-four hours heated editorials appeared, on both sides of the issue, across the nation.

More local ordinances were passed. In Pollux, Pennsylvania, the Sleepless could be denied an apartment rental on the grounds that their prolonged wakefulness would increase both wear-and-tear on the landlord's property and utility bills. In Cranston Estates, California, Sleepless were barred from operating twenty-four-hour businesses: "unfair competition." Iroquois County, New York, barred them from serving on county juries, arguing that a jury containing Sleepless, with their skewed idea of time, did not constitute "a jury of one's peers."

"All those statutes will be thrown out in superior courts," Leisha said. "But God! The waste of money and docket time to do it!" A part of her mind noticed that her tone as she said this was Roger Camden's.

The state of Georgia, in which some sex acts between consenting adults were still a crime, made sex between a Sleepless and a Sleeper a third-degree felony, classing it with bestiality.

Kevin Baker had designed software that scanned the newsnets at high speed, flagged all stories involving discrimination or attacks on Sleepless, and categorized them by type. The files were available on Groupnet. Leisha read through them, then called Kevin. "Can't you create a parallel program to flag defenses of us? We're getting a skewed picture."

"You're right," Kevin said, a little startled. "I didn't think of it."

"Think of it," Leisha said, grimly. Richard, watching her, said nothing.

She was most upset by the stories about Sleepless children. Shunning at school, verbal abuse by siblings, attacks by neighborhood bullies, confused resentment from parents who had wanted an exceptional child but had not bargained for one who might live centuries. The school board of Cold River, Iowa, voted to bar Sleepless children from conventional classrooms because their rapid learning "created feelings of inadequacy in others, interfering with their education." The board made funds available for Sleepless to have tutors at home. There were no volunteers among the teaching staff. Leisha started spending as much time on Groupnet with the kids, talking to them all night long, as she did studying for her bar exams, scheduled for July.

Stella Bevington stopped using her modem.

Kevin's second program cataloged editorials urging fairness toward Sleepless. The school board of Denver set aside funds for a program in which gifted children, including the Sleepless, could use their talents and build teamwork through tutoring even younger children. Rive Beau, Louisiana, elected Sleepless Danielle du Cherney to the City Council, although Danielle was twenty-two and technically too young to qualify. The prestigious medical research firm of Halley-Hall gave much publicity to their hiring of Christopher Amren, a Sleepless with a Ph.D. in cellular physics.

Dora Clarq, a Sleepless in Dallas, opened a letter addressed to her and a plastic explosive blew off her arm.

Leisha and Richard stared at the envelope on the hall credenza. The paper was thick, cream-colored, but not expensive, the kind of paper made of bulky newsprint dyed the shades of vellum. There was no return address. Richard called Liz Bishop, a Sleepless who was majoring in criminal justice in Michigan. He had never spoken with her before—neither had Leisha—but she came on the Groupnet immediately and told them how to open it. Or, she could fly up and do it if they preferred. Richard and Leisha followed her directions for remote detonation in the basement of the townhouse. Nothing blew up. When the letter was open, they took it out and read it:

> Dear Ms. Camden,
>
> You been pretty good to me and I'm sorry to do this but I quit. They are making it pretty hot for me at the union not officially but you know how it is. If I was you I wouldn't go to the union for another bodyguard I'd try to find one privately. But be careful. Again I'm sorry but I have to live too.
>
> Bruce.

"I don't know whether to laugh or cry," Leisha said. "The two of us getting all this equipment, spending hours on this setup so an explosive won't detonate...."

"It's not as if I at least had a whole lot else to do," Richard said. Since the wave of anti-Sleepless sentiment, all but two of his marine consulting clients, vulnerable to the marketplace and thus to public opinion, had canceled their accounts.

Groupnet, still up on Leisha's terminal, shrilled in emergency override. Leisha got there first. It was Tony Indivino.

"Leisha. I need your legal help, if you'll give it. They're trying to fight me on Sanctuary. Please fly down here."

Sanctuary was raw brown gashes in the late-spring earth. It was situated in the Allegheny Mountains of southern New York State, old hills rounded by age and covered with pine and hickory. A superb road led from the closest town, Conewango, to Sanctuary. Low, maintenance-free buildings, whose design was plain but graceful, stood in various stages of completion. Jennifer Sharifi, unsmiling, met Leisha and Richard. She hadn't changed much in six years but her long black hair was uncombed and her dark eyes enormous with strain. "Tony wants to talk to you, but first he asked me to show you both around."

"What's wrong?" Leisha asked quietly.

Jennifer didn't try to evade the question. "Later. First look at Sanctuary. Tony respects your opinion enormously, Leisha; he wants you to see everything."

The dormitories each held fifty, with communal rooms for cooking, dining, relaxing, and bathing, and a warren of separate offices and studios and labs for work. "We're calling them 'dorms' anyway, despite the etymology," Jennifer said, and even in this remark, which from anybody else would have been playful, Leisha heard the peculiar combination of Jennifer's habitual deliberate calm with her present strain.

She was impressed, despite herself, with the completeness of Tony's plans for lives that would be both communal and intensely private. There was a gym, a small hospital—"By the end of next year, we'll have eighteen board/certified doctors, you know, and four of them are thinking of coming here"—a daycare facility, a school, and an intensive-crop farm. "Most of the food will come in from the outside, of course. So will most people's jobs, although they'll do as much of them as possible from here, over datanets. We're not cutting ourselves off from the world, only creating a safe place from which to trade with it." Leisha didn't answer.

Apart from the power facilities, self-supported Y-energy, she was most impressed with the human planning. Tony had interested Sleepless from virtually every field they would need both to care for themselves and to deal with the outside world. "Lawyers and accountants come first," Jennifer said. "That's our first line of defense in safeguarding ourselves. Tony recognizes that most modern battles for power are fought in the courtroom and boardroom."

But not all. Last, Jennifer showed them the plans for physical defense. For the first time, her taut body seemed to relax slightly.

Every effort had been made to stop attackers without hurting them. Electronic surveillance completely circled the 150 square miles Jennifer had purchased. Some *counties* were smaller than that, Leisha thought, dazed. When breached, a force field a half-mile within the E-gate activated, delivering electric shocks to anyone on foot—"but only on the *outside* of the field. We don't want any of our kids hurt," Jennifer said. Unmanned penetration by vehicles or robots was identified by a system that located all moving metal above a certain mass within Sanctuary. Any moving metal that did not carry a special signaling device designed by Donald Pospula, a Sleepless who had patented important electronic components, was suspect.

"Of course, we're not set up for an air attack or an outright army assault," Jennifer said. "But we don't expect that. Only the haters in self-motivated hate."

Leisha touched the hard copy of the security plans with one finger. They troubled her. "If we can't integrate ourselves into the world .... Free trade should imply free movement."

Jennifer said swiftly, "Only if free movement implies free minds," and at her tone Leisha looked up. "I have something to tell you, Leisha."

"What?"

"Tony isn't here."

"Where is he?"

"In Cattaraugus County jail in Conewango. It's true we're having zoning battles about Sanctuary—zoning! In this isolated spot! But this is something else, something that just happened this morning. Tony's been arrested for the kidnapping of Timmy DeMarzo."

The room wavered. "FBI?"

"Yes."

"How … how did they find out?"

"Some agent eventually cracked the case. They didn't tell us how. Tony needs a lawyer, Leisha. Bill Thaine has already agreed, but Tony wants you."

"Jennifer—I don't even take the bar exams until July!"

"He says he'll wait. Bill will act as his lawyer in the meantime. Will you pass the bar?"

"Of course. But I already have a job lined up with Morehouse, Kennedy & Anderson in New York…." She stopped. Richard was looking at her hard, Jennifer inscrutably. Leisha said quietly, "What will he plead?"

"Guilty," Jennifer said, "with—what is it called legally? Extenuating circumstances." Leisha nodded. She had been afraid Tony would want to plead not guilty: more lies, subterfuge, ugly politics. Her mind ran swiftly over extenuating circumstances, precedents, tests to precedents….They could use *Clements v. Voy* …

"Bill is at the jail now," Jennifer said. "Will you drive in with me?" She made the question a challenge.

"Yes," Leisha said.

In Conewango, the county seat, they were not allowed to see Tony. William Thaine, as his attorney, could go in and out freely. Leisha, not officially an attorney at all, could go nowhere. This was told to them by a man in the D.A.'s office whose face stayed immobile while he spoke to them, and who spat on the ground behind their shoes when they turned to leave, even though this left him with a smear of spittle on his courthouse floor.

Richard and Leisha drove their rental car to the airport for the flight back to Boston. On the way Richard told Leisha he was leaving. He was moving to Sanctuary, now, even before it was functional, to help with the planning and building.

She stayed most of the time in her townhouse, studying ferociously for the bar exams or checking on the Sleepless children through Groupnet. She had not hired another bodyguard to replace

Bruce, which made her reluctant to go outside very much; the reluctance in turn made her angry with herself. Once or twice a day she scanned Kevin's electronic news clippings.

There were signs of hope. The *New York Times* ran an editorial, widely reprinted on the electronic news services:

PROSPERITY AND HATRED:

A LOGIC CURVE WE'D RATHER NOT SEE

> The United States has never been a country that much values calm, logic, and rationality. We have, as a people, tended to label these things "cold." We have, as a people, tended to admire feeling and action: We exalt in our stories and our memorials—not the creation of the Constitution but its defense at Iwo Jima; not the intellectual achievements of a Linus Pauling but the heroic passion of a Charles Lindbergh; not the inventors of the monorails and computers that unite us but the composers of the angry songs of rebellion that divide us.
>
> A peculiar aspect of this phenomenon is that it grows stronger in times of prosperity. The better off our citizenry, the greater their contempt for the calm reasoning that got them there, and the more passionate their indulgence in emotion. Consider, in the past century, the gaudy excesses of the roaring twenties and the antiestablishment contempt of the sixties. Consider, in our own century, the unprecedented prosperity brought about by Y-energy—and then consider that Kenzo Yagai, except to his followers, was seen as a greedy and bloodless logician, while our national adulation goes to neo-nihilist writer Stephen Castelli, to "feelie" actress Brenda Foss, and to daredevil gravity-well diver Jim Morse Luter.
>
> But most of all, as you ponder this phenomenon in your Y-energy houses, consider the current outpouring of irrational feeling directed at the "Sleepless" since the publication of the joint findings of the Biotech Institute and the Chicago Medical School concerning Sleepless tissue regeneration.

Most of the Sleepless are intelligent. Most of them are calm, if you define that much-maligned word to mean directing one's energies into solving problems rather than to emoting about them. (Even Pulitzer Prize–winner Carolyn Rizzolo gave us a stunning play of ideas, not of passions run amuck.) All of them show a natural bent toward achievement, a bent given a decided boost by the one-third more time in their days to achieve. Their achievements lie, for the most part, in logical fields rather than emotional ones: Computers. Law. Finance. Physics. Medical research. They are rational, orderly, calm, intelligent, cheerful, young, and possibly very long-lived.

And, in our United States of unprecedented prosperity, they are increasingly hated.

Does the hatred that we have seen flower so fully over the past few months really grow, as many claim, from the "unfair advantage" the Sleepless have over the rest of us in securing jobs, promotions, money, and success? Is it really envy over the Sleepless' good fortune? Or does it come from something more pernicious, rooted in our tradition of shoot-from-the-hip American action: hatred of the logical, the calm, the considered? Hatred in fact of the superior mind?

If so, perhaps we should think deeply about the founders of this country: Jefferson, Washington, Paine, Adams—inhabitants of the Age of Reason, all. These men created our orderly and balanced system of laws precisely to protect the property and achievements created by the individual efforts of balanced and rational minds. The Sleepless may be our severest internal test yet of our own sober belief in law and order. No, the Sleepless were not, "created equal," but our attitudes toward them should be examined with a care equal to our soberest jurisprudence. We may not like what we learn about our own motives, but our credibility as a people may depend on the rationality and intelligence of the examination.

Both have been in short supply in the public reaction to last month's research findings.

> Law is not theater. Before we write laws reflecting gaudy and dramatic feelings, we must be very sure we understand the difference.

Leisha hugged herself, gazing in delight at the screen, smiling. She called the *New York Times* and asked who had written the editorial. The receptionist, cordial when she answered the phone, grew brusque. The *Times* was not releasing that information, "prior to internal investigation."

It could not dampen her mood. She whirled around the apartment, after days of sitting at her desk or screen. Delight demanded physical action. She washed dishes, picked up books. There were gaps in the furniture patterns where Richard had taken pieces that belonged to him; a little quieter now, she moved the furniture to close the gaps.

Susan Melling called to tell her about the *Times* editorial; they talked warmly for a few minutes. When Susan hung up, the phone rang again.

"Leisha? Your voice still sounds the same. This is Stewart Sutter."

"Stewart." She had not seen him for four years. Their romance had lasted two years and then dissolved, not from any painful issue so much as from the press of both their studies. Standing by the comm terminal, hearing his voice, Leisha suddenly felt again his hands on her breasts in the cramped dormitory bed: All those years before she had found a good use for a bed. The phantom hands became Richard's hands, and a sudden pain pierced her.

"Listen," Stewart said, "I'm calling because there's some information I think you should know. You take your bar exams next week, right? And then you have a tentative job with Morehouse, Kennedy & Anderson."

"How do you know all that, Stewart?"

"Men's room gossip. Well, not as bad as that. But the New York legal community—that part of it, anyway—is smaller than you think. And you're a pretty visible figure."

"Yes," Leisha said neutrally.

"Nobody has the slightest doubt you'll be called to the bar. But there is some doubt about the job with Morehouse, Kennedy. You've got two senior partners, Alan Morehouse and Seth Brown, who have changed their minds since this … flap. 'Adverse publicity for the firm,' 'turning law into a circus,' blah blah blah. You know the drill. But you've also got two powerful champions, Ann Carlyle and Michael Kennedy, the old man himself. He's quite a mind. Anyway, I wanted you to know all this so you can recognize exactly what the situation is and know whom to count on in the infighting."

"Thank you," Leisha said. "Stew … why do you care if I get it or not? Why should it matter to you?"

There was a silence on the other end of the phone. Then Stewart said, very low, "We're not all noodleheads out here, Leisha. Justice does still matter to some of us. So does achievement."

Light rose in her, a bubble of buoyant light.

Stewart said, "You have a lot of support here for that stupid zoning fight over Sanctuary, too. You might not realize that, but you do. What the Parks Commission crowd is trying to pull is … but they're just being used as fronts. You know that. Anyway, when it gets as far as the courts, you'll have all the help you need."

"Sanctuary isn't my doing. At all."

"No? Well, I meant the plural you."

"Thank you. I mean that. How are you doing?"

"Fine. I'm a daddy now."

"Really! Boy or girl?"

"Girl. A beautiful little bitch named Justine, drives me crazy. I'd like you to meet my wife sometime, Leisha."

"I'd like that," Leisha said.

She spent the rest of the night studying for her bar exams. The bubble stayed with her. She recognized exactly what it was: joy.

It was going to be all right. The contract, unwritten, between her and her society—Kenzo Yagai's society, Roger Camden's society—would hold. With dissent and strife and yes, some hatred. She suddenly thought of Tony's beggars in Spain, furious at the strong because the beggars were not. Yes. But it would hold.

She believed that.

She did.

Seven

Leisha took her bar exams in July. They did not seem hard to her. Afterward three classmates, two men and a woman, made a fakely casual point of talking to Leisha until she had climbed safely into a taxi whose driver obviously did not recognize her, or stop signs. The three were all Sleepers. A pair of undergraduates, clean-shaven blond men with the long faces and pointless arrogance of rich stupidity, eyed Leisha and sneered. Leisha's female classmate sneered back.

Leisha had a flight to Chicago the next morning. Alice was going to join her there. They had to clean out the big house on the lake, dispose of Roger's personal property, put the house on the market. Leisha had had no time to do it earlier.

She remembered her father in the conservatory, wearing an ancient flat-topped hat he had picked up somewhere, potting orchids and jasmine and passion flowers.

When the doorbell rang she was startled; she almost never had visitors. Eagerly, she turned on the outside camera—maybe it was Jonathan or Martha, back in Boston to surprise her, to celebrate—why hadn't she thought before about some sort of celebration?

Richard stood gazing up at the camera. He had been crying.

She tore open the door. Richard made no move to come in. Leisha saw that what the camera had registered as grief was actually something else: tears of rage.

"Tony's dead."

Leisha put out her hand, blindly. Richard didn't take it.

"They killed him in prison. Not the authorities—the other prisoners. In the recreation yard. Murderers, rapists, looters, scum of the earth—and they thought they had the right to kill *him* because he was different."

Now Richard did grab her arm, so hard that something, some bone, shifted beneath the flesh and pressed on a nerve. "Not just different—*better*. Because he was better, because we all are, we goddamn just don't stand up and shout it out of some misplaced feeling for *their* feelings ... God!"

Leisha pulled her arm free and rubbed it, numb, staring at Richard's contorted face.

"They beat him to death with a lead pipe. No one even knows how they got a lead pipe. They beat him on the back of the head and then they rolled him over and—"

"Don't!" Leisha said. It came out a whimper.

Richard looked at her. Despite his shouting, his violent grip on her arm, Leisha had the confused impression that this was the first time he had actually seen her. She went on rubbing her arm, staring at him in terror.

He said quietly, "I've come to take you to Sanctuary, Leisha. Dan Jenkins and Vernon Bulriss are in the car outside. The three of us will carry you out, if necessary. But you're coming. You see that, don't you? You're not safe here, with your high profile and your spectacular looks. You're a natural target if anyone is. Do we have to force you? Or do you finally see for yourself that we have no choice—the bastards have left us no choice—except Sanctuary?"

Leisha closed her eyes. Tony, at fourteen, at the beach. Tony, his eyes ferocious and shining, the first to reach out his hand for the glass of interleukin-1. Beggars in Spain.

"I'll come."

She had never known such anger. It scared her, coming in bouts throughout the long night, receding but always returning again.

Richard held her in his arms, sitting with their backs against the wall of her library, and his holding made no difference at all. In the living room Dan and Vernon talked in low voices.

Sometimes the anger erupted in shouting, and Leisha heard herself and thought, *I don't know you.* Sometimes it became crying, sometimes talking about Tony, about all of them. Neither the shouting nor the crying nor the talking eased her at all.

Planning did, a little. In a cold, dry voice she didn't recognize, Leisha told Richard about the trip to close the house in Chicago. She had to go; Alice was already there. If Richard and Dan and Vernon put Leisha on the plane, and Alice met her at the other end with union bodyguards, she should be safe enough. Then she would change her return ticket from Boston to Conewango and drive with Richard to Sanctuary.

"People are already arriving," Richard said. "Jennifer Sharifi is organizing it, greasing the Sleeper suppliers with so much money they can't resist. What about this townhouse here, Leisha? Your furniture and terminal and clothes?"

Leisha looked around her familiar office. Law books, red and green and brown, lined the walls although most of the same information was online. A coffee cup rested on a printout on the desk. Beside it was the receipt she had requested from the taxi driver this afternoon, a giddy souvenir of the day she had passed her bar exams; she had thought of having it framed. Above the desk was a holographic portrait of Kenzo Yagai.

"Let it rot," Leisha said.

Richard's arm tightened around her.

"I've never seen you like this," Alice said, subdued. "It's more than just clearing out the house, isn't it?"

"Let's get on with it," Leisha said. She yanked a suit from her father's closet. "Do you want any of this stuff for your husband?"

"It wouldn't fit."

"The hats?"

"No," Alice said. "Leisha—what is it?"

"Let's just *do* it!" She yanked all the clothes from Camden's closet, piled them on the floor, scrawled FOR VOLUNTEER AGENCY on a piece of paper, and dropped it on top of the pile. Silently, Alice started adding clothes from the dresser, which already bore a taped paper bearing the words, ESTATE AUCTION.

The curtains were already down throughout the house; Alice had done that yesterday. She had also rolled up the rugs. Sunset glared red on the bare wooden floors.

"What about your old room?" Leisha said. "What do you want there?"

"I've already tagged it," Alice said. "A mover will come Thursday."

"Fine. What else?"

"The conservatory. Sanderson has been watering everything, but he didn't really know what needed how much, so some of the plants are—"

"Fire Sanderson," Leisha said curtly. "The exotics can die. Or have them sent to a hospital, if you'd rather. Just watch out for the ones that are poisonous. Come on, let's do the library."

Alice sat slowly on a rolled-up rug in the middle of Camden's bedroom. She had cut her hair; Leisha thought it looked ugly, like jagged brown spikes around her broad face. She had also gained more weight. She was starting to look like their mother.

Alice said, "Do you remember the night I told you I was pregnant? Just before you left for Harvard?"

"Let's do the library!"

"Do you?" Alice said. "For God's sake, can't you just once listen to someone else, Leisha? Do you have to be so much like Daddy every single minute?"

"I'm not Daddy!"

"The hell you're not. You're exactly what he made you. But that's not the point. Do you remember that night?"

Leisha walked over the rug and out the door. Alice simply sat. After a minute Leisha walked back in. "I remember."

"You were near tears," Alice said implacably. Her voice was quiet. "I don't even remember exactly why. Maybe because I wasn't going to college after all. But I put my arms around you, and for the first time in years—years, Leisha—I felt you really were my sister. Despite all of it—the roaming the halls all night and the show-off arguments with Daddy and the special school and the artificially long legs and golden hair—all that crap. You seemed to need me to hold you. You seemed to need me. You seemed to *need*."

"What are you saying?" Leisha demanded. "That you can only be close to someone if they're in trouble and need you? That you can only be a sister if I was in some kind of pain, open sores running? Is that the bond between you Sleepers? 'Protect me while I'm unconscious, I'm just as crippled as you are'?"

"No," Alice said. "I'm saying that *you* could be a sister only if you were in some kind of pain."

Leisha stared at her. "You're stupid, Alice."

Alice said calmly, "I know that. Compared to you, I am. I know that."

Leisha jerked her head angrily. She felt ashamed of what she had just said, and yet it was true, and they both knew it was true, and anger still lay in her like a dark void, formless and hot. It was the formless part that was the worst. Without shape, there could be no action; without action, the anger went on burning her, choking her.

Alice said, "When I was twelve Susan gave me a dress for our birthday. You were away somewhere, on one of those overnight field trips your fancy progressive school did all the time. The dress was silk, pale blue, with antique lace—very beautiful. I was thrilled, not only because it was beautiful but because Susan had gotten it for me and gotten software for you. The dress was mine. Was, I thought, *me*." In the gathering gloom Leisha could barely make out her broad, plain features. "The first time I wore it a boy said, 'Stole your sister's dress, Alice? Snitched it while she was *sleeping*?' Then he laughed like crazy, the way they always did.

"I threw the dress away. I didn't even explain to Susan, although I think she would have understood. Whatever was yours was yours, and whatever wasn't yours was yours, too. That's the way Daddy set it up. The way he hardwired it into our genes."

"You, too?" Leisha said. "You're no different from the other envious beggars?"

Alice stood up from the rug. She did it slowly, leisurely, brushing dust off the back of her wrinkled skirt, smoothing the print fabric. Then she walked over and hit Leisha in the mouth.

"Now do you see me as real?" Alice asked quietly.

Leisha put her hand to her mouth. She felt blood. The phone rang, Camden's unlisted personal line. Alice walked over, picked it up, listened, and held it calmly out to Leisha. "It's for you."

Numb, Leisha took it.

"Leisha? This is Kevin. Listen, something's happened. Stella Bevington called me, on the phone, not Groupnet; I think her parents took away her modem. I picked up the phone and she screamed, 'This is Stella! They're hitting me, he's drunk—' and then the line went dead. Randy's gone to Sanctuary—hell, they've *all* gone. You're closest to her, she's still in Skokie. You better get there fast. Have you got bodyguards you trust?"

"Yes," Leisha said, although she hadn't. The anger, finally, took form. "I can handle it."

"I don't know how you'll get her out of there," Kevin said. "They'll recognize you, they know she called somebody, they might even have knocked her out…."

"I'll handle it," Leisha said.

"Handle what?" Alice said.

Leisha faced her. Even though she knew she shouldn't, she said, "What your people do. To one of ours. A seven-year-old kid who's getting beaten by her parents because she's Sleepless—because she's *better* than you are—" She ran down the stairs and out to the rental car she had driven from the airport.

Alice ran right down with her. "Not your car, Leisha. They can trace a rental car just like that. My car."

Leisha screamed, "If you think you're—"

Alice yanked open the door of her battered Toyota, a model so old the Y-energy cones weren't even concealed but hung like drooping jowls on either side. She shoved Leisha into the passenger seat, slammed the door, and rammed herself behind the wheel. Her hands were steady. "Where?"

Blackness swooped over Leisha. She put her head down, as far between her knees as the cramped Toyota would allow. It had been two—no, three—days since she had eaten. Not since the night before the bar exams. The faintness receded, swept over her again as soon as she raised her head.

She told Alice the address in Skokie.

"Stay way in the back," Alice said. "And there's a scarf in the glove compartment—put it on. Low, to hide as much of your face as possible."

Alice had stopped the car along Highway 42. Leisha said, "This isn't—"

"It's a quick-guard place. We have to look like we have some protection, Leisha. We don't need to tell him anything. I'll hurry."

She was out in three minutes with a huge man in a cheap dark suit. He squeezed into the front seat beside Alice and said nothing at all. Alice did not introduce him.

The house was small, a little shabby, with lights on downstairs, none upstairs. The first stars shone in the north, away from Chicago. Alice said to the guard, "Get out of the car and stand here by the car door—no, more in the light—and don't do anything unless I'm attacked in some way." The man nodded. Alice started up the walk. Leisha scrambled out of the back seat and caught her sister two-thirds of the way to the plastic front door.

"Alice, what the hell are you doing? *I* have to—"

"Keep your voice down," Alice said, glancing at the guard. "Leisha, *think*. You'll be recognized. Here, near Chicago, with a Sleepless daughter—these people have looked at your picture in magazines for years. They've watched long-range holovids of you. They know you. They know you're going to be a lawyer. Me they've never seen. I'm nobody."

"Alice—"

"For Chrissake, get back in the car!" Alice hissed, and pounded on the front door.

Leisha drew off the walk, into the shadow of a willow tree. A man opened the door. His face was completely blank.

Alice said, "Child Protection Agency. We got a call from a little girl, this number. Let me in."

"There's no little girl here."

"This is an emergency, priority one," Alice said. "Child Protection Act 186. Let me in!"

The man, still blank-faced, glanced at the huge figure by the car. "You got a search warrant?"

"I don't need one in a priority-one child emergency. If you don't let me in, you're going to have legal snarls like you never bargained for."

Leisha clamped her lips together. No one would believe that, it was legal gobbledygook .... Her lip throbbed where Alice had hit it.

The man stood aside to let Alice enter.

The guard started forward. Leisha hesitated, then let him. He entered with Alice.

Leisha waited, alone, in the dark.

In three minutes they were out, the guard carrying a child. Alice's broad face gleamed pale in the porch light. Leisha sprang forward, opened the car door, and helped the guard ease the child inside. The guard was frowning, a slow puzzled frown shot with wariness.

Alice said, "Here. This is an extra hundred dollars. To get back to the city by yourself."

"Hey ..." the guard said, but he took the money. He stood looking after them as Alice pulled away.

"He'll go straight to the police," Leisha said despairingly. "He has to, or risk his union membership."

"I know," Alice said. "But by that time we'll be out of the car."

"*Where*?"

"At the hospital," Alice said.

"Alice, we can't—" Leisha didn't finish. She turned to the back seat. "Stella? Are you conscious?"

"Yes," said the small voice.

Leisha groped until her fingers found the rear-seat illuminator. Stella lay stretched out on the seat, her face distorted with pain. She cradled her left arm in her right. A single bruise colored her face, above the left eye. Her red hair was tangled and dirty.

"You're Leisha Camden," the child said, and started to cry.

"Her arm's broken," Alice said.

"Honey, can you ..." Leisha's throat felt thick, she had trouble getting the words out "... can you hold on till we get you to a doctor?"

"Yes," Stella said. "Just don't take me back there!"

"We won't," Leisha said. "Ever." She glanced at Alice and saw Tony's face.

Alice said, "There's a community hospital about ten miles south of here."

"How do you know that?"

"I was there once. Drug overdose," Alice said briefly. She drove hunched over the wheel, with the face of someone thinking furiously. Leisha thought, too, trying to see a way around the legal charge of kidnapping. They probably couldn't say the child came willingly. Stella would undoubtedly cooperate but at her age and in her condition she was probably *non sui juris*, her word would have no legal weight....

"Alice, we can't even get her into the hospital without insurance information. Verifiable online."

"Listen," Alice said, not to Leisha but over her shoulder, toward the back seat, "here's what we're going to do, Stella. I'm going to tell them you're my daughter and you fell off a big rock you were climbing while we stopped for a snack at a roadside picnic area. We're driving from California to Philadelphia to see your grandmother. Your name is Jordan Watrous and you're five years old. Got that, honey?"

"I'm seven," Stella said. "Almost eight."

"You're a very large five. Your birthday is March 23. Can you do this, Stella?"

"Yes," the little girl said. Her voice was stronger.

Leisha stared at Alice. "Can *you* do this?"

"Of course I can," Alice said. "I'm Roger Camden's daughter."

Alice half-carried, half-supported Stella into the Emergency Room of the small community hospital. Leisha watched from the car: the short stocky woman, the child's thin body with the twisted arm. Then she drove Alice's car to the farthest corner of the parking lot, under the dubious cover of a skimpy maple, and locked it. She tied the scarf more securely around her face.

Alice's license plate number, and her name, would be in every police and rental-car databank by now. The medical banks were slower; often they uploaded from local precincts only once a day, resenting the governmental interference in what was still, despite a half-century of battle, a private-sector enterprise. Alice and Stella would probably be all right in the hospital. Probably. But Alice could not rent another car.

Leisha could.

But the data file that would flash to rental agencies on Alice Camden Watrous might or might not include that she was Leisha Camden's twin.

Leisha looked at the rows of cars in the lot. A flashy luxury Chrysler, an Ikeda van, a row of middle-class Toyotas and Mercedes, a vintage '99 Cadillac—she could imagine the owner's face if that were missing—ten or twelve cheap runabouts, a hover car with the uniformed driver asleep at the wheel. And a battered farm truck.

Leisha walked over to the truck. A man sat at the wheel, smoking. She thought of her father.

"Hello," Leisha said.

The man rolled down his window but didn't answer. He had greasy brown hair.

"See that hover car over there?" Leisha said. She made her voice sound young, high. The man glanced at it indifferently; from this angle you couldn't see that the driver was asleep. "That's my bodyguard. He thinks I'm inside, the way my father told me to, getting this lip looked at." She could feel her mouth swollen from Alice's blow.

"So?"

Leisha stamped her foot. "So I don't want to be inside. He's a shit and so's Daddy. I want out. I'll give you four thousand bank credits for your truck. Cash."

The man's eyes widened. He tossed away his cigarette and looked again at the hover car. The driver's shoulders were broad, and the car was within easy screaming distance.

"All nice and legal," Leisha said, trying to smirk. Her knees felt watery.

"Let me see the cash."

Leisha backed away from the truck, to where he could not reach her. She took the money from her arm clip. She was used to carrying a lot of cash; there had always been Bruce, or someone like Bruce. There had always been safety.

"Get out of the truck on the other side," Leisha said, "and lock the door behind you. Leave the keys on the seat, where I can see them from here. Then I'll put the money on the roof where you can see it."

The man laughed, a sound like gravel pouring. "Regular little Dabney Engh, aren't you? Is that what they teach you society debs at your fancy schools?"

Leisha had no idea who Dabney Engh was. She waited, watching the man try to think of a way to cheat her, and tried to hide her contempt. She thought of Tony.

"All right," he said, and slid out of the truck.

"Lock the door!"

He grinned, opened the door again, and locked it. Leisha put the money on the roof, yanked open the driver's door, clambered in, locked the door, and powered up the window. The man laughed. She put the key into the ignition, started the truck, and drove toward the street. Her hands trembled.

She drove slowly around the block twice. When she came back, the man was gone, and the driver of the hover car was still asleep. She had wondered if the man would wake him, out of sheer malice, but he had not. She parked the truck and waited.

An hour and a half later Alice and a nurse wheeled Stella out of the Emergency entrance. Leisha leaped out of the truck and yelled, "Coming, Alice!" waving both her arms. It was too dark to see Alice's expression; Leisha could only hope that Alice showed no dismay at the battered truck, that she had not told the nurse to expect a red car.

Alice said, "This is Julie Bergadon, a friend that I called while you were setting Jordan's arm." The nurse nodded, uninterested. The two women helped Stella into the high truck cab; there was no back seat. Stella had a cast on her arm and looked drugged.

"How?" Alice said as they drove off.

Leisha didn't answer. She was watching a police hover car land at the other end of the parking lot. Two officers got out and strode purposefully toward Alice's locked car under the skimpy maple.

"My God," Alice said. For the first time, she sounded frightened.

"They won't trace us," Leisha said. "Not to this truck. Count on it."

"Leisha." Alice's voice spiked with fear. "Stella's *asleep*."

Leisha glanced at the child, slumped against Alice's shoulder. "No, she's not. She's unconscious from painkillers."

"Is that all right? Normal? For … her?"

"We can black out. We can even experience substance-induced sleep." Tony and she and Richard and Jennifer in the midnight woods …. "Didn't you know that, Alice?"

"No."

"We don't know very much about each other, do we?"

They drove south in silence. Finally Alice said, "Where are we going to take her, Leisha?"

"I don't know. Any one of the Sleepless would be the first place the police would check—"

"You can't risk it. Not the way things are," Alice said. She sounded weary. "But all my friends are in California. I don't think we could drive this rust bucket that far before getting stopped."

"It wouldn't make it anyway."

"What should we do?"

"Let me think."

At an expressway exit was a pay phone. It wouldn't be data-shielded, as Groupnet was. Would Kevin's open line be tapped? Probably.

There was no doubt the Sanctuary line would be.

Sanctuary. All of them were going there or already there, Kevin had said. Holed up, trying to pull the worn Allegheny Mountains around them like a safe little den. Except for the children like Stella, who could not.

Where? With whom?

Leisha closed her eyes. The Sleepless were out; the police would find Stella within hours. Susan Melling? But she had been Alice's all-too-visible stepmother, and was a co-beneficiary of Camden's will; they would question her almost immediately. It couldn't be anyone traceable to Alice. It could only be a Sleeper that Leisha knew, and trusted, and why should anyone at all fit that description? Why should she risk so much on anyone who did?

She stood a long time in the dark phone kiosk. Then she walked to the truck. Alice was asleep, her head thrown back against the seat. A tiny line of drool ran down her chin. Her face was white and drained in the bad light from the kiosk. Leisha walked back to the phone.

"Stewart? Stewart Sutter?"

"Yes?"

"This is Leisha Camden. Something has happened." She told the story tersely, in bald sentences. Stewart did not interrupt.

"Leisha—" Stewart said, and stopped.

"I need help, Stewart." *'I'll help you, Alice.' 'I don't need your help.'*

A wind whistled over the dark field beside the kiosk and Leisha shivered. She heard in the wind the thin keen of a beggar. In the wind, in her own voice.

"All right," Stewart said, "this is what we'll do. I have a cousin in Ripley, New York, just over the state line from Pennsylvania, the route you'll be driving east. It has to be in New York; I'm licensed in New York. Take the little girl there. I'll call my cousin and tell her you're coming. She's an elderly woman, was quite an activist in her youth. Her name is Janet Patterson. The town is—"

"What makes you so sure she'll get involved? She could go to jail. And so could you."

"She's been in jail so many times you wouldn't believe it. Political protests going all the way back to Vietnam. But no one's going to jail. I'm now your attorney of record, I'm privileged. I'm going to get Stella declared a ward of the state. That shouldn't be too hard with the hospital records you established in Skokie. Then she can be transferred to a foster home in New York. I know just the place, people who are fair and kind. Then Alice—"

"Stella's resident in Illinois. You can't—"

"Yes, I can. Since those research findings about the Sleepless lifespan have come out, legislators have been railroaded by stupid constituents scared or jealous or just plain angry. The result is a body of so-called law riddled with contradictions, absurdities, and loopholes. None of it will stand in the long run or at least I hope not—but in the meantime it can all be exploited. I can use it to create the most goddamn convoluted case for Stella that anybody ever saw, and in the meantime she won't be returned home. But that won't work for Alice. She'll need an attorney licensed in Illinois."

"We have one," Leisha said. "Candace Holt."

"No, not a Sleepless. Trust me on this, Leisha. I'll find somebody good. There's a guy in—are you crying?"

"No," Leisha said, crying.

"Ah, God," Stewart said. "Bastards. I'm sorry all this happened, Leisha."

"Don't be," Leisha said.

When she had directions to Stewart's cousin, she walked back to the truck. Alice was still asleep, Stella still unconscious. Leisha closed the truck door as quietly as possible. The engine balked and roared, but Alice didn't wake.

There was a crowd of people with them in the narrow and darkened cab: Stewart Sutter, Tony Indivino, Susan Melling, Kenzo Yagai, Roger Camden.

To Stewart Sutter she said, You called to inform me about the situation at Morehouse, Kennedy. You are risking your career and your cousin for Stella. And you stand to gain nothing. Like Susan telling me in advance about Bernie Kuhn's brain. Susan, who lost her life to Daddy's dream and regained it by her own strength. A contract without consideration for each side is not a contract: Every first-year student knows that.

To Kenzo Yagai she said, Trade isn't always linear. You missed that. If Stewart gives me something, and I give Stella something, and ten years from now Stella is a different person because of that and gives something to someone else as yet unknown—it's an ecology. An ecology of trade, yes, each niche needed, even if they're not contractually bound. Does a horse need a fish? Yes.

To Tony she said, Yes, there are beggars in Spain who trade nothing, give nothing, do nothing. But there are *more* than beggars in Spain. Withdraw from the beggars, you withdraw from the whole damn country. And you withdraw from the possibility of the ecology of help. That's what Alice wanted, all those years ago in her bedroom. Pregnant, scared, angry, jealous, she wanted to help *me*, and I wouldn't let her because I didn't need it. But I do now. And she did then. Beggars need to help as well as be helped.

And finally, there was only Daddy left. She could *see* him, bright-eyed, holding thick-leaved exotic flowers in his strong hands. To Camden she said, You were wrong. Alice *is* special. Oh, Daddy—the specialness of Alice! You were wrong.

As soon as she thought this, lightness filled her. Not the buoyant bubble of joy, not the hard clarity of examination, but something else: sunshine, soft through the conservatory glass, where two children ran in and out. She suddenly felt light herself, not buoyant but translucent, a medium for the sunshine to pass clear through, on its way to somewhere else.

She drove the sleeping woman and the wounded child through the night, east, toward the state line.

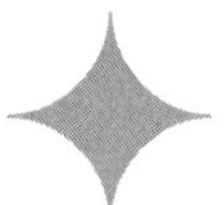